The Mirror

Series

Irish Born Trilogy
Born in Fire • *Born in Ice* • *Born in Shame*

Dream Trilogy
Daring to Dream • *Holding the Dream* • *Finding the Dream*

Chesapeake Bay Saga
Sea Swept • *Rising Tides* • *Inner Harbor* • *Chesapeake Blue*

Gallaghers of Ardmore Trilogy
Jewels of the Sun • *Tears of the Moon* • *Heart of the Sea*

Three Sisters Island Trilogy
Dance Upon the Air • *Heaven and Earth* • *Face the Fire*

Key Trilogy
Key of Light • *Key of Knowledge* • *Key of Valor*

In the Garden Trilogy
Blue Dahlia • *Black Rose* • *Red Lily*

Circle Trilogy
Morrigan's Cross • *Dance of the Gods* • *Valley of Silence*

Sign of Seven Trilogy
Blood Brothers • *The Hollow* • *The Pagan Stone*

Bride Quartet
Vision in White • *Bed of Roses* • *Savor the Moment* • *Happy Ever After*

The Inn Boonsboro Trilogy
The Next Always • *The Last Boyfriend* • *The Perfect Hope*

The Cousins O'Dwyer Trilogy
Dark Witch • *Shadow Spell* • *Blood Magick*

The Guardians Trilogy
Stars of Fortune • *Bay of Sighs* • *Island of Glass*

The Chronicles of The One
Year One • *Of Blood and Bone* • *The Rise of Magicks*

The Dragon Heart Legacy
The Awakening • *The Becoming* • *The Choice*

The Lost Bride Trilogy
Inheritance • *The Mirror*

eBooks by Nora Roberts

Cordina's Royal Family
Affaire Royale • *Command Performance* • *The Playboy Prince* •
Cordina's Crown Jewel

The Donovan Legacy
Captivated • *Entranced* • *Charmed* • *Enchanted*

The O'Hurleys
The Last Honest Woman • *Dance to the Piper* • *Skin Deep* • *Without a Trace*

Night Tales
Night Shift • *Night Shadow* • *Nightshade* • *Night Smoke* • *Night Shield*

The MacGregors
The Winning Hand • *The Perfect Neighbor* • *All the Possibilities* • *One
Man's Art* • *Tempting Fate* • *Playing the Odds* • *The MacGregor Brides* •
The MacGregor Grooms • *Rebellion* • *In from the Cold* • *For Now, Forever*

The Calhouns
Suzanna's Surrender • *Megan's Mate* • *Courting Catherine* •
A Man for Amanda • *For the Love of Lilah*

Irish Legacy
Irish Rose • *Irish Rebel* • *Irish Thoroughbred*

Jack's Stories
Best Laid Plans • *Loving Jack* • *Lawless*

Summer Love • *Boundary Lines* • *Dual Image* • *First Impressions* • *The Law
Is a Lady* • *Local Hero* • *This Magic Moment* • *The Name of the Game* •
Partners • *Temptation* • *The Welcoming* • *Opposites
Attract* • *Time Was* • *Times Change* • *Gabriel's Angel* • *Holiday
Wishes* • *The Heart's Victory* • *The Right Path* • *Rules of the Game* • *Search
for Love* • *Blithe Images* • *From This Day* • *Song of the West* • *Island of
Flowers* • *Her Mother's Keeper* • *Untamed* • *Sullivan's Woman* • *Less of a
Stranger* • *Reflections* • *Dance of Dreams* • *Storm Warning* • *Once More
with Feeling* • *Endings and Beginnings* • *A Matter of Choice* •
One Summer • *Summer Desserts* • *Lessons Learned* • *The Art of Deception* •
Second Nature • *Treasures Lost, Treasures Found*

Nora Roberts & J. D. Robb

Remember When

J. D. Robb

Naked in Death • *Glory in Death* • *Immortal in Death* • *Rapture in Death*
• *Ceremony in Death* • *Vengeance in Death* • *Holiday in Death* • *Conspiracy
in Death* • *Loyalty in Death* • *Witness in Death* • *Judgment in Death* •
Betrayal in Death • *Seduction in Death* • *Reunion in Death* • *Purity in
Death* • *Portrait in Death* • *Imitation in Death* • *Divided in Death* •
Visions in Death • *Survivor in Death* • *Origin in Death* • *Memory in Death*
• *Born in Death* • *Innocent in Death* • *Creation in Death* • *Strangers in
Death* • *Salvation in Death* • *Promises in Death* • *Kindred in Death* •
Fantasy in Death • *Indulgence in Death* • *Treachery in Death* • *New York
to Dallas* • *Celebrity in Death* • *Delusion in Death* • *Calculated in Death* •
Thankless in Death • *Concealed in Death* • *Festive in Death* • *Obsession in
Death* • *Devoted in Death* • *Brotherhood in Death* • *Apprentice in Death* •
Echoes in Death • *Secrets in Death* • *Dark in Death* • *Leverage in Death* •
Connections in Death • *Vendetta in Death* • *Golden in Death* •
Shadows in Death • *Faithless in Death* • *Forgotten in Death* •
Abandonded in Death • *Desperation in Death* •
Encore in Death • *Payback in Death* • *Random in Death* •
Passions in Death

Anthologies

From the Heart • *A Little Magic* • *A Little Fate*

Moon Shadows
(with Jill Gregory, Ruth Ryan Langan, and Marianne Willman)

The Once Upon Series
(with Jill Gregory, Ruth Ryan Langan, and Marianne Willman)
Once Upon a Castle • *Once Upon a Star* • *Once Upon a Dream* •
Once Upon a Rose • *Once Upon a Kiss* • *Once Upon a Midnight*

Silent Night
(with Susan Plunkett, Dee Holmes, and Claire Cross)

Out of This World
(with Laurell K. Hamilton, Susan Krinard, and Maggie Shayne)

Bump in the Night
(with Mary Blayney, Ruth Ryan Langan, and Mary Kay McComas)

Dead of Night
(with Mary Blayney, Ruth Ryan Langan, and Mary Kay McComas)

Three in Death
Suite 606
(with Mary Blayney, Ruth Ryan Langan, and Mary Kay McComas)

In Death
The Lost
(with Patricia Gaffney, Mary Blayney, and Ruth Ryan Langan)

The Other Side
(with Mary Blayney, Patricia Gaffney, Ruth Ryan Langan,
and Mary Kay McComas)

Time of Death
The Unquiet
(with Mary Blayney, Patricia Gaffney, Ruth Ryan Langan,
and Mary Kay McComas)

Mirror, Mirror
(with Mary Blayney, Elaine Fox, Mary Kay McComas, and R. C. Ryan)

Down the Rabbit Hole
(with Mary Blayney, Elaine Fox, Mary Kay McComas, and R. C. Ryan)

ALSO AVAILABLE . . .
The Official Nora Roberts Companion
(edited by Denise Little and Laura Hayden)

The Mirror

Nora Roberts

ST. MARTIN'S PRESS
NEW YORK

First published in the United States by St. Martin's Press, an imprint of St. Martin's Publishing Group

www.stmartins.com

Endpaper: Landscape © Folio Images / Alamy; ocean © Alberto Loyo/Shutterstock; trees © hakanyalicn/Shutterstock; clouds © VimerArt Studio/Shutterstock; house © Patrick F Infante/Shutterstock; moon © Efasein/Shutterstock; stars © codrinn/Shutterstock

The Library of Congress Cataloging-in-Publication Data is available upon request.

ISBN 978-1-250-28877-6 (hardcover)
ISBN 978-1-250-28878-3 (ebook)

Our books may be purchased in bulk for promotional, educational, or business use. Please contact your local bookseller or the Macmillan Corporate and Premium Sales Department at 1-800-221-7945, extension 5442, or by email at MacmillanSpecialMarkets@macmillan.com.

First Edition: 2024

This edition was printed by Bertelsmann Printing Group

10 9 8 7 6 5 4 3 2 1

To family
Those of the blood, and those chosen

PART ONE

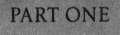

Witness

Can I get a witness?

—Brian Holland, Lamont Dozier, Eddie Holland

Prologue

The manor stood, as it had for generations, on the high, jagged cliffs above the thrash of the sea. Through the swelter of summers, against the bitter winds of winters, in blooming springs, and in dying autumns, it held its place on the rocky coast of Maine.

Within its stone and cladded walls, inside the gleam of its windows, it had seen births and deaths, it had known triumphs and tragedies. Both blood and tears had spilled on its polished floors; secrets and shadows lived in its many corners.

And it remembered them all.

From its turrets, its widow's walk, from the seawall beyond its grand entrance doors, many eyes had looked down toward the village of Poole's Bay.

Many eyes looked there still.

Since those grand doors opened in 1794, a Poole had walked those halls. A Poole had climbed the grand staircase, gazed from the many windows, dreamed their dreams. And some had lived their nightmares.

Some lived them still.

A murdered bride, the first of seven doomed, would—in all innocence—carry the curse that haunted the manor. Generation by generation, it passed its shadow to the next, and the next, through the rage of a jealous witch.

With those lost brides, others walked the labyrinth of rooms. Those who had lit the many fires, made the beds, cooked the meals continued their duties.

Others who had lifted a glass in toast, danced in the ballroom, or rocked a fretful baby in the night toasted and danced and rocked still.

In the many rooms, time came and went. Music played, clocks ticked, floors creaked as the manor waited for another generation.

As it waited for one who might break the curse.

More than two hundred years after Astrid Grandville Poole died in her wedding finery, more than two hundred years after her murderer cursed the manor and leaped off the cliffs to her own death, another with Poole blood walked through those grand entrance doors.

Those who'd come before her watched and waited as she made the manor her own. As she dreamed her dreams—or theirs.

As she walked the labyrinth where music played and clocks ticked and floors creaked. And to the mirror where time came and went.

Carved predators frame this mirror's glass and seem to snap and snarl and slither. And its glass opens a door to what was for her, and another with Poole blood.

Hands clasped, they step through the door together.

And become the ghosts.

Chapter One

Music that had been dim and distant poured around her now. Colors and shapes that had been blurred and indistinct on the other side of the mirror sharpened.

Sonya gripped Owen's hand—the hand of the cousin she hadn't known existed only months before. That hand was warm, that hand was real.

Instead of furniture stored, with white sheets draping it, people swirled around them. Women with hair piled high, long dresses flowing, and men in sharp, dark suits danced, laughed, drank. The room—the ballroom—smelled of flowers. There were so many of them. And of perfume. An orchestra played something lively and quick.

She heard a woman laugh, high and bright, over the music. She saw a line of sweat slide down the temple of a man with slicked-back hair as he led his partner in the dance.

And she heard her own heart pounding louder than the drumbeat.

When her hand trembled, Owen tightened his grip. And he said, almost casually, "This is fucking weird."

The bubble of hysteria in her throat came out in a breathless laugh. "I'll say. I've done it before, gone through, but this is the first time I was awake when I did. I thought, before, I thought I'd dreamed it. But it's not a dream."

"Nope." He scanned the room. "We know where we are. It's the ballroom. Any idea when?"

"1916. I read Deuce's Poole family history book and looked

through the pictures enough times to know this is Lisbeth Poole's wedding reception."

A man, obviously enjoying his gin, stumbled right through her. "Oh my God."

"That's beyond weird." Frowning, Owen turned to her, studied her with eyes a slightly lighter shade of Poole green than her own. "Okay?"

She managed a nod. "We're the ones out of place or time or whatever the hell. They don't see us, or feel us. Or most don't. She's not here."

"Who?"

"Hester Dobbs. Murdering witch. She's not here, not yet. This isn't her time either."

"Seeing as she'd be dead over a hundred years."

"Maybe we can stop her. It's not a damn dream, so maybe we're here to stop her. Thirteen spider bites, inside the wedding dress— that's how Lisbeth dies today. If we can just—"

"What, strip her clothes off?"

"I don't know. We have to try something. Where is she? Where the hell is Lissy?"

Owen pointed. "Other side of the ballroom? I'm taller, can see over more heads. I've seen pictures, too, and that looks like a wedding-type dress to me."

He shifted Sonya to the left.

"Yes! Yes, that's her."

As she started forward, people danced through her. Some gave her a jolt, like a mild electric shock, others a chill that shot straight through her bones.

"It's like walking through mud," Owen muttered, and shoved a frustrated hand through his unruly brown hair. "Or fricking quicksand."

"I know. I know. It happened like this before. I can't see her anymore. It's so crowded. Can you see her?"

"Just keep going. She's moving to our right. She's dancing. She's— Shit!"

"What? What happened? I—" Now she saw, through a break in the dancers as they glided. The look of shock and pain on the young, sweet face.

And then the shriek.

"We're too late, too late." But she kept pushing forward. "If we can't save her, we need to stop Dobbs from getting her wedding ring. She needs all seven rings. We need to get it first."

As Lisbeth collapsed in her husband's arms, Sonya felt the change in the air, the sudden brittle bitterness of it.

Hester Dobbs, her hard beauty glowing, her dark eyes sparking with venom, all but floated across the ballroom. Her waving fall of black hair seemed to stir in an unseen wind as she approached the dying bride.

Enraged, Sonya cried out, "Stop! You bitch. Leave her alone."

Dobbs snapped her head around. For an instant, just an instant, Sonya saw surprise, and maybe a hint of fear ripple over the hard beauty of her face.

Then that unseen wind struck her, slamming into her like an icy fist. It broke her hold on Owen's hand, sent her flying back, flying through people who rushed forward.

She landed hard enough to leave her dazed and dizzy. As she fought to draw in a breath, to push herself up, she watched a spider, wider than her palm, skittering across the floor toward her.

Real, she thought, it was somehow real, somehow *now*.

The room filled with screams, with weeping, with rushing feet as she tried to scramble up and away.

She saw its red eyes gleaming, and prepared for the first vicious bite.

An inch from her bare foot, Owen stomped on it. Her stomach rolled as she heard the ugly crunch.

"Up." He hauled her to her feet. "Move!"

"Did you get it? Did you get the ring?"

"It's gone, and so's the bride. We're not."

He dragged her through the chaos, shoved her through the mirror. And leaped after her.

She tipped straight into Trey's arms. And he wrapped them tight as the three dogs swarmed them.

"I've got you. Jesus, you're freezing."

"It got so cold." Now her teeth chattered with it.

"Are you hurt?" As he ran his hands over her, he looked at Owen. "Either of you hurt?"

"Sonya took a flight like you did outside the Gold Room."

"I'm okay. It just rattled me." Leaning into Trey, grateful for his warmth, she looked over at Cleo. "It was Lisbeth Poole. We couldn't stop it."

"Let's get you downstairs." Cleo stroked Sonya's hair. "Let's get you both downstairs."

"I need a drink." As he spoke, and his scrappy mutt, Jones, sniffed at it, Owen looked at the bottom of his shoe. "And a new pair of shoes."

"What is that?" Cleo demanded.

"Evil spider guts."

"Take them off! You can't track evil spider guts through the house."

"Yeah, that was my first thought."

Cleopatra Fabares, Sonya's best friend and housemate, took over.

"Trey, take Sonya downstairs. The kitchen. We all need a drink. You. Take those disgusting shoes off," Cleo ordered Owen again. "Leave them right here until we get something to put them in."

"Yeah, yeah, yeah."

"We're right behind you. You can pour us both a whiskey. A double."

As Owen bent to pull off his shoes, Cleo sucked in a breath that put him right back on alert.

"The mirror. It's gone. It's just gone."

He turned. "Son of a bitch."

"Get those damn shoes off," she insisted. "And let's get the hell downstairs. Then you and Sonya are going to start at the beginning, when the two of you just vanished inside that damn mirror."

"Whiskey first."

Though a MacTavish—emotionally if not by blood—Sonya wasn't one for whiskey. Tonight, she'd make an exception. Still shaken, she let Trey lead her down from the ballroom, down hallways, through the house as he snapped on lights.

"I don't remember anything before I was standing up there in front of that mirror."

She pushed at her hair, wished for a tie to hold it back, then just let the weight of it fall again.

"I don't remember getting out of bed, walking up there. And you were there."

"Cleo called."

"Cleo called," she murmured.

Cleo, her closest friend for a decade. Cleo, who'd moved into the manor with her without hesitation even knowing it held a curse, ghosts, and a crazed dead witch.

Being Cleo, Sonya decided, those elements had served as some extra motivation rather than any sort of deterrent. But then Cleo's Creole grandmother was a self-proclaimed witch—the good kind.

With the dogs, his Mookie and her Yoda, flanking them, Trey led her down to the main floor.

At the base of the stairs, she paused to look at the portrait of Astrid Grandville Poole. The first bride, so lovely, so tragic in her white dress.

"It started with her. Everything that's happening now started with her, and on her wedding day in 1806. When Hester Dobbs murdered her and pulled the ring from her finger.

"It has to end with me. It has to." She looked up at him, into those deep blue eyes she'd come to trust.

"You came. Cleo called, and you came. After three in the morning."

"Of course I came."

"But . . . you were with a client. The hospital." It flooded back. "Oh, that poor woman. Her husband—ex-husband—attacked her. Her kids—"

"They're okay." He kept his voice soothing. She was still so pale. "They're all going to be okay. Don't worry."

"You were worried. And so angry. I could hear it when you called to tell me."

"Her mom and sister are with her now." Trey turned her, steered her back toward the kitchen. "The police have him, and she's with her family. The kids are with them."

"And you'll take care of the rest, because that's what you do. Not just the lawyer business. Taking care's what you do." She tipped her head toward his shoulder as they walked. "I feel a little off."

"Really? I can't imagine why."

He turned on the kitchen lights, noted the fire crackling in the kitchen hearth, another roaring in the huge dining room.

Bringing the light, bringing the warmth. He wasn't the only one taking care.

Then he led Sonya to the table. "Sit. Do you want wine? Tea? Water?"

"Whiskey." She blew out a breath.

He thought of Owen getting a bottle only a few hours before when he'd needed to vent out that worry and anger, and all the frustration that came with it, to a friend.

"It seems to be the night for it."

With the worst of the cold fading as the fires snapped, she watched Trey get out biscuits for the hovering dogs, set out one for Owen's dog, Jones, before he walked into the butler's pantry, easy and confident in jeans and flannel shirt.

Like the first time she'd met him when he'd shown her through the manor, she mused with her head still swimming. The third-generation, long-limbed, lanky lawyer with his black hair, his deep blue eyes.

His seemingly infinite patience.

He knew the house as well as she did—better, she corrected. He'd roamed its rooms and hallways, welcomed from childhood on by the uncle she'd never known she'd had. Her father's twin—the classic separated at birth.

But they'd met through that same mirror, hadn't they? Those twins. As children, as men. Both artists, both so much alike in so many ways. Twin memory, Cleo called it.

One to become Andrew MacTavish of Boston, son of loving parents, husband of a loving wife, father of a loved and loving daughter. All of whom mourned and remembered him.

And one to grow up a Poole of Poole's Bay, to inherit the thriving family business, to inherit and live in the manor, as the son of a woman who was really his aunt, and all at the cold-blooded whim of the matriarch, Patricia Poole.

Just thinking about all of it hurt her mind, her heart. She covered her face with her hands, breathing slow as she tried to steady herself.

As Trey came back with a bottle and glasses, the phone in his pocket played Grand Funk Railroad's "Please Don't Worry."

On a half laugh, Sonya dropped her hands. "Clover never misses. Just a little musical pick-me-up from my nineteen-year-old ghost of a grandmother."

Trey set down the bottle. "Did it work?"

"I guess it did." When Yoda put his paws on her lap, she scratched his head. "And here's more," she said when the eye-patched Jones pranced into the room on his sturdy legs ahead of Cleo and Owen.

"We stopped by your room to get you a sweater in case you're still cold."

"Better now, but thanks." She took the sweater, then Cleo's hand. "Big thanks for looking out for me. For calling Trey and Owen."

From Cleo's phone, Dionne Warwick announced "That's What Friends Are For."

"True enough." Cleo sat, looked at Owen. "Buy me a drink, sailor."

He poured three generous fingers in each glass. "To being here," Owen decided. "Right here, right now. That's a damn good deal right now."

"It is." Sonya lifted her glass, took a gulp. Shuddered.

"All right. Okay. I know you want to know what happened, but can we start at the start? I don't know how I ended up in the ballroom, but you were with me, Cleo. Did I wake you up?"

"No. But somebody did." She took a long, slow sip, let it slide, let it settle. "I heard the clock at three, the piano, and someone crying, and someone who sounded like they were in pain. You know."

She looked at the others, shoved at her curling cloud of hair. "The usual middle-of-the-night manor entertainment. I'm just going to roll over and go back to sleep, but . . . Somebody touched me. My shoulder," she said, laying her own hand on it now. "And they said your name. 'Sonya,' just 'Sonya,' but there was an urgency in it."

"My name?"

"That's right. I turned on the light, and thought I'd probably dreamed it, but that urgency? It stuck, and I got up. I was going to check on you, but there you were, just coming out of your room. Sleepwalking, trance-walking, or whatever the hell it is. I ran back for my phone, and I called Trey as I followed you."

She turned to Trey. "Owen told me you were at his place. He filled me in on your client, your friend who was hurt by her drunk bastard of an ex. I'm glad she's going to be okay, her and her children."

"I was pissed off. You were right about that," Trey said to Sonya. "I went to get Mookie from Owen's, and dumped on him. Crashed in his spare room."

"A good thing you did," Cleo continued. "You went up to the third floor, Sonya, and I could hear that weeping woman, so clear. You stopped outside that room—a nursery once, right? You opened the door, and I swear, Son, I could see and hear the chair rocking along with the sobbing, and you said . . . Something like how night after night, year after year, Carlotta grieves for her boy."

"Hugh Poole's second wife, about six years after Marianne died in childbirth—having twins, Owen and Jane. They had three more kids, Carlotta and Hugh. One died as an infant." Sonya drank again, shuddered again. "It's in the book."

"I remember, too. I texted Trey so he'd know where we—you— were going, and I kept telling you I was there. I was afraid, I'm not ashamed to say, that you'd go down to the Gold Room, that bitch's room. I could see a red light glowing around it, and smoke curling out. You looked right at the door, and I thought, well, Jesus, just don't. You said she exists to feed, on fear and on grief. I should've turned the recorder on my phone to get it exact, but I didn't think of it."

"I wonder why?"

At Owen's comment, Cleo managed a snicker. "You said more,

about her drinking tears, night after night, year after year. Then, thank the goddess, you turned in the other direction."

She held out her glass to Owen. "Hit me again."

And she drank some more.

"Someone cried out in pain, in what had been the servants' quarters. You went to a door, and I swear to you I could smell the sick, and the bed creaking like someone was in it, tossing and turning. You said, sad, so sad, you couldn't help poor Molly O'Brian."

"Molly," Sonya murmured. The spirit who made the beds, lit the fires, tidied up.

"You said she came from Cobh and found a home here, how she loved to polish the wood, and you cried for her. You said you could only bear witness.

"When you turned, I thought: Shit, Gold Room. But you started toward the ballroom, so I let Trey know that. I turned lights on because it was so damn dark. Then you opened the ballroom doors, and I turned the lights on in there.

"And there was the mirror. It hadn't been there. We'd all been up there not long ago, and it wasn't there. But it was. It was so goddamn cold, and I could hear the pulsing from the Gold Room. Like the damn 'Tell-Tale Heart.'"

Now Cleo shuddered, just a little, before she continued.

"The way you looked at the mirror, Son, I knew, I *knew* you saw something I didn't. I couldn't. Then, oh, such relief, I heard Yoda barking, then the other dogs. I heard them running, and I told you to wait. 'Please, just wait.' Trey and Owen rushed in, the dogs, too. And you woke up."

"I don't remember any of that. Or . . . some, like a dream that's blurry and faded when you wake up. I heard you tell me to wait. I think. And the dogs barking. I felt half-in, half-out, I guess. Then I was awake and standing in front of the mirror."

She shifted to Owen. "You saw what I saw in it."

"Light, movement, color."

"Trey and I didn't. We're not Pooles. It's a portal," Cleo said with absolute certainty. "But not for everyone. You said it was pulling you."

"It was. There was music. I heard music."

"Yeah," Owen confirmed. "I didn't feel that pull, but I saw something, heard something."

"You didn't feel it, but you went with me."

This time Owen's phone sang out with "We Are Family."

"One weird trip," Owen said, and poured himself another shot of whiskey. "Five minutes, ten tops, but memorable."

"Closer to an hour," Trey corrected. "Fifty-six minutes."

"It couldn't have been." Shaking her head, Sonya looked at Owen for confirmation. "Just a few minutes."

"That just says time's different here than wherever you were. Where the hell were you?" Cleo demanded.

"Lisbeth Poole's wedding reception. In the ballroom, in 1916," Sonya said, and told them.

"She didn't expect us." Nudging her glass away, Sonya sat back. "When I called out, it threw her off. I . . . I don't think she saw us, but she heard me. And I think it scared her, for a minute. Half a minute. But it didn't stop her."

"It was already too late." Owen frowned into his glass. "No way to stop it, stop her."

"I thought if I could get to the ring first. Take Lisbeth's ring so Dobbs couldn't. But—"

"You flew," Owen said. "She didn't aim at me, but dead on at you. Shot you back, ten, twelve feet, and right through people who were running forward."

He picked up his glass a last time, drained the whiskey. "That's something you don't see every day. The spider was different."

"The one whose guts are on your shoe?" Trey asked.

"That's the one. Bigger than a wolf spider, but with black widow markings. People went right through it, as it went straight for Sonya. Fast fucker, too. I stomped its ugly ass, and we got the hell out of there.

"Lisbeth Poole was dead," he said to Sonya, "as she's always going to be dead on that night in 1916."

"Then what's the point of all this?" Sonya demanded, shoving impatiently at her long brown hair. "If it's always going to be too late, if there's no stopping her from killing them, what's the point?"

Cleo's phone played Ariana Grande's "7 Rings."

"It's never been about saving those brides, those women, Son." Cleo spoke gently. "It's about finding their rings, the seven rings, and breaking the curse. Expelling Hester Dobbs from this house, and breaking her curse."

"Dobbs has the damn rings."

"We'll figure it out." Trey laid a hand over hers. "We'll figure it out," he repeated, "but we won't figure it out tonight."

"This morning," Owen corrected. "I've got to be at work in . . ." He tapped his phone for the time. "Shit, about an hour and a half. And I need some damn shoes. I'm scrambling some eggs." He pushed up. "Got bacon?"

"You're scrambling eggs?"

"Cousin, if I'm awake to see the sunrise, I want breakfast. I'll take care of the bacon."

Trey gave Sonya's hand another pat. "I'm going to let the dogs out for a bit."

When he rose, Sonya shifted to look outside. Yes, morning was coming, and the night was dying away.

She had work of her own, and a life of her own. If the manor had given her a purpose beyond that, she'd do her best to fulfill it.

But morning was coming, and the day would follow.

She pushed away from the table to get started.

"I'll make coffee."

While the day bloomed, they sat and ate breakfast as they'd sat and shared whiskey and ghost stories.

After the dogs gobbled their own, Trey let them out again.

"I need you to drop me off," Owen told him. "I've gotta clean up, get to work. Have you got a bag or box I can dump those shoes in?"

"I'll take care of them," Cleo said.

"By take care of, you mean—"

"Burn them."

"Oh man."

"Outside," she added, "with a heavy dosing of salt."

"Jesus."

"That's how it's done," Cleo countered. "It's not like they were new. I could see that for myself."

"They were really well broken in."

She turned, patted his cheek, gave a couple days' worth of stubble a rub. "I'm sure you have others. A successful businessman and craftsman such as yourself."

"Is that a dig?"

She just smiled, sweetly. "You sacrificed your really well broken in shoes for my closest friend. No dig—this time. In fact, if I knew how to bake a pie, I'd bake you one."

"You could learn. I like pie. Come on, Jones. Gotta move, Trey."

"I'm with you. You're okay, cutie." Trey made it a statement as he took Sonya by the shoulders and kissed her.

His certainty served to boost her own.

"I'm okay. It's my house. As long as that mirror's in it, that's mine, too."

"Good. I owe you both dinner. I can pick you up at seven."

"Come for dinner. You, too, Owen. I'm making pot roast."

Trey blinked at her. "Really?"

"I did it once, I can do it again. I think."

"I'm in." Owen shoved his phone in his pocket.

Sonya stepped to him, rose up to kiss his cheek. "Thanks for the save."

"I could say anytime, but . . . Hell, anytime."

"Call if you need me," Trey said. "Come on, Mooks."

When they'd trailed out, Sonya turned to Cleo. "You were flirting with him."

Cleo widened her tawny eyes. "With Trey?"

"Owen. You had your flirt on. I know your flirt."

"He walked into that mirror with you—ahead of you, actually. He didn't think twice about it, just did it. And he saved you from harm. He earned my flirt."

"You're really going to burn his shoes, aren't you?"

"You're damn right."

Nodding, Sonya went in a cupboard for a garbage bag.

"Then let's go get them, get it done. Then I want a really long, hot shower before I start the rest of my day."

"There's a plan."

Chapter Two

Since Cleo volunteered to take the long list for the pot roast dinner and do the marketing, Sonya settled down at her desk in the library. She set down her water bottle, her tablet.

Over the past few months, she'd gotten into the habit of letting Clover, her house DJ, run the tunes. So without pulling up a playlist, she looked over at her mood boards.

Considering the early hour she'd eaten breakfast, she could afford to take a part of the morning to work on the Ryder Sports proposal.

She had time yet before she had to go to Boston and present it, and she thought she had a decent shot at the account. But her former bosses at By Design stood as formidable competition.

Matt and Laine had trained her well, and she'd worked hard for them for seven years. She knew how to put a major campaign together.

But she couldn't ignore the fact that she'd formed her own graphic design company, Visual Art by Sonya, less than a year ago. As a freelancer, a one-woman operation, she'd generated jobs since, and done some damn good work.

But the multigenerational, well-established sports equipment company would be, by far, her biggest client.

And she couldn't discount the point of pride when she knew she'd surely be in competition for that client with her ex-fiancé.

The cheating bastard.

Didn't matter, she told herself. Brandon Wise didn't matter.

All that mattered? The work.

She had a really good concept, and an excellent start.

"Time to push forward," she said, and opened the file.

With Yoda curled under her desk, she put in a solid two hours before she heard Cleo come back.

"Quick break." She saved the work and started down with Yoda following.

"Another two bags in the car," Cleo called out.

"Did we need that much?"

"Well, I was there."

Sonya ran out to fetch the bags, then stopped, breathed in air that tasted of spring.

She'd first come to the manor and the coast of Maine in the dead of winter. Now the air warmed, and daffodils bloomed. The big, bony weeper beside the house had fat buds, still closed and secret, on its branches.

Holding out her arms, she turned in a circle.

"This is my place now."

The view of the sun streaming down on the water, hers. The sound of waves crashing against the rocks, hers. Flowers blooming or budding, hers, too.

And if the curse on it was hers, too, now? She'd deal with it, somehow, some way.

She grabbed the bags and sailed back into the house.

In the kitchen, Cleo put groceries away. "That's a big slab of meat, Son."

"I know. It's scary, but I can do it. You bought an awful lot of apples. Are we getting a horse?"

"Oh, wouldn't that be sweet? But no. I'm making an apple pie."

"You're making an apple pie? From actual apples? Who are you, and what have you done with my Cleo?"

"I'm now Cleo, chief cook of the manor. Owen doesn't think I can do it, and I thought, well, I'll never know unless I try. So I called Mama, and she texted me her recipe while I was in the store. We had most everything except the apples anyway."

After getting out a bowl, Cleo began to put the apples in it. "And if I screw it up, nobody knows but you and me. And a houseful of ghosts."

"I'll never tell."

Sonya's phone popped out with Maroon 5's "Secret."

"Good, that's settled." Cleo tucked the cloth grocery bags away. "What time do you need to get started on that big slab of meat?"

"I think about one, one-thirty. I'm going to work until one for sure, then get it on."

"Then I'll meet you here by one-thirty. I'm grabbing a Coke and heading up to my studio. Want a Coke?"

"Yeah, I could use the boost. Don't go near the Gold Room, Cleo."

"Oh, you don't have to worry about that. It's mermaids for me today, not witches. And if the illustrations go well enough, I might work some on the painting."

They started upstairs together.

At the library, Cleo tapped her Coke to Sonya's. "Let's go get our art on."

Back at her desk Sonya put the Ryder proposal aside. While she didn't consider it pie in the sky, she needed to get down to her bread and butter.

She worked on her newest job, a store down in Poole's Bay.

Consistency, creativity, user-friendly, she thought as she disregarded Gigi's current, clunky, and altogether boring website.

Fun should be the theme there, she decided. Fun, casual clothes, surprising and fun scents in soaps and lotions, candles and bath salts. Toss in some—again—fun accessories.

She started a new mood board, keeping the fun up front.

The place really needed a fresh new logo. Though that hadn't been part of the package, she decided what the hell. She already saw it in her head.

The silhouette of a long-legged woman in heels, a short skirt, swinging a handbag, a scarf trailing behind. Just a hint of Paris, she thought as she worked. It fit with the name of the shop.

It said casual sophistication, female energy. And, of course, fun.

When her alarm beeped at one, she pulled herself out.

And as she began the process of saving her work, shutting down, for the first time she heard the bouncing of a ball in the foyer downstairs.

Jack, the little boy who hadn't lived to see his tenth birthday, loved playing with Yoda. And the love was mutual.

Maybe it was odd how easily she accepted that, but she'd lived in Lost Bride Manor long enough to learn not just to accept, but to embrace.

Because she didn't want to scare him—though how you scared a ghost was beyond her—she called out before she started down.

"I'm shutting down work for the day. I have work in the kitchen now."

She saw no sign of Jack until she got to the kitchen and found all the cabinet doors open.

"I guess you weren't finished playing with Yoda." She closed doors as she spoke. "But I'm on a schedule."

She got out the enormous heavy pot and Cleo's big slab of meat.

"Not as scary this time," she told herself. But she didn't actually believe it.

She seasoned the roast, began to brown it in oil. While it browned, she started peeling carrots.

She had a browned slab of meat and a pile of carrots and had started on the potatoes when Cleo dashed in.

"Sorry! I got caught up." Cleo grabbed an apron. "I started on a mer family. Cute little merbabies and toddlers. Then I thought: Where's Nana and Paw? They should have grandparents. I'll help you peel potatoes, and you can help me peel apples."

Before getting another peeler, Cleo pinned her cloud of burnt-honey hair up.

"I forgot a tie. Let me have that one." Sonya peeled the one off Cleo's wrist, tied her hair back. "When we were in college, did you ever see us peeling potatoes together?"

"I have to say no. But I didn't see myself peeling them with anybody." Cleo's eyes danced as she looked at Sonya. "Shame-the-devil truth? I kind of like it."

Sonya studied the mound of peels. "I like when it's all done, and doesn't suck."

"I kind of like the process, like art. The finish is what brings you pride, but you can't have the pride without the process."

"I'm working on the Gigi's job. I'm liking that process. And I can admit this process isn't as fraught as when I did it by myself the first time."

"I hung with you on FaceTime."

Sonya gave her a hip bump. "This is better. No regrets, right? About moving in?"

"Not a single one. I love it here. God, I love my studio. I'm going to love taking time to paint outside before much longer, and spending a Sunday afternoon sailing Poole's Bay when Owen builds me my sweet little Sunfish."

"I'd have stayed without you, because I knew this was my place, my home as soon as I saw it. But I wouldn't have been half as happy."

When they had all the vegetables prepped, Sonya heaved a breath. "Okay, here goes. You dump them in the oil and juices, with the herbs, stir them all around, let them cook awhile, brown a little maybe."

"All right, you've got that. I'm going to start on the pie crust."

"You're actually making pie crust. With flour and—whatever else is in pie crust."

"Process, Son, process. If you just do the inside part, it's sort of a cheat. I just—What is that noise?"

Sonya kept stirring even though her heartbeat sped up. "It's the dumbwaiter."

"The . . . well, God." Rubbing her hands on her apron, Cleo walked into the butler's pantry, frowned at it. "I'm going to look. It better not be something awful or it's going to piss me off."

Sonya held her breath, and didn't release it until she heard Cleo say, "Aww! Oh, it's sweet. Look here, Son. It's a pretty pie plate."

She carried it in. "Bright red, all fluted, and with an apple on the white inside bottom. It's perfect. I was just going to use this plain old glass one I found up here."

"Molly. She sent me up a platter for the pot roast I made for the Doyles. Lissy's platter. A wedding gift."

Cleo set the pie plate down, hugged Sonya's shoulders. "It's hard, I know it's hard, but Owen was right. We can't change what happened to her. Well, to either Lisbeth Poole or Molly O'Brian. To any of them."

"It's terrible watching them die, Cleo. Worse somehow knowing it's not just a dream, but that I'm somehow there and can't do anything to stop it."

"I know it. But, Sonya, you're bearing witness. Just like you said outside Molly's room. And I think it's important. And I think there's a reason Molly looks after us the way she does. Like sending me this dish, so I can make a pretty pie—hopefully. It matters to her. You matter."

"They all matter to me now. I want to stop Dobbs. I want to make her pay for all the misery she caused. I want—"

Doors began to slam; windows flew open and closed.

"Oh, blow it out your ass," Cleo shouted. "You blackhearted old bitch!"

Despite herself, Sonya let out a peal of laughter.

The iPad began to rock out, inviting them to celebrate good times.

"That's right, that's right, Clover." Cleo waved her fists in the air, shook her hips. "We're going to have a good time tonight."

"Come on!" Sonya sang, and plopped the roast on the vegetables. She picked up the wine she'd already opened, and poured it over the meat. "A whole damn bottle." She put the lid on the pot, then slid it into the oven, wagged a finger at Cleo. "Hours. No peeking."

"This already smells amazing. And I'm making pie."

"Show us how it's done."

It didn't live up to the phrase *easy as pie*, but they agreed it looked pretty when, after the measuring and the rolling and patching and peeling and slicing and stirring, Cleo slid it into the second oven.

"Son of a bitch! They better appreciate every bite of that. That's a ton of work."

"Let's take Yoda out, get some air."

Sonya waited until they walked outside in air cool after the heat of the kitchen.

"She stopped banging and bitching when we made fun of her."

"Yeah, I noticed." Cleo sent a smug glance back at the manor. "She feeds off fear and grief. That's what you said last night."

"We can't stop all of it, but we can fight back some with a few well-placed *Blow it out your asses*."

"I'm all for that. And we're going to throw that party, hold our Event in a few weeks. We need to start planning the details of that one."

"We do. We will."

"It's going to piss her off, having the house full of people. Happy people."

"It really is. We need to have your parents. I hope your grand-mère and my mom are up for that. And I should have my grandparents, all of them if they can make it. My aunt Summer and uncle Martin."

"We've got plenty of room for them." Cleo paused, looked back at the manor. "The house was meant for what we're doing in it, Son."

"And what's that?"

"Living, working, planning. And in your case," Cleo added, "having really good sex."

"It is really good sex."

"And as your friend, I applaud you. But she doesn't want any of that. She only wants the grief and the fear."

"We're going to give her plenty she doesn't want. And I'm going to find those rings, Cleo. I don't know how, yet, but I'm going to find them. And meanwhile, we're going to live and work and plan."

She watched Yoda chase a squirrel.

"You're going to get that slinky cat."

"I am," Cleo agreed. "I'm going to start that search real soon."

"And tonight we're going to serve a hell of a good meal, and we're going to do it in that big-ass dining room."

"That's what I'm talking about! When that pie comes out, we're going to get ourselves and that table looking extra."

"You always look extra. I should hate that about you."

"But you love me."

"I really do. Let's go check on your pie. And then I'm making beer bread."

Cleo smiled. "You figure Molly's cleaned up our cooking mess by now?"

Sonya didn't bother to look ashamed. "It's that obvious, huh?"

"Seems to me everybody's getting what they want."

They deserved a day like this, Sonya thought. A day to do good work, and to set that work aside early. A day to fiddle and fuss and spend time together.

With the scents of baking and cooking filling the kitchen—now spotless—they sat at the counter to work on the details of what they called An Event, scheduled, after some debate, for the second Saturday in June.

"The open house deal keeps it friendly, casual," Sonya decided. "But I vote for formal invitations."

"Make that unanimous. Adds elegance. An illustration of the manor."

"You read my mind. I'll go get a sketch pad."

By the time the pie and bread sat cooling on a rack, and they'd risked one quick peek inside the pot, they had their template of the manor in spring, with the weeping tree blooming, flowers spreading lush.

> *Sonya MacTavish and Cleopatra Fabares*
> *Invite you to The Manor for an evening of*
> *Food, drink, and fellowship.*
> *Saturday, June the eighth, at four p.m.*

"I like it," Cleo decided. "It's simple and welcoming."

"Not too simple?"

"I don't think so."

"Good. We need to include an RSVP." Sonya began to fiddle with the wording there. "A please respond by, say, May twentieth, so we have an idea of the count. Trey's mom will help us with names and addresses."

"We can hit Bree up for help with a menu. Head chef of the Lobster Cage, that's a solid connection."

"And she likes us, so yeah. We tap her for help on lining up servers, a couple bartenders. We order food from restaurants in the village."

"We're going to have to drag tables and chairs out of storage," Cleo pointed out. "Or rent them."

"Add glassware, dishes, linens. You know, I've designed invites for countless events, done websites for caterers, restaurants, bars. But neither one of us have ever planned and executed something like this."

"Scared?"

Sonya lifted her shoulders. "Little bit."

"Me, too. It adds to the fun."

"There are times your idea of fun and mine don't approach intersection."

When the tablet played the Beastie Boys, Sonya had to laugh.

"Okay, okay. We'll fight for our right to party."

"Which takes us to music. Do you think Trey and Owen can convince Rock Hard to play?"

"Won't know till we ask. It goes on the task list." Sonya noted it down. "Task for me: I'll generate the invitations."

"When you do, I'll get them mailed. You get the list from Trey's mom, and I'll talk to Bree."

"Good division of labor." Sonya clinked her water glass to Cleo's. "I know there are some folding tables in the basement. Not the scary basement where I'll never set foot again. I vote we assign Trey and Owen to hauling them up so we can clean them."

"Again, unanimous. Flowers. We're probably going to have to plant some, Son, and that's a learning curve for both of us. And we'll want some on the tables outside, and inside."

"So a trip to the nursery, and the florist. Both of us on those. I don't worry about making it pretty. We're good at that. I wanted to plant some flowers anyway. Like in the pots in the garden shed."

"I want to plant some herbs."

"You do?"

Cleo gave a decisive nod. "If I'm going to cook around here, I'm doing it right."

"You're in charge of those. Totally in charge."

"I can handle it. Now, let's go make ourselves pretty, and we'll come back and do the same with the table."

"What happened last night." Sonya gathered the sketch pad, her notes, her tablet. "It'll happen again. I know that, and so do you. But we're here, making a meal—with a freaking pie—and we're here, planning a party."

"An Event," Cleo corrected, and made Sonya smile as they walked from the kitchen.

"An Event. Sometimes my head says it's all crazy. But I know it's not. I know we're doing exactly what we should do."

"Live, work, plan," Cleo repeated.

"All of that. Just like I know there's so much more good in this house than bad. Some of the bad, it's just what happens when people live and work and plan in a house for over two hundred years. The worst of the bad? That's goes back to one . . . I won't call her a person."

"Entity."

"Entity then. And even with that, with what happened to them, Clover plays music, Molly makes the beds, Jack plays with Yoda."

They turned into the library, where Sonya put the notes and sketchbook on her desk. "And there's more."

"A lot more," Cleo agreed. "I feel them all the time."

"Why do they stay? The brides, and the ones who mourn them, maybe they stay because of the curse. But why do the others?"

"I don't know."

Sonya looked around the library, looked to the window where the African violet Cleo had given her years before bloomed.

"I think it's because this is home. I think they stay for the same reason I do—and you do now. This is home."

"I never thought of that," Cleo said as they walked out and down the hall. "And it feels right. It's a good house, Sonya, despite her. It's a really good house."

"It's our house, and it's their house. A year ago, I might've expected you to say something like that. But it's a hell of a surprise that I can say it, and mean it."

"And that's why they're with you, Son, because you say it, and you mean it. Now, go make yourself pretty."

She could do that. Funny, she thought as she continued to her room, though she'd gotten about three hours' sleep, she really wasn't tired.

She wanted an evening, this evening, of—well—food, drink, and fellowship.

She walked through her sitting room to the bedroom. There, under the late afternoon sun, the sea spread outside her windows, the terrace doors.

And there, on the bed, lay a dress she'd bought with her aborted honeymoon in mind. A dress she hadn't worn since trying it on.

Molly's choice, she thought, and why not.

She held it up, turned to the mirror.

She didn't wear pink often, but this color skewed more deep rose. A simple, sleeveless sheath she'd imagined wearing to a romantic dinner. As a bride.

"That would've been a mistake. But the dress isn't. Okay, Molly, nice choice. Thank you."

She took her time, and as she dealt with her hair, let out a sigh. Time, she determined, to bite the bullet and make an appointment with the local hairstylist. It had been way too long there.

And still many more weeks before she'd travel to Boston for the Ryder presentation.

Which still left time, if she hated what the new stylist did, to correct it.

"Nothing wrong with a little vanity," she told herself as she zipped up the dress. "And appearances for that presentation matter."

Clover agreed with "Looking Good."

Amused, Sonya turned in the mirror. "Yeah, I know I look good. Let's see if Cleo's ready."

Cleo had gone for lightning blue, a little shorter, a little flirtier, and was currently working her hair into a complicated braid.

Her eyes met Sonya's in the mirror. "I remember when you bought that dress. I talked you into it."

"I remember. Molly laid it out."

"Mine, too. She's got excellent taste. And considering we were both in watch-a-double-feature-and-go-to-bed clothes last night for our strange little party, it's nice to put on a dress."

"I'm making a hair appointment tomorrow. In the village."

Cleo's hands paused. "Are you sure?"

"I've gotta commit. And if they screw it up, I have time to fix it before the big presentation in Boston."

"I see your point, but hair adultery's a big step."

Sonya nodded solemnly. "The long-distance relationship isn't going to work out."

"I'll support you in your decision. I'm not sure I can be that brave with my multicultural do. Creole, Asian, a hint of Jamaica, a whiff of Brit? You've got white girl hair."

"I do. I'm risking it. Ready?"

Yoda pranced down with them, then danced in front of the entrance doors.

"Time to go out? You come around back when you're done." She opened the door for him. "You've got company coming, too."

"I thought I'd contact the one you got the adorable Yoda from. For that slinky cat."

"Lucy Cabot. She's great. Also works with a cat rescue. I'll send you her info. She'd know."

Sonya paused by what she knew Collin Poole had called the Quiet Place, where the old grandfather clock with its moon face stood silent. At three.

No matter where they put the hands, they always returned to three.

"I don't remember hearing it chime three last night. But I must have. I don't always, but I got up, made my way to the ballroom, so I must have. When I do hear it—when I'm aware I hear it—I don't feel that pull."

"If you ever do, you get me first."

"Count on it. Have you thought any more about making an office? Separate from your studio?"

"Maybe. The studio makes me so damn happy, but it might be smart to have a separate space for business."

"I like the idea of using more of the house. Really using it. That's why—"

She broke off when they walked into the big kitchen.

The pie and bread sat on the cooling rack and the air smelled glorious.

And the platter sat on the island.

"Oh, isn't that gorgeous. What a beautiful dish! It looks old and important."

"It is," Sonya murmured. "It's Lisbeth's. It's the one I used before. A wedding gift."

Lifting it, Sonya turned it over so Cleo could read the inscription on the back.

"She never got to use it, and that makes you sad. But, Sonya, I think using it—not just letting it sit somewhere in storage—it's a way of remembering her."

"I saw her, across the ballroom. Just for a minute. There were so many people. She was so young, Cleo, and she looked so happy. Honestly, she just glowed."

She set the platter down.

"You're right. It shouldn't just sit in storage."

They set the table, added candles, the good wineglasses. Since the April evening was cool enough, they lit the fires in the kitchen, in the dining room.

"How about some music to set the mood?" Cleo began.

Clover answered with "Tangled Up in You."

"Maybe a little direct," Cleo decided, "but I like it. Glass of wine, partner?"

"You pour. I need to take the pot roast out, make the gravy."

"Grab an apron for that. I'm going to be watching how you do it."

The minute Sonya took the pot out of the oven, lifted the lid, Yoda scrambled up to stand on his stubby back legs, wave his front paws.

"That's a Jack trick, and yeah, you'll get a taste test."

"I want one myself." Cleo poured the wine. "It just sits in there all damn day, then smells like that. I think the pie was harder."

"You're forgetting the mountain of peels that went into the composter."

"Some of those were apple peels. Just look at that," she added as Sonya set the roast in the center of the platter and began to surround it with vegetables. "I believe you've become a pot roast genius."

"Let's make sure." Sonya sliced off a bit, divided it into three. She handed one to Cleo, tossed one to Yoda, then sampled herself. "I believe you're right. I am, officially, a pot roast genius."

"There may not be room for my pie after this."

"They're men." Sonya put the platter in the warming oven. "They'll have room for pie."

Hip cocked, sipping wine, Cleo watched Sonya whisk up gravy.

"I am seriously impressed. Here, I'll whisk awhile. Take a wine break."

They switched positions.

Yoda scrambled up with a joyful bark to race toward the front of the house. The doorbell bonged, and Clover switched to the Black Eyed Peas singing about how tonight's gonna be a good night.

"I agree." Reaching over, Sonya turned down the heat. "Let's let them in and get it started."

Chapter Three

When Sonya opened the door, Mookie galloped in. Jones swaggered.

On the third floor, doors slammed like gunshots.

"Somebody's not happy to see us," Owen commented, and held out a bottle of wine. "He's flower guy, I'm wine guy."

"And both are appreciated." Sonya took the bouquet of white tulips. She kissed Trey, then Owen.

"I got a kiss last night," Owen reminded Cleo when she simply shut the door.

"Circumstances," she said.

"Come on back. Can I ask how your client is? The one in the hospital."

"She's good. Better. They'll keep her another day, maybe two. Owen spent more time with her than I could manage today."

"You went to see her?" Sonya asked.

"Her ex used to work for me. Us," he corrected. "She's doing okay. Looks like she got the crap beat out of her, but doing okay. She's counting on Trey to get her full custody of the kids and permission to move out of state with them. Back with her family."

"She can count on it. I remember this smell," Trey added. "And it's just as good as the first time."

"With special additions. Beer bread and apple pie."

"You made pie?"

Cleo smiled at Owen, and poured two more glasses of wine. "I learned."

"It looks good. You look good," Trey added. "Both of you."

"We had a good day."

"Did you actually burn my shoes?"

"We did," Cleo answered. "In a spot back near the woods, in a circle of stones and salt. Doused them with lighter fluid, tossed a match, and whoosh."

"It wasn't pretty," Sonya told him, "but effective." She got out three rawhide bones. "Now, you dogs take these and go behave yourselves. The humans are going to have dinner."

"How do they feel about cats?" Cleo wondered.

Trey watched his big Lab/retriever mix gallop off with his bone. "Mookie's fine with them."

"Depends on the cat," Owen told her.

"I'm getting one, as soon as I find the right one. I've got the gravy, Sonya. You get one of these big, strong men to take the platter to the table. We're eating in style tonight."

"So I see. I've got it," Trey said. "I remember from last time."

When Trey took it out of the warming oven, Owen blinked.

"Holy shit. That's a serious pot roast dinner."

"As the manor's pot roast genius, I don't do any other kind." Sonya grabbed the bread and board.

"You need help with that?" Owen asked Cleo.

"I've got it. Just going to ladle it into the boat. You get the wine."

At the table, Sonya plated the meal for all four of them before she sat.

"Compliments to the chefs," Trey said.

"Haven't tried it yet." Owen sampled the roast. "Okay, now I have. Kudos. It's better than your mom's, Trey."

"She knows. Thanks for this. It's a lot of work. A lot of trouble."

"You're welcome. Speaking of work and trouble, Cleo and I set the date for our Event. Open house the second Saturday in June."

"We're talking a bash here." As doors slammed, Cleo smiled up at the ceiling. "She hates the idea. And that just makes me love it more."

"This is how you're taking her on?" Owen wondered. "Throwing a party?"

"That's a nice little bonus." Cleo speared a chunk of carrot. "Mostly we want to open the house, fill it up with people, food, drink, music."

"It's made for just that," Sonya added. "When's the last time there's been a real event in this house?"

"I'm too young to really remember it, but I'd say Collin and Johanna's wedding. That didn't end well," Trey added.

"There won't be a bride for Dobbs to murder. And we won't let her dictate how we live here."

The lights flicked off, on, off, on. Sonya picked up her wine. Then laughed when, with boosted volume, the iPad in the kitchen rolled out with CeeLo's "Fuck You."

"Can't argue with that," she said, and drank.

"You want to provoke her."

"Sometimes." She met Trey's eyes and the worry in them. "She's responsible for the deaths of women in my family for over two hundred years. So yeah, sometimes I want to give her a good shot. But that's not the reason for the party. We're going to live here, in this house, in this community. We're going to be part of it. This is one way."

"He's not trying to talk you out of it." As he spoke, Owen sliced off some more beef. "He has to line up all the facts, suppositions, and motivations. Trey was born a lawyer." He forked some potato. "Now, if he were trying to talk you out of it, you'd end up talked out of it without realizing you'd been talked out of it."

Sonya nodded. "I've noticed that about him. Most of the time, you'd think going another way was your idea in the first place."

"You got it."

"I do. And"—Sonya looked back at Trey—"I like that about him."

"Good thing. So, how do you get all this done at the same time?"

"I have absolutely no idea," Sonya told Owen. "But that brings us back to the subject of food. Cleo and I thought we'd order food for our Event from the restaurants in town, and see if Bree could give us an idea on hiring servers and bartenders and all the rest."

"It's a good idea." Trey took a slice of bread. "People will come."

"Oh, hell yeah," Owen agreed.

"Will the Pooles?" Sonya wondered.

"The ones who are around? Probably, yeah. Everybody got what they wanted, Sonya. They've got no beef with you."

"People who knew Collin liked him," Trey added. "Those who didn't know him, they'll come out of curiosity. And because both of you are making connections in the village."

"I like the village," Cleo said. "I'm going to like seeing it from the bay when you build me that boat."

"He's got the design."

"Does he?" Over the rim of her glass, Cleo smiled. "I'd like to see it."

"Am I bugging you about the painting?"

"But," Cleo pointed out, "you've seen it in progress."

"I walked in on it. I don't do showings."

"What about Yoda's doghouse?" When Owen sent Sonya an exasperated look, she waved it away. "No, I'll come back to that. Getting off topic. The Event. Do you think we could get Manny's group to play?"

"You want the band?"

As Trey considered, Owen grabbed the bread. "Now we're talking. I figured you'd do some fancy formal deal where everyone's standing around like stiffs while somebody's playing the harp or whatever."

"We could get a harpist to play in the front parlor."

Owen pointed at Cleo. "Don't spoil it. Rock Hard? They'll jump on it."

"They'll jump on it," Trey agreed. "Just understand you're going to have people roaming all over the manor."

"That's why it's called an open house. But hoping for good weather,"

Sonya put in, "we're going to set up tables outside. We've got several folding tables in storage."

"You hear that, Trey?" Owen tilted his head as if listening. "That's the sound of you and me getting drafted into hauling up tables."

"And chairs," Cleo added. "And, Son, I think we should hang some party lights."

"Who doesn't love party lights?"

"The person who has to hang them," Owen said. "Then take them down."

"Maybe we'll leave them up. Cleo?"

"I love that idea. String them in that wonderful witchy weeper, around the deck over the apartment."

"Which is where we'd want the band to set up. It's a good thing, Trey." Sonya reached over for his hand. "A good, positive thing."

"It's a good, positive thing. And good, positive community relations."

"Another solid bonus on that. A woman has to earn a living."

"How's the Ryder proposal going?"

"I got some time in on it today before I switched to my revamp of Gigi's website."

"The girlie place on Bay off High Street?" Owen reached for a second helping. Of everything.

"Would you call it girlie?"

He shrugged. "Girl clothes, smelly girl stuff. That qualifies. Clarice—cousin—likes the smelly stuff."

"Make a note," Sonya told Cleo. "Have Gigi's smelly girl stuff in the bathrooms for the event."

"Right there with you."

"Now"—Sonya smiled as Trey topped off her wine. Then, lifting her glass, turned to Owen—"about that doghouse."

By the time they'd eaten their fill, Sonya had poured the last of the second bottle of wine. "I say we take this, walk around with the dogs before we come back for pie. And we'll tub up some of this, and some of that, for both of you to take home."

"I especially like that part. It was a damn good meal," Owen added. "Appreciate it."

"You're going to want a jacket. Both of you." Trey gave Sonya's bare arm a stroke as they rose. "April nights are cool."

The music on the iPad had Sonya frowning. "I don't know that one."

"'Pieces of April,'" Owen told her. "Three Dog Night."

"Owen knows music," Trey said.

"So I see. Well, speaking of dogs, we'll take them out the front, grab jackets."

All three dogs got up, stretched, and raced to the front.

"We'll take KP when we get back. It's only fair."

"I'll let you." Sonya glanced up at Trey as they walked. "I'm not sure Molly will."

"Invisible housekeeper. Handy," Owen decided. "I could use one of those."

"She's family now, too."

She paused outside the music room, and the two portraits she'd found in the studio. Of Clover and of Johanna—the sixth and seventh brides.

"Just like they are."

They stopped in the small parlor for jackets, then stepped out into a star-strewn night that struck between cool and cold.

"Going to see a freeze tonight," Owen predicted.

"Are you two warm enough?"

Trey took Sonya's hand. "We're Maine men, cutie. This is balmy."

"It's so clear." Shaking back her hair, Cleo looked up. "You never see stars like this in Boston."

"How about Lafayette?" Owen wondered.

"No, not unless you head into the bayou."

"Ever think about going back?"

"For visits, sure. To live?" Cleo shook her head. "I found my place.

I love this house." She turned, looked back at it. "Dobbs wants to spoil that. Chase us out. She doesn't understand who she's dealing with."

As she spoke, the window of the Gold Room slapped open. In the glimmer of starlight, something flew out. Something big, something fast, that let out a shrill, inhuman shriek.

Even as Owen shoved Cleo behind him, Trey shifted to stand in front of Sonya.

It took a heartbeat, no more than two, with all three dogs barking vicious warnings. And Jones actually leaping up as if to attack what flew at them.

Then, with the stink of sulfur, it vanished.

"She did that once before." Fighting for calm, Sonya bent to pick up Yoda, to soothe. "It didn't work then either."

"Hell of a show, though." Digging into his pocket, Owen pulled out three small dog treats, tossed them. "Jones doesn't back down."

"Do you always carry those?" Cleo asked.

"Don't you?"

She laughed. "I believe I'll start. Well. That may or may not conclude our show for the evening."

Sonya gave Yoda a kiss on the nose, then set him down. "Let's go have pie."

Trey took her hand, kissed it. "No, she doesn't understand who she's dealing with. I've got a bag in the truck. I'm staying tonight."

"I was hoping you would."

"I've got some gear in mine," Owen added. "I thought I'd bunk here if that's okay."

"Looking out for us, Cousin?"

"Maybe I figure I've had a lot of wine, and shouldn't drive."

"I guess Jones doesn't have a license."

"Suspended. He's a maniac behind the wheel."

Cleo looked down at Jones, scruffy and fierce with his eye patch. "I actually believe that."

They went in to find not only a spotless kitchen and dining room, but the leftovers divided into three tubs.

"Thank you, Molly. Well, I'm about to serve my first pie. Does everyone want coffee with that?"

"I'll handle the coffee." Trey stepped over to the machine while the iPad started a new tune.

"Johnny Cash," Owen told them. "'Cup of Coffee.'"

"I think you and Clover would get along very well," Sonya commented.

"Since Trey already told me—back when—and I've seen her picture? Hot babe. I try to get along with hot babes."

The music switched to Avril Lavigne's "Hot," and Owen grinned.

"Back atcha, gorgeous."

"You know, she's my grandmother, which makes her your—what, great-aunt?"

"Still a hot babe, and one with excellent taste in music."

"Pie." Cleo set four servings at the casual table.

"Coffee." Trey brought over the rest.

"Remember, it's my first."

Owen took a generous bite. "Hell of a good start."

It was, and Sonya decided also an excellent finish as the day—or more accurately the night before—began to catch up with her.

"I'm sorry to break this up so early, but I'm fading fast."

"I'm going to be right behind you," Cleo told her.

"Owen, do you know what room you want?"

"I'll crash in the one I had last time. I have to head out early, so thanks again if I don't see you."

Sonya caught the look that passed between the two men, and sighed.

"I don't give a damn about the mirror tonight. I'm going to sleep."

"We could all use it." Cleo covered the rest of the pie. "I'll see whoever's around in the morning after ten."

They went upstairs, with the dogs following, then parted ways.

In her bedroom, Sonya let out another sigh. "This was exactly the right way to spend the evening after how we spent last night."

"And you're tired." Lifting his hand, Trey laid it on her cheek.

"It's starting to hit. Don't let me get up and walk tonight if you can stop me."

"Don't worry. No walking tonight."

Trusting him, she got ready for bed, then curled up beside him.

"I'm really glad you're here."

"No place I'd rather be."

He felt her drift off within minutes, then lay listening to the manor. The sounds of settling, the rhythmic beat of the water against rock.

The sounds of murmurs and whispers that sounded like voices lost in the wind.

His dog and hers slept quiet, and after a time, so did he.

But he woke when the clock chimed three. She stirred against him, muttered in her sleep, then lay quiet again.

While she slept, he listened to the drift of piano music, the heartbreak of weeping, the creak of a door, the rattle of a window.

He heard something, a call or a cry from outside, over the sound of the sea. Quietly, he slipped out of bed, walked to the terrace doors, eased his way out.

And he saw the figure in black standing on the seawall. Saw her dark hair fly in a wind he couldn't feel.

She threw her hands up to a moon that hadn't been full when they'd walked the dogs.

When she leapt, her black dress billowing, his heart jolted.

The wind died, and the moon sailed as a crescent.

He stepped back in, closed the doors. When he got back into bed, the house lay quiet again.

Sonya woke alone. No Trey, no dogs. Thinking that was too damn bad, she sat up. She not only wasn't tired after the solid night's sleep, she'd have enjoyed sliding into a little wake-up sex.

Barely seven, she realized. And here she considered herself an early riser.

She took a moment to stand by the windows, looking out at the sun, the sea, all gold and blue. A fishing boat, white and red, glided by on its morning business, and a scatter of gulls winged by on theirs.

"This feels a lot better than yesterday morning, and so do I."

She grabbed her phone, shoved it in the pocket of her sleep pants.

She started down, past Cleo's room, the room Owen used—her door closed, his open, bed made.

She wondered if she'd ever come to take it for granted—the rooms, the beauty and history, the feel of the house that had become hers.

And decided, as she walked down the grand staircase, absolutely not.

She made her way into the kitchen, where Trey and Owen talked quietly over pie and coffee.

Conversation broke off when she came in.

She said, "Good morning," and headed for the coffee.

"Morning," Trey echoed. "The dogs are running off their breakfast out back."

Now she said, "Mmm. So you two are having pie for breakfast."

"It was right there," Owen pointed out. "No different from a Danish or a turnover, if you ask me."

She turned with her coffee, leaned back against the counter as she studied them. Two great-looking men, she thought. Friends, longtime friends. Longer than she and Cleo. Friends who could communicate with each other without words.

Like right now.

Her phone gave Lady Gaga's "Poker Face" a spin.

"Right. I've been known to play poker myself, so . . . You might as well tell me what's going on, as it involves me, directly or indirectly."

"Over to you, pal." Owen rose, took a tub of leftovers out of the fridge. "I've got to get moving." He picked up the bag at his feet and started toward the back door.

"Owen?"

He paused when Sonya said his name, turned as she walked to him. Then when she wrapped her arms around him, gave her back an awkward pat.

She could actually feel him look over her head at Trey.

"Thanks for being here." She let him go.

"No problem. Later."

When he went out the back, gave Jones a whistle, she turned back to Trey.

"I don't like you keeping things from me."

"I'm not doing that. Won't do that. I fully intended to tell you when you got up. Or if I had to leave before, I'd have called you to tell you."

She knew truth when she heard it, and nodded. "Okay. Tell me now. Did I try to walk last night?"

"No. When the three a.m. business started, you muttered something in your sleep. But I couldn't make it out. But besides the usual, I heard something outside."

"Outside the house?"

"Yeah. I got up, went over to look." He took a moment, drank coffee. "And I saw her. Dobbs. I saw her standing on the seawall—but under a full moon, with the wind really whipping."

"We didn't have a full moon last night."

"That's right. I'm going to bet the moon was full when Dobbs jumped off that wall. Like I watched her do last night."

"You—you watched her jump?" Instinctively, Sonya pressed a hand to her heart. "You saw her suicide."

"I did. She stood on that wall, raised her arms up, and just . . ." He tipped the flat of his hand over. "Just after three in the morning. Everything got quiet almost right after she jumped. The wind died, and the moon changed back."

His eyes, deep and eerily blue with the black rings around the irises, looked directly into hers. "It wasn't stepping through a magic mirror into another time, but it was a goddamn moment."

"You could've waked me."

"Why? It was over, and all of us needed some sleep."

She couldn't argue with that. Instead, she walked to him, set her coffee down, and wrapped her arms around him as she had Owen.

"She didn't hesitate, Sonya. She'd come here to end herself at the manor, and that's just what she did."

"And she's still here, a part of her is." Drawing back, she framed his face, kissed him. "That had to be beyond strange, and really hard to witness."

"Your instinct is to stop it. Just stop it, no matter what she did, what she is or was. But there was no stopping it."

"It wasn't for love of Collin Poole. That's not love, I don't believe that. It's not jealousy over a man."

"They'd have hanged her. For the murder of Astrid Poole. They'd have hanged her in the village, away from the manor. She needed to die here, at her own time, at his place, by her own means. I don't know much about witchcraft or curses, but I'm betting on that."

"Oh." She stepped back as it struck her. "Of course. It makes sense in the completely insane scope of it all. How could she doom a Poole bride every generation if she was hanged miles away? How could she take their wedding rings—because the rings, Trey, are part of how the curse holds."

"The spell you heard—when she killed Agatha Poole."

Closing her eyes, Sonya brought it back.

"'With my blade, I took the first, then by my blood this house was cursed. One by one they wed, they die, because they seek to take what's mine.'"

She opened her eyes. "'And with their rings of gold, my spell will hold and hold.'"

And shuddered.

"She stabbed Astrid—by her blade," Sonya began. "She killed herself here—by her blood. And yeah, the rings are the key to holding the spell, the curse."

"There's the other part. They—not she, not Astrid—*they* seek to take what's mine. Not Collin Poole, Sonya, or not just Collin Poole."

"The manor." On a long breath, she slid down onto a stool. "Not love for Collin Poole, however deranged. The manor. He'd inherited the manor from Arthur Poole, from his father, after his father had a riding accident."

"Was it an accident?"

Eyes wide, she pressed a hand to her heart. "You think—and God, I see why—she caused the accident."

"She has an affair with the oldest son, the son who'll inherit the manor—and all the prestige that goes with it. A lot of wealth besides. Get rid of his father so it passes to him? It's not a big stretch, considering."

"I guess it isn't."

"But then, he doesn't want Dobbs. He's not going to marry Dobbs."

"He marries Astrid Grandville. He loved her, Trey. They loved each other. I saw that. I saw them."

"I'm not disputing that. In fact, that's part of it."

Rising, he slid his hands in his pockets. Paced to the window to check on the dogs.

"He loved someone else, married someone else. Someone who'd live here, make a family here. So she killed Astrid, the first bride. On her wedding day."

"But Collin still didn't want her."

"No, he grieved, ordered that portrait painted. And Dobbs will be hanged for murder—and I'd say in no small part for witchcraft. She escapes long enough to come here, cement the curse with her own blood and death."

"So she can stay." Sonya nodded as it played out in her head. "In some twisted way hold the manor. Hold it by causing the death of a Poole bride, one every generation."

"Taking their rings to bind it. It's good. I guess it's good to have what feels like a logical explanation."

"Collin, in his grief, hanged himself. His brother inherited the manor, lived here with his wife, his children.

"Until his daughter Catherine—here, on her wedding night. Lured outside in a blizzard, where Dobbs waited. And froze to death. Dobbs took her ring. I saw that, too."

"And down the line," Trey finished.

"Except for Patricia Poole. My great-grandmother. She refused to live here, closed the manor. Her son Charles opened it again against her wishes, married Lilian Crest—Clover—against her wishes, no doubt. Clover dies giving birth to my father and his twin, and Charles hangs himself—like Collin did."

"She separates the twins, puts your father up for adoption and passes your uncle Collin off as her daughter's son."

Down the line, Sonya thought.

"I need to know more about Patricia Poole. More about Gretta, the daughter. I know she's in Ogunquit, that she has dementia. I need to know more."

"I'll help as much as I can there."

He took her mug over to the coffee station, made her a second cup.

"I know Gretta Poole never lived here," he continued. "I don't remember her ever coming here. Patricia Poole either."

"I should talk to your father. I should talk to Deuce. He and Collin were close friends. If anyone can fill in some blanks, he could."

Trey pulled out his phone. "I'll text him. Let me set this up, have him come here. He'd want to come here for something like this."

"If you're sure."

"I am. And I've got to go." He took her shoulders. "You're okay."

"I like that you make that a statement of fact and not a question."

"Because it is a fact. I'm going to have things to clear up with Marlo—my client. She's being discharged from the hospital sometime today or tomorrow. And if she's up to it, there's paperwork I have to have her sign so I can file. I don't know if I can get back. And . . ."

"I'm okay," she reminded him. "Don't forget the leftovers."

"Not likely. Look, if something's not okay—"

"I'll call you."

"Expect Deuce around two." He kissed her, lingered over it.

He got the tub, kissed her again. "Any chance you can put all this away awhile?"

"A very big chance. I've got stuff to do."

"Good. We'll talk later."

When he went out the back, she held the door open to let Yoda in.

"I know, you'll miss your pals." On his whine, she bent down to give him a good rub. "But I'm here. Right here. And that's where I'm going to stay."

She decided apple pie for breakfast was an excellent idea. With it and her second cup of coffee, she sat down to check her email and line up her day of work.

Chapter Four

Sonya knew Cleo's morning routine as well as her own, so when Cleo passed the library shortly after ten, Sonya answered the grunt with a wave.

She gave her housemate ten minutes, time enough for that first, mind-clearing cup of coffee, then with Yoda, headed down to the kitchen.

Cleo sat at the island with coffee, a toasted bagel, and her phone. After grabbing a Coke, Sonya gave Yoda the option of outside, which he took. Then she sat beside her friend.

"I take it our overnight guests are gone?"

"They are. Owen at the crack of dawn, and Trey not long after."

"Makes me very glad I don't have work that requires me to come near the crack of dawn." She lifted the bagel, got a good look at Sonya's face. And set it down again.

"Well, shit. Just shit! What happened? Did I sleep through something?"

"Apparently everyone did but Trey."

As she listened to Sonya's recount, Cleo nibbled on the bagel.

"Three a.m., binding the curse with her own blood. And I'm a hundred percent on your conclusions. Not for love of the 1800s Collin Poole, but pure jealousy and avarice. She wanted to be lady of the manor. And she still does."

"When Patricia Youngsboro married Michael Poole Jr., she didn't have her wedding or reception here, and refused to live here," Sonya said. "Closed the manor until her son Charles inherited, and he opened it, moved in—with Lilian Crest. But for those twenty years or so, the manor stayed closed—maintained, but with no occupants. Why would she do that? Unless she knew of or believed in the curse?"

"I'm going to say both."

"Both," Sonya agreed. "Everything I've read says she was a hard-ass, status-symbol type of person. A controller, one who ruled her business and her family."

"Yeah, I'd say separating her dead son's twins qualifies as controlling. And downright mean."

"She embraced all things Poole." Sonya held up a finger. "Except the manor. The historic family home, a major status symbol. Her other son, Lawrence, never lived here. Her daughter, Gretta, never lived here. Why?"

"Because she didn't want them to." Instead of a finger, Cleo held up a fist. "Iron fist. That's what you're thinking, and again a hundred percent. But she couldn't do a damn thing about it when her husband left the manor to Charles—Charlie—and he moved in."

"Exactly," Sonya agreed. "Charlie said no to the control, no to her rules. So Dobbs had her sixth bride, after a couple of decades of holding the manor."

Sonya pushed up. "From what I can tell, Clover was already pregnant when they moved in. But Dobbs didn't go after her, or her wedding ring, until the birth of the twins."

"You think, after that twenty-year gap, Dobbs wanted more. More blood, more rings, more power?"

"I think it's possible."

"And I'm right there with you."

"I need to find out more about Patricia Poole. She must've been in this house before she married. At parties, for dinner. Something. Then she shut down one of the biggest—aside from the business, the biggest—Poole status symbol, and had a house built on the other side of town. And as far as I know, she took nothing out of the manor. No furniture, no family heirlooms.

"Deuce—Trey's father—is coming to talk to me about it this afternoon. And I want to know more about Gretta Poole. She lived a lie, pretended to be Collin's birth mother. And she never married, raised Collin in her mother's house. She never lived on her own."

"Under her mother's thumb. Or we could go to Gilead, because I bet Patricia could've given Aunt Lydia a run. Under her eye."

"Yeah, with the manor closed again, until Collin inherited it, and moved in."

Clover let loose with "Sweet Child o' Mine."

"It's interesting," Cleo commented, "having a three-way conversation that includes a ghost, through her musical selections."

"But I think she can only tell us so much, all of them can only tell us so much. That's why we need the living. I'm going to go back to work."

She walked to the door to let Yoda in. "If you're not in the middle of your own and can break off, feel free to join us when Deuce gets here."

"I think I will. I not only want to meet him, but I'd like to hear what he has to say firsthand."

"You'll like him. Come on, Yoda. Break's over."

She went back to work on Gigi's, and thinking of Owen's "girlie" comment, worked on some potential ads and taglines about gifts—for the women in your life.

She worked on some choices specifically targeting Mother's Day. Embrace the girlie, she decided.

As it neared two, she shot off an email with those drafts attached. Let the client get a feel for the direction, she thought, before she put too much time and effort into it.

Downstairs, she put a coffee service together, added a plate of cookies.

She carried the coffee service into the front parlor, stopped, and looked around.

The piano gleamed under the vase of white tulips. All the pillows were plumped, and the air smelled faintly, very faintly, of orange oil.

"Thank you, Molly," she said just as the doorbell sounded. "Right on time."

She thought of the first time she'd opened the door to Oliver Doyle II, on a cold winter day in Boston, and without any idea how that visit would change her life.

She wouldn't have this house without Deuce, she considered as she went to let him in. And looked down at Yoda. "Plus, I wouldn't have you."

She opened the door to cool April air, and the man who'd helped change her life.

It was easy to see Trey in him, in those wonderful blue eyes—his behind silver-framed glasses. His full head of hair had gone silvery gray, but those distinctive eyebrows remained dramatically black.

Sonya reached out both hands to him. "Thank you so much for coming."

"Sonya. It's always a pleasure to see you, and to visit the manor."

She heard the door to the Gold Room slam like cannon fire.

"Really?"

"Yes." He stepped inside, then bent to pet Yoda. "Trey's caught me up on events, and tells me you and your friend Cleo are handling it all very well."

"I think we are. It helps that Cleo loves the manor as much as I do. Come in and sit down. I made coffee."

"Much appreciated." Then he looked over and up as Cleo started down the stairs. "And this must be Cleo. I've looked forward to meeting you."

"I'll say the same." She held out her hand. "I really like your wife."

"So do I."

Cleo flashed him a smile. "Sonya said I could sit in on your talk, if that's all right with you."

"More than. I hope I can fill in some blanks, though some of that will be speculation, gossip, and opinion."

"We'll take all three." Cleo hooked her arm through his as they walked into the parlor. "But gossip not only often rings true, it adds the fun."

"I'm not ashamed to agree." Sonya poured out the coffee. "And I think adding all three together helps us get a clearer picture of my father's biological family. And could help us evict a certain element from the manor."

From the library, the iPad blasted the Allman Brothers Band and "Black Hearted Woman."

"Clover agrees."

He smiled at that, all the way into his eyes.

"It seems you've developed a relationship with her. And adjusted, in a matter of months, to—we'll say—the eccentricities of the manor."

"It's funny. I stopped thinking about leaving almost from the moment I moved in. It casts a spell. A positive one," Sonya added.

"Son always wanted a house like this," Cleo told him. "The history, the character, the quirks. Maybe even, deep down, the ghosts."

"That would've been really deep down," Sonya said. "And I'm not thrilled about walking through the house in my sleep, or watching the brides die. But if that leads to that eviction, I'll take it."

"You're exactly what Collin would have wanted," Deuce murmured.

"Tell me about his grandmother. Tell us about Patricia Poole."

"She was a force," Deuce began. "A strong-willed woman. Well-respected, if not well-liked. My own parents have said Michael Poole Jr., her husband, had a great deal of charm, and little interest in the business. He had no problem turning the reins there over to her so he could travel and—let's use a word that fits their time frame. *Cavort.*"

"Good word," Cleo decided.

"Their marriage—and here we turn to gossip—was, by and large, one of convenience. Each did as they chose. I remember her as a hard woman who ruled both the business and her family with an iron fist."

Once again Cleo held hers up. "Exactly my phrase."

"Then you already have some understanding of her. Collin's childhood under that rule was very restricted. He escaped whenever he could—and he was good at it," Deuce added with a smile. "It seemed she deemed me an acceptable companion, and I was also very good at being polite, well-spoken, and well-behaved in her presence. It helped that she was busy with Poole Shipbuilders, with her various clubs, social engagements and had little interest in young boys."

He sipped his coffee, smiled. "I was fortunate to have two grandmothers. They both disliked Patricia Poole, and were both very good at putting on a pleasing face when necessary. But children hear more than adults tend to think, and I'd catch snatches when her name came up. *Bully* is a term I'll use in polite company."

"She bullied her daughter into pretending to be Collin's mother."

Deuce nodded at Sonya. "I agree with that speculation. I knew Gretta Poole better than Patricia, and always found her easily cowed. A nervous sort of woman. I would call her a dutiful mother, but not particularly affectionate. I wouldn't know the reason behind all of that until I did the Poole genealogy for Collin."

"It's clear my father got the better end of that deal. But to go back, and I understand it was before you were born, it feels like the manor should have been a showplace for Patricia Poole. Instead, she refused to live here, and closed it."

"I agree. From all my research and from the snippets overheard and remembered, Patricia embraced all things Poole. Except the manor. I thought of a comment—my grandmother Doyle at Collin and Johanna's wedding. She said Collin's grandmother hadn't stepped foot in the manor since Patricia and Michael's engagement party."

"So she had her engagement party here. She did visit the manor often before she married Michael Poole?"

"As the Youngsboros and Pooles were on equal steps on the social ladder, and according to my research, Michael and Patricia's engagement was expected, I'd say yes. And."

He opened his trim briefcase. "When I worked on Collin's book, I made copies of some clippings, some photos. Society pages, you see. Gossiping about Patricia and Michael stepping out, him escorting her to parties, galas."

When he offered the folder, Sonya began to look through.

"Handsome couple, they'd say," she muttered. "And this one's a shot of them at a holiday event. 'Will Christmas Bells Lead to Wedding Bells?'"

"So you see, their engagement was anticipated."

Cleo studied the photo. "They're striking together. So formal, but striking. She looks . . . formidable, even at this age."

"Look here, this was taken out back." Sonya pulled out the copy. "'Summer Soirée: Garden Party at Poole Manor.' You can see her here, with her hand on Michael's arm. And it's dated the summer before they were married. Before the Christmas article. So she certainly came to the manor prior."

"Here's another, announcing the engagement. A picture of them, at the foot of the staircase, Son. 'Valentine's Day Engagement Announced.' I have to give her props for knowing how to dress. In all these pictures."

"Something she was known for," Deuce put in. "Always perfectly presented."

"Something put her off the manor," Cleo said. "I bet we can guess who—or what."

Clover played "Black Magic Woman."

"I tend to agree." Deuce reached for a cookie. "I wouldn't have said Patricia Poole was an easily frightened or intimidated woman, but I tend to agree. I had assumed she simply wanted a more modern house, a bit more manageable, closer to the village and the business. But knowing all we know now?"

He shook his head.

"She never used it, not for parties, fundraisers. She couldn't sell it. It comes down through the Pooles, and I can speculate that however much Michael Poole accommodated her, he drew a line there."

"So it came down to Charles."

"The son she couldn't control. The one who stepped out of her orbit as soon as he could. He came into money at eighteen, took it, and lived as he wanted. From what I can put together, he dropped out of college and traveled awhile."

"More like his father than his mother?" Cleo asked.

"From what people who knew him say, yes. My father knew him, liked him. He's described as charming, generous, and definitely free-spirited."

McCartney's "My Love" trailed down the stairs.

Deuce smiled a little. "I've no doubt they loved each other. And no doubt Patricia wasn't pleased when he brought back a young wife, a pregnant wife, along with friends they'd picked up along the way, and not only opened the manor but moved in."

"I don't understand." Genuinely baffled, Sonya lifted her hands. "He moved back, with Lilian Crest, his pregnant wife. But no one questioned Collin was Gretta Poole's son?"

"According to my mother, the group Charles brought with him largely kept to themselves. Neither she nor my father were aware, until I dug up the marriage license and so on, that Charlie had married. They were only here a few months, when Lilian—sorry, Clover—died in childbirth. Charlie hanged himself. Patricia took over. She unquestionably bribed or bullied those in authority to cover it up, to lay the groundwork for what would become the dark family secret."

"And her daughter let herself be used that way. Lived with that every day."

"She would never have defied her mother," Deuce told Sonya. "Not like Charlie."

"Speculation, gossip, and opinion? Why?" Sonya wondered. "Why did she keep one baby? Why not keep both or put both up for adoption?"

"Lawrence Poole had no children, no heirs—and like his father, little interest in the business. And physically, his health wasn't robust. Gretta—shy, nervous, awkward—would likely never marry and have children. Charlie was gone."

"Bloodline."

"Yes, Cleo, I believe exactly that. Collin was her chance—perhaps her only chance—to continue her direct bloodline. She didn't need two, just one."

"Did she try to stop Collin from opening the manor?" Sonya asked.

"As boys, we'd find our way inside." Deuce looked around now. "I don't think she ever knew, or understood, his pride and fascination in this house. In its history—his history, too. But he understood her well enough to make it a fait accompli. As he was of age, and the manor his, there was nothing she could do.

"Do you mind?" he asked as he reached for the coffeepot.

"Help yourself."

"He told me once, not long after he'd moved in. We were playing chess upstairs, just the two of us, and he was full of plans for the manor, the business, his life. God, we were young!"

With a wistful smile on his face, he doctored his coffee.

"He said his grandmother threatened to disinherit him if he didn't relent. Now, she couldn't have cut him off from the business, the Poole inheritance, but her own wealth. And when he refused, she said she'd wasted her time and resources on him. She said he was as big a fool as his father, as useless as his mother."

"Poor Collin," Sonya murmured.

"It didn't cut him deep, I promise you. At that time, we didn't know his true parentage, only the lie Patricia had carved into the family tree. I commented that how would she know his father was a fool when he'd died before Collin was born? Collin shrugged that off. Just her way, and told me she'd said he'd rue the day. Rue the day," Deuce repeated, "and he laughed at that. So did I.

"She never set foot in this house. She didn't attend his wedding; she didn't come to Johanna's funeral. Though they worked together until she died, they remained estranged on a personal level."

"Yeah, my dad got the better end of the deal."

Even knowing it, Sonya felt tugged in two directions. The cold cruelty of it on one side, her father's happy life on the other.

"She could've told Collin why she'd closed the manor," Sonya continued. "If she'd been genuinely concerned for him, she would have. He might not have believed her, might have dismissed it, but she didn't even try to tell him."

"He'd have told me if she'd spoken of it. And," Deuce added with a slight shrug, "we very likely would have laughed again. Did we believe the manor haunted? Absolutely, as we'd believed since we were boys. But that was exciting. People already called it Lost Bride Manor, but that was local superstition as far as we were concerned—and intriguing."

Looking back, thinking back, Deuce sipped his coffee.

"Even when I began to do the Poole genealogy, write their history, I didn't see those deaths as anything but a tragedy of their times— the first a murder, yes, but the others accidents or medical issues."

"Did Gretta know?" Sonya pressed. "She never married—and that may have been her choice. But I wonder if her mother *discouraged* her on that, particularly after Collin and my father were born."

Deuce sat back. "That's a very good point, Sonya. And it would fit Patricia snugly."

"If her daughter fell in love," Cleo continued, "got close to some-one, she'd almost certainly tell that person the entire story. Blow the lie up right there. Can't have that."

"I want to talk to her—to Gretta Poole. Am I allowed to do that?"

"Since Collin's death, I've been her custodian, and the trustee of what he left to take care of her. I've been to visit her twice now, but she doesn't know me. You're a blood relation, and certainly allowed to visit. But her condition's advanced. She rarely speaks to anyone, and when she does, it's generally nonsense. Though she's usually passive, she can be disruptive. Anxious again, frightened. Even angry."

"I'd like to try. I won't know if it'll do any good until I do."

Nudging up his glasses, he gave her a long look.

"You have Collin's eyes—well, your father's. It may spark some-thing. I'll see you're put on her visitation list. That way you can pick a time that suits you."

"I appreciate it, very much. All of it. Did you know about the mirror?"

"I've never seen it. Collin told me, again even back when we were boys, that he dreamed of it. A mirror framed with predatory birds and animals. And of the boy, who looked just like him, in the glass. I thought they were dreams, and later, when I found out about your father, assumed some sort of twin memory or connection."

Reaching out, he closed his hand over Sonya's. "Now that I know it's not, I worry about it, and you. And I worry I didn't know enough of what has, can, and does happen in this house when I knocked on your door last winter."

She turned her hand to link her fingers with his. "You changed my life, and I'm grateful. I want to be here, and I want to do everything I can to end whatever power Hester Dobbs has in this house."

When Sonya said the name, doors slammed, something pounded against the walls, and the ceiling light swayed as if in a sudden, wild wind.

"She will have her tantrums," Cleo said, and picked up a cookie. "Sonya said she feeds on fear and grief. We're not giving her a damn thing to eat."

"I'm glad Sonya has you, Cleo. I'm glad you have each other."

"And we're not alone here." Sonya gave Deuce's hand a squeeze in turn. "They're all here, all seven brides. Others, too, others here in the manor. I know that absolutely. And they all want her gone. I don't know why it's for me to do—us," she corrected. "But it is."

She smiled as the noise died. "So I'll go see Gretta Poole at some point. Maybe she can add something, maybe not. And in a few weeks, Cleo and I are throwing a major event."

"I heard about that. It's quite an undertaking."

"The manor was made for big, happy parties."

"It counteracts, I think," Cleo put in. "People and fun and light and music."

"How it used to be. After Johanna . . . Collin lost his heart. But before? He'd often have a summer party, and always one during the holidays. Smaller gatherings in between. Maybe it does counteract. One thing I can be certain of is people will come. So be prepared."

He rose. "I'd better be on my way. I'm going to do some more research on Patricia. The originals of these clippings and photographs should be tucked away in here somewhere."

"I hadn't thought of that. We can look."

"In any case, I'll leave these with you. My mother or Ace may have some filed away, too. So we'll see. We'll do whatever we can to make sure you live here safe and happy. I'm glad to have had some time here, and to have met you, Cleo. I had a friendship like yours and Sonya's, and I know how much it matters."

"Give Corrine my best," Cleo told him. "I really enjoyed my day with her. She made me look damn good."

"I'd say that would be the easiest job she's ever had."

"And now I see where Trey gets his charm."

"She's been a real asset to my work," Sonya added as they walked him to the door.

"She'll be happy to hear that. Everyone at Doyle Law is thrilled with your work on the new website and the rest. I mentioned it to a colleague in Ogunquit. You should be getting a call from Peter Stevenson."

"Thank you! I love new clients. Thanks for coming."

"Anytime, and I mean that. Take care of each other."

"That's what we do." Cleo draped an arm around Sonya's shoulders. "I can see that."

They watched him walk to his car, waved him off.

"I feel better." Sonya closed the door. "I feel like I have a clearer picture of Patricia Youngsboro Poole."

"And it ain't flattering. I'm surprised she and Dobbs didn't get along—and I have to figure they didn't. They're poured from the same mold, if you ask me. Now, Oliver Doyle II? Top marks there. Now that I've met both Trey's parents and his sister? You better grab on, Son. As my mama would say, that boy's from good stock."

"I've got a pretty good hold, but—"

She broke off as Yoda, tail wagging, trotted down the hallway with the ball clutched in his jaws.

"Now I know where you got off to." She bent down to pick up the ball he dropped at her feet. "You've been playing ball with Jack."

"You've got a built-in dog sitter."

"Apparently." Since Yoda eyed the ball with joy and kept wagging, Sonya gave in. "Okay, not done yet? We'll take ten minutes for ball play outside."

"I'd join you, but I've got work now. Y'all have fun."

As Cleo headed up, Sonya grabbed a jacket. "It really has to be ten minutes, pal. I want an hour on the Ryder proposal, and I have other things to deal with first."

But she stepped outside and reveled in how spring seemed to slip closer every day. Overnight freeze or not, the daffodils waved their buttery heads. And she swore the grass seemed greener when Yoda chased the ball across it.

As she tossed the ball for the tireless dog, she scanned the sea, hoping to see a whale sound. She glanced up at the balcony off her bedroom, and imagined what Trey had seen during the night.

It made her shudder.

To die that way, to choose to, she thought, and condemn yourself to decade after decade of anger and, yes, evil. All because you didn't get what you wanted in life.

"It makes no sense, does it, Yoda? But at the core, she's insane. An insane witch. But she can't beat us." She tossed the ball again. "She won't. That's the last time, Yoda. Your human has to earn her living."

As she started back toward the house, one of Cleo's studio windows flew open. Sonya braced, but Cleo called out.

"It's not her, but, Son, you're going to want to come see this."

"On my way."

She hurried to the door, then scooted Yoda in before she ran for the stairs and bounded up. As if it was a new game, the dog bounded up with her.

A little breathless, she arrived at Cleo's studio.

"What is it? What happened?"

"I needed something and went in the closet."

Cleo gestured toward the open door.

Inside stood a portrait, beautifully painted. Her dark hair fell in pretty curls down the right side of her head toward the lace inserts on the sleeves and bodice of her white silk wedding gown.

Her ring sparkled on her finger, a slim gold band crusted with diamonds that seemed to flash even in the dim light of the closet. She carried a bouquet of pale pink peonies and trailing greenery.

Her eyes, Poole green, radiated joy.

"It's Lissy. Lisbeth Poole Whitmore. Not my father's work. Collin's. It's Collin's signature in the corner."

She looked at Cleo. "First I found Johanna's portrait, then Clover's, now you found Lisbeth's."

"And your dad painted Clover—the mother he never knew, and in her wedding dress—so before he was born. Collin painted this, all that detail, a woman who died years before he was born."

"They went through the mirror." Laying a hand on Cleo's arm, she steadied herself. "Not just Collin, but somehow my father went through the mirror. Like I have."

"And more than once, I'd say."

"We'll take her downstairs, hang her with Johanna and Clover."

"One more thing, Son? The portraits, the three of them, are all the same size, and use the same type of frame. Like they're meant to hang together."

"And that's what we'll do."

Sonya carried the painting down, and for now, propped it against a wall in the library. She and Cleo would hang it in the music room that evening.

But now she had work, and was grateful to have it. Quitting her job and going freelance the previous fall had been exciting and terrifying.

She supposed she could rate her move into the manor on exactly that same scale.

Now the manor was home, and she had a business. Maybe not thriving at this point, but steady. And incredibly satisfying.

She supposed, in a twisted way, she had Brandon Wise to thank for where she sat right now.

He'd been low enough to cheat on her—just weeks before their wedding—with her own cousin, in her own house, in her own bed. She could wonder now if it had been luck or fate that had brought her home early enough to catch the two of them naked in bed.

Either way, she decided, a lucky escape for her.

And when she'd broken the engagement, refused to listen to his lame excuses, he'd gone on a mission to undermine her at work.

"Corrupting my client files, letting the air out of my tires," she muttered. "So screw any sort of twisted thanks. I'm here because I took the steps, I did the work, and I took the risks."

She glanced toward Lisbeth's portrait and thought she was there, in the manor, to live, to work, and to stand up for seven women who'd come before her.

She buckled down to work.

When she had enough on the layout to send to the client for approval, rejection, changes, she shifted to work on a book cover.

Since the Adirondacks and deep winter set the stage for the thriller, she began with the protagonist's isolated cabin, under a cold moon. Blue shadows, she thought, that isolation, a sense of dread and danger in the thick line of snow-drowned trees.

Maybe footprints across the snow. A single light in a window—and a silhouette behind it.

Sonya worked on the concept, tried two more for comparison.

While she liked the first design, the sense of cold, of danger lurking, she set them all aside to consider fresh in the morning.

She scrubbed her hands over her face, then dropped them when she heard the Beatles and "I'm So Tired."

"Yeah, maybe. But not done yet."

Chapter Five

The Ryder proposal. She looked at her mood board, then opened her file.

Because she had to admit her brain was tired, she told herself she'd just review for now.

This represented an opportunity to take her business from steady to thriving. She really wanted to thrive.

And on a personal level, she wanted to beat Brandon. No doubt, she thought, just none, that he'd head up the team on her main competitor's proposal.

For all his many miserable flaws, when it came to the work, he excelled.

So she just had to be better.

She started the review, began to tweak. And . . .

Looked up, blinking, when Cleo tapped her fist on the doorjamb.

"Sorry. I thought maybe you should come up for air. But if you want to dive back, I fed Yoda."

"Fed . . ." She checked the time. "How the hell did it get to be seven?"

"It comes after six, which is about when I passed by earlier, and Yoda followed me down." Angling her head, Cleo studied Sonya. "I'm not going to tell you to stop if it's rolling, but you look like you could use a break."

"I'm past that point, and I'm going to screw something up if I don't stop. I'm going to shut down."

"We're having open-faced roast beef sandwiches and the rest of the leftovers. How about I go pour you a glass of wine?"

"How about you do? I'm right behind you."

Sonya saved and closed down the work she hoped wouldn't turn out to be a hot mess when she opened it again. She'd slid into the zone for a while, true, but then she'd slipped into autopilot.

Now she left it behind, left it to simmer like one of Cleo's pots, and taking the portrait, went downstairs.

She propped the painting in the music room, under the other portraits they'd found in the studio closet.

A kind of tryptic, she thought, invisibly connected.

"We'll put you in place after dinner."

For a moment when she stepped back, just a fleeting moment, she thought she caught a scent. Her father's aftershave. It came to her like a brush of lips on her cheek, like a hand sliding to smooth down her hair.

"But you're not here." She sighed it out. "I wish you could be."

She walked down to the kitchen, where Cleo had wine waiting and Yoda sprawled under the table in anticipation.

"You are my queen," Sonya said as she took the wineglass.

"I worked a little late myself, since all I had to do was warm things up."

"How's it going?"

"The contract work? I don't think I've ever had a job I've enjoyed more. And the painting I'm trading for my boat? I'm trying not to regret giving it up."

Cleo's brows drew together as she picked up her own wine.

"Owen better build me a fabulous boat, and he'd better give her a place of honor."

"Ready to eat?"

"Absolutely."

When they sat at the table, Sonya smiled over at Cleo. "The way Owen wanted your mermaid painting the minute he saw it—and way before you finished? He's going to put her in a place of honor."

"I'll harangue him if he doesn't." Cleo cut into the beef and bread and gravy. "People don't know how to harangue properly, if you ask me. But I do."

"I can attest," Sonya said, and made Cleo laugh.

"That studio, Son? It's something I needed and wanted without ever knowing it was what I needed and wanted. I honestly think my work's better because of it."

"I feel the same way about the library. And Xena?" she added, thinking of her African violet. "She just blooms and blooms."

"I'd say all of us were meant to be planted here, at this time, in this place. What were you working on when I pulled you out?"

"Ryder. I sent off the Gigi proposal—and I really think it works—and another draft layout for some ads for Baby Mine. I did some work on another book cover."

"Busy, busy."

"Just how I like it. Maybe you could take a look at the book cover designs. Then I just wanted to review what I've done on the Ryder job. And one thing led to another."

Sonya picked up her wine. "Confession."

"I'll always be your priest."

"I want the Ryder job because it's an amazing opportunity, especially for someone with only a few months' freelancing under her belt."

"Don't forget the years working in your field."

"I don't. But compared to By Design, I'm incredibly small-time."

"And incredibly talented."

"Thanks, Father Fabares. Snagging Ryder as a client would push my business to another level, and why wouldn't I want that? But there's this petty little part of me that wants the job because I'd beat Brandon."

"Well, duh." Cleo waved her glass. "That's not petty."

"It feels petty."

"Then you're looking at it wrong. You want the job because it's a major client, and you're offering them a clever, creative campaign. You want it because it'll give your company a big-ass boost. Beating Brandon the asshole Wise? That's just the proverbial cherry on top."

Sonya considered. "You've got to respect the cherry on top."

"Of course. Now, let me say as someone who knows you in and out, if not for this job—which I firmly believe you'll get—you'd barely give that cheating bastard a thought at this point. You moved on—in every way. You have—in no particular order—a business you're building yourself, a hot, interesting man who, by my view, doesn't have a cheating bone in his body. You have this amazing house, and all that comes with it. And part of that is a mission to, at its core, right wrongs.

"And"—she smiled and speared some potato—"you've got me."

"You're right. If I don't get the job—" She held up a finger before Cleo could object. "I'll still have you, and all the rest. I'll keep right on building my business. But *when* I get the job—"

"There you go."

"I'll enjoy that cherry on top. Not as much as the whole rich, gooey sundae, but I'll enjoy it."

After dinner, they went to the music room. Once they took a seascape down, they carefully hung the third portrait in its place.

"I guess this is part of righting those wrongs." Sonya stepped back to study the three brides. "To acknowledge them this way. To display them together this way."

"They're meant to be. The same size canvas, the same frame. And the styles, Sonya? They're so similar. We can see the differences, and your mom can and will. But to the untrained eye?"

"I know. The twin thing again, I guess. The other thing? They painted each at a happy moment—maybe the happiest moment of their lives. No shadows, no sense of tragedy. I like that."

From upstairs something crashed. On the wall, the portraits shook.

"She doesn't," Cleo muttered. "But whatever power she has, there's an opposing one. We're part of that. So . . ." Cleo aimed her middle finger at the ceiling just as the phone went with Queen's "We Will Rock You."

With a laugh, Sonya tossed back her hair. "And let me add an *Up yours* to round it off."

Something banged against the ceiling and set the light swaying. The portraits shook, but they didn't fall.

At three, the clock chimed. Piano music slid through the air like tears. Sonya stirred awake, and though her heart ached when she heard the weeping echoing from the nursery, she felt no pull.

Before she could drift back to sleep, her balcony doors blew open, and an ice-edged wind swept through.

Yoda woke with a wild bark and sprang out of bed.

Cold covered her like a second skin as she struggled against the lashing wind. Something pounded against the entrance doors below like a battering ram, and her fireplace roared to furious life.

Dimly, under the shrieking wind, the roaring fire, the pounding, she heard the phone by her bed play "Bad Moon Rising."

Afraid for him, Sonya scooped the shivering dog up under one arm and pushed her way to the balcony doors.

Behind her, Cleo shouted, but Sonya kept her focus, all her energy, on reaching the doors.

When she closed her fingers around the door handle, she let out a cry. It was like holding on to an iceberg.

But she held on, put her shoulder against the door. As she fought to close it, she saw the figure on the seawall.

Not facing the sea, but the house. The white ball of moon illuminated her as the wind she conjured whipped at her hair, her dress.

Gritting her teeth, Sonya put all her strength against the door.

"Go ahead, bitch!" She shouted it. "Take that first step to hell. I swear I'm going to kick your ass the rest of the way there before I'm done."

"And I'll help her." Cleo, hair flying, put her shoulder to the second door.

They fought the doors closed and, braced against them, watched Dobbs turn toward the sea. And jump.

The moon waned to a crescent; the wind died. Downstairs, the furious pounding stopped as the flames in the fireplace snapped off.

Both Sonya and Cleo slid to the floor, and with the shivering dog between them, clung together.

"We're okay." Sonya pushed the words out as her heart sprinted from her chest to her throat and back again. "You're okay?"

Nodding, Cleo whooshed out a breath, then another.

Sonya kissed Yoda's nose. "We're all okay."

"I'd say hanging that third portrait seriously pissed her off."

"Looks like it. Did you see her? Dobbs? Standing on the seawall?"

"Yeah. Looking at the house. I don't know if she looked at us, or it was a replay of what happened a couple hundred years ago."

Exhausted, Sonya shifted to lean her back against the door.

"She lured Catherine Poole outside, took her wedding ring outside. I think when she pulls enough power together, she can use it out there. But it's stronger in the house. She's stronger in the house."

"And you think she used some of that up tonight, to put on this show. I can see that," Cleo decided. "She wanted you to see her, wanted you to be afraid."

"She still jumped. At the end, she still jumped."

"Didn't she have to? You can't take back death, Son. And it was her suicide, her death, her blood that sealed the curse."

"You can't take back death," Sonya repeated, and the truth of that squeezed her heart like a vise. "I'm never going to be able to help the brides."

"That's not true. You can't save their lives because their lives are already gone. But you help them just by being here to start. And we hung three portraits—that's help. Hell, Sonya, you—both of us—have a really sweet relationship with your grandmother."

Clover responded with "We Are Family."

"She was here. She used John Fogerty to shout out a warning. And you came running."

"I heard Yoda barking, then the booms downstairs and all the rest. She's backed off now, you can feel it. The manor's settled for the night. I can stay with you."

"No, I'm fine. I really am. I won't say I wasn't scared, but you know what, Cleo? I was a lot more mad."

"You think I don't know that face?" Cleo tapped a finger to Sonya's cheek. "You were way more mad. I really think she's used herself up tonight, so we'll get some sleep." Cleo faked a yawn and grinned with it. "That's a nice insult right there."

In full agreement, Sonya gave Cleo another hug before they rose. "Thanks for the assist."

"Anytime. See you in the morning."

Yoda curled up in his bed, and Sonya did the same in hers.

Volume low, her phone played James Taylor's quiet ballad "You've Got a Friend."

"I know I do."

And Sonya slipped into sleep before the song ended.

She woke early and energized—and determined to stick with routine. Since she'd skipped a workout for a few days, she decided to start with one.

A quick coffee first while she let Yoda out to start his day. She stepped out with him, breathed in as she looked out to the woods.

Maybe later, she considered, on a work break, she'd venture into the woods.

She gave Yoda his breakfast, added a quick pat.

"Gonna work out."

And she considered it another insult to open the hidden door on the landing and go alone down to the gym Collin had set up in part of the old servants' quarters.

She streamed a cardio session, then, thinking of the night before, chose another with weights.

Stronger's better, she thought.

Twice she heard one of the servant bells ring, and ignored it. The Gold Room, she had no doubt.

She hoped Dobbs considered it another insult.

When she came up, she heard the bounce of the ball on the main floor, and smiled at the idea of her built-in dog sitter.

A young boy playing with a dog—another insult.

She showered, changed, then called down from the top of the stairs.

"I'm coming down for coffee and a bagel."

When she walked down, Yoda sat waiting in the kitchen. And the cabinet doors were all neatly closed.

"Thanks, Jack."

While she ate, she answered early texts from her mother, another from Trey, then scanned her emails.

Nothing yet from Gigi's, but since it was still early, she didn't worry.

"Let's go to work, Yoda."

With her water bottle in hand, and the dog at her heels, she headed up to the library. At eight-forty-five, she sat at her desk.

"We're going to pick up where we left off on Ryder. One hour only." To make sure of it, she set an alarm on her tablet before booting up the computer.

She opened the file, rolled her shoulders.

Pleased with her progress, Sonya got right to it.

She could see it, she could envision the entire campaign and the appeal to regular people with the images she'd designed.

People—not actors, not professional athletes—using Ryder equipment and gear to play ball, to bike, do yoga, shoot hoops, and all the rest.

Color and movement, children, young people, older people. Corrine's photographs nailed exactly what she'd wanted. And her layout worked, her text worked. A little more polishing, she thought, but it was a damn good proposal.

When her alarm went off, she winced. But she stuck with the plan. Another hour here, another hour there, and she'd take it up, put it on the big screen upstairs.

Make any necessary adjustments, improvements.

But for now, she closed down the Ryder files.

To her delight, she found an email inquiry from the law firm Deuce had spoken of. Before answering, she checked out their website.

"Oh yeah, I can do better."

She glanced up as she heard Cleo coming down the hall.

"Morning. Sleep okay after the performance?"

"Like a rock. Now must have coffee." She turned toward the steps, then back again. "Forgot. Going into Poole's Bay later. Groceries and some other errands. Anything you want?"

"Getting low on butter and Cokes. I guess beer, too, if we have beer-type company. But tonight, Trey's taking both of us to dinner."

"You know he doesn't have to drag me along."

"He wants to. I imagine he'll drag Owen, too, if he can. Lobster Cage. He'll pick us up about six-thirty."

"Okay, I'm for it. If we have enough of the rest to last until tomorrow, I'll put off the errands today. Now coffee."

Routine, Sonya thought again. She liked it.

She crafted a response to the inquiry, suggested a phone or video consultation at the potential client's convenience. In case Deuce hadn't provided it, she added a link to her own website.

Which, if she said so herself—and she did—crushed it.

As she sent the first email, one came through from the owner of Gigi's.

When she read that the client loved the new logo, Sonya pumped a fist in the air.

She nodded through the email. Some questions, some concerns, some wondering if. All valid.

She answered them all, offered some suggestions on the wondering, tried to alleviate the concerns, but offered options if those concerns remained.

Since one of the wonderings involved the possibility of a new sign with the new logo, Sonya got to work on it.

So deeply involved, she barely noticed when Yoda scooted out from under her desk. Then he leaned, wagging, against her leg.

"What? Oh, time to go out? Just one more minute. How did it get to be past noon?"

Because routine, she decided as she found the point to break. A good, solid routine.

Downstairs, she let the dog out, slapped together half a PB and J, added some chips, grabbed a Coke.

She gave Yoda a midday treat, but when he didn't follow her back upstairs, she assumed his pal Jack lingered nearby.

Before she made it back to her desk, she heard the ball. And this time, to her absolute pleasure, the sound of a young boy's laughter.

She worked until nearly four, then made herself close it out for the day.

She no longer heard the ball, and Yoda hadn't curled under her desk or anywhere else in the library. She found him sleeping in the kitchen. He opened one eye, batted his tail on the floor.

"Did Jack wear you out? I want some air, and I bet you could use some, too."

And the woods beckoned. She'd studied them drenched in snow, watched a deer come to their verge, wondered what it felt like, looked like, beyond that verge.

Now with spring almost ready to bloom, she'd find out.

Grabbing the old jacket she kept in the mudroom, she led Yoda out. He started to race around the yard, the circular pattern she often took, then stopped, head cocked, when she walked across the slope of lawn toward the sheltering trees.

"The city girl wants to explore a little," she told him. "Trust me, we won't go far."

As she walked, she could still hear the steady beat of water on the rocks and see buds forming on trees, shrubs. Something green pushed up its stalks from the ground.

Not only had the air warmed, but so had the light. She wondered if she'd notice that change in the same way in Boston.

Probably not, not in this way.

At the edge of the woods, she glanced back toward the house, then tapped her pocket where she'd put her phone.

Just in case.

"This path right here, Yoda. And we stick to it."

Under the trees, the air cooled and the light went soft. She smelled pine, and earth—such a different perfume from the scent of the sea. Yoda stuck to her side as they ventured along the narrow track.

She wondered how many others had walked here, and how long it had been since anyone wandered in the dappled sunlight. Now and then birds called, and a breeze, gentle as a stroking hand, stirred the trees.

Otherwise, she had silence where even the relentless beat of the sea on rocks came muffled and distant.

She noted downed branches, and wondered if they'd fallen during a winter storm, and if John Dee—who plowed the driveway, the road, stacked firewood by the shed—got any of those logs from these woods.

She'd have to ask.

Other tracks veered from the one she and Yoda walked. Considering them, she shook her head.

"Not today, but maybe later. Maybe."

She heard a kind of bubbling, and to her surprise and absolute delight, spotted a narrow stream, running—sluggishly, she thought, but running—over rocks.

"Would you look at that! We have a stream. A creek? Whatever, we have one."

A branch, thick and sturdy, had fallen over it, forming a kind of bridge. As if to prove its use, a fat squirrel dashed across it. Her quick laugh turned into a gasp as Yoda instantly gave chase.

"No! Yoda! Stop!"

But his stubby little legs had already carried him across where his joyful barks echoed back to her.

Panicked, she left the path for the banks of the stream. The branch might hold a squirrel and her little dog, but it wouldn't take her weight. So she stood, shouting for Yoda as it struck her just how far they'd walked.

She could count the number of times she'd walked in the woods on one hand—and none like this.

Deep woods, she thought now as pleasure turned to anxiety. Deep, with all the wildlife that lived in the deep.

Now the humming silence felt ominous, and the soft, dappled light a threat toward dark.

With no choice, she started to ease her way down to the gurgling water to try to wade through. And Yoda came prancing back, scrambled across the branch, then wagged his way to her with a look of satisfaction in his eyes.

"You!" She scooped him up, tried for her sternest glare. "Don't ever do that again. No running off in the woods."

He body-wagged, licked her cheek, and didn't look the least bit penitent.

Heading back, she carried him until she felt reasonably sure they were close enough to the edge of the woods to risk setting him down again.

"Pull that one again, and it's the leash for you, puppy."

Maybe she should buy a compass, she considered, then realized she'd probably find one somewhere in the house.

Of course, she didn't actually know how to use a compass, but she could learn.

Maybe she felt a wave of relief when she saw the manor, heard the sea, stepped out into the stronger light. But it wouldn't stop her from walking in the woods—sometime.

"They're ours, right, Yoda? I can learn to use a compass. I can buy hiking boots. Because they're ours."

She pulled out her phone, checked the time.

"Let's go find Cleo."

Chapter Six

Inside, Sonya left Yoda lapping at his water bowl and headed up to Cleo's studio.

She gave a light rap on the doorjamb before walking in.

"I'm about to go make myself presentable for . . . Oh, Cleo!"

Sonya stepped closer to the painting on the easel. "She's stunning. She's gorgeous. She's amazing."

"I think she's finished." Cleo stood at her worktable, cleaning her brushes. "I'm going to leave her there, take another good look tomorrow. And if I still think she's finished, put her in the drying rack."

"She's magic," Sonya murmured.

The mermaid sat on the rocks, her tail a glory of jewel colors as it swept the water. And while day broke in a symphony of golds, pinks, blues, and a whale sounded out to sea, she sat, holding a glass sphere.

In the sphere she held sat another, and in that sphere yet another.

"The detail, Cleo, inside the globes." Sonya pressed a hand to her heart. "I'm awestruck. Sincerely."

"I'm going to credit the mermaid lamp we found in storage, the happenstance of the job illustrating a book on mermaids, and this view for inspiration."

She walked over, laid a hand on Sonya's shoulder as she studied her own work.

"Screw bullshit modesty." Cleo tossed back her hair, rocked her hips. "She's special."

"Owen should build you a frigging yacht for her."

"A pretty two-person Sunfish is what I want. But he'd better appreciate her."

"You didn't sign her."

"Tomorrow, after I'm a hundred percent sure. I guess you're wrapped for the day. And now so am I. Let's go get pretty."

"Not only wrapped," Sonya said as they started down. "I wrapped, then took a walk in the woods."

"By yourself?"

"I had Yoda. Not far in, but maybe a little more than I planned. I liked it—though there was a moment after I found this little stream, or creek. What's the difference?"

"A creek's a small stream."

Frowning, Sonya looked over as they stopped on the second floor. "How do you know that?"

"We have lots of them in Louisiana, Son."

"True. I guess a creek."

"Or a brook."

"I like *brook*. I'm saying brook. Yoda chased a squirrel over this branch over the brook. But he came back. It was probably half a minute, but it seemed longer. I need a compass."

"At least. Next time, you tell me you're walking in the woods. If I can't go with you, I'll know where you are."

"Deal. What are you wearing to dinner?"

"Haven't decided."

"I bet Molly has."

They went into Cleo's room together. On the bed lay a dress, belted at the waist, in a coppery color. With it lay a lacy black sweater.

"Nice choice," Sonya decided.

"I have to agree. Thanks, Molly."

Sonya continued to her own room and found her navy, square-necked dress paired with her cream-colored, waist-length suede jacket.

"I don't think I've ever put those two pieces together. I like it. Thanks, Molly."

Deciding she'd gotten used to having a fashion consultant, among other things, Sonya took her time.

She thought of all that had happened since she'd dressed for dinner with Trey—and he'd had to cancel.

She'd walked through the mirror, Owen beside her. She'd seen Lisbeth Poole die at her own wedding reception. Watched Hester Dobbs glide through, a ghost among ghosts, to take Lisbeth's ring.

And she'd pulled herself into the normal so she and Cleo could make dinner for the men who'd stood with them, stood by them. Trey had watched Dobbs leap to her death off the seawall.

Cleo found Lisbeth's portrait—what was surely the third in a series. Now it hung in the music room.

They'd withstood Dobbs's three a.m. tantrum—it felt good to think of them as tantrums—then watched her, as Trey had, leap from the seawall.

Through it all, she thought, as she added earrings, they'd worked, and laughed, and lived.

And she'd taken a walk in the woods with her dog.

Her life, Sonya reflected, had grown so much richer, so much fuller since her move to Maine and the manor.

Though she'd spent, excepting the past few months, her whole life in Boston, she felt her roots digging deep into the rocky coast of Maine.

She missed the easy access to her mother, and suspected she always would. But the rest? No, she'd left that part of her life behind.

Stepping back, she did a half turn in the mirror. Then slid into her shoes, and with Yoda trailing behind, walked down the hall. She peeked into Cleo's room.

"I'm nearly there!" Cleo called out. "I got distracted. A text from Lucy Cabot about a cat. I'm going to go see it—her, it's a girl cat—tomorrow when I go into town for supplies."

After perfecting her lipstick, Cleo stepped out of the bathroom and looked at Yoda.

"If she's my cat, and I bring her home, you have to be sweet to her."

"Lucy wouldn't have called you if the cat didn't get along with dogs. And Yoda's already been field-tested with cats. This could be fun."

"This is really just a look-see."

"Yeah, that's what I said about Yoda." He wagged when Sonya gestured toward him. "Look and see."

They started downstairs just as the doorbell bonged.

"Talk about timing."

"Doesn't that man have a key?" Cleo asked.

"He does, but he's Trey. He'd think emergency only."

Yoda was already dancing at the door, and bulleted out to greet Mookie when Sonya opened it.

"He thinks he's the lucky one," Trey commented. "But I'm the one taking two beautiful women to dinner."

"Has the Mook had his?" Cleo asked.

"He has."

"Then I'd say we're set." She picked up the tug rope, offered it.

And the games began.

"You boys behave." She stepped out, rose up to kiss Trey. "More luck, going out to dinner with a handsome man. Or will it be two handsome men?"

"Owen's meeting us. Apparently Jones is staying home and watching his favorite movie."

"And what might that be?" Cleo wondered as they walked to Trey's car. "*Scooby-Doo*? *101 Dalmatians*?"

"*King Kong*, the original."

"You're kidding."

Trey shook his head as he held car doors open. "Don't ask me why, but Jones goes for it. And clearly roots for Kong."

"I get the second part." Sonya glanced back at Cleo, got a nod of agreement. "You take a giant ape out of his kingdom, try to merchandise him, what do you expect?"

Then she touched a hand to his arm. "Can you tell us how it went with your friend, and her kids?"

"It wasn't pretty, but in the end, he won't fight her for custody or for relocating. He's angling for a deal on the charges."

"I hate that," Cleo muttered from the back seat, and Trey glanced at her in the rearview mirror.

"I understand that. The deal, if it happens, helps clear the way for my client to get herself and her kids back with family out of state. More, it'll spare her the need to return here for a trial. I don't see the prosecutor going for less than fifteen for that guilty plea."

"Is your client okay with that?" Sonya wondered.

"She just wants to feel safe, for her kids to feel safe. That means going back with her mother and her sister. And that's my priority."

Cleo leaned forward, put a hand on Trey's shoulder. "Of course it is, and should be. I'd never make it as a lawyer because I'd want to burn his balls off with a lighter. It would take a long time to manage that."

Trey flicked her another glance. "Remind me to stay on your good side."

"I'd say you're safe there. I met your daddy yesterday, and I liked him too much to ever burn his son's balls."

"Thanks, Dad. How'd that go? I didn't have a chance to talk to him today."

"I think we understand Patricia Poole a lot better now, and I'm going to try to talk to Gretta Poole, at some point anyway. And we had some things happen I haven't told you about yet. I thought we'd wait and tell both you and Owen. We were fine," Sonya added. "We are fine."

"After that business with the mirror," Cleo put in, "it's clear the four of us are in this together. So."

"Fair enough."

But as he drove into town, he shot Sonya a look as if to assure himself on one single fact. She was fine.

"And more news," Sonya began. "Cleo finished the painting she's trading to Owen. And it's breathtaking."

"Probably finished," Cleo corrected. "But I'm happy to take the *breathtaking*."

"If you can stay tonight, we'll go up so you can see it."

"Sounds like a win all around for me." He parked, sent her a smile. "I've got a maybe bag in the trunk."

The same young hostess greeted them in the Lobster Cage, and cast her wistful eyes on Trey.

"She's got it bad," Cleo commented when the hostess had passed out menus and walked back to her station.

"She's twenty," Trey muttered.

"I had a serious crush on my art history professor. I was nineteen," Cleo remembered. "And I'd have to guess he was more than twice that. I'd have been in serious trouble if he'd taken advantage."

"Got over him, didn't you?" Trey asked.

"Yes, but the memories are sweet."

Sonya remembered their server with his orange-streaked dark hair in a topknot. An environmental engineering student who'd shifted from in-person college to remote when his father had fallen ill.

"Good evening, ladies, Trey. Can I start you off with some drinks while you wait for the rest of your party?"

"He should be right along. How about a bottle of sauvignon blanc?" That got the go-ahead. "Bring four glasses, Ian. If Owen wants something else, he'll tell you when he gets here. Which is right now," he added as Owen walked in.

While his hair looked windswept and fell wherever it chose, he'd obviously put on a fresh shirt, fresh jeans.

He dropped down in the booth beside Cleo. "Sorry," he said. "Got busy."

"We just got here. I ordered a bottle of sauvignon blanc."

"Great. What are the rest of you drinking?"

"That busy?" Trey commented.

"And then some. Hey, Ian."

"Hey, Owen. I'll get your wine right out to you."

"Good busy?" Cleo wondered as the server left the table.

"Busy's usually good in business."

"It sounds like things have been busy at the manor, too. You wanted to wait for Owen to tell us. Well, here's Owen."

"Tell us what?"

"Cleo found a portrait of Lisbeth in the studio closet."

"No shit. Huh." Owen sat back. "Who painted it?"

"Collin. Your uncle," Cleo specified. "It's absolutely beautiful."

"A wedding portrait again. Even if it wasn't obviously a wedding dress, I'd have recognized it. Since you and I, Owen, both saw her wearing it."

"We hung it in the music room with the others."

Owen shifted slightly to Cleo. "Good. That's where it belongs." He flicked a glance at Trey. "There'll be three more. Maybe four if they don't count the one of Astrid in the entrance."

"Is it like the other two?" Trey asked. "Size, frame?"

"Exactly," Sonya told him.

"Four more then, in my opinion. Neither Collin nor your father painted the one of Astrid, and it's much bigger, different style frame. This is going to be a set."

"Or a series," Sonya agreed. "From the last bride to the first."

Ian returned with the wine. Once Trey had tasted and approved, he told them the night's specials as he poured all four glasses.

Before he could step away to give them time, both Sonya and Cleo opted for specials. Trey and Owen went for old favorites.

"That's what I like," Owen decided. "Four different meals. You're never going to eat all that lobster Cantonese," he said to Cleo.

"I'm going to give it a serious try."

"Trade him a sample for one of his lobster potpie," Trey advised. "You won't regret it. Now, there's more after the portrait. How did Dobbs take it?"

"Not well." With a shrug, Sonya lifted her wine. "A lot of banging, slamming, wind blowing, lights flickering. But she ran out of steam."

"Mostly," Cleo added.

"Mostly."

Sonya told them about the events at three a.m.

Trey's eyes narrowed. "Facing the house?"

"Yes, at first. She wasn't when you saw her."

He shook his head at Sonya. "No, her back to the house, then the jump. And no banging or blowing the doors open."

"No CCR warning from Clover?"

Now Trey shook his head at Owen. "The clock, the piano music, and something that pulled me to the window to watch her jump. Nothing else."

"You're about to say I should've called or texted you, but there wasn't any need." Sonya gave Trey's arm a squeeze. "We got the doors closed, and she jumped. And it was done for the night. I worked out in the gym this morning."

"Rubbed her face in it," Owen said, and got a smile from Sonya.

"Maybe. She rang the Gold Room bell a lot, but that was it. Cleo thinks she ran low on power after the night. I agree with her there. Dobbs stayed quiet the rest of the day. She stayed quiet. So quiet Cleo finished the mermaid painting."

"Wait a minute. It's done? When can I have it?"

"I'm not sure it's done. I'll be sure tomorrow. Then it needs to dry, then it needs to be framed."

"I can make the frame. I'll make the frame."

"Nothing ornate, and it shouldn't look shiny and new. I can—"

"I'll make the frame," Owen repeated. "I just want another look at her first. How long before I can have her?"

Cleo picked up her wine, smiled sweetly. "Where's my boat?"

"I'll bring the design when I come to look at her."

"Then we'll talk. Now tell me how your dog became a fan of *King Kong*—the old one."

"Original," he countered. "And who isn't? I can come by tomorrow, after work. About five maybe."

"Fine, as long as you understand, you can't take her or frame her for several weeks."

"Months? That's longer than you took to paint her."

"Yes. Welcome to my world. I wanted to use oils," Cleo explained. "I used a medium that cuts the drying time. Otherwise, you'd be looking at six months, not two."

"That's the way it works?"

"It is."

"Then that's the way it works."

When the meals came, conversation drifted into general areas, easy talk.

Halfway through, Bree Marshall bolted out of the kitchen, chef's hat over her short red hair. Nudging Owen over, she scooted onto the edge of the booth.

"I've got five minutes. Tell me about this event. How many people?"

"Well, we don't know yet," Sonya began. "But—"

"You need to get a ballpark soon. You're going to order food from all the restaurants in the village?"

"That's the plan, so—"

"You want to nail down what you want from each. You don't let them choose, or you'll have a mess of it. You want servers, bartenders, a kitchen crew. And you need somebody to monitor the bathrooms. People will want to pee."

Cleo leaned forward to look around Owen. "How would you feel about helping coordinate all that?"

"Like you're smart," Bree said, and grinned. "I need to see the venue. I can come up next Monday, about eleven."

"Perfect," Sonya told her. "We appreciate your help."

"You're gonna need it. Open houses are chaotic, and I live in the chaos." She smiled over at Trey. "That's why we'd never have made it." Then she gave Owen an elbow bump. "We'd have been a better match."

"I tried to tell you."

"No, you didn't."

"Subliminally."

"Oh. I missed that." She gave him a smacking kiss on the cheek that made him laugh. "Too late now. Manny's got me by the heart and hormones. Gotta get back. I'm ordering you two ramekins of chocolate lava cake and two of strawberry shortcake to share. You'll thank me."

And just like that, she was gone.

"Why do I feel we were run over by a flash flood of whipped cream?" Sonya wondered.

"She does that." Then Trey angled his head, looked at Owen. "Subliminally?"

"She's hot." Owen shrugged. "She's always been hot. But I stood by the code. Anyway, she's right. You're smart to enlist her for this deal you're doing."

"She lives in the chaos because she knows how to manage the chaos," Trey said.

"And people," Sonya added. "Which is why we're sharing chocolate lava and strawberry shortcake for dessert. To which I have no objections."

"Which, again," Trey said, "makes you smart."

When desserts arrived, Sonya couldn't argue about the smart.

"I've got it," Owen said when Trey signaled for the check. "You covered the last time we grabbed a meal—and I've had more than a few up at the manor."

"It's all yours."

"Thanks." Sonya sent a look toward Cleo, got a nod. "Since you're coming by around five tomorrow, why don't you stay for dinner? And you, Trey, if you can make it."

"I think I'm going to try my hand at jambalaya. My grand-mère sent me her recipe. It's got some heat on it."

"Then I'm there." Owen paid the check, grinned at Trey. "I like the hot. I have to take off. I need to get an early start tomorrow."

"Then we'll see you around five. And thanks for dinner," Cleo added.

"Welcome." He slid out, turned to Sonya. "Maybe I can crash at your place tomorrow night. I wouldn't mind seeing Dobbs take a header off the cliffs, if she does an encore."

"Plan on the first, who knows about the second. And you should both see Lisbeth's portrait."

"Tomorrow," he said, and left.

The others didn't linger long, and drove home in a soft, quiet spring rain.

The dogs greeted them like war heroes before rushing outside.

"We'll let them back in through the mudroom so they don't track wet through the house. Cleo and I will show you the portrait."

"Just waiting in the closet?"

"That sounds right," Cleo decided. "Waiting. I put some supplies I'd ordered in there a few days ago. Nothing then. Went in today to get something out, and there she was."

They turned into the music room.

Trey said, "Wow," and walked closer. "Beautiful, the subject and the work. She's the first biological Poole up here, and it shows. The resemblance." He turned to Sonya. "Old photos don't show it as clearly. You have the same eyes, the same shape of the face."

"I guess that's true. Someone—maybe several someones—wants us to have these. And hanging them here, that's felt right from the first one."

"And you're both right about the set. These are painted to go together."

"I think, before it's done, we'll have all seven. One generation missing," Cleo added.

"Patricia Poole. I think she must've had some altercation, some event, with Dobbs. Deuce had old newspaper clippings. Society news, and so on. She'd been to the manor any number of times before she married a Poole."

"She met Michael Poole Jr. here," Cleo put in. "We found a gossipy article on that—dinner party deal. She had her engagement party to him here. Another society article, with a photo of them."

"But not the wedding, and nothing after." Trey stepped back to study all three portraits together. "I'd bet on that altercation happening at the engagement party. Not all facts in evidence, but—"

"That's it!" Thrilled, Sonya clasped her hands together. "Talk about smart, and screw all the facts. That makes genius sense."

"I'm going to agree with Sonya. If something happened before to scare her enough, why consent to the engagement party here? The wedding was, what, Sonya, like nine months later?"

"Ten, and a big, important one, so they'd start planning right off.

She went from swanning around for her engagement into breaking Poole tradition and refusing to hold her wedding reception here. Refusing to move into the most important house in the area."

"Facts not in evidence," Trey repeated, and slipped his hands into his pockets as he studied the three portraits. "And I'd put money on it. I don't know what it really tells you, but I'd place that bet."

"It says Dobbs scared her off, and where and when. I wonder if she showed herself to any of the others before their weddings."

"I don't know, but I can't think she wanted to scare Patricia off." Cleo spread her hands. "I don't see why she would when that meant she had to wait another twenty-odd years for her next victim."

Clover used Sonya's phone for the Beatles' "I Me Mine."

"Yeah, that was you." Gently, Sonya touched the frame of Clover's portrait. "Maybe . . . maybe she taunted Patricia somehow, went too far, and it backfired. That's what makes the most sense."

"And now what makes the most sense is for me to go up and read myself to sleep. I'll see you in the morning, Sonya. Probably not you, Trey, but tomorrow night?"

"I'll be here."

"Night, Cleo, and we should bring the dogs in."

At the doorway, before she turned off the light in the music room, Sonya took one last look at the portraits—thought of the past, thought of the future.

Then she turned off the lights and focused on now.

The dogs rushed in as happily as they'd rushed out—and a lot more sloppy.

While they dried wet paws, Sonya opened what she considered the next door with Trey.

"I want to say a couple things to you."

His eyebrows lifted as he glanced at her. "Okay."

"First, you have a key to the manor. I don't want you to feel you have to ring the bell. You can just use your key. And next . . ."

She rose, started to walk with him and the dogs through the house.

"If you wanted, you could leave a few things here so you don't have to pack a bag whenever you stay. I'm not saying all this to box you in. I just—"

"I already built the box for myself," he interrupted, and took her hand. "It's a nice box. It's roomy."

She tipped her head toward his shoulder. "So I can fit in there, too?"

"It's a nice box," he repeated as they started up the stairs. "There's a lid if it starts to crowd you."

"You said it was roomy," she reminded him. "And it feels like a really good fit."

They walked into her sitting room, through to her bedroom. As the dogs headed straight to the bed they shared on visits, Sonya closed the bedroom door, leaned back against it.

"Leave a few things, Trey. I've got plenty of space in here, and in my life."

"I'll leave a few things." He set down the bag, stepped to her. "Because I want that space in here, and in your life."

"I'm glad you're here." She lifted her arms, circled them around his neck. "I'm always glad when you're here."

When their mouths met, the hunger leaped in her, so fast, so fierce it stunned her.

She wanted this, the physical, wanted him to stir up all those needs until they boiled over and burned them both.

As if sensing it, he pressed his body to hers, trapping her against the door while the kiss leaped from hungry to desperate.

Raw need, she realized. For whatever reason, tonight the need ran raw in both of them. Surrendering to it, she took her arms from around him long enough to struggle out of her jacket. As their mouths took and took, she rushed to unbutton his shirt.

And moaned in pleasure as she stripped the shirt away to find warm flesh, hard body.

He yanked down the zipper at the back of her dress.

The dress fell, and before she could step out of it, his hands were everywhere. With none of his usual patience, those hands demanded, possessed, aroused until those raw needs boiled over.

Until she felt the burn she'd craved.

She let out a moan. "Don't stop."

"Couldn't."

Her fingers wanted to tremble as she tugged at his belt. Now, it had to be now, or the need would tear her to pieces, a wild animal of greed.

When she freed him, took him, hard and ready, in her hand, she felt him pull at her briefs.

"Tear them. God! Just tear them. I have more."

When she heard the thin fabric rip, she let out a laughing gasp. "Now! Right now!"

He lifted her so her back slid up against the door. Her fingers dug into his shoulders.

Then their eyes met, and they held. And something new wrapped around that raw need. Just as strong, just as urgent.

Looking into his eyes, feeling the strength of his hands, the heat of his body, she said, "Yes." Then again, "Yes."

He slid inside her, slowly, a deliberate torment for them both. With every inch, her body shuddered, and it rejoiced.

When he was sheathed deep, their eyes remained locked.

He watched her, watched her as he saw pleasure swamp those green eyes, as the heat they brought each other flushed her skin, and slicked it.

Their bodies slid together, and slapped together, until she gasped with every beat.

He watched her fly. Even as her legs wrapped around him, as he took her weight, she flew. Just as she went limp, he flew after.

Chapter Seven

Though she felt so used up, so loose, so sated she thought she could sleep through an alien invasion, Sonya pulled on a T-shirt and sleep shorts.

"If I walk," she told Trey, "I don't want to walk naked. That's just weird on top of weird."

"You look good naked."

"I'll take that compliment, and still." In bed, she snuggled up against him. "You look good naked, too."

"And still, I'll pull on pants if you walk. I'll be with you."

"I know."

With a hand over his heart, she slid straight into sleep.

At three, with the chime of the clock, the drift of piano music, she stirred. And she sighed.

Even before she turned from him, Trey knew she'd walk. He grabbed his pants from the foot of the bed, yanked them on as she got out of bed and started for the door.

"I'm coming," she murmured.

As he followed her, the dogs woke.

"Quiet," he told both of them. "Stay quiet."

They trailed behind him out of the doorway, and down it, he saw Cleo step out of her door.

"It felt like I should get up," she whispered. "I really wish Owen had come back with us."

When Sonya passed her, Cleo fell into step with Trey.

"Is she out there? Dobbs? I didn't take time to look."

"Neither did I."

At the end of the hall, Sonya looked toward the nursery, the weeping. "So sad," she said. "So sorry."

But rather than walk that way, Sonya turned toward the stairs.

For reassurance, Cleo reached for Trey's hand. "Maybe it's—the mirror's—in a different room tonight."

Trey nodded as they followed. "Maybe. But she knows where she needs to go. Not hurrying, but no hesitation either."

Halfway down the stairs, the music changed from the lament of "Barbara Allen" to something lively, and to Trey unrecognizable.

"That's new, the music change."

"It's happier," Cleo decided. "Do you hear voices? I sort of do."

"Like an echo. Distant. Singing?"

"I think so."

At the base of the steps, Sonya turned to walk down the hall. She stopped at the door to the music room, then stepped just inside.

"The music, the voices—all still distant. But she hears something."

"Sees something, too?" Cleo wondered. "Do you see anything? There's not much light, just some backwash from the night-lights we plugged in, but I don't think we should turn them on."

"No. We won't turn them on. And no, I don't see anything but the music room."

Sonya saw the music room, and to her eye it was brightly lit. Flowers painted on pale blue globes shined from the lamps gracing side tables, and the candles in a silver candelabra on the piano flickered.

Their glow illuminated the room as dark pressed against the windows.

She saw a trio of men in suits, and women—two of them young—in pretty dresses that swept toward their ankles.

She recognized Owen Poole as he looked on indulgently while the woman—his wife, second wife and mother of his children—played the piano. Behind her, Lisbeth, her dark hair wound in a braid around the crown of her head, sang a song about the seaside.

As it had once before, a different tableau, it all went still. The young man, Edward, Lisbeth's fiancé, stopped with a glass halfway to his lips and a wide smile on his face.

Lisbeth's mother sat, her hands still on the piano keys, her head tossed back in a laugh.

The hem of a blue dress stilled on a swirl as the young woman wearing it stopped in mid-turn.

The fire in the little hearth stopped crackling and remained frozen like one of the paintings on the wall.

In her pink frock with its flounced skirt, Lisbeth turned to Sonya.

"We were so gay that night! Mama played and played. I loved my Edward. Isn't he handsome?"

"He's very handsome."

"We'd be married in just a few more weeks. My dress is a real dilly, too. Papa didn't mind the cost one bit. Not for his little girl. Everyone's coming. It'll be an absolute crush."

"I know."

"You know," Lisbeth agreed. "It hurt, when I died, and I was so afraid. I was sad, too. And for a while it made me even sadder that Edward moved on. He found someone else to love, and he got married, had a family. It made me so very sad. But then I loved him, so much. And I wouldn't have wanted him to stop living, like I did."

She smiled, simply beamed. "Though wouldn't that be romantic? Tragic and romantic, like a novel! But I loved him too much for that. I never believed in curses. Such silliness, that's what I thought. Now you have to stop her. You have to break the curse. Find the rings, Sonya."

"How? Where?"

"Well, silly, I don't know." She looked over at Edward again, smiling with the glass partway to his lips. "I wish we'd had one night together. Even just one night."

The tableau broke. The fire crackled in the hearth. Edward sipped from his glass, and the girl in the blue dress turned.

Behind her mother, Lisbeth sang.

"You and me, you and me, oh, how happy we'll be!"

Then it all vanished in the dark.

Trembling, Sonya fumbled behind her for the light switch, then jolted when Yoda brushed against her leg. On a half turn, she saw Trey and Cleo.

"Did you see her, see them? Did you see?"

"No. Here." Trey drew her against him. "You're cold."

"No, no, just . . . overwhelmed. I think I'm going to sit down a minute." She turned again, walked unsteadily to a chair. "You didn't see them? I was asleep, then I wasn't, and I was here, and there were people, and music, and Lisbeth."

"We heard music, and singing, but like it was far off." Cleo squeezed her hand. "I'm going to get you some water."

"No, I'm fine. Well, not fine, but okay. You didn't see anything?"

"What did you see?" Trey asked.

"It was a little party. I recognized Owen—not our Owen, Lisbeth's father, and her mother was playing the piano. Lisbeth was singing. She was wearing a pink dress and singing, ah . . . By the sea," Sonya sang, "by the sea, by the beautiful sea. And Edward—her fiancé—was watching her and smiling. And one more couple, young like them, a girl in a blue dress, a man in a suit."

As she stared at the piano, she stroked the head Mookie laid in her lap. Warm, real, she thought.

"Then it all stopped, froze. Just the way it did when I saw Astrid and that party in the parlor. Except for Lisbeth. She looked at me. She saw me. She spoke to me."

"You talked to her."

She looked up at Trey. "That wasn't just in my head? You heard me?"

"Your side of the conversation." Cleo sat on the arm of the chair, rubbed a hand on Sonya's arm.

"She told me how happy they'd all been that night, though I could see it for myself."

Sonya told them the rest.

"The room was different, but not much. Different paintings on the wall, and of course, the portraits weren't there. But the Victrola we brought down? It was right there, just where we put it. I think it was new."

"It wasn't Dobbs," Cleo said. "Not this time."

"No. Not this time. They were so happy. It was like when I saw

Astrid in the parlor. Just friends and family having fun, an evening together with music. She wanted me to see that."

"And feel that," Cleo added.

"I did. I did feel it."

"There's more of that in this house, that feeling," Trey said, "that history, than what Dobbs brought into it. And that's what you're bringing back to it."

"I know it. And though it's way beyond strange, I'm glad I had the chance to see her, talk to her. They really loved each other, Lisbeth and Edward. It was young and sweet, but it was love.

"There's a lot of that in this house, too. People who loved each other. I'd say I'm sorry I got you all up at three a.m., but it's not the first time, and I don't think it'll be the last."

Taking a breath, Sonya rose. "What do you say we all go back to bed?"

"I'm for it. You two can walk me to my room on your way. Well, you four since we have our canine escort."

At the door, Trey took one last scan before he turned out the lights. All quiet, he decided. All settled. For now.

In the morning, he talked her into the shower, so her day started out in the best possible way.

Downstairs, the dogs—their morning ritual slightly delayed— dashed outside. By the time they'd dashed back in for breakfast, Sonya, absolutely content, sat down next to Trey with coffee and bowls of cereal.

"If you don't count middle-of-the-night conversations with dead relatives, this feels so normal."

Trey tapped his mug against hers. "It's our normal."

"You take it all so . . . well, just in stride."

"I grew up in and around the manor, with the legends, the rumors, and with a couple of my own experiences. You've had a hell of a lot more to adjust to. And I don't see a hitch in your stride, cutie."

Oh, she'd had more than a few hitches, she thought.

"When I first moved in, it was easy to dismiss things, mostly little things, as old house, imagination, coincidence, whatever."

He remembered how she'd looked that first day, standing there, the ground blanketed with snow, her hair dancing in the cold wind under her knit hat. He remembered the look of wonder and excitement on her face.

"It didn't take you long to accept and deal."

"Falling in love with the house, and I have to admit at first sight, factored into that. But . . . And I've never believed what I'm about to say. Do you think some of it comes through the blood? The Poole blood. I don't know if I'll ever really think of myself as a Poole. Born and raised, and happily, as a MacTavish, but."

"But," he agreed. "And I think your ancestry could play into it. Clearly, you and Owen—both Pooles—could see something in the mirror Cleo and I couldn't. And could—Jesus, what a moment—walk into it. You saw and heard what you did last night. Cleo and I only barely got a hint of it."

"But you both hear Dobbs when she goes on one of her fits, and you've seen her twice now. Once in the Gold Room—and that was another moment—and out on the seawall. Cleo saw her out there, too."

"Dobbs wasn't a Poole."

Swallowing a spoonful of cereal, Sonya sat back. "She wasn't a Poole. That's so simple and logical, it went right by me. Counselor."

"Simple, logical. It doesn't explain why I've seen Clover twice, and you haven't."

"Oh, that just shows you're not a girl."

"Guilty as charged. But how does that apply?"

"Obviously, she's soft on you, and has been."

Suddenly, Trey's phone rang out with the classic "Holding Out for a Hero."

Raising her eyebrows knowingly, Sonya pointed at him. "I rest my case."

"Who am I to argue with a hot babe? Make that two hot babes. Mookie and I have to get to the office. You'll text if you need me?"

"Yes. I intend to have a very good, very productive day. You have one, too."

He rose. "Any day that starts out with shower sex is already good and productive."

"I can't argue with that," she said, and kissed him. "Bye, Mookie. Be a good boy and a wise legal consultant."

Alone, Sonya dealt with the breakfast dishes as she imagined the ever-vigilant Molly had already made the bed.

"Come on, Yoda, let's go to work."

Upstairs, she started with checks of her texts and emails. Though it tempted her to dive right into the Ryder proposal, she ordered herself to work on current clients. She could end the day with the big potential.

She'd barely begun when she saw Cleo.

"A little early for you."

"When you're up, you're up. I'm going to pull myself together and hit the market. I'm hoping to score some andouille sausage because Grand-Mère claims it makes all the difference."

"Listen to you." Not a little amazed, Sonya sat back. "I'm not sure I knew there were types of sausage. What's andouille?"

"Spicy," Cleo said, with relish. Then frowned, cocked her head. "You had morning sex."

"How could you know that?" Astonished, Sonya threw up her hands. "How could you possibly know that?"

"Because I can see you're relaxed in a way I envy. I really miss morning sex. And afternoon sex, and bedtime sex. And now, damn it, I'm thinking about sex I'm not having. I'm going for coffee."

"It was morning shower sex!" Sonya called out.

"Damn you, Sonya!"

Laughing, Sonya went back to work.

Less than an hour later, Cleo, in spring-weight khakis, a lavender cashmere sweater, stopped at the doorway.

"I'm off. Did you think of anything you want me to pick up?"

"No." But the glory of her friend's hair had her vowing to call the salon at her first break. "I have a consultant call in about thirty, so if I don't answer when you come back, I'm still on it. And I bet you come back with a cat, so I'm timing my break for then so I can cuddle her."

"I'm just going to look."

"Uh-huh. See you and Miss Kitty Cat later."

As it had before, the barrage began before Cleo could have turned down Manor Road.

The iPad roared out with Springsteen's "No Surrender."

"Don't worry. I won't."

When Yoda tried to crawl into her lap, Sonya picked him up, stroked him as her pocket doors slammed closed, slammed open, then closed again. Wind, bitter and cold, lashed through the room and plucked a few books off their shelves. Under her feet, the floor seemed to lift and fall.

On the second floor of the library, the wall screen screamed on with the sound of bullets blazing.

Sonya's heart hammered in her throat; Yoda trembled in her arms. But she stayed where she was.

"Keep it up, bitch. You don't impress me."

Fog crawled into the room. Feeling the ice flow from it, Sonya lifted her feet, crossed her legs under her before it slithered under her desk.

She watched her own breath expel in clouds as the cold dug into her bones.

"We're staying right here." She shouted it, but nearly reached for the phone to call Trey when she heard the main doors crash open.

Then it stopped, it all stopped.

She heard her own tattered breathing as the silence fell, and the air warmed again.

"We're okay." As he shook, she hugged Yoda against her, stroked his soft, brindled fur. "We're okay."

When Christina Aguilera's "Fighter" filled the room, Sonya let out one long breath. "Yeah, I'm learning to be one."

She made herself get up, replace the books. When she went out, looked down, she saw the main doors stood closed.

But she could feel the remnants of cold still sneaking down from the third floor.

"Nice try. Keep wasting your energy, bitch."

She checked the time and decided she had enough of it to spare. Though he'd stopped trembling, she carried Yoda downstairs.

She let him take a run outside, in the sun, and while he did, girded her loins and made an appointment at the salon.

"More courage," she congratulated herself.

She rewarded herself with a Coke, and got a rawhide bone for Yoda before she called him back in.

Then she went back upstairs, settled him, settled herself. And waited for her consult to begin.

Cleo came back with groceries. And a cat.

Since Yoda had already raced down at the sound of the door, Sonya followed. Halfway there, she saw Cleo, a bag of groceries in one hand, a young, sleek black cat in the other.

"I *knew* it!" Sonya jogged the rest of the way down. "Oh, Yoda, don't disappoint me," she said when he put his front paws on Cleo's legs to sniff at the newcomer.

Who, Sonya noted, looked at him regally from her superior height.

"She's just six months old. She's already been spayed, so I don't have to go through that. Lucy said she's fine with other animals and kids. And hell, Son, her eyes did it. Look at them! I've gotta say, they're Poole green. It was meant."

"Well, she's beautiful." Gently, Sonya stroked the soft, pure black fur. "And why am I not surprised you have a black cat? What's her name?"

"She's Pyewacket. She's Pye."

"Like the math thing?"

"Not pi, P-y-e. Pyewacket. It's from an old movie, one of my mama's favorites. *Bell, Book and Candle*, about witches. We'll watch it sometime."

"We'll watch a movie about witches in this house?"

"Fun, interesting witches, with a romance. Anyway, Kim Novak's cat is Pyewacket. Her familiar."

"Okay then, welcome to Lost Bride Manor, Pye."

"Lucy's just wonderful," Cleo gushed as she snuggled the cat. "She gave me most everything Pye needs, and I stopped back into the store for a few more things."

"I'll go get them."

"There's more groceries, too, but I don't want to leave her alone in the house just yet."

"I'll get everything. It's break time anyway. I got the job."

"The other law firm job? Woo, Son!"

"And Dobbs had a big tantrum. I'll tell you about it when we put the groceries away." She ran out.

"I don't like when she goes after Sonya and I'm not here. We've got ourselves a witch, Pye, a mean-ass ghost. And more. You'll get used to it."

Cleo looked down at the dog, who danced in place, tail swinging.

"I'm going to put you down to get acquainted with Yoda. You both better make friends."

She set Pye down, then crossed her fingers. Yoda wagged, whined, sniffed. The cat turned this way and that as if waiting for the dog to scratch an itch.

Then she stretched herself under his jaw as if to take care of it herself before slinking off toward the parlor to, Cleo assumed, begin exploring her domain.

"Isn't she perfect?" Cleo said. She turned as Sonya came in, arms loaded. "And they got along fine. Here, let me take some of that. Just leave the welcome basket and so on here. I'll start on the groceries. I'm going to put her litter box in the mudroom if that's okay."

"That should be the place for it."

"But I'm going to teach her to go out with Yoda."

At the door, ready to go out for the rest, Sonya paused. "You're going to housebreak a cat?"

"I'm going to housebreak this cat. The litter box will be for emergencies only when I'm done. Come on, Yoda, let's see if she follows."

Pye followed, in her own time, and in her perfectly slinky way.

When Sonya came in, Cleo grinned. "I'm going to put her food and water bowls with Yoda's so they learn to eat together. That's the first stage of learning to poop together."

"If you say so."

"I do. I ordered a cat tree. I've been looking at them online, and went with Lucy's pick, which actually looks like a tree. It can go up in the studio. And I ordered the cutest little bed. It's like a little pink cave."

"Pink."

"She's a girl. Now, tell me everything."

"I'll start with the good stuff. The law firm wants something like what I did for the Doyles. Updated, photos, bios. It's not a family firm, but I can work the same type of feel, just a bit more formal. They've already sent back the contract. I owe Deuce for the speed there. They were already sold."

"You did the work that sold them," Cleo reminded her, "but we'll give Deuce a big hug."

"They know Corrine, and liked her work so much on the photos, they're going to contact her, hire her if she's available to do theirs. So I know going in I'll have excellent shots to work with.

"Is this that sausage you wanted?"

"Yes. Score! Now if I can make it half as good as my grand-mère. Tell me about Dobbs."

"Like that other time, you were barely on the road when she started."

"She thinks divide and conquer, but that's bullshit." Cleo's tiger eyes flicked upward. "There's no dividing here. What did she do?"

Sonya started at the beginning as they finished putting away groceries, set out Pyewacket's food and water. And Cleo put the litter box in the mudroom, where Sonya believed it would become a house staple.

"I hate you were alone through all that."

"I think it's good, actually. It proved—to her and to myself—I can handle what she tosses out.

"And while I nearly called Trey, I feel incredibly satisfied I got through it on my own."

"No shame calling him, or me. You remember that."

"I will," Sonya promised. "When I need to. But now I've got work, especially if I want to carve out a little time for the Ryder presentation. What time for cooking? I want to give you a hand."

"After Owen checks out the painting and I see his design for my boat."

"Sounds good."

"You go on. I'm going to walk out with Yoda and Pye, get them started on that part of her training."

Surprised, Sonya glanced down at the sleek little cat. "You're going to let her outside?"

Cleo answered dryly, "Outside's an essential aspect of housebreaking, Son."

"Aren't you worried she'll take off?"

"Lucy said she'd been in their yard. It's fenced, but she could climb it. She knows when she's got it good. And around here, she'll have it more than good."

"All right then." Sonya gave the cat another dubious glance, but went back to work.

When she heard Cleo coming up the stairs, cooing to the cat, she relaxed.

"She peed!"

Amused, Sonya gave her friend a thumbs-up.

Yoda didn't prance up the stairs, but in a few minutes, Sonya heard the bounce of the ball and his running feet.

She thought: All's well in the manor.

Chapter Eight

By late afternoon, Sonya dug herself so deep into the work she didn't notice Cleo going downstairs. Just after five, she surfaced with a jolt at the bong of the doorbell.

"I've got it!" Cleo called up.

Shortly after, Cleo and Owen stopped at the library doors. Yoda raced out to greet Jones. Jones responded with a dignified wag, and pointedly ignored the cat, who slunk behind them.

"We're going up to the studio. If you're not done when we're done up there, don't worry about it. I can draft Owen as sous chef."

"I'm about ready to shut down. Brain's starting to fizzle."

"I'll just dump my gear in the room first," Owen said.

When he walked down the hall, Cleo gestured. "Look at that. She's following him just like the dogs. When he came in the house, she went right to him, started winding around his legs."

"Hussy."

"I know, right? She and his dog didn't even acknowledge each other. But when Owen reached down to give Pye a stroke, Jones looked away. It was disgust, Son, I swear it. And Pye? She purred. Orgasmically."

"I think you're jealous."

"Maybe. A little bit." She shrugged it off, and when Owen walked back, trailed by the cat and two dogs, told Sonya, "We shouldn't be long."

"Take your time. I'll be ready when you are."

Cleo started up the stairs. "I didn't figure you for a cat person."

Owen glanced at her. "Why not?"

"Eye-patch dog."

"Dogs, cats. Whatever. Animals are usually easier to deal with than a lot of people. Dead or alive. Did she show up last night to take her dive?"

"Can't say, but we have stories to tell. Let's do this first."

On the third floor, he looked down toward the Gold Room.

"Quiet now."

"She rumbled a little this afternoon."

"And yet you spend a lot of time up here."

"No way in hell she's robbing me of my studio."

When they stepped in, he saw why. Because all he saw was the painting.

The beauty on the rocks, the colors, the details down to the water streaming from the sounding whale.

And the magic in the globe.

He set the tube he carried on the worktable.

"She's going to be worth the wait. Jesus, she's . . . I haven't got the word for her, and I've got plenty of words when I need them."

He took his eyes off the art to look at the artist. "I knew you were good. I didn't know you were this good."

"I think she's the best thing I've ever done, so you'd better take good care of her."

"You don't have to worry about that." He stepped closer.

"Don't touch!"

"Right." He shoved his hands in his pockets. "You're right about the frame, and I can make one that suits her. I need the measurements."

"Twenty-four by thirty inches, one and three-eighths deep."

"Is that exact?"

"It is."

"Okay then. Got it. You'd better see the design, because once I start, I start. No changing your mind."

"When I make it up, I stick." Cleo planted a hand on her hip. "When I make a deal, I keep it."

"Then take a look, and make it up."

The cat jumped on the back of the love seat, where she watched the dogs like a queen watched her subjects.

At the worktable, Owen slid out and arranged the drafting papers.

Cleo said nothing as she stared at the sketches, from port, from starboard, from bow, and from stern.

Carved mermaids swam up the sides. Another, hair flowing back, graced the bow.

Her mermaid, she realized. He'd replicated the face, the hair, on the boat she'd traded her for.

He said it to her, and now she thought it of him.

She hadn't known he was this good.

"Unexpected," she managed. Pressing her fingers to her lips, she turned away.

"Listen, you want something else—"

She just waved a hand, breathed out, turned back to him. The evening sun streamed in the windows behind her, shot a halo around her hair.

"I haven't had my own pet or my own boat since I moved to Boston. Other things took priority. Like school, then getting my toe in a career. I moved here, and there was Yoda, so I had him, even though he's Sonya's. And today I got Pye. You knew where her name came from when I told you what I'd called her."

"Sure. It's a great movie. I like old movies."

"Yeah, so do I. I knew you'd build me a boat that was sound, would handle well. A boat I'd enjoy sailing in the lovely bay. But I didn't expect you to come up with one that speaks to me like that one would. Can you really do that? Those carved mermaids?"

"Well, yeah. Why would I spend time designing what I couldn't build?"

"Well, it's perfect. More than perfect. And before you tell me to, I'll promise to take good care of her. How long do I have to wait to take her out?"

He glanced back at the painting. "Several months."

She laughed, shook her head. "Really?"

"Because I've already started on her. If you didn't want her, someone would."

"You already started on her," Cleo murmured. "I want her. Nobody else captains *The Siren*."

He had to smile. "Named her already?"

"No other name would do."

"Good name." He walked to her, held out a hand. "Deal."

"Deal," she agreed. "But let's be real. This exchange deserves more than a hearty handshake."

She moved right in on him, laid her hands on his shoulders. The look in her eyes told him she intended the kiss to be light and playful.

He had other ideas.

So when she brushed her lips to his, he gave her a little jerk forward and turned on the heat.

It had been simmering for a while, and if it hadn't simmered in her, too, he figured she'd let him know real quick.

He felt her surprise, but no resistance. Then the hand on his shoulder slid up until her fingers threaded through his hair.

She turned up the heat a few more notches.

He had a way, and that wasn't a surprise to her. Good strong hands gripped her hips, and his mouth was confident and experienced on hers.

She let herself fall into the moment, rode the storm of it that tossed testing and teasing aside and embraced unapologetic lust.

And in that moment what happened inside her body wasn't a stirring but an eruption. She not only accepted it, but clung to it, grateful.

From her pocket, Marvin Gaye suggested "Let's Get It On."

Not yet, not quite yet, Cleo told herself.

And in the next moment, they stood, bodies still molded together, faces close, eyes open and watchful.

"Time to step back," she decided.

"Seriously?"

"Seriously. And regretfully. We'll just . . ." She put a hand to his cheek, then eased back. "Put this aside for a while."

"A while."

"We're grown-up people, so we both know the next step, if we take it, is sex. I have rules about that."

"Hey, me, too. What are yours?"

"First, no sex with married men, or men in serious relationships. Even those in casual relationships get a pass. First round can be a one-off, no harm, no foul. But no second round or beyond unless it's exclusive on both sides. Any who want to sleep with other women, go right ahead, but I won't be one of them."

"Is that it?"

"Oh, the list goes on and covers things like respect and honesty and so forth, but those are the broad, essential terms. Yours?"

"No married women, no women tangled up with some other guy—that's just stupid. No problem with a one-nighter if things fall that way. She says no—and there's more ways to say no than a two-letter word—you suck it up and take no. And I'm not going to have sex with a woman who's going to bounce off me to someone else. I'm not going to roll off her and roll onto someone else. Either way, that's just insulting."

Jones walked over to sit beside him, like a wingman.

"If I'm reading this right," Owen continued, "you're saying no to me climbing in your bed tonight."

"I am." She gave him a long look out of amber eyes. "Regretfully."

"But not no altogether."

"I like you. I liked you right off. You never pressured Sonya, never made her feel guilty about coming out of nowhere to inherit this house and all the rest."

She held up a hand when he started to speak.

"You could have, if you were someone else. But that's not you, so I liked you. And I know a true friend when I see one, because I'm one. You're a true friend to Trey, and loyalty ranks high with me. I've got a lot of respect for the no-bullshit types, which you seem to be.

"But what went beyond that, for me, is the way you went with Sonya, no hesitation, through that damn mirror."

"Look, I'll take credit for that if it cuts down on the *a while*, but what the hell else was I supposed to do?"

She smiled at that. "And that you'd ask that, have that mildly an-noyed attitude when you do is exactly why I like you and find you attractive."

"Then why aren't I climbing into your bed tonight?"

"Because once we start, it'll be hard to stop if either of us decide to." She spread her hands. "Friendships. Yours to Trey, mine to Sonya, mine to Trey, yours to Sonya. I don't know about you, but I've never been able to stay friendly with an ex. On the surface, maybe, but not underneath. Because, well, they're an ex for a reason."

"You got me there. Trey and Bree manage it, but I think that's an exception."

"So a while."

"Deal," he said, and put his hands on her again.

She laughed. "Sneaky. I like sneaky."

He hadn't been wrong about the simmering, and if he was any judge, it wouldn't be long to flashpoint.

So he could wait. A while.

Sonya stepped into the doorway just as they broke apart. And im-mediately stepped back. "Oh, well. Sorry."

"It's fine," Cleo told her, her eyes still on Owen. "We were just seal-ing a deal."

"You were up here longer than I . . . I thought I should check. Sorry."

"It's fine," Cleo repeated. "Come take a look at my boat."

When Cleo walked to the worktable, a clearly flustered Sonya fol-lowed.

"Maybe I'll just . . . Oh my God! This is the boat? Mermaids! Oh, this is so you, Cleo. Owen, this is so absolutely Cleo. It's perfect."

"Say that again when I finish building it. Got any beer?"

"Yes. Oh, I love this. It almost makes me want one of my own."

"You're getting a doghouse."

Smiling, Sonya looked over at him. "Am I?"

"We made a deal."

"Deals all around," Cleo said. "And I need to start dinner."

"Ready to help."

"I'm going to roll the plans up, stick them in my room. I'll be right down for that beer."

As they walked out, Sonya looked at Cleo, waved a hand in front of her face as if fanning away heat. Cleo just rolled her eyes, gave Sonya a poke with her elbow.

"I want to hear all about it," Sonya muttered.

"Later. Dinner needs to happen, and I'm behind there."

"Because you were busy kissing Owen."

"Among other things. Not those things." Another eye roll. "Looking at the boat design, discussing."

"It's going to be beautiful, and so uniquely yours. I have to say, he really gets you."

As they came down the main stairs, the door opened. Mookie charged in, followed by Trey.

Pleased he'd used his key, Sonya went straight to him, wrapped close, lifted her mouth for a kiss.

"We've been up looking at the design for Cleo's boat. It's amazing."

"I've seen it, and agree."

"Dinner's going to be a little later," Cleo told him. "Sonya and I have to get started."

"I'll put my stuff up and give you a hand where I can. Hey," he said as Owen came down with Jones, and the cat.

"Who's this?"

"My cat. Pyewacket. She's apparently attached herself to Owen."

Trey bent down, gave her a long, smooth stroke. And she arched under his hand, purred like a well-tuned engine.

"And appears to be fickle," Cleo added. "We'll let the dogs and Pye out, and get started."

"You're letting the cat out with the dogs?"

"I'm housebreaking her," Cleo told Trey.

"Okay, well, that should be interesting."

"Getting a beer," Owen said. "You want?"

"I do. Two minutes."

"Hurry down. We have a lot to tell you. And Cleo and I will fill Owen in on last night."

"Sounds like I'm going to need that beer." Owen headed straight back to the kitchen. Paused at the music room.

"That's the newest one."

"Lisbeth. I found her in the closet, in the studio. She's just the beginning."

"I'll start." Sonya opened the kitchen door for the animals, and began the story of the night before.

While she weighed in with a few details, Cleo got out the pot she wanted, turned the heat on under it.

Owen had a beer ready for Trey when he came in.

"Busy night," Owen commented.

"For a while. You saw the portrait?"

"Yeah, and then you saw her." He turned to Sonya. "Can't say in the flesh, exactly."

"It seemed like it. She was so vital, so vivid. I wondered if you'd have seen her, the rest of the party, like I did."

"I think he might have. Sonya, start cutting the chicken into bite-sized pieces." Cleo added the red bell pepper, the onion, and the celery she'd chopped to the sausage she'd already browned in the pot. "I think since Trey and I heard something, it's different from the mirror anyway. But Owen's a Poole, so I think so."

"Maybe Collin saw something, too." Sonya started on the chicken, with less speed and more precision than Cleo on the sausage.

"Maybe." Owen gave the vegetables in the pot a stir. "I'm betting the paintings in there add a punch."

"Agreed." Trey got out wine, poured two glasses.

"Well, she didn't like us hanging them, that's for certain. Thanks." Sonya stopped work on the chicken to take the wine. "And today?"

She took a gulp of wine, then put it down to work as she told them.

"Pulled out some stops." Owen watched as Cleo added garlic and herbs to the vegetables, stirred.

"The fog didn't touch you?" Trey asked.

"No. I pulled my legs up. I really think I'd have those ice burns if I hadn't. I nearly called you. I'm not ashamed to admit I was close to the edge of panic. But it stopped. Just stopped, all of it.

"Clover was there," she murmured. "I think the whole time, now that I look back. I think . . . I think I felt her."

Her phone played Tom Petty's "I Won't Back Down."

"That's right, and neither will we. Did I do this chicken right, Cleo?"

"Couldn't be righter if you'd used a ruler. I need to sauté it. How about letting the kids in?"

"I've got it." Owen went to the door, laughed. "Cat chases dogs. You should see this. She's even got Jones going for it."

"It's like a game of tag," Sonya said when they looked out. "She chases one, rounds back for the next. I guess she's permanently It."

"Smart girls take charge." Pleased, Cleo went back to sauté the chicken. "I guess they can stay out awhile since they're having fun."

While Cleo stirred, the meat sizzled and the scent rose up.

"How long does that take?" Owen wanted to know when she put the browned chicken in with the rest.

"This part? According to my grand-mère, about ten minutes, then I add the spices and the rest, bring it all to a boil. Turn it down, cover it up. Forty-five minutes, stirring several times."

"So about an hour. I think I'll poke around a little." He looked at Trey. "You in?"

In answer, Trey set down his beer.

"Not the Gold Room."

Frustration darkened Trey's eyes as he turned to Sonya. "Eventually, cutie, we're going to have to open that door again."

"Not tonight. Between last night and this morning . . . Not tonight. Eventually . . . You're right, I know you're right."

"It'll wait."

"You're looking to stir her up like I'm stirring up what's in this pot." Cleo glanced back over her shoulder. "Good. You'll have to wait until I can put this on low for us to go with you."

Sonya took a long, deep sip of wine. "And we need to let the pets in for that. She might send something after them. We stick together."

When the phone played Bon Jovi's "Livin' on a Prayer," Sonya gave it a dubious look.

"It's about sticking together," Owen pointed out. "And I figure we've got three portraits, and you and me? We went through the mirror, both ways. If we're not halfway there, we're damn close."

"She's been quiet since this morning. Recharging her evil batteries."

"Cleo said she made some noise this afternoon."

At Owen's comment, Sonya spun around. "You didn't tell me."

"Oh, she makes some noise most days. And this wasn't even as much as usual. She just wants me to know she's there."

Judging it time, Cleo added cayenne and paprika to the mix, blended it in. She dumped in crushed tomatoes, chicken broth, then because in her opinion it never hurt, added some of the wine before measuring out the rice.

"Needs to boil, then I'll set the timer for thirty-five."

"You said forty-five."

"The last ten's for the shrimp," she told Owen. "And some prayers I didn't screw anything up."

"Smells great." Trey rubbed a hand on Sonya's shoulder. "I'll let our four friends in. Third floor. I want to see Cleo's—Owen's painting anyway. And we'll check the closet in there. In case. We won't touch her door."

Sonya nodded. "But it'll piss her off, all of us going up there. Yeah, she deserves a slap after this morning. You're right. You're all right."

When he let in the pets, Pye strutted over to leap on a chair at the casual dining table and began to wash.

All three dogs flopped down on the floor as if exhausted.

"She wore them out," Trey observed.

"She's already right at home." Sonya nodded. "I know just how she feels. And it is home. I should be able to go right up to that door and say get the hell out of my house."

"You were alone this morning," Owen pointed out. "It shook you up, but it would've shaken anybody up."

"It did, and maybe that's part of the reason I'm saying don't open that door. But I feel, honestly, it's not the time to confront her like that. I think we need more first. But I don't know more what."

She huffed out a breath. "I need to arrange to go see Gretta Poole. I've been dragging my feet there, too. I'm angry, angry about what was done to my father and to Collin, to Clover's babies. And Gretta Poole was part of that."

"I didn't—don't—know her very well," Trey began. "I guess she always seemed old to me. Old and . . ." He broke off with a shrug.

"He doesn't want to dis a woman in her condition." Owen sniffed at the pot. "I don't have a problem with that. She is what she is, was what she was. Weak. My grandmother used to say a jellyfish had more spine than Gretta Poole. I never saw anything to contradict that.

"This is boiling."

"I'm giving it a minute." And another stir. "I'll go with you, Sonya."

"Thanks, but I think two strangers might be too much."

"Cutie." Trey stroked Sonya's hair. "Everyone's a stranger to her at this point."

"I guess that's true. Still, maybe it should be one-on-one. Especially since it might come to nothing."

"If you change your mind, I'll go. Otherwise? It might be interesting to spend some time in the manor alone. I really haven't yet, except when I first got here and you were out."

"And you went down to the servants' quarters. Alone, in an empty house you knew was haunted."

"See?" Satisfied, Cleo turned the heat to low, stirred a last time, then covered the pot. "Interesting. Every time I run errands you're here alone—if not alone-alone."

"And what happened today?" Sonya tossed back.

"Something you handled," Cleo pointed out as she set the timer on her phone. "You don't think I can do the same?"

"It's not that. I just—"

"You're going to make me think this isn't my home, too."

"Oh, that's a low shot!"

"Why aim high?" Cleo stuck the phone in her pocket.

"Why don't we—"

Trey broke off at two hot female looks. He held up both hands, stepped back.

"I'll be gone longer than your errand runs. I can at least coordinate the visit to Ogunquit to the next time you plan to go into the village.

And you could hang out there longer. Maybe have lunch with Anna, or scout out painting spots."

Once again, Cleo planted a hand on her hip—a sure sign she'd dug in.

"You arrange the trip for when you can arrange it, and I'll either go with you or stay here and take care of myself. Just like you do when I'm not here. We take care of each other, Son. But we both have to stand up for ourselves."

"Will you call Trey or Owen if something happens?"

"Like you did today?" Now Cleo waved a hand for peace. "Well, you nearly did, so I'll do the same. If something happens and I'm really frightened, I'll SOS. Promise."

"All right."

"Good. Now let's go rattle that bitch's cage."

Four phones blasted out "Times Like These."

"Foo Fighters." Owen shook his head and grinned. "If she wasn't married, either way too young or way too old for me, depending, Clover'd be the girl of my dreams."

Chapter Nine

When Sonya thought of the Gold Room, she thought of blood on a white wedding dress, of a woman crying out as she froze to death in a snowstorm, or another desperately birthing her twins before her body gave out.

She thought of murder and madness.

As if he read those thoughts, Trey took her hand. "It'll be fine."

He spoke so matter-of-factly as they climbed the stairs, she almost believed him.

But.

"As Han Solo and others have said, I have a bad feeling about this."

"You have to believe the Force is with us," he countered. "It's always with the good guys."

Behind him, Owen mimicked Darth Vader breathing, and got a punch on the arm from Cleo.

"Hey, I'd take Vader over Dobbs anytime." Owen glanced back as they started past the library. "Hold on a minute." And walked in to study Sonya's mood board.

"That's the Ryder thing? Got your multigenerational representation," he said. "Smooth. Smart. You know what you're doing."

"Most of the time."

"You know what you're doing," he repeated, and this time got one of Cleo's smiles.

Two men, two women, three dogs, and a cat started up to the third floor.

From the Gold Room came a slow, steady thud, a heartbeat, dull and thick.

When they reached the landing, a red glow outlined the door.

"I guess she doesn't like everyone coming up at once. Well." Sonya got a good grip on Trey's hand. "We've come this far."

The sound increased in speed and volume as they walked down the long hall where the sunlight through Cleo's studio windows pierced the shadows.

The animals reacted, Mookie with a low growl, Yoda with a snarl, Jones with a trio of throaty barks.

When the cat hissed, Cleo picked her up.

"Getting colder." Trey glanced at Cleo. "Does that happen when you come up to work?"

"Not so far. If she tries it, well, I've got plenty of sweaters."

At Cleo's studio, Trey stopped, and with Sonya's hand still in his, stepped in to study the painting.

"That's a major wow. A major magic wow. Owen, I'd say you're going to need a better boat, but I've seen the design. Fair trade.

"Why don't we check the closet?"

Sonya crossed over to it, opened it. And saw only Cleo's currently well-organized supplies.

"It should be Agatha next. But not tonight." Sonya closed the door again.

"It's warmer in here than it is in the hall," Trey observed. "And not just because you've got sun coming in."

"I have a few little things in here to block her, or muffle her anyway."

"What, like crystals and incense?"

Cleo gave Owen a cool stare. "If you believe in ghosts, like the one making all that racket, why not the rest?"

"Okay, your point."

From the Gold Room, the noise increased with the sound of windows slamming open, crashing closed.

"I'd say her cage is rattled," Trey remarked, and stepped back into the hallway.

The glow around the door burned fiery red now as the door itself bowed out, bowed in, as if breathing.

Beside him Owen hooked his thumbs in his pockets. "I hate to give her credit, but that's pretty cool."

In obvious disagreement, Jones bulleted down the hall to bark wildly at the heaving door.

"Come on, man."

As Owen started down to his dog, Sonya called out, "Don't touch the door. She's at peak."

"We won't. Stay." Trey pointed at Mookie before he jogged down after Owen.

"Okay, you're the big dog. Let's just—" But when Owen leaned down to haul Jones up, the door slammed open.

And the dog rushed in.

"Oh, hell no." Without hesitation, Owen pushed in after.

Trey glanced back at Sonya. "I have to," he said before he leaped in. And the door slammed shut.

"Shit! Shit. Hold her." Cleo shoved the hissing cat at Sonya. "I have something that might help."

When Cleo ran back to the studio, Sonya stood with two growling dogs and an angry cat.

"Fuck it. Just fuck it." She fed on fear and misery, Sonya remembered. So she wouldn't give Dobbs either. She strode forward, and her phone played Santana's "Evil Ways."

"Yeah, she's got them. She's also got my goddamn boyfriend, my cousin, and a dog in there."

"Wait!" Cleo ran down the hall with a smoking stick of white sage.

"Really, Cleo? Against this?"

"My grand-mère made it herself. Don't dismiss it. Believing's half of it. Jesus, Sonya!"

The door beat, and a cold wind seeped around its edges to lash through the hallway. What beat and crashed behind it sounded like a war.

"What the hell's happening in there?"

"We have to stay calm." As her hair blew back, Sonya set the cat down, took Cleo's free hand. "It's the opposite of what she wants from us. Calm."

"Working on it." She began to circle the smoking sage at the door. "Ah, here is light against the dark. Peace against violence. Love against hate."

Inside the room, the wind rose to a gale. Smoke billowed up to fly like birds out of the windows.

The bed rose six feet off the floor, then dropped like a stone. Under it, the floor cracked in jagged black lines.

And the walls bled.

"Do you see her?" Owen snapped it out while his breath expelled in white vapor.

"For a second. Not now."

"I see her."

She stood, a foot off the floor, arms outstretched. Her long black dress whirled around her, and her hair streamed like black smoke.

Her dark eyes fixed on Owen, gleaming with glee and madness, while Jones, teeth bared, barked below her.

"A Poole." Her voice came silkily through the wind. "You've the look of him, rougher, but the look of him who pumped his lust into me one night, then cast me aside for a biddable little whore. Be damned to him, to you, to all Pooles. I rule here."

"All this over a one-night stand? Bullshit, pathetic bullshit. Go haunt hell."

Though Trey didn't see Dobbs, when Owen charged forward, he moved with him. Then Owen's head snapped back, and Trey grabbed his arm to keep him upright.

As Owen swiped at the blood streaming from his nose, as the dog leaped, snarling, he saw her hands curl like claws and braced himself for another blow.

A drop of his blood fell on the floor. White smoke trickled under the doorway.

Rather than strike, Dobbs screamed. Rather than strike, she whirled like her hair, like her dress. And vanished.

The room was just a room.

"What the fucking fuck?" Trey demanded.

"She clocked me, and I tell you she was going to do it again. Then poof. Goddamn it. Jones, you asshole." But he said it with pride as Jones strutted toward him.

"He's got something." Trey crouched down, and after a short tug, took the scrap of black fabric from Jones. "Son of a bitch." He looked up at Owen. "This has to be from her dress. He tore off a piece of her dress."

"Good man, Jones. You fucking maniac."

"Let's get the hell out of here. The women are either going to be pissed or frantic. Probably both."

"Yeah, well, what was I supposed to do? Nobody messes with Jones."

Trey opened the door.

Sonya and Cleo stood, hands clasped, with a smoking cone in Cleo's other hand. The two dogs and the cat sat calmly enough. Then Mookie rushed him, wagging and whining.

"Fine. We're all fine. Sorry, but—"

"You didn't have a choice," Sonya finished, and glanced at Owen. "Neither of you. I'd have done the same if it had been Yoda, Cleo."

She held herself back from embracing Trey in desperate relief. "Owen's bleeding."

"Sucker punch." He shrugged. "Not my first or last bloody nose."

"Bathroom there. Go clean it up," Cleo said. "Do you need help with that?"

"No, I got it."

"I need to go check dinner."

"How long were we in there?"

"Forever." Now Sonya did put her arms around Trey. "But really probably not five minutes. Let's all go and talk downstairs."

But she walked to the bathroom door first. "If you go in there again, I'll punch you myself."

"Well, that's terrifying." Leaning over the sink, Owen pinched his nose. "She's done for now. Me, too. I want another beer."

Satisfied, Sonya joined the others. All but Jones, who sat at Owen's feet at the sink, headed down.

"We'll wait for him to talk it through. I caught a glimpse of her in there, but he got more. And I think they had what passes for a conversation."

Cleo stopped in her studio to tap out the smudge stick.

"What is that?"

"White sage," she told him. "From my grand-mère."

"Works against negativity," Sonya added.

"Okay. It was definitely negative in there. I broke my word to you."

"I meant it when I said I'd have done the same. You said you had to, and you did. Plus, you didn't really break your word. You didn't open the door. Except from the inside to come out, and that's different."

Sonya added, "I want a really big glass of wine."

They moved straight to the kitchen, where Cleo lifted the lid and stirred.

"I'm going to feed the dogs, and the cat. Got cat food?" Trey asked Cleo.

"Of course. And only the best for Pye."

She replaced the lid, got out a can while Trey filled dog bowls, and Sonya got out two beers before topping off the wine.

When Owen came in with Jones, Jones went straight to the food, and Owen to the beer.

Trey studied him. "Might have a shiner tomorrow."

"I don't think so. I'm not going to say she hit like a girl considering present company, but it didn't have the punch she gave you that time."

"We're going to sit. Cleo, can that just keep doing what it's doing so you can sit?" Sonya took her wine to the table. "We need to hear it all."

"I can start by telling you it was a lot like the first time I went in there. Cold, wind, bed floating up and crashing, walls bleeding. Some smoke this time, and pouring out the windows. I caught a glimpse of her, like before. Owen got more than a glimpse."

"Jones, too. He saw her. She's a looker if you go for that type. I'd say sultry, but it's more edgy. Plus, she's crazy as fuck, and it shows. She was standing about a foot over the floor."

He began to recap the rest.

"One night?" Sonya repeated. "Not an actual affair, but one night?"

"That's how she put it, and went on about how she rules this house."

"That's where your 'bullshit' comment came from," Trey assumed.

"It is bullshit, and she pissed me off. My family—ours," he corrected, "built this place. It's not hers, and it's never going to be."

"You went at her."

With a shrug, Owen lifted his beer to Trey. "Well, I was pissed off. Plus, you went at her with me. Then bam, she took her shot. She was winding up for another, but . . . Something changed. Like that."

He snapped his fingers.

"She spun like a, well, a top, and screamed, then gone."

"Everything stopped," Trey added. "Maybe she ran out of juice."

"Maybe the smudging helped." Cleo rose again when her phone alarm sounded, and this time got the shrimp out of the refrigerator. "I could see it trickling in under the door. The pissed off—and I'm not blaming you—feeds her, I think. Like fear, pain, sorrow."

"It does. And Cleo and I stayed calm. She hates that."

"I stayed calm after you ordered me to." After adding the shrimp, she turned. "Blood."

"Again?" Owen reached for his nose.

"No, not now, then. I bet some of it hit the floor. So theory." She came back, sat, picked up her wine. "Smudge stick made by a good witch, calm, and blood. Blood's life, it's power."

"And it was Poole blood," Sonya added.

"You think that combination shut her down?" Sipping his beer, Trey considered. "Maybe. Interesting, and it makes as much sense as anything."

"Add one more. Jones got a piece of her."

Sonya widened her eyes. "He bit her?"

"I don't think he managed that. But he gave it a shot."

"He got this." Trey took the scrap of black fabric from his pocket.

"Is that—it's from her dress?" When he set it on the table, Sonya hesitated, then brushed her fingers over it. "How can it be real, be solid? What am I saying? How can Molly make the beds, clean the house? How can Jack play ball with Yoda, and all the rest?"

"He ripped her dress." With no hesitation, Cleo picked up the scrap. "Good boy, Jones."

"He prefers *man*."

"Naturally. Maybe we can use this. I'm going to ask my grand-mère."

"You need to keep it somewhere secure. I don't think we should keep it in the house, at least for now."

"I'll take it." Owen held out his hand. "It's Jones's trophy anyway. I'll bring it back if you find out you can use it, but this way it's at my place."

He looked toward the stove. "Isn't that done yet?"

Cleo held up five fingers, and went back to stir.

"We'll set the table." Sonya rose.

"I'll let the dogs—sorry, dogs and cat out. How did you keep them calm?" Trey wondered.

"I honestly don't know." Sonya got out plates then handed them to Owen. "It seemed like they settled down when we got calm, and Cleo started with the smudging. What's this?"

Sonya noticed the dish on the counter, and lifted the dishcloth that covered it. "Cake?"

"Corn bread. Grand-mère again. She said if I was doing her jam-balaya, I had to make her corn bread to make it right. I sampled some, and think I pulled it off."

"We could all have used a sample."

"You can have more than a sample in just a minute, Owen, be-cause this looks ready to me."

When they dished it up, Owen dived right in. "Got a real nice kick to it."

"Chef's kiss," Trey agreed.

"It's wonderful, Cleo. When I think how you buried this talent."

"Didn't bury it, Son; didn't know I had it to bury. It's like a fun hobby now. I never had a hobby."

"Shopping."

Cleo shook her head. "Shopping's a calling, even a mission."

Clover came out with some honky-tonk-type piano, then a rough, ready voice.

"Dr. John?" Owen grabbed some corn bread. "'Mama Roux.' Oh yeah, Clover's the girl of my dreams."

"You know Dr. John? That's Creole music. Grand-mère's a major fan."

"Then she's got damn good taste," Owen said.

"It's spooky."

"Meant to be, Son."

"Well, here's to the chef, and her grand-mère."

The rest raised their glasses with Trey.

Since Cleo had cooked, Sonya split leftovers into three tubs. "Anyone up for a movie? Down in the movie room."

"What kind of movie?"

Recognizing Owen's caution, Sonya smiled. "Don't worry, Cleo and I save our rom-coms and weepers for girls' night. Only thing off the table are horror flicks, which pains me, as I love them. But after the last couple of days, I'm not waving a red flag."

"The last *Indiana Jones* is a good one."

"You've already seen it?" Sonya asked.

"Yeah, but if a film's only worth watching once, it's probably not much worth the first time."

"Sounds like popcorn for dessert. Coffee, beer, Coke?" Cleo asked.

"Coke, thanks."

"I'm with Trey on that," Owen said.

"Popcorn, Cokes, and Indy." Sonya nodded. "Sounds really good, and a little like giving somebody who deserves it a return punch in the face."

They settled into the cushy seats with the dogs piled up on the floor for naps. Pye sprawled over the back of a seat to take hers.

When the movie ended, Sonya actually clapped. "The end of an era done really well. And such a good way to close out this strange and ultimately excellent day."

"I've got an even better way," Tray murmured in her ear.

"I sincerely hope so. And she didn't make a peep."

They trooped back upstairs to let the animals out for a last round, to deal with movie dishes.

Once more, all together, they walked upstairs. This time stopping on the second floor.

"See you in the morning. Either at three a.m. or," Sonya added, "hopefully later."

She waited until she and Trey reached her bedroom before turning to him. "So, what's this even better way?" Then laughed when he scooped her up.

Sonya slept through the three o'clock hour, and all it brought. Trey saw her, Dobbs, as he'd expected to.

He hadn't expected to see Owen, Jones beside him, standing on the lawn. Easing the doors open, Trey stepped out on the balcony.

"For fuck's sake, Owen."

"Wanted a closer look," Owen called up, and watched as Dobbs jumped off the wall. "And to test a theory."

"I'm coming down."

"Yeah, meet you inside."

While Sonya slept on, Trey pulled on pants. He went quietly out and down the stairs where Owen stood at a window in the front parlor.

"Looking for another bloody nose, or worse?"

"She didn't see me. I wondered about that, so I set my phone for quarter to three."

With a shake of his head, he grinned. "And son of a bitch if Clover didn't come on with Sinatra's version of that old song. Anyway. I went outside."

He turned to Trey. "We're heading toward a half moon, and you can smell spring. Air's still got a bite at this hour, but you can smell it.

"I left the front door open, so I heard the clock, heard the piano start. Straight 'Barbara Allen' tonight. Then it changed out there."

He stepped to the window, looked out at the seawall.

"Full moon, and I'd say late summer from the feel of it. There she was, Trey. Just poof, there she was. The way Sonya and Cleo said they saw her."

"Facing the house."

"Like that. But she didn't see me. I'm standing right there, and Jones is growling. We saw her, but she didn't see us. She turned around, and I heard her say her blood sealed the spell. You called down."

"She didn't hear me," Trey realized. "Didn't see you, didn't see me. She's not as strong out of the house, and this is like a loop."

"Yeah, that's how I see it. I'm guessing she geared up the night she blew the doors open up there, but she didn't try that tonight. Just jumped. Then everything changed back."

Aligning the steps, the known, Trey paced, and factored the not-quite-known in with them.

"And we're thinking she's taken that leap every night at three a.m. since, what, 1806."

"My money's on it."

"I hope it hurts, every time. You decide to do this again, come get me first."

"She didn't even know I was there. I wondered, because Poole."

"She didn't know you were there because you weren't there. Not when she jumped, and it's a loop. Same time, same night, same moon."

"Huh. I didn't figure that one. Sounds right."

"The house was here, not exactly the way it is now, but here. And even when she jumps, she's in it."

At sea, Owen dragged a hand through his hair. "Now you're losing me."

"It's a loop, Owen, like a replay. But what she is, is in the house. So she can still bang and pound and blow, whatever, even as what's out there takes the dive."

"That's crazy." For a beat, Owen considered it. "And yet somehow sounds right."

"It's done for tonight. I'd say it's all done for tonight. Let's get some sleep."

"I'm for that."

In the morning, Sonya beat Trey downstairs, and found Owen filling a go-cup with coffee.

"Hey, listen," he began. "I let the dogs out, and the cat came down right behind them, went to the door, so she's out, too. I took one of the Toaster Strudels—it was a full box. And I'm taking this go-cup. I'll bring it back."

"Okay. I was going to scramble some eggs if you want some."

"Now she tells me. I've gotta go."

"Don't forget the jambalaya. And, Owen"—she got out a mug for her own coffee—"you can leave some of your things here in your room, or whatever room you want. Anytime you want to stay, you stay."

"Thanks." He glanced over as Trey came in. "I'm heading out, and you're getting scrambled eggs. You can fill her in on last night."

After grabbing his share of leftovers, he started out the back for Jones. "Later."

"Last night?"

"Scrambled eggs?"

"Trey."

He held up a hand. "Just let me get coffee, okay? You slept through it, probably because it wasn't anything much. Three a.m., the usual. I got up just to see if Dobbs took her dive. She was on the wall, like before."

He took his first hit of coffee.

"And?"

"And Owen was outside."

"He—he went out there?"

"Set his alarm for before three, got up, went out. And no, I didn't know he planned to, but I'm going to say it was a good idea."

"Of course you are. You would—" She broke off, narrowed her eyes at him. "Don't tell me you went out there, too."

"I went out on the balcony to call down to him. Are you really making eggs, because now I want them. I can do it if you're too irritated."

"Irritated." She got out a frying pan. "Why should I be irritated because the two of you pull this after Owen ended up bleeding?"

"First, let me point out, I didn't pull anything."

"But you're okay that he did?"

"I am. And you might not be as irritated if you hear the rest of it. Would you like to?"

Reasonable, always reasonable Oliver Doyle III could make her crazy.

She tossed a pat of butter in the heating skillet, then broke eggs in a bowl.

"I'll take your silence as assent," he decided, and told her the rest.

"You should've woken me up."

"Why? She'd jumped before I went down to talk to Owen. And you're letting your annoyance block off the point."

"What point?" She poured the eggs into the pan.

"She didn't see us." Trey dropped two slices of bread in the toaster. "She didn't see us, didn't hear us."

"Let me repeat. And?"

"I think you need more coffee." Helpfully, he topped off her mug. "I'll feed the dogs, and oh yeah, cat. She didn't know we were there, Sonya. Because we weren't."

"Excuse me?"

"We weren't there when she jumped because she jumped a couple hundred years ago."

Knowns and unknowns, the logic, to his mind, was solid.

"I think what this is, is a kind of loop. A time warp, or slip. You saw her facing the house, and so did Owen. But by the time I looked out, both times, she was facing away."

"And she blasted the doors open," Sonya reminded him.

"Because she's in the house."

On a frustrated breath, Sonya pushed at the eggs with a spatula. "She was on the seawall. You just said so."

"She was out on that wall in 1806. Owen's got that scrap of her dress in his pocket," he added as he opened the door.

Two dogs and a cat ran inside and immediately pounced on their food bowls.

"It hit me this morning, I don't think her dress had a tear in it. And it wouldn't have, because what happened in the Gold Room yesterday hadn't happened in 1806."

She yanked out plates. "I don't see why . . ." Then set them down slowly.

"Coffee's kicking in." Taking the spatula from her, he divided the eggs himself.

"You're saying Dobbs jumping off the wall is like, like a tape set on repeat, timed for the three o'clock hour. It's not her as much as a kind of recording of her."

"Close enough." Since her temper appeared to have cooled, he leaned down, kissed her. "Let's sit down and eat."

"What she did when Cleo and I saw her, or that night when I heard someone calling and banging on the door, when I saw the snowstorm that wasn't there, in that three o'clock hour, that's her. In the house."

"When you think about it, she doesn't use that hour much. Probably costs her more."

"She doesn't, now that you point that out. It's not Dobbs pulling me when I walk, I absolutely know that. Does she watch herself? I wonder. Stand at the window and watch herself die, night after night?"

"I lean yes. Since she's as crazy as Rochester's first wife, wouldn't she consider that one of her finest hours?"

"Yes. And points for *Jane Eyre* over breakfast." She looked at him, the wonderfully deep blue eyes, the just-a-little-longer-than-lawyerly dark hair, and that air of calm and confidence he wore as comfortably as his jeans.

"Warning. It's unwise to tell an irritated woman she's irritated."

That simply rolled off him.

"Facts are facts, cutie. I've got a family thing later, then a work deal tonight. But I can come by after if you want."

"I officially give you the night off. I need to put in some solid extra time on the Ryder proposal. Presentation's coming up, and it has to kill."

"From what I've seen, it already does." He took their empty plates to the sink. "You've got a lot going on. Are you sure you want to do this big party?"

"Completely. It's just what I need, what Cleo and I need. And honestly, I think it's what the manor needs."

"Then I'll plan on the weekend here, digging out tables and chairs. I'll rope Owen into it. Now Mookie and I have to take off."

She went to the fridge, took out a tub of jambalaya. "Your parting gift."

"That takes care of lunch." When she put her arms around his waist, he cupped her chin in his hand, lowered his head to kiss her. "I won't say don't work too hard because why would I, and why would you listen? So how about go up to your office and kick ass."

"Just exactly the right thing. You go do the same, because yeah, we love what we do."

After Trey left with Mookie, Sonya glanced at the dishes. "And Molly loves what she does, so I'll leave those for her. Let's go get to work, Yoda. You can come, too, Pye."

But when they reached the second floor, the cat veered off. Sonya watched her slink down the hall and into Cleo's room.

Sonya put in a solid two hours, undisturbed, before she saw Cleo and the cat come out.

Sonya saved her work, rose. "I'm coming down with you. FYI, Pye's been out this morning, and she's had breakfast."

"Thanks. I should've gotten up earlier and done that myself."

"Owen let her out, Trey put out the food. But I don't mind doing both, since I'm already up and doing that for Yoda. And Owen opened your Toaster Strudels."

For a moment, Cleo frowned, then she shrugged. "I guess he's entitled. I thought she'd curl up in bed with me, but she's not a nighttime cuddler. She slept on the window seat."

"I wonder if she watched the show."

"What show?" On a yawn, Cleo walked into the mudroom. "And see! She hasn't used the litter box once! I'm going to let her out again. Yoda, be a sweetie and go with her. What show?" Cleo repeated.

"Get your coffee." And Sonya got a Coke for herself while she explained.

Irritation, mild but there, surfaced in Sonya when Cleo instantly got the implication.

"It's like an echo, a repeat. She didn't see or hear them because it's not actually happening now."

"Well, yeah. I was getting to that."

"It's fascinating. And now I'm annoyed I didn't think of it before. Setting an alarm and going out there." She sulked for half a minute. "I wish Owen had told me he was going to do it."

"You'd have gone out there with him?"

"Bet your ass." She made a Toaster Strudel for herself. "I'd say we should do it, but that time frame is for other things, for you. And no, I won't, because I'm not leaving you alone in that time frame."

After biting into the pastry, she pointed at Sonya. "I bet, seeing as she's batshit, she loves it. It's a big moment for her, and she gets to relive it every night."

Cleo's phone played Green Day's "Basket Case."

"She's all that," Cleo agreed.

As if to prove it, doors slammed upstairs.

"That one's getting old," Sonya called out, and made Cleo grin. Still, Sonya went to the door, called to Yoda. The cat led the way back in.

"I don't really want them out there when she's acting up. And I've got to get back to work anyway. I'm planning to put in some time this evening. I'm going to get the Ryder proposal up on the big screen."

"You let me know when you're ready to do that. I want to see it."

"I was going to ask if you would. I could use the input. It's just you and me tonight. Well, you and me, cat, dog, and our bevy of spirits."

Chapter Ten

Late that afternoon, Trey sat in the conference room on the second floor of the old Victorian that housed Doyle Law Offices, with his apartment above on the third.

The family held this semiannual meeting at the offices, once the family home, to cloak it in a business setting rather than a free-for-all family dinner.

Ace, in his three-piece suit, his mane of white hair, sat at the table's head. His wife, the quietly elegant Paula, faced him from the opposite end. Deuce sat on his right, with Corrine beside him, Trey on Ace's left, with Trey's sister, Anna, beside him, and her husband, Seth, across.

Sadie, Deuce's admin, who ruled all—as she had for decades—swept in with a tray of cheese, crackers, and fruit.

"You eat some of that." She pointed at Anna. "Growing another human takes energy. Energy needs fuel."

"Yes, ma'am." Anna patted her baby bump. "And I'm always hungry these days."

"And you." She gave Deuce a hard look. "You have a client due in an hour and . . ." She checked the watch on her wrist. "Ten minutes. No lollygagging."

"I'll be there."

"If he gags his lollies, Sadie," Ace assured her, "we'll give him the boot."

"See you do."

When the door closed behind Sadie, Ace pointed at the tray. "Grab it if you're going to, and let's get down to it."

The firm's founder and family patriarch ran this show. He adjusted his black-framed bifocals and began.

"I'm going to start by putting up our new website. I know we've all seen it and agree it's a major improvement. So, thanks to Trey for getting Sonya MacTavish on board. And to my lovely daughter-in-law for her excellent photography."

"I had good subjects," Corrine said, "especially Mookie."

Under the table, the dog batted his tail at his name.

"Ace," Paula warned as she caught him sneaking some cheese to the dog.

"He's entitled. It says right on the website he's our legal consultant. Which takes me to another section of our new and improved website. Interns. I'm going to propose, when Eddie's passed the bar, we offer him a position as associate."

They discussed the ins and outs, moved on to other business that required updated documents and signatures.

"I should say that Sonya recommended me for the photographs in an update of Stevenson, Kubrick, and Wayne's website. You all know Pete Stevenson, and my lawyer assures me there's no conflict of interest."

"As long as she doesn't make Pete look better than me."

"As if I could." Corrine gave Deuce's hand a quick smack.

"The girl keeps rolling, doesn't she?" Ace gave an approving nod. "While we can't discuss any of the legalities of her inheritance here, I'd like to know how she's doing outside her work. Trey?"

"She just keeps rolling. I have to admit, before I met her, I doubted Collin's decision to leave her the manor and what goes with it. I didn't think she'd meet the terms of her inheritance, even stay to the end of the year. But she's no pushover, whoever or whatever's doing the pushing."

"Since we didn't speak as attorney/client," Deuce began, "I'll tell you she plans to go to Ogunquit and speak to Gretta Poole. Or try to."

"Oh dear." Paula's eyes clouded with concern. "I can understand why she feels she must or should, but I'm afraid she'll be disappointed."

"Very likely," Ace agreed. "I doubt Gretta's capable of adding anything to the family history for her. Or anything else, for that matter."

"She was always weak-willed," Paula murmured. "Looking back, I wonder that I believed she'd met someone, gotten pregnant. She never once in my memory went outside the lines, and certainly never stood up to her mother. Then, few did."

"You did." With obvious pride, Ace beamed at her.

"That's old business." She waved it away like a pesky fly. "Ancient business."

"And as fresh as ever." Grinning, he blew her a kiss. "Collin had just come into his inheritance—the manor and the rest—and decided to open it again, live there."

"I remember." Deuce picked up his water glass, smiled into it. "I was nearly as excited as he was. We'd managed to sneak in plenty as boys."

"*Sneak* isn't accurate," his mother said dryly. "I knew what the two of you were up to."

"Did you?" Amused, impressed, he angled his head. "You never tried to stop us."

"Trying to stop two young boys from exploring a haunted house?" She gave a light laugh at the thought. "I'd have failed, so why not let you think you were getting away with something? I wasn't the least surprised when Collin decided to move there. But apparently Patricia was."

"I never met her," Seth said, "but I've heard tales—my parents have a few. I think this is going to be a good one."

"She came knocking on our door—"

"Now, Ace."

"Now, my own darling. This house," he continued. "We were still living here. I wasn't home, and that's a shame. Though my own darling took care of the old . . . I'll use another *B* word. Bully."

Shifting in his chair, Deuce turned to his mother. "She came here, to you, about Collin living in the manor?"

"All right then." Paula threw up her hands. "More about you, Deuce. At first very polite, in that cold, cutting way she had. She believed you had influenced Collin to make this move, and she expected I would speak to you, demand you remove that influence. My response didn't suit her."

"Which was?" Trey wondered.

"Basically, that both her grandson and my son were of age, and knowing Collin as I did, I believed he made his own decisions. When her continued soft-pedaling—as I'm sure she saw it—didn't move me, she threatened my family."

"Uh-oh," Anna murmured.

"She would ruin us in Poole's Bay, see that we were ostracized, that Ace was disbarred and my son disgraced so he would never have his law degree."

"Let's go back to that first *B* word," Trey suggested, and got a wide grin from his grandfather. "She could never have done any of that."

Paula took a delicate sip from her water glass. "She may have believed she could, or that I would wilt under such threats. She was in an absolute rage."

"My own darling told her to get the hell out of our house, that she would never be welcome there again. And—my favorite part—to stick her threats up her skinny ass. If she tried to harm our family, she'd find out just what the Doyles were capable of."

"Go, Grandma!" Anna applauded.

"You never said a word," Deuce spoke softly. "Not a single word about any of this."

"I wasn't nearly as pleased with my own language and temper as your father. Not once I'd calmed down in any case. And we agreed, your father and I, not to say anything that would worry you or Collin."

"Did she try anything?" Trey asked her.

"No—at least not that I'm aware of. Bullies often fall back when confronted, don't they? I think she simply threw Collin in with our

family. She dismissed him," Paula added, and some hints of that former temper came through again. "Just dismissed him. She couldn't do
anything about his inheritance—the manor, the business, the money.
So she worked with him, but on a personal level he wasn't important
any longer."

"He knew you loved him." Deuce looked down the table at his
mother. "He knew we were his family."

"Yes. We didn't know then about the true facts of his birth, about
his brother and the heartless decision Patricia made all those years
ago. But he was our family. He was a brother to you, Deuce, and a son
to your father and me.

"Now that family extends to Sonya."

"It would," Anna agreed, "even if I didn't like her as much as I do.
What's going on at the manor, Trey?"

"I'll start that saga by telling you they found another portrait in
Collin's studio. Well, Cleo's studio now. Lisbeth Poole on her wedding day."

"Lisbeth," Deuce murmured. "First Johanna, then Lilian, now
Lisbeth. Reverse chronological order."

"It has Collin's signature. Like the others, it wasn't in the inven-
tory. They've hung it in the music room with the other two."

"You know that's creepy." Looking around the table, Seth lifted
his hands. "Am I the only one here who thinks that's creepy?"

"No," Anna assured him.

"Then brace yourself."

Trey told them the rest, weaving his way through interruptions as
his family talked over each other.

"Maybe I should change *creepy* to *terrifying*."

"It's actually not," Trey told Seth. "At least most of the time the
manor's how I remember it whenever I'd visit Collin. This big, fascinating house, with just a little extra. And the extra added, and still
does, makes it more fascinating.

"But," Trey added, "when Dobbs winds up, she packs a punch.
And that can be literal."

"Is she safe there, Trey?"

He looked over at his mother. "I have to believe she is. She matters to me, so I have to believe that. What I know is Dobbs is outnumbered, and not just by a couple of steel-spined women."

"I want to meet this Cleo." Ace sent a wink to his wife. "I have a soft spot for steel-spined women."

"Can we clear the decks for Sunday dinner?" Corrine looked around the table. "I'll invite them. And Owen, as he's part of the family, and part of this. All right, Deuce?"

"More than all right."

"Sounds good to me. And I've got to go up," Trey added, "change for a dinner meeting."

"With Sonya?" Anna wondered.

"A client thing."

"Then, unless there's any other business . . ." Ace looked around the table. "We're adjourned."

In the manor, Sonya set up her laptop on the second floor of the library. She'd worked straight through until six, and knew she'd created the best proposal possible for the Ryder project.

But Cleo's eye would tell her where and how she'd missed.

As she synced the computer with the screen, Cleo came up the stairs with two glasses of wine.

"For your anxiety, and my enjoyment."

As if anticipating a show, Yoda already perched beside the sofa. The cat followed Cleo up and wandered the new space before choosing the window seat.

"I'm not very anxious, but I will be when this is real. And I won't have wine there, so I'll take it now. Absolute honesty, Cleo."

"I'll never give you anything less." Cleo took a seat on the sofa, lifted her glass. "When you're ready."

"I did the voice-overs myself. I needed to time them, coordinate them. And if Ryder goes for it, they can hire their own voice actor. But tell me if that part fails, and I'll contract a pro."

Too revved to sit, Sonya stood with the wine in one hand, her remote in the other.

"I'm going to start with the visual of the logo, with the changes I made. And with a collage I want to add to a drop-down History tab on their website."

The logo flashed on-screen, and yes, she thought, she liked the hint of motion.

"For three generations, Ryder Sports has stood for excellence and innovation." Her voice flowed over the logo, and continued as the images changed to public domain shots of the Boston flagship store, and the Ryder family.

She'd blended images of the Ryders and athletes, more of their philanthropic work, sports camps for disadvantaged and disabled children, scholarships, sponsorships.

"Ryder excels," she ended, *"so you can."*

She paused the screen.

"Too much, not enough?"

"I think you hit it, Son. Who doesn't want to hear about their good works, their longevity, their successes? And anyone clicking on that tab wants to learn about the history."

"I'm torn between starting there, or with the website itself. Or one of the ads."

"The history's not the big bang, but it builds to it. Keep going."

"Okay." She put up the website. "No voice-overs here. I'll do my pitch."

"Let's hear it."

With a nod, Sonya took a sip of wine. Then one more.

"While I headed the team that designed Ryder's website, I feel it needs some updates and refreshes."

She used her tablet to demonstrate the drop-downs, the links, the streamlined review section. Then the flash to the new store in Portland.

"As work progresses on the new store, this section will update, and include the countdown to opening."

She wound up all the hows and whys of that area, paused again. "Too technical?"

"A little bit." Legs crossed, Cleo tapped a finger on her thigh as she considered. "I can see the site's user-friendly. It always was, since I've used it—and that's you again. I'd save the tech stuff because people who aren't into tech will just tune out. Since you don't want that, you go into it if someone asks a tech question."

"You're right. I got caught up in the tech," Sonya realized. "I'll cut that down, and that should, hopefully, shorten all this so I can get to that bang."

She brought up the next. "Digital ads."

"Yes! Hot guy pumping iron," Cleo said as Owen's picture came on-screen.

"Whether you're pumping iron," the voice-over streamed as the photos scrolled, *"or shooting hoops, Ryder's got you covered. If you're fielding a ball or riding to work, Ryder's got you covered. Whether it's yoga, tai chi, your first time on two wheels, or throwing a spiral, Ryder's got you covered. Because . . ."*

The visual ended on the field where Ryder equipment spread, with the tag beneath.

Game On!

"In work, in life, Ryder's got you."

"All right, baby, that is gold! I mean it, Sonya. I want to go order a new yoga outfit, a new mat, and I feel a sudden need to start lifting weights."

When Sonya laughed, Cleo pointed at her. "I actually mean it. I mean, naturally, about the outfit, as I'm due for one. But your arms are happening, and I think I want mine to."

"They are?" Frowning Sonya looked down and flexed. "They sort of are."

"Anyway, show me the rest."

She went through in-store ads, billboards, signage.

She ended with an image that spanned ages and interests from a little girl on a tricycle to a group of seniors doing tai chi in a park.

Ryder Sports
For Any Age, For Any Interest
For Everyone

"You sure as hell sold me. And you ended with the bang. A number of bangs. Tone down the tech stuff."

"Got that."

"Do you know who from the Ryder family's going to be there?"

"No. I know Burt will—Burt Springer, and I owe him for even having this chance."

"Make eye contact. During your presentation, make eye contact, especially if any of the family's there. You know how to give a presentation—you've done plenty of them. Do what you do. The work is gold, Sonya, absolute honesty."

"Thanks, I can polish it up a little more." Pacing, she nodded. "Yeah, just a little shine up here and there, let most of the tech stuff go unless asked. And I'll know when that's done, it's the best I can do. It won't be as slick as By Design, but—"

"Maybe not. You went for the heart." Cleo laid a hand on her own. "In my book, heart wins. If they go with slicker? Their loss. Now, how about putting all this away for the night? We'll have leftovers and a nice, fluffy movie."

Clover had Ariana Grande and Victoria Monét singing about besties in "Monopoly."

"You may be Sonya's grandmama, but you're our best friend, too."

The air suddenly carried the scent of wildflowers in a meadow. A mix of sweet and spice, just drifting.

"Do you—"

"Yeah." Sonya gathered her laptop, tablet. "I do. Every time I worry too much about an entity I won't name tonight, I think about Clover and Molly and Jack, and the other six brides, and whoever else is here. I think about Collin and my dad, and this house. I think about you and me doing our best work and eating leftovers for dinner."

"Me, too. Let's go down. Since I fed Pye and Yoda before I came up, we'll let them out while we get those leftovers ready." Cleo glanced over her shoulder as she started downstairs. "She hasn't used the litter box."

"I don't know if your continued success in that area is you, the cat, or the manor."

"Why not all three?"

Halfway down, both their phones signaled a text.

"It's from Corrine Doyle. An invitation to dinner on Sunday."

"Same here," Cleo said. "That sounds like fun. We're saying yes, right?"

"We're saying yes. Do some juju so my hair appointment on Friday doesn't make me look like a freak."

"Would Anna use a salon that does that?"

"No, but things could go wrong," Sonya said darkly. "Maybe I should—What are you doing?"

As they walked into the kitchen, Cleo continued to wave her left hand over her cupped right. "I'm consulting my Magic 8 Ball. Outcome good. There, no need to worry."

She decided not to, especially since leftovers and a fluffy movie hit all the right notes.

And as she settled into bed to read herself to sleep, she got another text.

> Just checking in. Dinner meeting ran over. I am unsurprised by that. Are things quiet? If not, I can head up.
>> All quiet, but thanks. Worked late anyway, then practiced the presentation for Cleo. We're fine here.
> Then I'll see you tomorrow. Maybe you can practice on me. I'd like to see the presentation. If the quiet doesn't hold, text me.
>> I will. See you tomorrow.

And what the hell, she added a heart emoji. Then smiled when he sent one back.

She didn't wake at three, but she dreamed.

First came music. Mick Jagger couldn't get no satisfaction. Then the voices, a man's sounding shaky, nervous. A woman cried out in pain.

As the dream cleared, she saw the fire first, one set to roar in the hearth. Then the room. Her room, she realized. This room, though the walls were papered, and the paper patchy and faded.

But her bed, and in her bed, a woman—barely more than a girl— with her long blond hair tangled, sweaty, her pretty face pale, her blue eyes glazed.

Lilian Crest Poole. Clover, laboring to deliver her sons.

My father, Sonya thought, frozen in place. My father and Collin.

A man—barely more than a boy—knelt beside her, gripping her hands. His dark hair fell nearly to his shoulders, and his eyes, Poole green, swam with tears.

"It's okay." Clover turned her head toward him. "That one's over. I didn't know it would hurt so much! It hurts so much, Charlie."

"We were supposed to have more time to practice. Weeks more. Fucking storm." He looked toward the glass doors, where thick snow whirled. "We're stuck, babe. And everyone else took off when they said this was coming."

"It's you and me." She smiled at him as he wiped a cloth over her face. "You and me and our babies. Because there's two of them, like I told you. I felt two of them. That's why it's early. We read all the books on home births. And we've got music."

"As long as we've got batteries, you're going to have music. All the ones I recorded for you. Hey, 'I Only Want to Be with You.'"

"It's crazy but it's true," Clover sang, then broke off with a moan, a sob. "Another one's coming. Oh God, oh God, oh God. Charlie!"

"Take a hit, Clove, just one hit. I've got a joint right here. It'll help."

But she shook her head as she struggled to breathe through the contraction. "Not good for babies. Charlie!"

"I'm here, right here. Look at me, babe. I only want to be with you," he sang as she let out another cry, as her head swiveled on the pillow as if to find some relief.

But as contraction built on contraction, no relief came.

"I have to push!"

"I see a head! Holy shit, Clove! It's happening. It's really happening." She pushed, and she wept; she fought, and she laughed.

And in blood and pain and sweat, delivered a son.

"I got him!" Tears rolled down Charlie's cheek even as his Poole green eyes lit with wonder. "Wow, listen to him yell! Rock star. He's really small, but he's perfect. Look, we've got a boy. I'm going to tie off the cord, like we read, cut it."

She held out her arms for the squalling baby, gathered him in. "He's beautiful. Isn't he beautiful?"

"You are. You're the most beautiful thing in the world. You're my life, Clove."

"He's our life now. Look at his perfect little fingers! Oh, oh, it's not over!" Her body arched in pain. "Take him! Take our baby, wrap him up warm, Charlie. It's not over."

She shook with the next contraction, her body overwhelmed.

Charlie wrapped the baby, set it in a box padded with blankets and decorated with flowers and peace symbols.

When he came back to her, sweat ran down her face faster than he could wipe it away. And still she shuddered, shivered as if cold.

"I'll nurse them, nurse them both together." Breathless, she reached for Charlie's hand. "Then they won't cry."

"We'll plant the placenta with a tree. Our family tree."

He dabbed at her face, held her hand while the baby wailed and the recorder played Dylan's "The Times They Are a-Changin'."

"Everything's changing, babe, for us. We're going to be free, you, me, our kids." He brought both her hands to his lips, kissing them as she moaned through the pain. "We'll grow our own food, and we'll really open this house up to art and music and love."

"I have to push. I have to push again. Oh fuck, oh fuck! It hurts!"

"I know, Clove. I know."

"Tell me you know when you have to push a baby out!"

"Okay, okay. I see the head, and it's coming. This one's coming faster. Almost here!"

Sonya watched the birth of her father. She couldn't say how she knew the younger twin would grow up as Andrew MacTavish in Boston, but she knew it.

The dying girl took him in her arms.

"Help me sit up some more, Charlie. More pillows. I can't nurse them both unless I can sit up more. They're hungry, and the first milk's got all the good stuff they need in it. Help me, Charlie."

He propped her with pillows, dried her face, kissed her, kissed the baby in her arms. "I'll get our first. We've got two sons, Clover. We've got two baby boys."

"So beautiful, so sweet. He's already latched on. You kinda gotta help him find my nipple, Charlie. Yeah! Like that. Oh my God, it feels so amazing. I'm feeding our babies, Charlie. We're a family."

She smiled. She smiled, though Sonya could see the shadows in the room. She could see far too much blood on the sheets, the towels.

"I'm getting cold. I can't believe it. I was so hot, but I'm getting cold."

He built up the fire, laid a blanket over her.

"I can change the sheets, or at least take them off if I can lift you to the other side."

"It's okay. Look, our sons are sleeping. Can you do the diapers? I don't think I can get up yet. I'm so tired now. Just so tired."

"I've got it. You just rest. Holy shit, Clover, you're a frigging goddess. I'll bring down a rocking chair in the morning from the attic. I'm going to clean up our boys, then go down and get some of that soup you made. I can heat it up in the fire. You need to eat. I'm going to take care of you, Clover. Take care of you and our family."

"Okay, Charlie. I love you."

"I've never loved anyone like I love you. I never will."

He used squares of white cloth and diaper pins, then swaddled each baby and laid them together in the box covered in flowers and peace signs.

He turned the music down, then took a candle and started for the door. "Soup, some of that bread we made the other day. And some goddamn wine. I wish I had flowers for you, Clover."

"I have everything I need."

When he left and the shadows in the room deepened, the girl in the bed turned her head to Sonya.

"I'm dying, so that bitch is coming. She'll take my ring. The ring Charlie gave me. Get it back for me, okay? Get them all back."

As more blood pooled on the sheets, Sonya tried to rush forward, only to fall back.

She could only watch as Dobbs came into the room.

"With your death in this hour, your blood feeds my power. I feel it rise, I feel it surge. And your only song becomes a dirge. Onto my hand slides the ring of this Poole bride. All others who come, I will cast aside.

"For all time, the manor is mine."

As Dobbs vanished, Clover's eyes, almost lifeless, opened. "My poor Charlie, my poor babies. I couldn't stop her. You can. You can."

Sonya woke on the floor beside the bed. Yoda nuzzled against her as she wept.

PART TWO

Knowledge

Knowledge is power.

—Sir Francis Bacon

Chapter Eleven

As she drew the dog to her, pressed her face to his neck, the phone beside her bed played INXS and "Baby Don't Cry."

Sonya just shook her head and held Yoda closer.

As she wept, her heart stuttering with pain inside her, the air chilled; the glass doors rattled.

Grief fed her.

Choking back a sob, Sonya struggled to fight her way through it. Should she call Trey at this miserable hour? She could run to Cleo for comfort.

And why? Why burden them in the middle of the night for what had been? For what she'd witnessed.

"No, no, I'm not doing that."

Instead, she got up, and with the dog trailing her, went into the bathroom to splash cool water on her face.

"I was there." Straightening, she looked at her own face in the mirror, saw the sorrow shadowing her eyes. "You needed me to be."

In agreement, Clover answered with Marvin Gaye's "Can I Get a Witness."

"You can. You did. And I won't forget. It's all right, Yoda. We're all right now."

When he settled back in his bed, she settled in hers. And lay quiet.

She'd remember every detail, every detail of her father's birth. She'd remember the strength and sweetness of the woman who'd only had minutes to be their mother. And in those minutes had shown them such love.

She'd remember the love she'd seen, even felt between the two people who'd created those lives. Brothers who, because of one woman's dictates, never had a chance to be brothers.

She'd remember that tiny, squalling life had grown into a good man, a loving one who'd given her life.

"Thank you, Clover," she murmured as she closed her eyes. "I wouldn't exist without you. I wouldn't be here. I promise you, I won't forget."

When sleep finally overtook her, she didn't feel the presence watching over her, or the hand, slender, ringless, that lay gently on her cheek.

But she dreamed again, and again of the girl and the boy.

Now they stood in the sunlight, faces alive, so alive with love and laughter. He wore a flowered shirt, strings of beads around his neck.

She had flowers in her long blond hair, flowers in her hand, and a gold ring, two hearts entwined, on the third finger of her left hand.

Slowly, sweetly, they kissed under blue skies, in a field of wildflowers. They laughed into each other's eyes, like two children with a secret.

"Love you forever, Clover."

"Love you forever, Charlie, and one day more."

There was music. Dusty Springfield sang "I Only Want to Be with You."

The girl's white dress billowed as she danced barefoot in the meadow.

In sleep, Sonya smiled.

In the morning, Sonya let Yoda and Pye out, fed them their breakfast, and freshened their water bowls. She had her first cup of coffee looking out at the woods. And was rewarded with a glimpse of a doe.

When she went downstairs to work out, it surprised her the cat followed. Thinking of Cleo's comment about her arms, Sonya selected free weights.

While she curled, lifted, pressed, the servants' bell rang. The cat walked toward the sound of it, then arched her back and hissed.

"I feel the same way." Stretched out on the mat for chest presses, Sonya gave a hiss of her own. "And that's all she gets from us. Hisses."

After she finished, showered, dressed for the day, she tied back her still-wet hair. Downstairs, she made another cup of coffee and took it upstairs to Cleo.

Her friend sprawled over the bed with her mountain of pillows.

Sitting on the side of the bed, Sonya thought of their college days when Cleo had an early-for-Cleo class. And did now what she'd often done then.

She waved a hand over the coffee to send the scent closer, and said, "Cleo."

Cleo's tawny eyes blinked open.

"Is it morning? Is that coffee?"

"Earlier than your usual, but morning. And coffee to ease the pain."

Cleo pushed herself to sitting, and as the cat leaped onto the bed, took the coffee in both hands. "Why are you bringing me coffee in bed earlier than my usual?"

"Did you hear the clock last night?"

"Um." Cleo sipped coffee, closed her eyes. "No, at least I don't think so. I just—" Her eyes popped open, and her hand shot out to grip Sonya's. "Oh God, Sonya, did you walk? And I wasn't there with you. I slept through it. I—"

"Not like that. Or I don't think like that. I don't remember hearing the clock either, or the piano, and I don't think, I just don't, that I left my room. I think the mirror came to me, and I went through it. I went through it, Cleo, and back to when Clover had my father and Collin. Collin first—I don't know why I know that, I just do."

To clear her head, Cleo took a deep gulp of coffee. "You saw your dad being born?"

"I saw it all. Let me tell you from the beginning."

She related the dream that wasn't a dream, careful to include every detail.

"Oh, Sonya." Setting the coffee aside, Cleo wrapped around her. "I'm sorry, so sorry."

"I came out of it sitting on the floor by my bed. Cleo, I don't think I left the room. My bedroom, and the room where it all happened."

"Maybe that's why. It was the ballroom for Lisbeth, so that's where you went. You've seen the others."

"I'm not sure where I went. The first couple of times, I thought I was dreaming. Just dreaming. I think, after Marianne Poole, the third bride, I started accepting it was more."

"Accepting could be why you've been more aware."

"I still couldn't do anything. Still couldn't help, couldn't stop it. When I tried . . . I think that's when I ended up on the floor.

"It's one thing to understand I can't change death, and another to stand helpless and watch it happen. And to Clover."

"I can't imagine how hard and hurtful. She saw you, Sonya. Clover saw you, she spoke to you. She knew you were there. Bearing witness."

"She confirmed that with 'Can I Get a Witness.'" Sonya frowned now. "It wasn't the Stones, though."

"Baby, the late, great Marvin Gaye did it first. And isn't that just like her? Sonya, I know it had to be brutal, but think of this. You saw your father's birth. You witnessed the person who, along with your mama, brought you into the world coming into it. That's a kind of miracle, and a powerful thing."

"She nursed them. She was dying. Maybe she didn't fully understand that, but she was exhausted and she was dying, but she wanted to feed them, hold them. And he, Charlie, he pinned these little cloth diapers on them, wrapped them up warm when they fell asleep, tucked them up together before he went down to get her some soup.

"She died while he was gone, I could see it. Dobbs came when he was gone."

"Did you write down what Dobbs said?"

"No. I remember every word."

"I'm going to."

In her POUR YOUR ART OUT sleep shirt, Cleo rolled over to grab a pad, a pencil.

"Say them again." Cleo wrote them down. "We're documenting everything."

"Yes, that's next on my list."

"You could've come to me, Son."

"I nearly did. Nearly texted Trey. Then I didn't see the point. More? I wasn't going to give her another ounce of my grief and fear. Just hisses, right, Pye?"

"Hisses?"

"Pyewacket went down to the gym when I did this morning. And we hissed at the Gold Room bell. Yoda was right there when I came out of it last night, to comfort me, and she was down there this morning hissing at Dobbs."

"We've got us a couple of damn good furry friends here."

"We do. They've had their first-thing-in-the-morning outside time, and breakfast. I'm going to let them out, the post-breakfast thing, and fill my water bottle for work."

"I'll pull it together and let them back in. I wish I'd been with you."

"I knew you were here, and that matters."

She pushed off the bed, started to call the pets. And it struck her.

"I had another dream."

"Oh God."

"No, no, the opposite of awful. I nearly forgot. I saw them, Clover and Charlie. Their wedding day. Not here, not at the manor. I wonder if anyone knows when they moved in here. Anyway, it was so sweet, Cleo. They were dancing on the grass somewhere, and the sun was shining. They looked so young, so happy, so in love. The song he played for her during labor—'I Only Want to Be with You.' That's the music I heard."

It played again on the phone in Sonya's pocket.

"She took you there." Tears gathered in Cleo's eyes. "She wanted you to have that, to see that, and feel it. The bright pushes away the dark."

Believing it, Sonya herded cat and dog downstairs, where they both seemed happy to go out into the April sunshine. She filled her water bottle. She met Cleo on the stairs.

"Nothing but litter in the box."

"She's a very smart girl. You're also a very smart girl, so you're going to let Trey know what happened last night."

"I'm going to text him now, let him know the basics, and that I'll fill in details when I see him."

Cleo smiled. "It's good to have someone you understand and who understands you in your life, isn't it?"

"It is. Then again, I've always had that with you. And since you're in gym shorts, I assume you're making good on your idea about working out."

"I'm getting my own water bottle, then giving it a half hour. Twenty minutes with the damn weights, then a ten-minute yoga capper. My day started a little early, so why not?"

"You know, your arms are already happening."

"That's the yoga, but now I want more."

Knowing if Cleo wanted more, she'd get it, Sonya walked up to the library.

Taylor Swift's "Shake It Off" greeted her.

"Working on that, and getting there."

She sent Trey a brief text, and by the time she'd booted up and started writing what she thought of as documentation, he texted back.

> I get why you didn't let me know when it happened, but
> I'm sorry you were alone when it did. Why don't I pick up
> dinner, and you'll tell me in more detail. Want pizza?

Yeah, she thought. He got her.

Because she heard her friend start up to the servants' passage, she called out, "Cleo, Trey's going to bring pizza tonight."

"All about it."

Pizza's great, and I will tell you all. But I wasn't alone. Clover
was there. We'll see you when you get here.

She wrote it all down, added it to the file she'd already started.

Because she hadn't shaken it all off, she sent a quick thinking-of-
you text to her mother, with added assurances all was well.

Another rapid response told her she was loved, she was missed.

When she opened her first email, she noted her Baby Mine clients
wanted a digital ad and a trifold, coincidentally, to her mind, targeting twins.

With ideas already running through her mind, she answered,
promising to have some concepts by the first part of the next week.

Anna Doyle came next, with an attachment. New products for the
web page.

My energy level's up!

Anna told her in the body of the email.

> So I've been spending a lot of time in my studio. New pieces,
> descriptions, and pricing attached. I'm not sending all, as
> I'm doing some specifically for the event in May.
> Also so glad you and Cleo can make dinner on Sunday. I'm
> hoping both of you have time, whenever, to meet up for lunch
> in the village. I'm reaching a point of all work and no play.

Before she answered, she downloaded the attachments.

"May be all work," Sonya muttered, "but really excellent work."

> Beautiful pieces, perfectly photographed. I'll have them up
> by this afternoon. As it happens, I'm in the village tomor-
> row to risk having my hair dealt with. I'll bring a hat if it
> turns out wrong, and would love to meet you for lunch. I'll
> ask Cleo if she can make it. We could both use a break, too.
> How about one o'clock?

She sent, moved on to the next email, and the one after.
And Anna's response popped up.

One's great. Just tell me where! I need an infusion of women.

Smiling, Sonya glanced up as Cleo stopped at her door, flexed.
"Does it show?"

"Holy shit, you're ripped!"

"Liar, but I'll take it."

"How about lunch in the village tomorrow with Anna? After my
hair experiment. One?"

"I'm there. Where?"

"I'm going to let the pregnant woman decide."

"I'm there, wherever. Going to switch to work mode."

Cleo's in. Your pick of venue.

**Waterside. It's the casual restaurant at the hotel. And I
have a connection that'll get us a good table. Girl lunch!
Yippee.**

Sonya sent a *Yippee* back.

Then, like Cleo, switched to work mode.

She didn't break, even though Clover played "A Hard Day's Night,"
loudly, until Yoda whined and wiggled.

"Okay, sorry. You want to go out. And I got the hint, Clover, but
when you're rolling, you're rolling."

When she rose, Yoda ran to the top of the stairs, whined, wiggled,
and actually danced in place.

"I'm coming."

She saved her work, started out in time to see Pye streak past her
and downstairs with Yoda chasing after. She paused when she saw
Cleo coming down from the third floor.

"I'll let them out," Sonya told her. "Yoda's a little desperate, and I
need a Coke."

"I want one myself. She must've known you were letting him out. One minute she's on the windowsill looking out, the next she's flying out of the studio."

"Ears like a cat. It was rolling for me, so he waited longer than he should've. How about you?"

"I already peed, thanks." Cleo opened the door for the pets. "Oh, you meant the work. It's going so well, I'm going with you to Boston next month. I'll be done, and not only will I serve as your assistant for the presentation, but I get to hang with Winter. And if my editor needs to meet with me, I can do that."

"Cleo!" Sonya threw her arms around her friend and bounced. "This is everything. Feel my nerves about the presentation effectively cut in half."

"Son, you could've asked me."

"I wasn't going to ask you to go to Boston and be my emotional support. Especially when you're working on a major project."

"Which will be done." Lifting her arms, Cleo turned a self-congratulatory circle. "Then I'm taking a break—which I can afford to do, thanks to you—and using that time to work on painting, for my own wants and needs."

"This is turning into a really good day. Mom's going to be thrilled."

"I texted her right before Pye ran out, and she is."

Deciding she wanted more than a Coke, Cleo grabbed a yogurt. "Do you want one?"

"No. I'm going for chips. And pretending that's healthy by adding some grapes."

"Take what I'd rather be eating back up. You can eat at your desk; I can't at this stage of the work. I'll let Pye and Yoda back in."

Upstairs, and with the contract signed and sealed, she started on her new law firm client.

Slightly more formal, she thought, more urban than the Doyles'. She wouldn't want to mimic their colors or look in any case.

She began to experiment with a color wheel. Selected three two-combination choices for the template.

As she worked, she heard the ball bounce downstairs, and smiled when Yoda deserted her.

So he'd be entertained while she worked.

Eventually, Clover played "Five O'Clock World."

"Okay, okay, nearly ready to stop anyway. Take another look in the morning. And when a man's bringing you pizza, you should spruce up a little."

She went to her bedroom to do just that. She hadn't intended to change her work clothes, but Molly had laid out a blue sweater and gray pants.

"I was just going to do some makeup, but okay. This is nicer." When she came out, Cleo walked out of her own room.

"You changed." Cleo pointed at her.

"You, too."

"I was going to anyway, but Molly cut the time in half by laying out this very pretty shirt and these flattering pants. Good day's work?"

"Yes. You?"

"Same. I say it's glass-of-wine time, and we take it outside, drink it to the sounds of the sea."

"Let's do just that."

Outside, the air blew cool and light, and the sky held a pale, tender blue. Daffodils blew their fluttery trumpets with the scent of hyacinths answering the call.

Spring flirted around the edges of everything.

As they walked to the seawall, Yoda trotted around sniffing at the greening grass, scouting out places to lift his leg and make his mark.

"It's so clear." Cleo pointed toward the bay, where like the sky, the water spread blue. "It's like the village, the lighthouse, and the cliffs are etched in glass. I may set my easel out here sometime and paint from this perspective."

"And sail in the bay in your mermaid boat on a summer Sunday."

"Absolutely." When the cat leaped onto the wall, sat as if taking stock of her empire, Cleo smiled and sipped. "Maybe I'll take Pye sailing. I bet they make life jackets for cats."

Sonya joined Pye on the wall, then looked back at the house. "I want to see that tree bloom. That's my major spring goal."

"I've got a four-season project in mind, painting it in every season. You should paint with me. We haven't done that in forever."

"Because my canvas work looks like a moderately talented high schooler's beside yours."

"Not true." Cleo gave Sonya's leg a light slap. "And we'd have fun. I'm going to have a lot of fun when I take my short sabbatical and paint when I want, whatever I want."

"Are you thinking about giving up illustrating?"

Shaking her head, Cleo scooted up on the wall beside Sonya. "No. Not only does it pay for my shoe collection, but I like it too much. I'm in a position now to be pickier about the jobs I take, though, and space them out so I can do more fine art.

"There's a shadow on your bedroom window," she murmured.

"I see it. I think it's Molly." Testing, Sonya lifted a hand, waved. The shadow waved back.

"If not Molly, at least a friendly."

Yoda let out a yip and raced to the edge of the grass. Seconds later, Sonya heard the sounds of someone driving up the road.

She slid off the wall. "I'm betting it's pizza time."

"I can be ready for that."

Not just Trey's truck, Sonya noted, but Owen's right behind it. "Looks like it's pizza for four."

Mookie leaped out first, ears flying as he and Yoda had their madly happy reunion. The eye-patched Jones strutted over.

"I ran into Owen, so got an extra pie." Trey gestured as Owen got out of his truck carrying a six-pack. "He's got the beer."

"We started without you." Sonya rose up for her own happy re-union. "It was so nice out, we drank our wine on the seawall."

"Gonna snow tonight."

Genuinely stunned, Sonya stared at Owen. "No! No more snow. Look, it couldn't be more clear."

"Temps drop with the sun," Trey told her. "Then the clouds roll in."

"Couple inches, tops." Owen shrugged it off as the cat came over to ribbon around his legs. "Hitting mid-fifties tomorrow, so it won't last."

"But it's almost May."

"In Maine," Trey pointed out.

As he spoke, a window in the Gold Room slashed open. What flew out was huge, black as midnight. Wings spread, their span was taller than a man and seemed to slice the sky.

The sun caught a glint of talons, beak, sharp as razors as it swept over the lawn.

"House. Now." Trey gave Sonya a push toward the house as he stepped in front of her.

Even as he moved, what flew went to smoke.

"Sulfur," Cleo murmured under the wild barking of the dogs. "I can smell it from here."

"She went with a vulture. Biggest bastard I've ever seen," Owen added.

"Vulture." Since the glass remained in her hand, Cleo downed the last of her wine. "Aren't those the ones that hang around till you're dead?"

"They're still birds of prey."

"Ten-foot wingspan?" Trey asked him.

"Right around, yeah. Didn't get it very far, though."

"Far enough." Sonya heaved out the breath that had clogged in her lungs. "She's been mostly quiet all day, saving up for something like this, I guess. I bet it just burns her ass the four of us are going to enjoy some pizza."

"So let's go do that." Cleo scooped up the cat and started for the house.

"Yeah, let's do that," Sonya agreed. "Just another evening at the manor."

When they trooped in, Clover greeted them with "Peaceful Easy Feeling."

"An optimist." Trey carried the pizza boxes into the kitchen, where Cleo had already started the feeding routine for the animals.

Sonya poured more wine into her glass and Cleo's before she reached for plates.

"I gave Owen the brief overview you gave me. Now spill the details."

"I will. Let's start on the pizza before it gets any colder, and I will. I also wrote it all down, so if it ever fades from my memory—as if—I can refresh it."

"I never heard a thing," Cleo said as they gathered around the table. "Slept right through it all."

"I don't think there was anything for you to hear, since it all happened in my room. Then and now." She put a slice of pizza on her plate, then just let it sit.

"I had to have gone through the mirror again. But I didn't go to it. It came to me."

When she teared up in the telling, Clover played "Tragedy + Time."

"She sure learned to laugh again," Owen commented.

"I think she's amazing." Sonya swiped at a tear. "And seeing how much love she gave Collin and my father in the little bit of time she had, that's going to stick with me forever."

"Part of the point, I think." Trey laid a hand on hers. "Eat some now."

She nodded, picked up the slice. "And bearing witness. I think that's the big guns here. Dobbs took her ring—slim, gold, interlocking hearts, just like in the painting."

"And she said . . ." Cleo took the paper out of her pocket, read off the words.

As she did, windows shook.

"Oh, bite me, you hideous, heartless hag."

Owen tapped his bottle to Cleo's glass. "Points for the alliteration." Then turned to Sonya. "It wasn't like it was with you and me? Awake and aware going through?"

"No, like dreaming, then not. But like before, I could smell the candle wax, feel the heat from the fire, hear their voices. Like being there, but not.

"But when I finally went back to sleep, I did dream. I wasn't there, like through the mirror, but it was absolutely clear. Their wedding, Clover and Charlie's—she was wearing her wedding dress. It was just full of light and happy. She wanted me to have that, too. Now I do."

"And today, quiet, you said."

She nodded at Trey. "Yeah, until smoke vulture."

"She rang the servants' bell when I was downstairs working out. Pye hissed at her."

"You work out?"

Cleo raised her eyebrows at Owen. "Mostly yoga, but I'm trying a new routine."

"I'm figuring to stay Friday and Saturday nights, since you've got us hauling more stuff on Saturday. If you don't want company down there, let me know when you plan to hit the gym."

"It wouldn't be before ten on Saturday, and Sunday." She batted her eyelashes. "That's a day of rest."

"And dinner at your parents'. Cleo and I are looking forward to it."

"I'm hoping it's ham. Nobody makes ham like Corrine." Owen flicked a glance at Cleo. "If you take care of dinner Friday, I'll cook Saturday. Only fair."

"You'll cook?"

"Keep it simple after digging up tables and chairs. I can make mac and cheese."

"Opening a box isn't actual cooking—I have changed my stand on that," Cleo added.

"He makes it from scratch," Trey told her. "And it's awesome."

"Really? Well, in that case, consider the kitchen yours on Saturday."

"Done. Sonya, I'm taking you up on your offer to leave some stuff upstairs. I'll dump some in there tomorrow."

"Good." She rose to open the door for the pets as all four sat in front of it. "Stay out back. She never does anything out back. At least so far. More wine, Cleo?"

"No, thanks. I'm going up to do some sketching in a bit."

"Beer?"

"I'm good," Trey told her.

"One does it for me. I need to take off after this slice."

"You could stay, Owen."

"Can't. Got work waiting. I just came for the pizza. Wouldn't mind a Coke for the road."

"Would the work involve my boat?"

"Might, later. Depending. I'm building a doghouse."

"Yoda's doghouse!" Sonya hurried back to the table, threw her arms around his neck from behind. "Is it wonderful?"

"Not yet."

"Can you take a picture? Can I see a picture?"

"No."

"He'll be firm on that," Trey warned her.

"Couple of weeks, and you'll see it. You don't like it, remember it's your design."

"I'm going to love it, and so's Yoda."

"Witnessed." He pointed to Trey, to Cleo. "I'm going to take off."

Sonya got his Coke, hugged him again.

"I'll walk out with you. I've got some things in the truck. To leave upstairs."

Once out of earshot, Owen looked over. "Look, man, if you're worried, I can shuffle things around and stay tonight."

"No, I got it. And hell, Owen, most of the time, they've got it."

When they went outside, Owen walked out far enough to look up at the Gold Room. "It's the bird thing."

"The bird thing. Sonya's had it happen before, but she'd have said if the damn thing was that big. And those talons? They looked real enough. Didn't last, but while they did . . ."

"*Didn't last* is key. And we can worry about it lasting longer." He started back to his truck. "But I don't see there's anything we can do about it."

He opened the door so Jones hopped in.

Not yet, Trey thought as his friend drove away. But there would come a time, had to come a time, when they did more than react, more than play defense.

He heard a window open in the turret above, the library window, and looked up.

Clover, blond hair shining against the twilight, leaned out.

He stopped in his tracks, started to speak.

But she only blew him a kiss, and was gone.

Chapter Twelve

It snowed.

Sonya looked out at the fluffy layer of white over what had been a wide stretch of green. And cursed.

The fact that daffodils waved over the thin blanket of snow didn't stop the next curse.

Sure, they might get a dusting or whatever—and an occasional spring dumping—in Boston in late April, but she'd been completely into the idea of spring.

So she blamed Maine.

Trey simply shrugged it off, kissed her goodbye, and left with just a hooded vest over his flannel shirt.

She consoled herself that she'd had a night of what, in her previous life, had been normal. She'd slept nearly eight full hours, undisturbed.

And woken to snow and a fire lit by ghostly hands in the bedroom hearth.

They hadn't been wrong about the drop in temperature either.

When Cleo surfaced just before ten, Sonya sat, fully dressed, makeup in place at her desk.

"I'm thinking I'll cancel the hair appointment, and just work until we go meet Anna for lunch."

"Stop it. You're going."

"It's not your hair!"

"And yours needs shaping up, and you want your nice, subtle

highlights refreshed. They really bring out that maple syrup color. And I need coffee!"

Scrambling up, Sonya followed her down. "Maybe I don't want to leave you alone in the manor while I give in to my shameful vanity over my hair."

"Stop that, too. And didn't you say before I went up last night you were going in early enough to stop by the bookstore?"

"That was last night. Oh, and it snowed."

"Did it?" Cleo went to the window in the kitchen. "Damn if it didn't. But it's already melting. There's a lot of sunshine out there. Coffee. But that explains why my fire was going when I got up."

"She lit the one in the library, too. I realized I've sort of missed that."

"We're having pork chops tonight."

"Okay, but—"

"And you should get ready to go. You know how much you like browsing in bookstores, and you should go by Gigi's. I'll let Yoda and Pye out and back in before I leave." Leaning back against the counter, Cleo drank coffee. "Son, your hair needs work. Go get your hair done."

"Fine. Fine. And if I come to lunch with orange highlights and hair that looks like somebody whacked it with garden shears, it's on you."

"I accept that responsibility."

"On you," Sonya repeated darkly, then stalked off to get a jacket, her purse.

And a hat.

She did love spending time in bookstores, and A Bookstore had become a favorite stop. It calmed her nerves. At least until she brought the two books she'd selected to checkout, and they came roaring back.

"I read an advance copy of this one." Diana tapped the top book. "Just loved it. Twisty mystery, and a swoon-worthy romance. What more could you want?"

As she started to ring up the sale, Diana glanced back. "Everything okay?"

"Oh, I'm just a little nervous. I've got a hair appointment. My first since moving here."

"At Jodi's?"

"Yeah."

"Oh, no worries. Jodi does my hair. Anita's, too."

"Did I hear my name?" Anita came in from the back with more stock.

"Sonya's heading to Jodi's."

"Oh, who's doing your hair?"

"I'm not sure." Nerves, more nerves, balled in her stomach. "Does it matter?"

"Diana and I both go to Jodi. Jeannie goes to Carly, doesn't she?"

"Jeannie?"

"Our weekend manager. Pretty sure she uses Carly. And Aileen—my sister, she works here part-time—she goes to Micah."

"Who's adorable." Diana bagged the books. "A new salon's scary, but you'll be in good hands."

With no choice but to hope that was true, and having lingered too long to stop in anywhere else to procrastinate, Sonya walked down the skinny sidewalk.

The snow that had greeted her that morning might not have fallen. Not a trace of it remained as she wandered down to the salon.

And at the door, she reminded herself it made no sense to be more fearful of a new hairdresser than she was of the entity in the Gold Room.

She went inside.

Less than two hours later, she walked out a very happy woman. She tossed her newly shaped, highlighted, and styled hair as she walked back—hatless—to where she'd parked.

Unashamed, she pulled down the vanity mirror, turned her head right, left.

"I'm back!"

As she drove through the village, she sent out loving vibes to the shops, the restaurants, the houses and apartments. And especially to the old Victorian that housed Doyle Law Offices.

A woman wasn't truly all the way home, she thought, until she found her hairstylist.

Though she'd driven by the hotel, just to take a look, she'd yet to go in.

She knew Anna's husband Seth's family owned it, ran it, and from the exterior, it looked like they knew exactly what they were doing.

The snow-white brick on a rise above the bay, the sea, spoke of a mix of grand service and quiet comfort.

She saw rooms with small terraces facing the water, a circle centering the drive currently alive with daffodils and hyacinths and tulips that brought spring right back.

On the far side, she spotted paved pathways winding through gardens she imagined would burst very soon.

It made her remember, when she'd looked at hotels for her aborted wedding, she'd wanted something just like this. With history and that welcoming aura, rather than the slick and grandiose Brandon had insisted on.

Then she set that memory well aside.

She parked in the lot near those gardens and walked in the warming air to the front entrance and the doorman.

"Good afternoon. Checking in?"

"No, I'm here for lunch at Waterside."

"Straight back through the lobby, on your right. Enjoy."

She walked in, and fell in love with the coziness and the melding of grand and rustic. Light showered down from the candlestick bulbs on iron chandeliers. The big fieldstone fireplace with logs snapping under its floating mantel added warmth and more welcome.

People lounged in chairs or sofas having coffee or a drink—and she noted some had shopping bags beside them from the village.

The art on the walls depicted different views of the village, the bay, the marina. And one where the manor stood, high above on its rugged cliff.

Recognizing the style, she walked closer and read Collin Poole's signature in the corner.

So, in his way, he was here, too, she thought. And so was the manor. Because of that, she felt only more welcome.

She crossed the tile floor with its central mosaic of a gull in flight over the bay, and turned into the restaurant.

A smaller fire simmered here, and wide windows brought in the bay. Anna sat at a table with that sweeping view beside her.

She wore a knee-length red dress that showed off her baby bump with pride. Short black hair framed a face that lit up with a smile when she saw Sonya.

"I just got here. I was about—Oh! Your hair. It's fabulous."

"I owe it all to Jodi of Jodi's."

"She knows what she's doing. Really, it looks terrific."

"So do you. And I love this hotel! God, what a view."

"One of my favorites."

When the waiter stepped to the table, offering drinks, Sonya ordered water, flat.

"I warn you," Anna said when he stepped away, "I'm allowed one glass of wine a week. I intend today to be that day, and I'm not going to drink alone."

"Cleo and I won't let that happen. What's a girl lunch in such a great place without one glass of wine? And there's Cleo now."

"God, she always looks amazing."

"I know. If I didn't love her, I'd hate her."

"Am I late?"

"We both just got here," Sonya told her.

"Good. I hate to be late for fun. And look at your hair!"

"I'm now suitably chastised about my anxiety, and a devoted fan of Jodi's Salon. I'd almost forgotten how much I like salons. The vibe, the gossip, the chance to focus on yourself for an hour or two.

"And"—she gave Cleo a poke—"Micah is the one for you. According to everyone in there."

"True," Anna agreed. "He's a genius with curls."

"Plus, I was told, then saw for myself, he's adorable."

"An adorable genius? I'll check that out. And how's Baby Girl?"

Smiling, Anna gave her bump a gentle pat. "Feisty. And I'm enjoying every minute—so far. I'm so glad you could both make it today. I know you're busy."

"You're not sleeping at the wheel. Get it? Cleo, wait until I show you Anna's new pieces."

They ordered those single glasses of wine, salads, and, at Anna's suggestion, mini quiche appetizers to share.

"You weren't wrong about these," Cleo said after a sample. "I've never made a quiche. I should try that. I should try making cute tiny quiches."

"Cleo's embraced cooking."

"See, busy. Trey let the family know what's going on at the manor. It's a lot. I want to say it's way more than I ever experienced when I visited Collin. It always struck me as playful and interesting, but that's not what you're dealing with."

"Most of the time it is," Sonya told her. "Other times? Other times it's hard to believe it's happening even when it's happening."

"Hester Dobbs thinks she's going to drive us out. But she won't. It's our place, and we love it, love everything in it. Even back in college Sonya talked about having a house with history and character."

"I did. I just didn't anticipate the *characters*." She emphasized the plural. "But with one nasty exception, we're enjoying those characters. I'm getting to know my biological grandmother, and she's wonderful. Oh, Trey saw her again last night."

"What!" Cleo dropped her salad fork. "And you didn't tell me?"

"You'd already gone up by the time he came back in, and I was hair obsessed this morning."

"Sorry." Anna held up a hand. "Let me echo: What? Trey saw the ghost of your grandmother? And that's 'again'?"

"It's the third time."

"Okay, back up." Now Anna circled a finger in the air. "Rewind."

"He was just a kid the first time. He told me he was trying to learn how to play the guitar and was in the music room at the manor. I think your dad and Collin were playing chess. And there she was. Hot babe, he told me. She talked to him about music for a minute, then gone."

"He never said a thing," Anna muttered.

"Then, a few weeks ago, when he was checking the clock in the Quiet Place, she—well—appeared. Last night, he walked Owen out. After Owen left, he heard the window in the library open, looked up, and she leaned out. Blew him a kiss, then?" Sonya flicked her wrist. "Gone again."

"I think your grandmother's soft on your boyfriend, Son."

"And how weird is that?"

"How weird is any of this?" Anna, who'd nursed her once-a-week wine through the meal, now took the last sip. "He told me he'd once seen a woman in white on the widow's walk, but he never said anything about this."

"I caught a glimpse once of the boy—Jack. He plays with Yoda, teaches him tricks. And sometimes, if he's annoyed, opens all the cabinet doors in the kitchen."

"When I let them out before I left today, Pye was playing with a little ball of string. I hadn't given her one. So I assume Jack likes cats, too."

"You have a cat?"

"I have a cat," Cleo confirmed. "Pyewacket."

"Oh! Great name. From the old movie."

"Has everyone seen that movie but me?" Sonya wondered.

"We'll watch it," Cleo said.

"Seth and I want to get a dog, and a cat. We decided to wait until the baby comes, plus six months, then gauge our ground. But we want her to grow up with pets. Since we're just starting to talk about outfitting the nursery, pets are down the list."

"Now your rewind." Cleo mimicked the finger roll. "I believe Sonya and I were to be consulted on nursery art and such."

"Yes, but you're both so busy, I—"

"Cleo, in particular, is never too busy for anything connected to babies. Are you thinking pinks because girl?"

"Actually, no. Are you sure you want to hear all this?"

"Start talking. Wait." Cleo signaled the waiter. "We need to order dessert. What's good?"

"Their peach melba's amazing. And really generous."

"We'll share."

With that settled, Cleo gestured to Anna. "Not pink."

"Nothing too girlie, because what if she's not a girlie girl? Plus, we want at least two, and the next could be a boy. Seth and I liked the idea of a forest sort of theme, and animals. Cute animals."

"What about magical animals?"

Anna's eyes went dreamy. "Magical animals?"

"Unicorns, winged horses, friendly dragons, griffins. Throw some elves and fairies in there because, you know, they live in magic forests."

"A magic forest. Uh-oh." When her gone-dreamy eyes filled, Anna waved a hand. "Don't worry, hormones really bring them on. Can you imagine going to sleep and waking up in a magic forest?" She swiped a tear away. "It's so sweet. It's so perfect."

"I could do a mural."

"You're going to have me sobbing in a minute. You really could?"

"Trust me," Sonya assured her. "I'll assist, but Cleo shines here."

"Talk it over with Daddy. If you both like the idea, I'll come look at the room, sketch some things up."

"I know Seth, and he's going to love it. Name your price!"

"You can pay for the supplies, but that's it."

"But—"

"That's it, or no deal."

"You drive a hard bargain." And had another tear spilling. "But I'm buying lunch."

On the way home, Sonya stopped at the florist for fresh flowers. She drove home in a happy mood with their scent filling the car.

To be greeted at the door by Yoda with crazed joy, and Adele's "Hello."

"Yes, hello! I'm home. Were you a good boy? Did you play with Jack? Did Clover look after you?"

Yoda wagged all the way back to the kitchen with her, where Cleo sat at the counter with a sketchbook. Cleo looked up, raised her eyebrows at the armload of flowers.

"Did you buy them out?"

"Came close. We ditched all the faded ones the other day, so it was time to go a little crazy. What are you doing?"

"Oh, playing a little in a magic forest. You were a while at the florist."

"Apparently." On her way to choose vases, she stopped, looked over Cleo's shoulder at the trees with their curving branches, the waterfall dropping into a winding stream. An arched bridge spanned it.

"Yeah, you shine."

"It's going to be fun. I hope they go for it, and let me have my way with the colors, the animals. Like maybe something between a monkey and raccoon hanging off a branch."

She reached over to stroke the cat, who'd perched on the stool beside her. "A cat, but with a long, braided tail."

Sonya carried back the first of the vases. "If she teared up thinking about it, she's going to fall to pieces when she sees your sketches."

"Hope so. Flowers," she said as Sonya began arranging. "But nothing you'd find at the local florist. Anyway, I'm going to play with it. I really enjoyed having lunch with her."

"Me, too. And I will help in the nursery, but assisting as I sometimes do when you're cooking."

"You downplay your fine art talents."

"Maybe, but I know I wouldn't come up with an animal that's a cross between a monkey and raccoon."

When she'd filled the last vase, she carried a couple at a time. Another homey task she enjoyed, Sonya thought. Walking through the manor with flowers, finding just the right place for the right arrangement.

Sometimes, she'd found, Molly disagreed with those choices, and she'd find flowers moved. But she had to admit, she'd come to enjoy that, too.

Once she'd spread flowers out on the first and second floors, she carried an arrangement to the third for Cleo's studio. As she did, she realized she hadn't come up to the third floor alone—at least knowingly—for weeks.

When even her brief hesitation irritated her, she walked straight down to the studio.

With the mermaid in the drying rack, Cleo had a blank canvas on the easel. Sonya suspected it wouldn't stay blank for long, as the rigorous organization in the studio had slid into Cleo's creative jumble.

Since sketches, folders, pads, pencils littered the old desk, Sonya put the flowers on the table by the sofa.

Then she walked to the closet, held her breath. Opened it.

She saw nothing but Cleo's still-organized supplies.

"Okay, not yet."

But she didn't doubt that sooner or later, either she or Cleo would open that door and find Agatha, the fourth bride.

She'd just closed the door when the banging started.

Steeling herself, she walked out.

The door of the Gold Room bowed out, sucked in as she walked toward it.

My house, she thought. Mine, not yours.

She said just that, then repeated it, lifting her claim over the banging.

The door flew open, and wind rushed out with it.

The cold bit into her bones.

Hester Dobbs stood in the center of the room, arms outstretched, palms up.

Under the wind, she heard whispering, urgent, but couldn't make out the words. Her phone blasted out with the chorus of Nirvana's "Stay Away."

"This house is mine!" Dobbs shouted, and her voice blew cold like the wind. "You'll die here. You'll all die here."

When the walls bled, even the whites of the witch's eyes went black. "Poole blood."

Sonya watched it drip from her cupped hands.

"It's all Poole blood."

On her wild laugh, the door slammed shut.

Silence fell.

"You'll die again tonight," Sonya spoke with a calm that surprised her. "And the next night, and the next. That's your hell for the time being. I can live with that. For now."

As she walked away, her phone played "It's Gonna Be Alright."

"That's right, Clover. That's goddamn right."

When she reached the kitchen, Cleo held a potato on a wooden spoon with one hand, and carefully made slices in it with the other.

"What are you doing to that potato?"

"Making it an accordion. Then you do this butter and herb thing. Meat and potatoes. Men coming."

She looked up, and quickly set the knife aside. "What happened?"

"You didn't hear anything?"

"No, it's been quiet. I thought after your flower delivery you might've gone back to work awhile."

"I saw Dobbs. In the Gold Room."

"Jesus jump-roping Christ, you went in there?"

"No, no. She blew open the door, and I saw her inside. You didn't hear all that banging and booming?"

"No, nothing."

"So just for me this time," Sonya murmured. "As Trey would say, interesting."

"You saw her? What were you even doing near that damn door, Sonya?"

"She started up with the banging, and, I don't know. It pissed me off, and I guess I needed to stake my claim. My house, you know. Then while I'm standing there, she blew the door open, and I saw her in there."

She sat because now that it was over, maybe her legs were a little shaky. And told Cleo the rest.

"I like your slapback, but, baby, stay away from that room."

"You're up there every day."

"I don't go near that room. Take Clover's advice. Stay away."

"Her dress was torn. Down by the hem of her skirt. I wouldn't have gone in even though in that moment I was more mad than scared."

She shook it off.

"Done now, so maybe that'll be it for a while. Now I want to watch you make potatoes into accordions."

Sonya flipped open the sketchbook, and laughed at the image Cleo had drawn while she'd carried flowers through the house.

"It *is* like a part monkey, part raccoon."

"I settled on moncoon."

As Cleo picked up the knife again, Sonya looked at other sketches. "These are fabulous. Magical. Oh! You made Yoda a butterfly!"

"He's got such an interesting body type, that brindle coat, so I thought add wings, miniaturize, and we've got a butterhound. This is pure entertainment for me."

She set the first potato in a baking dish. "One down," she said, and picked up another. "Three to go." She smiled over at Sonya. "We're doing fine, Son."

More than fine, Sonya thought when Cleo put the potatoes in the oven, prepped the chops. To contribute, she did what she now considered her baking specialty. She made beer bread.

Yoda barked and raced out of the kitchen. The cat slithered down from the stool.

A minute later, they heard answering barks and male voices.

"We've got company."

Trey walked in. "Owen went up to put his stuff away. Hey, your hair."

Deliberately, Sonya tossed it. "What about it?"

"Looks great. It always does."

"Good answer." She kissed him, then leaned into him, wrapped her arms around him. "I'm glad you're here."

Because he heard something in her voice, he looked over her head at Cleo.

"Everything okay here?"

"It is," Sonya assured him. "But it's not often we get through a day at the manor without something. And today wasn't one of those without-something days."

"We're having wine," Cleo decided. "We're all having wine be-cause this meal is going to deserve it. I'm going to open a bottle, pour it out. Then Sonya will tell her latest tale."

"Dobbs?" Trey asked, and Sonya nodded.

"Dobbs."

Chapter Thirteen

They waited for Owen. Sonya had to give Trey credit for patience, because he didn't push.

Then again, he never really did push, she admitted. And when he nudged, it was so subtle you didn't realize you'd been nudged until you stood where he wanted you.

She considered that his superpower.

Instead of a push, he fed the dogs and the cat while Cleo put string beans on to steam.

They waited.

When Owen wandered in, all eyes turned to him. He stopped, frowned.

"What?"

"We were waiting for you." Cleo handed him the fourth glass.

"Why?"

"So Sonya can tell you both what happened about an hour ago."

"Before I do, I'm going to say it's all part of living in this house. It's part of my inheritance, and if I accept the manor, I take the rest with it."

"Since I live here," Cleo added, "the same."

Sonya told them, then waited for the reaction.

"Sounds like you handled it."

"She—they," Trey corrected, "have handled it all along. You're up there every day, Cleo. Nothing like this?"

"Not since she shut me in the bathroom up there, and went at

Sonya in the library at the same time. I admit that scared the crap out of me. Other than that, just banging and shaking now and again."

"Her dress was torn." Trey looked at Owen.

"Fearless Jones."

"Point being he damaged the dress."

"So maybe we can damage her?" Letting out a breath, Sonya slid onto a stool. "I like the idea of some payback, but I don't see how you hurt a dead woman."

"We could try an exorcism."

Sonya shook her head at Cleo's suggestion. "*The Exorcist* is classic, and a favorite movie of mine."

"Hell of a book, too," Owen put in.

"Hell of a book," Sonya agreed. "But I'm not playing around with that in real life. Plus, if we did manage to evict her, wouldn't she still have the rings? Maybe we'd be a lot more comfortable, but it wouldn't necessarily break the curse, would it?"

Beyoncé sang out with "Single Ladies (Put a Ring on It)."

And Sonya let out a half laugh. "I'd say that's Clover's upbeat way of saying I have to put the ring—or all seven of them—back where they belong."

"Which she's wearing," Trey pointed out.

"Exactly. She goes, they go—or maybe. And I won't risk the maybe."

"It's not just because you fell for the house."

She shifted to Trey. "No, not just. I've witnessed what she did to women on what should've been one of the happiest days of their lives. What she did to the woman who brought my father into the world.

"It's personal. And that, seeing that? Only more personal."

"Collin left this place to you for a reason." Trey skimmed a hand down her hair. "He never had kids, but his brother did. His twin did."

"He loved this place. I'd say he left it to you because he figured you had the best chance of stopping her before the next bride comes along and makes it eight."

Owen took a look in the oven as he spoke. "Hey, this looks good," he added. "Anyway, I also figure he must've tried to do it himself at some point."

"He did love the place," Trey confirmed. "And Johanna, so I can't imagine he didn't at least try. He never said anything about it, but wouldn't he have to try?"

"It has to be a woman." Cleo spoke decisively as she got down plates. "What was done was done by a woman, to women. It has to be a woman, a Poole woman."

"I hadn't thought of it exactly that way," Sonya considered. "But that sounds right."

"I think it's more than that." Trey took the plates for the table. "I hadn't thought of the woman thing either, but Cleo makes a strong point. A Poole woman, that follows."

"I can handle these," Owen said, and began to deal with the beans. "Not just any Poole woman," he continued. "His twin's daughter."

"I was going to add some butter and herbs to those."

"I've got it," Owen told Cleo, then continued. "His twin's daughter who can and has gone through the mirror."

"And bore witness six times," Trey finished.

Sonya got up to help. "It's going to take all seven, isn't it?"

"I think so." Trey gave her shoulder a squeeze.

"Add one more element." With one eye on Owen and her green beans, Cleo took the rest out of the oven.

"The paintings. It follows," Sonya decided. "We need all seven brides. I don't know what the hell happens then, but we need all seven. On the wall, and through the mirror."

She set the bread on the table, then looked around.

Trey, letting the pets in, giving them treats to entertain them while the humans ate. Owen tossing beans in butter and something she couldn't identify. Cleo arranging chops and potatoes on a platter.

Just a normal dinner with friends.

"I don't know whether to be nervous or comforted by all that hasn't happened yet. I do know I'm glad you're all here."

Clover added her presence as "With a Little Help from My Friends" played.

"And you, too, Clover. All of you."

Owen carried the bowl of beans to the table. "What did you do to those potatoes?"

"I made them musical instruments."

It took him a second, then he sat and put one on his plate. "Accordions. Cool. Let's see how they play."

They played very well and added to an easy dinner at home. At Cleo's suggestion, they had a glass of post-dinner wine in the solarium.

"When I finish my mermaid project, I want to find out more about all these plants. Look, Son, we got more blooming."

"We'll both find out more. I need to spend more time in here anyway. It's so pretty, and it's nice on an evening like this. I've popped in to water, but they never seem to need it."

"Same here. Everything's always thriving."

"I wonder if Molly handles this, too."

Clover answered that with "Eleanor Rigby."

"Eleanor." Sonya leaned her head against Trey's shoulder. "I wonder what happened to Eleanor. I hope she was happy here."

"I think anyone who wasn't wouldn't spend their afterlife taking care of plants, or making beds, playing with dogs."

"And cat." Cleo lifted her glass to Trey. "And I agree. If you put all things Dobbs aside, this has been a good house for a couple hundred years."

"Here's a thought." With Jones sprawled beside him and Pye curled in his lap, Owen stretched out his legs. "Do they all know each other? They're all not from the same time frame, right? Do they have like ghost meetings? Holiday parties?"

"That's actually not a completely stupid question."

Owen only grinned at Cleo, and scratched the cat between the ears.

"I'm going with aware, at least aware of each other. And maybe time frames don't matter so much after death," Trey added with a shrug. "I think place matters more. They had to die here. Of course, that's applying the logical to what should be illogical."

"We're living in the illogical—or what used to be illogical for me," Sonya pointed out. "And I really hope they have holiday parties."

"Clover'd bring the music."

Sonya grinned at Cleo. "Wouldn't she? And I agree about place over time. We've all seen Dobbs now. Trey's seen Clover three times. I caught a glimpse of Jack, and I really think it's Molly in the window of my bedroom. Cleo's seen her in the window, too. Just the shadow, the silhouette, but it's real."

"Add the guy with a cigar in Collin's office for me, and the woman on the widow's walk. But I've been coming around the manor since I was a kid.

"You, too," he said to Owen.

"Sure. Heard the doors opening and closing, all that kind of thing. No Dobbs until recently. If it's Molly up in the window, then yeah, caught sight of her a few times. And once . . ."

He trailed off, drank some wine.

"Keep going," Cleo insisted.

"I brought Collin up an order of books from the bookstore. I saw this guy raking leaves. Older guy, little gray beard. He stopped a minute, tipped his cap. He was wearing one, so I waved and went in. I asked Collin when he'd hired the new guy to deal with the lawn. He just laughed. He said, like, 'Oh, he's been around awhile.'"

"And," Cleo prompted.

"When I left, I went looking for him. I wanted to give him my number in case he needed something, but I couldn't find him anywhere."

"You never mentioned that."

He shrugged at Trey. "Didn't think much of it. It was just a couple months before Collin died. Then it hit me. There wasn't any truck or car up there. Just Collin's."

"Raking leaves," Sonya murmured. "I wonder if that's who filled the log holders for the wood-burning fireplaces over the winter."

Always helpful, Cleo answered with music.

"Barenaked Ladies—nice choice," Owen decided. "'Jerome.'"

"Jerome. Well, here's to Jerome, who spared me from hauling wood so I'd have a warm, cheerful office to work in."

"I'll go one better." Cleo raised her glass. "Here's to the staff of Lost Bride Manor. They take loyalty to a whole new level."

At three, Sonya turned toward Trey, and in the quiet wash of moonlight, saw him watching her.

"I hear it," she murmured. "But that's all. I hear it, but none of it's her."

"Okay. Go back to sleep."

Outside, Cleo stood with Owen and stared at the seawall. Seconds before, she'd watched Dobbs leap off.

"Satisfied?" Owen asked her.

"Yeah. She didn't see us, you had that right. And no tear in her dress. I needed to see for myself. What happened there happened there in 1806."

"And we don't need a magic mirror to see it."

"I wonder if you could always see it, or if we can now because Sonya's here, because she's made this place hers. I guess that doesn't matter much."

She rubbed her arms. "It's cold. Let's go in."

"She died out here, on the rocks." Owen opened the entrance door. "She didn't die in the house, not even on the property technically. So how is she in the house?"

"She did something to make sure of it before she jumped."

As they walked up the stairs, Cleo lifted her hands.

"I don't know what, but she had to be sure of it. The whole point was being here, forever, and killing a bride every generation. She missed with Patricia. Did that gap add to her power or detract from it?

"Something to think about."

When they reached her bedroom door, Owen gave her a long, silent look. Cleo didn't need words to read it.

"Still under consideration," she said, and went inside.

* * *

In the morning, Sonya came down first. Or so she thought, until she saw Owen in the kitchen.

"You're an early riser."

"Jones is. Then the cat came in and jumped on my chest. She got pretty insistent."

He shuffled aside so she could get to the coffee machine, and let out the two dogs who'd trailed her downstairs.

"That screwed any idea of sleeping in some."

He waited until she had coffee in her hand.

"So, what do you think about omelets?"

"That I like to eat them, and don't have a clue how to make them."

"I was afraid of that. I have a clue. Mine aren't pretty, but they're relatively tasty."

Sonya drank more coffee. "I can make toast to go with them. Trey should be down in a minute. And Cleo won't be too long. She told me she'd set an alarm so we could get started on finding what we need for The Event."

"I'm going to do that bacon-in-the-oven thing she does. That takes twenty, so she might make it. If she doesn't, she'll have to make her own omelet."

While he dealt with the bacon, she filled the pet bowls. Then watched him hunt in the refrigerator for cheese, eggs, butter.

"Owen?"

He grunted, found a bowl.

"You're my favorite cousin."

His lips curved as he worked. "How many you got?"

"Well, there's the one I found naked under my at-that-time fiancé."

"So I scaled a low bar."

"She has a brother, and I like him fine. He moved to Atlanta so I don't see him much, but I like him fine."

"Proximity's lifted me over that second bar."

"Not just that. Then again, I haven't met the rest of my Poole cousins. One of them may knock you out of first place. Do you think they'll come to the open house?"

"Maybe. The ones who can, anyway. Cathy and Cole are in Europe, so not likely. Connor travels for the business a lot, so he'd be a maybe. My brother Hugh's in New York, but he'd make the trip, depending on his schedule. I figure Clarice and Mike will come by at least."

"So many."

"More, but they're all scattered."

"More. It's strange to have so much family I knew nothing about. Same for all of you. You didn't know about me."

He shot her a look as he started whisking eggs. "We know now. Cheese omelets," he said when Trey walked in. "Bacon and toast on the side."

"Sounds good. Look, if lunch happens, I'll handle that."

"You're going to cook?"

Owen set the eggs aside. "He means sandwiches."

"I do. My fried bologna and American cheese slices sandwich is legendary."

"And that's no baloney," Owen confirmed.

"I'll take your word on that, since we don't have any bologna."

Cleo made it just under the wire. The omelets weren't pretty, but in Sonya's judgment, more than relatively tasty.

"You maintain your position as favorite cousin."

"Good for me. I'm going to grab a shower before we start digging through storage."

"I thought you wanted to use the gym."

"I got a quick workout in before you came down. We starting up or down?"

"Let's start down, but not scary basement down." Sonya drained the rest of her coffee. "Ever again."

"Then I'll meet you back down here."

Cleo watched him go. "He worked out and made omelets? How early does he get up?"

Trey considered. "I figure if Owen lived on a farm, he'd wake up the rooster."

Cleo pondered over her coffee. "That's a problem. Anyway, we have a list."

"We like lists," Sonya concurred. And deciding to give Molly a Saturday break, rose to deal with the dishes.

"Not a problem. What's on it?"

Cleo took out her phone, hit her app, and began to reel them off. "Folding tables and chairs. Potential deck or lawn furniture, planters and/or pots for the deck."

As the list continued, Trey got up to help Sonya.

"Have you considered the convenience of paper and plastic plates and glasses?"

"An Event, Trey," Sonya reminded him. "Not a let's-throw-some-burgers-on-the-grill gathering."

"I stand corrected. Let's try this: Hire help."

"On the list." Cleo rose to pitch in.

Hair still damp from his shower, Owen came in. "Molly, I guess, made my bed, and put my jeans and sweatshirt on it. Like here, wear these."

Sonya just smiled. "She'll do that."

"It's weird, the clothes thing's weird."

"You'll get used to it. And if you didn't, make sure you thank her next time." Cleo held up the list on her phone. "Let's get started."

They went down to the storage area that had once been part of the servants' wing.

In under five minutes, Cleo dug out a treasure.

"Son, look at these—I guess they're urns. They could be planters, couldn't they? They look like rusted metal, in a good way, but they're stone."

"I love the pedestal, the classical style. Oh, wouldn't they look great flanking the front entrance, those fabulous doors? We could try it."

Resigned, Owen looked at Trey. "This is going to take a while."

"Tables." Trey made his way through to the back wall, pointed to a stack of them. "Folding. I thought I remembered these."

"Those are perfect. How many are there?" After a quick count, Sonya nodded. "Five. Good start."

Owen crouched down. "You know what these are? They're field tables. Military field tables. They're old, man. In good shape, though."

"Can we set one up? They look right," Sonya said, "but they have to be sturdy."

"Some chairs here." After she called out, Cleo lifted one, unfolded it. "Old but sturdy. Not enough, but another good start."

"We need to test them. If any of them need a little work"—Sonya glanced over at Owen—"maybe?"

"The lawyer can handle simple repairs."

Within an hour they had a collection of tables, chairs, two urns, a three-legged stool, and an assortment of vintage chafing dishes.

"Some of these are silver, some are copper, but there's no sign of tarnishing." Sonya ran her fingers over a domed lid. "I really hope Molly has help. I bet these were used for big parties, for weddings. I think . . ."

"Can't say I paid too much attention." Owen studied the assortment. "But yeah, they had this kind of thing set up in the ballroom for the one we crashed."

"We'll use them again, and Molly's—or whoever's—work gets appreciated. I want to go through the serving platters, bowls. Here's what I'm thinking, Son. We rent the plates, glassware, flatware, but we use some of our own. It doesn't have to be uniform."

"It shouldn't be uniform," Sonya agreed. "Mixing patterns and styles adds charm. I say we keep going, keep knocking down the list. Same thing upstairs. Then when we have what we're going to have, we move it into the apartment. Use that as a staging area."

"You want to move all this up into the apartment?"

Sonya gave Trey's arm a pat. "Not the tables and chairs. No point moving them twice, but the rest?"

"This is going to take a while," Owen repeated.

The servants' bell began to ring, followed by barking, hissing. And the lower basement door creaked open.

"Absolutely no." With purpose, Sonya strode over, started to shove it closed. "God, need a hand. It's like someone's pushing it back."

Trey rushed over, and over her head, gave it a hard shove. "Cold to the touch."

"Fine. She deserves the scary basement. She can have the scary basement."

"She can't, cutie. You've got furnaces, water heaters, and more. The Gold Room's one thing, but this is another."

Owen pulled a flashlight off a shelf, switched it on. "Let's go check it out."

"Isn't that just what she wants you to do?" Cleo pointed out.

"Why disappoint her?" Owen got another flashlight, tossed it to Trey. "Hang back here," he told Jones.

Trey opened the door. "We won't be long."

"Oh, but—" And as the door closed behind them, Patsy Cline sang out on Sonya's phone:

"Crazy."

"You can say that again" was Sonya's opinion.

Trey tried the light switch. "Light's working."

"Colder down here than it should be." After turning off his flashlight, Owen looked around. "As clean down here as the rest of the house. Not even a stray spiderweb."

They worked their way through the labyrinth of rooms.

"If Sonya's not going to come down here, and she really isn't," Trey added, "she should find another place to store these tools."

"Got some nice ones, and all clean. No dust. This old hand planer's a beaut."

"Take it. You know she'd tell you to take it. What the hell's she going to do with it?"

"Maybe. I don't like to just . . ." Frowning, Owen trailed off. "It's not as cold now, is it?"

"No. You're right, it's not. Lights stayed on, and it's warming up. Looks like she just—"

As it struck him, Trey broke off, stared at Owen.

"Well, shit," Owen said an instant before it started.

On the other side of the door, all the servants' bells rang in insistent cacophony. The doorbell bonged, bonged, bonged. Above, the ceiling seemed to sag as if from a great weight.

"Everybody calm down," Sonya ordered herself as much as the barking dogs and hissing cat. "We're all staying calm."

As much as she dreaded it, she thought of Trey and Owen, then reached for the basement door.

The lights went out.

As Sonya dug for her phone and its light, it played "Psychotic Girl."

"Tell me. Cleo!"

"Here. Right here!" As Cleo's phone light came on, she let out a scream, rushed forward. Grabbing Sonya's hand, she dragged her back.

"Behind you. She was behind you."

The dogs lunged like a unit. As the men burst through the door, the noise stopped; the lights came on.

Dazed, Sonya fought to get her breath back as Trey rushed to her.

"*Let's split up*, they say. In every horror movie ever."

"Are you hurt?" He stroked her face, her arms.

"No."

"She was behind Sonya. The lights went out, then I saw her behind Sonya."

"She's okay." Because she trembled, Owen put an arm around Cleo's shoulders. "Everybody's okay."

"I could see her face, like I did in the bathroom mirror that day. It was just full of . . . well, damn it, evil."

"The dogs went after her." Steadier now, Sonya crouched down to pet all three. "And Pye, too, I think. Dobbs ran, or whatever her version of retreat is. Such brave boys, such a kick-ass girl," Sonya crooned.

"She wanted to lure Owen and me down there, so she could go at you and Cleo here."

"Yeah, but if she wanted to prove some point, we proved a bigger one." Steady now and defiant with it, Sonya tossed her hair back. "She's the one who ran.

"Okay?" she asked Cleo.

"Yeah, sorry for the panic. But she was right behind you."

"So you ran right to me and pulled me away." Crossing over, she wrapped around Cleo. "And we're okay. Let's pick out some serving dishes."

They sent some up in the dumbwaiter, carted out more to stack in the kitchen.

The guys hauled the urns up and set them by the entrance doors where Sonya and Cleo deemed them perfect.

They scoured the upstairs areas for more.

"I swear every time I come up here, I see something I missed. Son, look at these chairs."

"Love! Wouldn't they be great on the lawn?"

"If you want them trashed after a couple rains. They won't take the weather," Owen told them. "You want to put something like that outside, you need teak, maybe cedar, larch, or something that's sealed and waterproofed."

"Oh. See anything? Furniture for the back deck over the apartment's on the list."

After a hunt, he came up with two Sonya/Cleo–approved chairs and a table.

A dustcover slid down and to the floor. "Somebody likes that bench," Sonya decided.

"Somebody's got a good eye."

Hands in pockets, Trey studied it. A graceful curve of woven metal, it had a fanning back, arms, and sadly peeling white paint.

"You'd need a scour brush to take off the old paint, then pick out your color—waterproof metal spray paint."

"See. Minor repairs. And . . ." Owen pointed over to where another dustcloth fluttered to the floor. "Somebody likes those chairs to go with it."

"They're great!" Cleo wove her way over. "Metal again, and the backs are like scallop shells. We could clean these up and paint them, Sonya."

"They'd look perfect on the deck. We could sit out and watch the sunset behind the trees. Vintage, not new and modern. They really suit the house."

"I remember those. Collin used to put them out just where you're talking about. The bench? I think I've seen pictures with that bench in it. Wait."

Trey closed his eyes, tried to visualize.

"His wedding. You flipped my memory switch," Owen told him. "I've seen some pictures of him and Johanna on that bench. Wedding day stuff."

"That's it. Only they had it in the front. I don't remember ever seeing it there, so probably just for the wedding. She's in the white dress, he's in a gray suit. And there's one with my parents on either side. Mom's got that on the bookshelf in the living room."

"I'd like to see it when we're there tomorrow. Cleo and I can bring the bench, the chairs back to life. Right, Cleo?"

"Absolutely."

"Cleo and I can handle a chair each if you guys can handle the bench. We could just take them outside, leave them there until we pick out the paints and fix them up. We still have to hit the garage and the shed, but I'll stop and get the keys to the apartment."

As Trey and Owen got on either side of the bench, they exchanged a look.

"'A while,' he said," Trey muttered.

With the women out of earshot, Owen risked a mutter of his own. "They're going to want us to come back and haul down that *darling* piecrust table and that *adorable* plant stand."

"Don't forget the *majestic* ten-ton bench for the foyer."

"I'm trying to. Why am I always the one backing down the stairs?"

"Your bad luck. Easiest way is take it out the back once we get down there."

"'Easiest,' he said."

They caught up with the women, who'd paused in the grand foyer to discuss bench placement.

"I know it's a lot," Sonya said as they continued back. "But every time we bring something down, it's like making it more ours. We'll take a break after the shed, promise. We could have a drink out on the deck."

When she got to the kitchen, Sonya set the chair down with a clang. "Did I dream it, or did we pile a mountain of serving dishes on the island that aren't there now?"

"God, you don't suppose Molly cleaned them and put them all back." Setting her own chair down, Cleo shoved her hair out of her eyes.

"She's too smart for that." Trey shifted his hold. "Keep going, Owen. Get the key to the apartment."

"The apartment!" Leaving the chair where it stood, she rushed over to dig out the key, then ran outside with the animals flying after.

She unlocked the door.

It smelled fresh with a hint of orange oil. Cushions plumped, furniture gleaming.

The folding tables and chairs they'd earmarked were neatly stacked against the side wall. All the serving dishes were organized, according to type, on the kitchen counters.

"This is amazing," Sonya murmured. "Just amazing, and so kind. Dobbs thinks she can scare us away with her meanness, her tantrums? Never going to happen. Not when we have others, so many others, who'll do so much without being asked, without any of it expected."

Clover responded with TobyMac and "Love Is in the House."

Trey walked in behind her, wrapped his arms around her waist, set his chin on the top of her head.

"Love's in the house," he said. "And the house is packed."

Chapter Fourteen

After unearthing pots, planters, and other useful things, they sat out on the deck with Trey-made sandwiches and ice-cold Cokes.

Cleo and Sonya huddled over paint colors.

"This!" Sonya said.

"That, oh yeah. Ocean Mist? Couldn't be more perfect. For the bench, right?"

"Definitely, then what about Sea Green for the chairs?"

"We have a winner. Two winners. Sonya, how about we find little copper tables for either side."

"Copper tables is genius."

"Rob Farmer can make them." Eyes shut, Owen leaned back in the old metal chair. "He might have something already in his shop."

"Rob Farmer."

"Metalworks," Trey answered Cleo. "He's got some pieces at Bay Arts. He's got a shop out on Red Fox Road, two miles out of the village."

"How long would it take?" Sonya wondered.

"Won't know till you ask." Owen took out his phone. After scanning his contacts, texted the number.

"Now you've got his number. My job is done."

"And I'm using it right now."

She got up, wandered off to make the call.

"A coffee table, too," Cleo decided. "Not copper. Too matchy. Wood. Nothing fancy—a rustic, raw-hewed sort of thing. Even better, one of those live-edge tables."

Feeling her gaze, Owen opened one eye. Then closed it again.

Cleo just sighed, knowing she'd planted the seed.

"It's really nice out here. We tend to gravitate to the front, that view, but this is a nice place to just sit. What we need out there is some pretty bird feeders."

"Yeah, the bears'll love them." Owen put a foot up on Jones, rubbed.

"Really?"

"And the cat would be thrilled with the all-she-can-eat buffet."

"She wouldn't—Of course she would. I'll settle for the planters, some wind chimes, maybe some witch bottles."

Sonya rushed back. "Cleo, he says we can come out to his shop right now."

"Now." Automatically, she patted her hair. "Sure, okay."

"We're fine here," Trey said before she could ask. "Just fine right here."

She walked over, kissed him. "We won't be long."

Owen waited until he heard the car start. "Quiet. You won't be getting a lot of that from here out."

"I won't?"

"Not saying she's a motormouth, because she's not. Neither of them are. But your quiet, sitting-in-your-boxers-watching-the-ballgame nights are coming to an end."

"Says who?"

"The one who knows you as well as I know me. You're good and stuck on her, and I don't blame you a bit. After all, we share the devastating Poole good looks."

"Yeah, I often think of you when I look at her."

"It's in the genes, brother. Plus, she's smart, got the creative thing going, and she doesn't take any crap, even from a two-hundred-year-old witch with an attitude. Add the damsel, even one who can absolutely handle herself, in some distress angle.

"You're sunk."

"It's not any of that, and it's all of that. Something just clicked. It clicked the minute I saw her standing out in front of the manor, the minute she smiled at me. Son of a bitch. It's not supposed to happen like that."

"Why the hell not?" Owen stirred himself enough to shift in his chair. "You move slow, that's how you're made. Nothing wrong with that. Sometimes circumstances move faster. It's easier to sail with the wind than into it."

He settled back. "Anyway, I'm going to enjoy the quiet, then go in and put some mac and cheese together."

He had it together and in the oven by the time they got back, flushed with pleasure and carrying a flat-topped copper stand with a honeycomb pattern.

"Isn't it great! He's going to make us another one. I'm taking it out to see how it looks. Oh, and we stopped and bought the paint!"

Considering the rousing success of the day, Cleo got out the wine. "You didn't mention Rob Farmer's about a hundred and fifty."

"But spry," Trey added.

"Very, and very talented. Also a bit of a hound dog. He flirted hard with me. Not as hard with Sonya, as he's heard—he told us—she's seeing the young Doyle boy."

"What did you do?" Owen wondered.

"Flirted right back. He's also very cute. And with the flirting and ordering a second table, he took fifty off. So a bargain."

She opened the oven. "Well, well, that looks like a very high-class mac and cheese. How much time have we got?"

He moved next to her, looked in. "About ten more to cook. You want it to rest a couple after."

"Perfect. I'm going to run out, take a look, then I'll set the table."

When she went out, Trey gave Owen a big smile. "About that quiet time."

"I've got plenty left in the bank."

"If you say so."

After Owen's very successful mac and cheese, and a friendly argument over the best rock bands of all time, the women issued a challenge.

"I think it's time we heard some Head Case, don't you, Cleo?"

"Couldn't agree more."

Trey carted plates over to the sink. "Sadly, Head Case is no more."

"We have two members of the band right here." Sonya spread her hands. "We'll imagine the rest." She pushed away from the table. "Music room."

"They think we're gonna suck," Owen said.

"Sometimes we did."

"Sometimes we didn't." Owen rose with a shrug. "I'm game. You should grab that wine," he told Cleo. "We sound better if you're a little drunk."

Trey got two beers. "We play better if we are."

With wine, beer, three dogs, and a cat, they trooped down to the music room. Owen picked up a guitar, gave it a strum, started tuning it.

With obvious reluctance, Trey did the same.

"Do y'all play any other instruments?" Cleo wondered. "It's such a great collection. It should all be played instead of just displayed."

"Owen can handle the piano."

"*Handle's* about right." After some testing chords, Owen nodded. "You improvise better there." As he played an opening riff, he looked at Trey. "Not as much punch as with an electric, but this'll do. Remember the lyrics?"

"Yeah, I remember the lyrics."

"Okay then." He played the opening again while his foot tapped the beat.

Trey filled in the rhythm and added his voice.

"A million miles away, your signal in the distance."

Acoustic or not, they rocked out Foo Fighters' "Walk," with Owen coming in on the chorus.

The audience broke into applause.

"I'm not anywhere near drunk," Sonya said, "and you do not suck. Do another!"

"There's wisdom in quitting while you're ahead."

Owen just grinned and played another riff. When they went with Aerosmith's "Livin' on the Edge," Cleo grabbed a tambourine. Laughing, Sonya joined in as backup dancer.

As they rocked through what she decided equaled Head Case's greatest hits, the banging started.

She shot a middle finger at the ceiling and kept dancing.

"Play it louder!"

Trey stomped his foot, clapped his hands.

"That's right!" Sonya shot up her fists. "That's damn right. 'We Will Rock You'!"

With Cleo, she joined in, defiant voices singing out both threat and promise.

"And that, ladies and gentlemen, about wraps up tonight's performance."

"We've still got at least some of it," Owen said to Trey. "We shut her down."

"One more." Cleo lifted her glass. "We've got just enough wine left for one more."

"Let's finish with the Boss." Owen flexed his fingers. "I've got one more in me."

When they ended with Springsteen's "Fire," Sonya decided there was nothing sexier anywhere, anytime, than a good-looking man and a guitar.

"That's the way to put a cap on an evening." Cleo scanned the instruments. "I've got to learn how to play something in here."

"You've got some pipes."

She smiled at Owen. "You should hear me sing in the shower."

He smiled back. "Looking forward to it."

She only laughed. "Time to let our four-legged friends out before bed."

When they reached the door, opened it, Sonya let out a whoosh. "Wow, that's some fresh air! You know, I think I reached the little-bit-drunk level."

"If a woman can't get a little bit drunk on a Saturday night among friends in her own house, when and where?"

She gave Owen a light punch on the arm. "My favorite cousin, and my second-favorite rocker. I'm going to bed with my favorite rocker."

"That's probably for the best."

She slept without dreams, or without dreams remembered, without a stir, without a murmur when the clock struck three.

She slept while Trey stood at the window and watched Hester Dobbs take her fall.

On Sunday, since Trey went off with Owen to work on Yoda's doghouse, she and Cleo handled domestic chores. They divided laundry detail, then in the blissful April sunshine washed out planters and pots. And finalized the open house invitations.

"Corrine said a hundred and fifty invites would do it."

Sonya sucked in a breath between her teeth. "That could mean like three hundred people. Holy shit, Cleo. Can we really do this?"

Clover returned to the Boss and "You've Got It."

"Do we?"

Sonya squared her shoulders. "If we don't, we're gonna. But let's hold off until Bree comes over tomorrow. Then we pull the trigger."

"Good plan. Now let's pull the trigger and get ready for dinner at the Doyles'."

Upstairs, Sonya decided to go with Molly's pick of a simple and classic blue wrap dress and low-heeled booties.

For Cleo, she'd gone with a soft spring pink.

"Good choices." Sonya gave Cleo a nod when she did a turn. "Not too fancy, not too casual."

"When we're in Boston, we need to squeeze in some shopping time so we can give Molly some new choices."

"I find no objection to that. I'd say we're ready, with a stop for flowers on the way." Bending down, she nuzzled Yoda. "Be good. I know Jack will come out and play with you both."

As they drove, Sonya glanced over at Cleo. "I know you're serious about coming to Boston with me, but are you really serious about standing in as my assistant for the Ryder presentation?"

"Absolutely. I can help set up the visuals, and if I run the video, you can focus on your pitch. It's a good one."

"I've refined it a little. I'd need to run it through with you again.

And I have to ask Trey if he'd keep Yoda while we're out of town. Or, if it's easier for him, to just stay at the manor."

"I think I'm going to see if Owen'll take Pye, unless Trey's going to stay. And even then, he'd be at work all day. She's so clearly stuck on him. Owen, I mean."

"Have I missed anything since my very awkward interruption in your studio?"

"No. It's all under consideration."

"He really is my favorite cousin."

"That's a low bar, Son."

Sonya had to laugh. "He said the same thing."

They stopped for flowers, rich purple tulips, then drove the climbing road just outside the town proper.

"We haven't seen it in daylight," Sonya said when the GPS announced they'd reached their destination. "What a beautiful house. It's not as big and sprawling as the offices, but it has the same feel to it."

"It's really wonderful. Who doesn't love a wraparound porch, especially with a turret over it?"

"I sure do." She eased across the slate-gray, paved drive to pull up beside Trey's truck.

"Trey's here, and that's Anna's car. So we're not too early."

"I don't see Owen's truck, so we're not too late either. I bet those azaleas are spectacular when they bloom."

"Won't be long now."

They walked to the covered porch, rang the bell.

Anna's husband, Seth, answered. "Sonya, good to see you. And you must be Cleo. Seth," he said, and offered a hand. "Come on in."

They'd kept the Victorian style inside with a graceful fireplace flanked by bookshelves in the living room and the gleam of honey-toned floors.

"Action's back here," Seth told them as he guided them through.

"The action smells delicious."

He smiled at Cleo. "Wait till you taste Corrine's glazed ham."

They passed a manly-looking office where Sonya expected Deuce put in some hours, and a more feminine style with walls lined with photos where Corrine put in her time.

Voices as well as scents flowed back from a big, serious kitchen where the family gathered around a large island or sat at a table by a wall of glass that opened into an expansive garden.

Already early blooms showed their color.

Trey, dress shirt untucked over khakis, slid off a stool and leaned down to kiss her. The easy greeting with his family all around gave Sonya a little glow.

Corrine took a baking dish out of the lower of double wall ovens, and after setting it aside, came around the island to kiss Sonya, then Cleo on the cheek.

"Aren't these gorgeous! And tulips mean spring. Thank you both."

"Thanks for having us. Your home's just beautiful."

"We're happy here." She patted Sonya's hand. "You've both met Deuce. He and Trey were just arguing baseball, so your arrival's a reprieve."

"Oh, we'll get back to it," Deuce promised.

Ace—no three-piece suit and tie today, but just as handsome in an open-collared shirt—unfolded himself from the table where he'd been sitting with his wife and granddaughter.

He winked at Sonya, gave her a bear hug, then turned to Cleo.

"Cleopatra, at last." He took her hand, and with a twinkle in his eye, kissed it. "Come meet my own darling, then you can tell me your life story."

"I'd love to, as long as there's a semicolon after it. I'm not finished yet."

"I do love a beautiful young woman with some sass. Paula, meet Cleo."

"That'll keep them busy awhile. Sonya, let me get you a drink."

"I had a lot of wine with last night's concert. But I'd love some water."

"Trey didn't mention you went to a concert."

"He and Owen performed in the music room."

"'Performed' might be overstating it." Trey tugged her down to a stool.

"Not for me. We haven't had live music at the manor since you came to dinner, Corrine. We need to have it more often."

Obviously too at home for bell ringing, Owen came in. Not with flowers but a live plant.

"Owen! Is that—"

"Old-fashioned weigela," he finished, and kissed his hostess. "I heard you had a spot for one."

"I do! Deuce may curse you when I watch him dig the hole."

"I already am," Deuce said as Owen carried it straight out to the deck. "Well, since the gang's all here, I'll carve the ham."

Owen lit right up. "Score!"

It was just that easy, a Sunday dinner around a big table, conversations winging. Baby talk, baseball talk, gardening, cooking, art, local gossip, and plenty about the planned open house.

And none, Sonya realized, about what lurked in the manor in the Gold Room. Maybe the Doyles decided to give her a kind of reprieve.

Corrine didn't brush off offers to help deal with the dishes, which to Sonya's mind made it a true family dinner.

It brought chaos with it, but she enjoyed that, too, as well as a tour of the gardens, which gave her too many ideas to fit in her head.

"The gardens at the manor are well established," Corrine told her as they walked. "But Collin filled in with annuals every year, added planters."

"We're hoping to do the same. But how do you know what everything is? What goes together? And where to fill in?"

"Experience. And if you make a mistake? There's always next year."

Though the living room didn't boast a baby grand, it had a spinet. It took very little to coax Paula to play, and Ace to form a duet.

Seth sat with his arm around Anna's shoulders, murmured something in her ear that had her smiling and bringing his hand to her belly under hers.

Deuce and Corrine sat together, his hand on her knee, her head tilted toward his shoulder.

It struck Sonya she wanted that, every stage of that unity.

The young just starting, the deeply established, the long-lasting. A home filled with generations and music and arguments over baseball.

One day, she thought, she wanted a chance to begin all of that.

Just one more reason to find the seven keys, break the curse, and rid the manor of what shadowed it.

When Paula lifted her hand to pat the one resting on her shoulder, Sonya took it as her cue.

"This has been wonderful, just wonderful. I can't thank you enough for having us."

Cleo picked it right up. "If we didn't have a cat and dog waiting at home, you'd have a hard time getting rid of us."

Goodbyes took time before Trey walked them out.

"Sonya told me," Cleo began, "but now I've seen for myself. You have a terrific family. I wondered how three generations managed to work together, but question answered. Love, respect, rhythm. You've got them."

"Born lucky. Staff meeting in the morning."

"You told me." Still feeling wistful, Sonya wrapped around him. "We're fine, and yes, you'll know if that changes."

She kissed him again before she got behind the wheel.

Cleo lingered by the open passenger door another minute. "You know, I really liked your grandmother. Easy elegance, humor, style all wrapped up in one. If I didn't like and admire her, I might break my number one relationship rule and have a wild affair with your grandfather."

"And that's a damn clever way to flatter them both."

Cleo got in, sighed as Sonya waved and backed out of the drive.

"That was fun, and illuminating."

"Illuminating?"

"Seeing them all together that way. Each one their own person, but all a part of a whole. I think Collin must've been a good man. I don't see Deuce being lifelong friends, brothers really, with someone who wasn't."

"Neither do I," Sonya agreed. "The wedding photo—the one of the Doyles with Collin and Johanna on the bench. You saw it, right?"

"I did. It tells me Johanna must've been a good woman. Corrine's style's all over that house, and that picture wouldn't be there unless she loved both of them."

"They didn't have the chance to make what the Doyles made. But we will." Sonya glanced over. "We will, Cleo, when it's right."

Cleo looked toward the bay as they drove by it.

"When it's right," she said after a moment, "I don't see either of us settling for less."

Then she turned back. "We've got some time before dark. Let's free the furries and walk around. Corrine packed my head with so many garden ideas."

"Mine, too. We have to figure out what we've got first."

"That's where we start. Owen said no bird feeders because bears like them."

"Oh." A beat. "Oh! That's a very disturbing thought."

"So no bird feeders, and unless a lot of it's already there, I doubt a garden to rival Corrine's—at least not our first year."

"What are you doing?"

Cleo kept working her phone. "I'm looking up that plant Owen brought her. If I can figure out how to spell it. Maybe we have one. Okay, here it is. And that's beautiful. If we don't have one, I want one."

"Right there," Sonya said as she turned onto Manor Road, "is a good place to start."

She parked, and they walked to the house. Cat and dog greeted them at the door before both streaked out.

"I guess we did test their bladder control. How about we change," Cleo suggested, "and take that walk around in pj's?"

"Now, that's what I call being home."

Clover sang it out with Steve Perry's "Missing You."

"Okay," Sonya said with a laugh, "that's being home."

When they'd changed, they joined Yoda and Pye. As they walked, Sonya used an app on her phone to take pictures of bushes and iden-tify them.

"I need that app." Cleo pulled out her phone. "I'm downloading that app."

"It'll work better—lots—when everything has leaves. Better yet flowers. If they get flowers, because we don't know that yet. And there's stuff poking out of the ground over there, over there. I don't think they're weeds."

"Rosebushes over there. You don't need an app to recognize rosebushes."

"Or hydrangeas. So we've got those. And you know what else we've got? Gardening books in the library."

"Then let's get to it."

Since the air had chilled by the time they went in, they brewed a pot of tea to take up with them. Where a fire already crackled in the hearth.

"That's nice. Thanks, Molly—or Jerome," Cleo considered. "Either way, it's nice."

They pulled out books, and Cleo grabbed one of Sonya's sketch pads. As they sat, Sonya opened one of the books, blew out a breath. "It's a lot."

"We can handle it. While it's fresh in my head, I'm going to sketch out what we've got—or think we've got."

They spent an hour and more, peaceful, by the fire thinking of gardens, imagining flowers.

Each took a book with them to bed.

Sonya fell asleep thinking of gardens, imagining flowers.

And dreamed.

Chapter Fifteen

1964

We did it! Charlie and me got totally hitched.

We weren't going to. I mean, get real, like Charlie says, marriage is just another establishment construct. Like you need a license to love?

That's serious bullshit.

I mean, man, my parents got the license, the house in the burbs and all that. And as long as I can remember they spent most of their time bitching at each other, bitching about each other, or ignoring each other.

Sure wasn't a lot of love in my house.

When they weren't doing that, they were ragging on me. I figure they blamed me for not just calling it and moving the hell on.

So I moved the hell on and took off. Freedom, baby! Rode my thumb all the way to San Francisco. I met a lot of cool people along the way—and some not so cool for sure. Picked up some work here and there when I needed to—hungry isn't fun, let me tell you.

But waiting tables means you're going to eat.

If you're open, and man, I was wide open, you find people who'll give you a place to flop awhile. And you talk about this bullshit world and how you'd fix it. You listen to music, get a little high.

I stayed at this farm, a commune thing, for a time. Really, really cool. Everybody took care of everybody. We grew our own food, had these cool chickens, some cows. A lot of work, yeah, but I liked it. I learned a lot, too.

A couple of the guys fixed up this old VW bus, and we all painted it. Birds, butterflies, rainbows. Totally psychedelic!

I was going to stay on the farm. It was nice there and nobody hassled us. But something told me to get on that bus and ride, so I did.

Even when it broke down somewhere in Bumfuck, well, I still had my thumb. I don't know why I needed to keep going, but I did. It was like some part of me knew I had to get somewhere.

Somewhere turned out to be San Francisco.

It was happening. It *was* A Happening!

I made a lot of friends there, people who understood, really *got* what it was like to be held down by the man. Who said fuck no to war. This was our moment, and we were going to change the world. Live in peace and harmony, live off the land, and share the freaking bounty.

And that's how I met Charlie. That's when I *knew* why I'd had to keep going until I did.

It wasn't just that he was handsome, though oh yeah, those green eyes just did me in. He was so smart, and like me, so open. He loved music like I did. And like me, he wanted a world where you could just be, just live, just take care of each other.

Sometimes we'd talk all night about how we'd build that world. For each other, for our friends, for everyone.

Then I got knocked up. But I was really happy, and when I told Charlie, he was really happy, too. We were going to have a baby! And we were going to bring that baby into the world with love, raise that baby in love like neither of us ever had.

It was the idea of a baby that had Charlie telling me things he hadn't before, even when we talked all night. Like he said, he'd put all of that out of his life because his family was mostly everything he stood against.

Hey, mine, too!

It turned out his family was rich, like really rolling. I didn't care about that. Like Charlie was an artist, and he worked his street art, sold enough for us to get by. And I waited tables at this vegetarian place.

We got by fine, and didn't need all that material bullshit that screws people up.

But he told me about this house, this great big house, and some land, way over in Maine. But right on the Atlantic, man. And how the house was his now.

We could build our life there, and have a place for art, for music, for peace. We could have chickens and raise vegetables. Maybe we'd get a nanny goat!

Our baby could be born there and grow up by the sea.

They called it The Manor. Lost Bride Manor because way back this woman got stabbed to death on her wedding day. Harsh, man! And it was haunted, which is wild!

So we got this camper, and Charlie and me and some friends started across the country. He told me about his mother—a complete bitch who tried to run his life like she did everyone's. How she tried to push him away from his art. Tried to make him be a lawyer.

My Charlie, a lawyer! Just makes me laugh.

He wanted us to get married, like legal, license, the works. Because of the baby (I told him babies, because I could just feel two in there) and because he didn't want his old lady bitch mother to try anything with me or our kids.

You know what surprised me? The minute he said it, I wanted it, too. I didn't care about the legal shit, but I wanted us to make those promises to each other, to our babies.

We headed to Maryland because you can get a license there pretty quick and without much hassle. I bought a dress, this beautiful white dress at a secondhand shop with a high waist and a skirt that would work because I was showing.

While we camped, we met this guy who had a brother, and the brother had a place in the mountains. Not mountains like out west. These were all green and soft.

We got married there, in a kind of meadow. Even though it was almost October, it was as warm as summer. So I picked wildflowers and made a ring of them to wear, and more to hold.

This old guy in overalls married us—he was a traveling preacher—and he was cool with us saying our own words. Like me telling Charlie I'd live with him in love and how we'd fill our lives with the riches of nature, and him telling me how I'd made him a better human and brought all the color into his life.

He even had a ring for me, and it was perfect. Two hearts hooked together like our hearts were. I knew when he put it on my finger, it was the only material thing I'd ever really need.

That symbol of our hearts joined forever made me cry a little, but a happy cry.

Then we were married! Life mates. Husband, wife? No! Those are establishment labels.

We had music, and we danced and danced and danced in the meadow in the sunlight, and in the moonlight. A perfect day, and I put it on my list of the happiest.

When I left home. When I met Charlie. When I found out I was pregnant. My wedding day.

I had plenty of fun, and some not so fun mixed in there, but those were my most perfect and happiest days.

That night, Charlie and I made love as life mates, and the two hearts shined on my finger.

The next morning, we left for Maine, and the manor.

Sonya woke in the quiet just after dawn. Outside the windows, the sun bloomed like roses over the sea with streaks of gold shimmering through them.

And the sea drummed, a quiet thunder.

For a moment, just a moment, she caught the scent of flowers. Not the ones on her dresser but a scent like a mountain meadow basking in the sun.

She lay there, revisited the images that had flowed in the dream.

"All right, Clover," she murmured. "I won't forget."

She got up, and since Yoda yawned and stretched his way out of his bed, went downstairs. She watched the cat slink her way out of Cleo's room.

"An early start for all of us."

She stopped by the library, took her tablet off the charger, and carried it with her.

Downstairs, she let the dog, and the cat who streaked by him, out. She made coffee, and taking a mug to the counter, sat to write out all she remembered.

As she expected Bree late morning, Sonya dressed—no house/work sweats today—then settled in to work until Cleo surfaced.

When she did, Sonya rose to hand her the story she'd printed out.

"Read this, will you, over your coffee?"

With a nod and grunt, Cleo continued downstairs.

Inside ten minutes, Cleo, wide awake, came back. She waved the papers in her hand.

"Did you walk? Did you go through the mirror? I didn't hear a thing. I'm so sorry I didn't—"

"Don't be sorry, and I don't know. I woke up in bed, and I felt her, Cleo, I felt her right there when I did."

Annie Lennox's voice sang from the tablet: "Sweet Dreams (Are Made of This)."

"It was sweet, yes, very sweet and very vivid. Here, let's sit down a minute."

She went to the sofa, waited for Cleo to join her. Yoda padded over to lie at her feet, and the cat leaped onto the armrest.

"Were you there?"

"It was . . . like she was telling me a story—her story—but I could see it happening, and hear it. Hear her narrating it. I watched her leaving home with a backpack and a duffel. God, Cleo, she was just a kid. Hitching rides—this lovely teenage girl climbing into cars and trucks with strangers.

"When you think what might've happened to her. It didn't," Sonya reminded herself. "Or she didn't show me the bad parts."

"She gave you a kind of antidote, didn't she? From watching her die. Because she loves you, and because she wants you to know more about her, and to know you come from love. Not just your parents, but from her and Charlie."

"I could see her at different points. Sitting in some room talking with people about Vietnam, about civil rights, about standing up against oppression. Listening to music, getting stoned."

Clover told her, via Tom Petty, "You Don't Know How It Feels."

"I guess I don't, and I swear, no judgment. My parents loved each other. Not that they never argued, but I did come from love, and I grew up in it. You, too, Cleo."

"Yes, me, too."

"I saw her waiting tables, and traveling, and on that farm she showed me. Hoeing weeds, harvesting carrots—I think. The psychedelic bus she left in."

"I thought the hippie thing, the counterculture thing, was later. Like late in the sixties."

"I've researched it some. Its roots go back further. She and Charlie missed the full bloom, but they were in on the bud, you could say. I saw when they met. He was—not holding court, that's wrong, but talking to a group of people about peaceful protests. He talked about Gandhi and Martin Luther King, how he'd gone to DC, heard King's speech, heard Joan Baez, Bob Dylan. About using art and music to spread the message of peace and justice and equality."

"He was magnetic, Cleo. Young and passionate and magnetic. When I saw him before, when the twins were born, he was so scared, struggling to hold on to Clover, to help her, to be strong. But he was terrified."

"She showed you another part of him, too."

"Yeah. He came back here for her, for the family they were making, for the world they wanted to build. And he wanted marriage not just because he loved her, and he did, but to protect her—legally— from his mother. He was smart enough to understand that.

"I saw them on their wedding day, two young, happy people making promises to each other, dancing in a country meadow. It was so lovely."

"She gave you a gift, and through that a gift to me." Moved, Cleo swiped at a tear. "You're going to share it."

"With Trey, yeah. And Owen."

"And your mom. You should send this to her, Sonya. Send your mom what you wrote. I think it's a gift to her, too."

"I hadn't thought of that, but you're right. You're a hundred percent. I will."

"Good." Now Cleo let out a long sigh. "This hit all my feels. Every one of them. I need to pull myself and everything else together before Bree gets here. Unless you want to postpone that."

"Absolutely not. They were going to open this house, Cleo. We're not doing it in the same way—I'm not going to deal with chickens and goats—but we're opening the house to people and art and music. To community."

"Glad to hear the no-go on chickens and goats." She gave Sonya a pat, rose. "We're going to do those herbs, though, maybe some tomatoes and peppers, but that's as close to farm girls as we'd ever get."

"Just close enough. I'll send this to Mom, but I think I'll wait until after her workday. Then we can talk if she wants."

"Maybe FaceTime so I can get in on it."

"Done. I'm going to work until Bree gets here."

She got in a solid hour before Yoda took his barking race down the steps. For the first time since her Saturday tantrum, Dobbs banged doors.

"Don't like that company's coming?" Sonya saved her work, shut down. "Suck it."

She started downstairs as the doorbell bonged.

Bree, red hair a cap of fire, tattoos displayed below the pushed-up sleeves of her sweater, stood a few steps back from the door, goggling.

"Big wow. I'm talking big-ass, giant wow."

"This can't be the first time you've been up here."

"Yeah, it can. Oh, you mean since Trey and me had a thing back when." She stepped inside, goggled some more. "More big-ass wow. He used to come up, hang out, play video games or whatever. I wasn't into gaming back then, and I worked summers, weekends, and all that. I'm surprised we found time to have sex."

She stopped, winced. "That's weird, isn't it?"

"Weirder if you didn't."

"There is that. So this is Yoda, and the cat." Crouching, she used one hand on each to rub. "I'll make sure to tell Lucy they're happy, healthy, and living in fucking splendor.

"Talk about a staircase made for your grand entrances. Hey, Cleo. Well, I want a tour. I want to at least see what you're going to let people poke into."

"I think we'll leave the downstairs closed. At least unless one of us is with them. There's a gym and a movie theater, but also a lot of storage areas."

"And the attic," Cleo added. "The ballroom."

Bree goggled again. "A freaking ballroom?"

"A lot of things stored up there, too," Sonya explained. "It may take years to sort through it all. But there's plenty of other house."

"You're telling me." She looked up at the portrait. "That's the one, right? The murdered bride."

"Astrid, yes."

"Okay, show me around."

They started with the main level, which brought on more goggling. Sonya thought of her first tour, guided by Trey, and understood exactly.

"This place is something else. I'm more a clean lines, modern, open concept in my dream-house dreams, but this is something else."

When they reached the kitchen, she put her hands on the hips of her cargo pants. "I'd give up those dreams in a heartbeat for this kitchen. You've got a chef's kitchen here. More farmhouse than my style, but I have deep, painful kitchen envy."

She wandered.

"The dining room's a little spooky, but it's big. Yeah, yeah, this'll work.

"I want to go outside first before we see more in here."

She stepped out. "Jesus, you've got a lot of mowing in your future. You've sure got the room for a shit-ton of people. If it doesn't rain."

"Don't say *rain*!"

Bree sent Sonya a grin. "A lot of room inside, too, but we'll plan for dry. You could do tents, but you know, it's such a freaking sight, as it is. And some of this stuff will be blooming in June."

"You know about gardening?"

She shook her head at Cleo. "Not much of a damn thing, but I know the seasons around here. Are you leaving those ugly chairs on that deck deal?"

"They won't be ugly when they're sanded and painted."

"I'll take your word. Still, that's a good spot for the band. Manny and the rest of them are juiced up about playing here at Spook Manor. No offense."

"Absolutely none taken." Sonya gestured out. "We can put the chairs, the bench out in the yard. We've got a start on tables and chairs to set out, too. We'd need to rent bar stations."

"Uh-huh. Show me the rest."

They went upstairs, where Bree's jaw all but dropped on the library floor. She picked it up as they continued down the wide hallway.

"Now I have bedroom envy," she said by the time they'd reached Sonya's. "None of this is my style, but I've got the envy anyway."

She wandered back. "Okay, so a couple of really nice powder rooms main level, a couple of guest baths and sitting rooms up here. I'd close your own bedrooms off, again unless you're taking someone through. And no food tables up here. Maybe a bar in the library. What's up there?"

"Third floor," Cleo told her. "Most of those rooms are already closed off. My studio's up there."

"Close it off, yeah, but I'd like to see it. I want to see this mermaid I've heard about."

As they started up, a door slammed as if blown in a hard wind.

"I didn't realize somebody else was here. You've got a guest?"

"Not exactly," Sonya murmured. "Spook Manor."

Bree didn't goggle this time. Instead her eyes ticked right, then left. "You're not serious."

"One of the reasons we're going to block off this floor is to keep people from wandering in—or trying to wander in," Cleo added, "to a room occupied by a very unwelcome presence."

More doors slammed.

"Yeah," Cleo called out, "I'm talking about you, Dobbs."

"Hester Dobbs," Sonya explained. "The woman who killed Astrid Poole on her wedding day. The rumors are true, Bree. The house is haunted, and it's full of ghosts. She's the only one who's an asshole!"

Sonya shouted the last word.

"You're not shitting me." Bree rubbed the chill from her arms. "And you work up here?"

"Nothing and no one can push me out of my studio." Cleo gestured as they reached it. "See why?"

"I'm running out of holy shits. This is . . . It's just freaking awesome. I don't know how I'd handle what's going on down the hall, but it's awesome. You must—"

She turned, saw the painting.

"You hung her," Sonya said.

"I decided to let her dry on the wall so I can enjoy her until she leaves me. Don't touch," Cleo warned.

Slipping her hands in her pockets, Bree admired the frameless painting. "She's really, well, she's just spectacular. I get why Owen's willing to build you a boat for her. Or them, seeing as there are more of her in the glass ball."

R.E.M.'s "Redhead Walking" rocked out of Sonya's phone.

"Ringtone?" Bree asked.

"Biological grandmother. She likes music."

"Okay." Bree drew out the word. "So, let's head back down and talk about all this."

They settled at the casual dining table with Bree's choice of Cokes for all three. Then she took a breath, and dove straight in.

"How many invites?"

"Corrine—Trey's mom—said about a hundred and fifty."

Bree raised her eyebrows at Sonya. "You guys aren't screwing around. So potentially three hundred. I wouldn't bank on much of an attrition rate. Let's start with booze. Beer, wine, and soft or full bar?"

"We thought full bar," Cleo began.

"Here's what you do. Set up for a full bar out back, another maybe in the big parlor. Then you have two more, wine, beer, soft, outside, and one in that sitting room, the turret one back there. You're going to want to talk to Jacie at the liquor store and work out a decent discount."

"Jacie." Sonya noted it down.

"Or you could cut one of the wine bars down, have some servers passing through. Add a signature drink."

"Signature drink." Sonya exchanged a look with Cleo.

"Like The Manor Cocktail or . . ." When a sound like thunder rolled through the house, Bree looked up, warily. "Ghost in the freaking Machine."

"Spirit of The Manor."

Cleo clapped her hands together. "You're good at this, Son. Maybe a twist on a Bellini."

"Talk to Sylvia, head bartender at the Cage. If you can get her to work the party, you've got the best. Food stations."

She took them through it almost faster than they could note it down.

"You never talked about budget."

"We'd never have been able to do anything like this before," Sonya told her. "Collin, the manor, all of it changed that. We want"—now she looked up, defiantly—"a serious bash. A way to open the manor up, fill it with people, make it—and us—a real part of the community again."

"This should do it. It's smart, and community-minded, to order your food and drink from all the locals. More complicated than just having a caterer handle everything, but smart."

"I'm going to create signs for each dish, name of the dish, name of the venue that made it."

"Really smart. So let me tell you what you're going to want from those venues, at least top of my head on that, and how much. I'm wrong on the attrition, you can adjust. Then we'll round up the number of servers, bartenders, the dishes and glassware you'll need to rent, and all that."

"Before you do that, I'd like to consult with my co-host. Give us one second. Cleo."

"Don't go far," Bree called out, and glanced at the ceiling again.

When they came back in under two minutes, Sonya sat, folded her hands on the table. "We did toss around the idea of having the whole thing catered in some of our earlier stages of planning, and rejected that for this plan. So, no single caterer. But at this stage, with all the details and suggestions from you, we realize we could really use an event coordinator."

"Are you interested?" Cleo asked. "And can you estimate your fee?"

Sitting back, Bree pursed her lips. "I could be interested."

"You'd create the menu. Cleo and I would approve. You'd select the staff. You know who's best a lot better than either of us could, and would save us hours, maybe days of time. You'd help supervise the setup. We wouldn't ask you to actually work the event, but like us—and the Doyles have volunteered, our moms will both be here—just help keep an eye on things."

"I could be interested," Bree repeated. "I like you, both of you, and I like what you're doing here. So I'd give you the friends and family discount."

She named a fee, stiff but not harsh, and got nods.

"Fair," Sonya said.

"But I prefer *Event Goddess* to *coordinator*."

"As our Event Goddess," Sonya said, "what do you think we should serve?"

By the time Bree finished and left, details crowded Sonya's brain.

"We should've thought of Event Goddess before. I think we could've—would've—pulled this off. But not like she will. And not without going a little crazy."

"We'll still go a little crazy, but you're right. The more she talked, the more I could see how much smoother it'll all go with someone who knows what they're doing taking charge. We approve, we handle the decor, deal with the invitations and RSVPs. There's more, but my brain's clogged."

"Right there with you." As if to unclog it, Cleo pushed back her hair. "I'm making a PB and J and going back to work where I know what I'm doing. Want me to make two?"

"Do that. I'll let Pye and Yoda out awhile."

With her PB and J and a full water bottle, Sonya settled back at her desk. After she pulled the trigger and sent the invitation graphic and the order to her printer, she opened her first file.

It took some effort, but she put all things Event-related out of her mind.

By the end of the day, she pulled another trigger and sent another order off for the displays she'd created for her Ryder presentation.

"Done," she told herself, and firmly. "Don't look back, look ahead."

As she started to shut down, Trey sent a text.

> I got slammed right at the end of the day. Have to deal with it, and it may take a while. Can I mooch dinner tomorrow night?
>> Sorry about the work. I'm just shutting mine down. Dinner tomorrow includes a story. A good one, so don't worry. FYI, had a very productive meeting with Bree, who accepted the role as Event Goddess. Don't work harder than you have to. I'll miss you.
> I could use a good story after today. Bree won't let you down, not at a risk of losing goddess ranking. I'll miss you, too.

Clover reached back for an old one with the Searchers and "(I'll Be) Missing You."

As the tablet played, Sonya took it with her downstairs.

Cleo turned from the stove.

"Since the cooking part of my brain got crowded out, and I just beat you down here, we're having my pasta in vodka sauce."

"I love your pasta in vodka sauce."

"How much am I making?"

"Trey got held up with work, so it's just you and me. Look, if you haven't started that yet, let's FaceTime Mom, then we'll just make a big salad for dinner."

"A big salad, and girl movie night. I have to let the whole Event stay quiet awhile."

"I ordered the invitations. And the displays for my presentation. I feel just a little queasy about that."

"Get over it. Let's sit down and have some time with Winter."

While they did, Trey stood in front of his client's house. Or what had been her house. Police tape stretched across the broken front door. Both front windows had been boarded over.

He muttered a curse, then took photographs for his files.

He turned when Owen drove up, got out of his truck.

"I heard. Figured you'd be here." Owen studied the house alongside Trey.

"How the hell did he make bail?"

"His parents mortgaged their fucking house—that's the word. And Milt Treeter agreed to take him in until the trial."

"Treeter's always been an idiot."

"They slapped restrictions on him. No contact with Marlo, no drinking, no travel outside the county, mandatory addiction therapy, anger management."

Owen chin-pointed to the boards, the police tape. "That worked out well."

"Under two hours out, he gets drunk, punches Treeter in the face, knocks him down and out—busted nose, concussion—he steals Treeter's car, comes here, busts in."

Trey scrubbed his hands over his face. "I got a look inside before they closed it up. He trashed what he could, busted up furniture, broken glass everywhere. Jesus, if Marlo and the kids hadn't gotten out, gone back to New Hampshire, it would've been worse than last time."

"They can thank you for that. Fuck it, Trey, that's a fact. You pushed that through so she could take the kids the hell away from him."

"She only took what they absolutely needed with her. She was still hurting from when he went at her. She didn't want much else, sent me a list a couple days ago, and we were arranging for the rest of her stuff to be sold, donated if it didn't sell."

"Does Marlo know?"

"No." Thinking of it, Trey rubbed at the tension in the back of his neck. "Informing her's the happy duty I've got coming up. Then we'll deal with that wreck in there when I'm cleared to go back in."

"I'll help with that part. I'll help," Owen insisted. "You're not doing all that as her lawyer. He could've come after you, but he didn't."

"I'm not a woman he's got fifty pounds on, or a kid. Or a goddamn empty house."

"That's exactly why he didn't. Go do what you have to do." Owen laid a hand on his shoulder. "I'll pick up some takeout. You got her out and away, Trey, her and the kids. This? It's just stuff."

"Yeah, but it was her stuff. She didn't have a hell of a lot, but it was hers."

Chapter Sixteen

Trey spent most of the next day dealing with the fallout of Wes
Mooney's drunken rampage.

He spoke with the landlord, met with the chief of police. He did
his best to reassure and advise Marlo and her family.

And when cleared, went back to the house to salvage what he could.

In under ten minutes, after wading through the destruction, he realized he'd easily fill the bed of his truck with what couldn't be salvaged.

Looking at the kids' room and the scatter of toys Wes had kicked,
stomped on, heaved against the walls added a fresh and vicious punch
to the gut.

Just stuff, as Owen had said, but here, especially in what had been
a cheerful room with its bunk beds and bright blue walls, innocent
stuff, little treasures of childhood.

Monster trucks crushed underfoot, a Spider-Man play set in pieces.

And the worst of the worst?

Wes had used his sons' crayons to write on their bedroom wall.

Your mother's a whore!

Because his mind continued to circle to what could have happened
if those boys hadn't been tucked away in a spare room at their grandparents' home, he left their room for last.

He hauled out broken furniture, bagged broken dishes, glassware,
lamps.

Systematically, he worked his way from the living room and kitchen back to the main bedroom.

While Marlo's mother and sister had packed some of her clothes and essentials, clothes for the kids, some of their toys, what they'd left for later now joined the debris.

"Pissed on the bed, for fuck's sake."

As the rage rose up, Trey pushed it down and stripped the bed.

When he heard footsteps, he turned, then his fists unclenched when his mother stepped into the doorway.

"Mom. You shouldn't be here."

"And you should do this alone?" Dressed for physical labor in her oldest jeans and a sweatshirt, Corrine looked around the room. "It's so sad, isn't it, how a disease like alcoholism can destroy lives?"

"I'm not in the mood to give him much of a damn right now. Marlo's terrified he'll get out again and come after her and the kids. She can't afford to come back here, financially or emotionally, plus she's still recovering physically. She can't deal with what he did here."

"So you are."

"She's not just a client, Mom, she's a friend."

Despite the bite in his tone—maybe because of it—Corrine gave him a look of utter patience.

"I know that, Trey, just like I know you. I didn't need your father to tell me you're handling all this pro bono."

"She's got two kids to support, and she's doing the right thing and getting them all counseling."

"She's doing the right thing, and so are you." Once again, she looked around. "And you've made a good start here. I haven't been in the house before. Is there a washer and dryer?"

"Yeah, back in the—Don't touch those!" He snapped it out as she walked to the soiled bedding. "He—"

"Trey, I have a nose, and it wouldn't be the first time I've washed sheets someone peed on. I'll get these in the wash, then I'll go through her clothes. I'd have a better eye for what's ruined, what's not, than you."

She hauled up the bedding. "Tom and Loreen Arbot own this place, don't they?"

No stopping her, Trey admitted. And realized her practicality cooled the worst of his temper.

Being mad solved nothing. Doing did.

"Yeah, I talked with them both. Insurance will cover the damage to the house. They're upset, but not at Marlo. Worried about her, and they asked me to let her know they're sorry this happened."

"They're good people. There are more good people than not, but most of the time, the nots make more noise."

They were still at it when Owen came by to pitch in. Not long after, Marlo's neighbors the Baileys did the same. At some point, Corrine huddled with Marcia Bailey.

"Here's the plan," Corrine announced. "I've spoken with Marlo—"

"You—Mom."

"Not on any legal issue. I'm hardly a novice at this, Trey. Doyle Law Offices—Sadie is arranging—will ship the boxes of items Marlo needs and wants to her."

Pausing, she sighed a little. "Basically nothing more than her clothes and some things for her boys."

"Clean slate." With a push broom, Owen cleared the floor in the small ell of a dining area. "Makes sense."

"It does," Corrine agreed. "And with that in mind, we have her permission to hold a yard sale for everything that we've salvaged and she no longer wants."

At the thought of it, Trey pressed his hands to his eyes. "A yard sale?"

"That's right, and you can stop looking for complications there, as Marcia, Lorna, and I, along with a few other ladies, will handle it. We'll leave it to the rest of you to be the muscle, dispose of what's beyond salvaging, and move what is salvageable outside on Saturday morning. Bright and early. Anything left, donated."

She swiped her palms together. "Then done."

"I still need to—"

Corrine pointed at her son. "Stop worrying about it tonight. What needs to be done will be. Now I'm going home to clean up and change because I've decided your father's taking me out to dinner."

She went to Trey, hugged him hard. "Walk away for tonight. Go see your girl."

Owen waited while Trey secured the house.

"Your mom's a born organizer. And she's right. You should head up to the manor."

"Can't shake the mood, the pissed-off mood."

"So a beer, a hot meal, and sex should take care of it. I'd come up for the first two, but I want to finish Yoda's doghouse."

"I'll help with that."

"Don't need you. And didn't Sonya say she had a story to tell you?"

"Yeah, right." Annoyed on every level, Trey dragged his hand through his hair. "I forgot about that."

"Well, it's not like you had a few other things on your mind. Tell them I've invited myself up tomorrow."

"All right."

He did his best to cool the anger still simmering inside him. But he kept seeing the soiled sheets, the broken toys, the holes in the wall where Wes had punched his fist.

He told himself an evening with Sonya was just what he needed, and the least productive thing—what he felt more inclined toward— would be to brood at home trying to figure out what he could have done, might have done, should have done to prevent any of it.

So he picked up his dog and drove both of them to the manor.

A light rain with hints of wet snow blew in as he topped the hill. A reminder of April in Maine.

He told himself he'd shrugged off the worst of the last two days when he let himself and the delighted Mookie into the house.

While Yoda and Mookie greeted each other like long-separated brothers and the cat slunk in for some adoration, Trey walked back to the kitchen.

And God, she looked good. Her hair pulled back in a tail, those green eyes full of smiles for him.

He drew her in, held on.

And didn't see the concerned look she sent Cleo over his shoulder.

"It's fish and chips night at the manor." Though she answered Son-ya's look, Cleo kept her voice cheerful. "Let me get you a beer."

"Sounds good. Appreciate it."

He let Sonya go, skimmed a hand down her hair. "Before I forget, I'm supposed to tell you Owen invited himself over tomorrow."

"Oh, hot date tonight?"

He shot Cleo a smile that didn't reach his eyes, then took the beer she offered. "Yeah, with a doghouse for a certain Jedi Master. So, how about I feed the pets, and you tell me this story you've got? You said it's a good one."

Sonya took his hand to stop him. "After you sit down and tell me what's wrong,"

"Nothing. Just some work stuff."

"No, it's not. You're so angry, and more than just angry, so it's more. It's easy to hide that in a text like last night, though I don't know why you would. We are in a relationship, aren't we?"

"I'll feed the rest of the crew," Cleo announced, and got busy.

"It doesn't have anything to do with that."

"If you being angry and upset doesn't have anything to do with that, which also means me, what are we doing here?"

"Jesus, Sonya, give it a rest."

She gave that due consideration for about two seconds. "I'm going to say no to that, even though you're clearly ready to take out your pissed-off mood on me."

"I should take my pissed-off mood back to my place."

"That would be one choice."

"I'm just going to step outside awhile," Cleo began.

"Don't. It's snowing some."

At Trey's announcement, Sonya glanced toward the windows. "Well, that just adds to it. And you stay right where you are, Cleo, while Trey decides whether to treat me like some helpless female."

"How am I—"

"By assuming you can take on all my problems, but I'm not capa-ble of helping you with yours."

"I'm not doing that. That's bullshit." And, he realized, they'd hear about it all anyway, so fighting about it equaled stupidity.

"Wes Mooney made bail yesterday, toward the end of the business day."

"Wes . . . Isn't that your client's—that's Marlo?—her ex-husband?"

"Right." And because it was still in his hand, he took the first draw on his beer.

"After what he did?" Outrage vibrated in every word. "How did he get out on bail?"

"They set it high, out-of-reach high, but his parents mortgaged their house. It helped he didn't fight custody of the kids, or Marlo moving out of state. So along with his lawyer slow-walking any plea deal, he made bail.

"He had restrictions," Trey added, "travel, contacting Marlo. He agreed to attend AA, had a friend agree to give him a place to stay."

Sonya gripped his free hand. "God, Trey, did he hurt her, the kids?"

"No. Her mother and sister had already packed up some of her stuff and taken her back with them. But he got drunk, punched his friend, stole his truck, and went to Marlo's. She still has furniture, some clothes, things, toys—stuff she was going to have shipped or sold when she's in better shape."

He took another pull of beer before setting the bottle down with a snap.

"He broke in the door, busted windows, trashed furniture, smashed toys they hadn't taken with them, ripped what clothes she left, or just heaved them around. Goddamn it, he pissed on her bed. He's got both hands in casts now, breaking bones when he smashed his fists into walls."

"Too drunk to feel the pain," Sonya murmured.

"Yeah. And for what? For fucking what? If Marlo and the kids had been there—"

"But they weren't." Her tone might've sounded calmer than she felt, but Sonya cut him off. "They weren't there because you helped get them away. You did everything you could as her lawyer to keep them safe. So they're safe."

"If he hadn't been too drunk to think of it, he might've headed toward her family home."

"Or come after you. You helped her get the divorce, then you helped her and the kids get away."

"Too much of a coward. Sorry," Cleo said quickly.

"Don't be, because you're right. She's right, Trey. You wouldn't be half as mad if he'd come after you, but it's easier to go after a woman and a couple of kids than you. You've got every reason to be mad, but here's the thing. Now I can be mad along with you."

She looked at Cleo. "We can be mad along with you. What happens to him now?"

"His parents lose the bail money, and maybe their house. I can't care about that. I get you want to do everything you can for your kids, but he's a grown man, an alcoholic, a man who put his ex-wife in the hospital, who hurt his own kids—their grandkids."

"So you're pissed off there, too, because they didn't do what was best for him, or for the mother of their grandchildren, or for their grandchildren. They didn't do what was right."

"And now they forfeit the bail, and he's facing more charges. They'd have had the plea deal sewn up in a matter of days, but the parents pressured him and his legal counsel to push for bail first. Stupid. More than stupid—dangerous."

As the hot edge of anger cooled, he finally sat. "With a guilty plea, his cooperation in giving Marlo full custody, not fighting her taking the kids out of state, they'd probably have knocked it down to fifteen. Now? He could do twice that."

Trey shook his head. "Add the additional assault, stealing the truck, the B and E, the destruction of property, he will do twice that."

"Are you actually sitting there asking yourself what you could've done to prevent this?"

Mookie came over, laid his head on Trey's knee. Trey reached down to stroke. "Maybe. Yes. Some."

"Did you, as her legal counsel, look out for the best interests of your client?"

"I did. I can know that and still wish I'd found some way, or anticipated his level of anger. Last night was bad. And today, going through her place, seeing the extent of the damage, the rage that fueled it, brought it all back.

"I could see where the son of a bitch hurled his own kids' toys against the wall, or stomped on them."

"I don't feel sorry for him," Sonya said carefully. "I can say while his addiction is at least part of the reason, it's not an excuse. And I can say I imagine part of what fueled that rage is grief. He's lost everything."

"So he gets drunk and blames her. Anyway, we got most of the wreck cleaned up."

"'We'?"

"I was working on it when my mother showed up. I didn't want her in there. And I know what you'd say to that, so don't bother."

"I'll just think it then. Cleo and I will both think it."

"And Pye," Cleo added as she coated cod fillets, "since she's also female."

"I could use a slight break on those thoughts, as my mom, then Owen shows up, then the next-door neighbors. Anyway, it's mostly dealt with. And my mom—Owen's right, the born organizer—she's gone down some list in her head. She's got Sadie on shipping what we boxed up for Marlo and the kids, and has a group of women to run a yard sale on what we salvaged."

"When?"

"She wants it Saturday, and I'm not even going to think about how they can get it all done by then. But she wants it done, so it will be."

"I'll text her. We can make up some flyers and signs."

Trey put an arm around her waist, drew her over, pressed his face to her shoulder. "Thanks. And I'm sorry."

"You don't have to be sorry."

Then Clover played "Macho Man" and made him laugh.

"I think that's a dig, but I'll take it. It wasn't the macho thing," he began, then laughed again at the raised-eyebrow look he got from both women. "Maybe slightly. Not so macho I can't admit you were right. Owen was right, too."

"Owen?"

"He told me to get up here, have a beer, a hot meal, and sex, and I wouldn't be so pissed."

"Happy to help with the first two," Cleo told him, and dropped a coated fillet in hot oil. "But I leave the third up to my good friend."

"I can handle it." She leaned down, kissed him. "But if you mean right now . . ."

"After the first two, and the story. I could use a good story."

By the time they sat down to the meal, Sonya had nearly finished the tale.

"It was more than a dream," she said again, "because at times I could hear her, like narration. And it was all so clear. I saw her life, or what she considered the best parts of her life up until the day after the wedding."

"When they headed north, to the manor."

"Yeah. And it was beautiful, and adventurous, and foolish, and profound all at the same time.

"She had joy. She had Charlie. When I woke up, I knew that. And that feeling's stayed with me since. We FaceTimed my mom last night and told her. She cried, but the good kind."

"We all cried, the good kind. You can see it all in her portrait," Cleo added. "But this gives us more of her."

"She's meant something to me for a long time, and this," Trey said, "adds more. But you didn't walk?"

"At least not out of the room—I really don't think I left my bedroom. I didn't the night I saw her die."

"The mirror shows up, I guess, when and where it wants to. Or needs to," Cleo decided.

"And Dobbs?"

"She put up a little fuss when Bree was here yesterday. Otherwise?" Sonya shrugged. "She's been pretty quiet. Cleo—slight pause—this is really good."

"It is, right? More authentic with mushy peas, apparently, but I couldn't bring myself to make anything that looked like mush."

"We'll thank you for that. I forgot Bree was coming."

"You've been a little busy. And Bree's another story. Some slams and bangs, especially when we went up to show her Cleo's studio."

"How'd she take it?"

"Loved the house, because who wouldn't? Was a little bit freaked out by Dobbs, but she didn't run for the hills."

"And the best part?" Cleo stabbed a chip. "She's agreed to be our Event Goddess."

"Heard that. Which means what exactly?"

"We're excited," Sonya told him, "because she's going to coordinate. The menu, the staff, the bars, what goes where. It's a load off."

"She can do it. It sounds like both of you've been pretty busy yourselves."

"Gearing up. I give my presentation—with my invaluable assistant—in Boston in three weeks. Cleo's sending off the final illustrations for her mermaid project in . . ."

"Next week. It should be next week."

"Then we're going to hit the nursery and hit it hard, start planting. Then The Event. But Boston first, and I wanted to ask if you could keep Yoda."

"Sure. He can go to work with me and Mook for a couple days. We can stay here the night or nights you're gone."

"You wouldn't mind?"

"No."

"Do you think Owen would keep Pye?"

He glanced at Cleo. "I don't see why not. If Owen's got a weakness, it's animals."

"He could stay here, too, if he wants."

"Worried about me staying here alone?"

"No. Maybe. Yes, a little bit."

Clover reassured Sonya with the Pretenders and "I'll Stand by You."

"It's true. She will." Reaching out, Sonya squeezed Trey's hand. "Thanks in advance."

"Not that far in advance. The last time you made excuses about showing me the presentation."

"It wasn't fully polished. And I just ordered the posters and displays."

"I bet it's polished now, and I saw the mock-up for the posters. So how about tonight?"

"As the assistant, I say yes. We both need the practice, Son, if we're going to crush it. Which we are. Let's practice with a receptive audience."

"Fine. You're right. No yawning if you're bored."

"You haven't bored me yet."

He was far from bored.

On the second floor of the library, he sat, a pair of dogs at his feet, a cat on his lap. Though the snow had turned to rain, a fire crackled.

As he watched her, listened to her, studied the visuals she presented, he realized this was who she'd been in Boston.

This smooth and professional woman who exuded both confidence and expertise was as much Sonya as the woman who worked at her desk in sweats. As the woman who'd made dinner for his family, the one who loved dogs and accepted hauntings as part of her life.

The woman who'd welcomed him into her life, and her bed, who'd embraced his community as her own.

The woman who walked through the mirror.

And all those parts of her pulled something in him no one ever had.

"This campaign highlights the rich history and traditions of Ryder Sports, and demonstrates that Ryder has always, will always value their loyal customer base while opening its doors to the needs and interests of the next generation.

"Thank you for giving me the opportunity to present my vision for a business rooted, as I am, in family and community. And you have my very best wishes on your grand opening in Portland."

She blew out a breath, and her easy, professional smile lit into a grin. "Done! So?"

"I have this irresistible urge to pull up Ryder's website and buy sports equipment."

She laughed, took a little bow. "But seriously, did you notice any glitches, dead ends, wrong turns?"

"Maybe a hockey stick," he considered. "I don't play hockey, but I feel this sudden need to own a hockey stick. Sonya, I don't know much about marketing, advertising, but I know smooth when I see it, and I just did. Smooth and smart. Playing up the history of the company, the family? Smart."

He set the cat aside and rose.

"I—more or less—got what you were doing with the photos you had my mother take. But seeing how you've used them, put this all together? That's a different level.

"And I really want that hockey stick."

"Crushed it." Cleo rubbed her hands together. "Told you."

"It feels right. It may be my first major presentation for my own company, but it feels right. I don't know what angles By Design's going for, but it'll be smart and slick and sleek."

"Yours is smart," Trey reminded her. "It's not slick and sleek. Smooth is different from slick and sleek."

"It is. Yes, it is. Nothing much more to do than see if Ryder prefers slick and sleek or smooth."

"I said it before and don't mind saying it again. Crushed it. Now I'm going to make some tea and head up to play with a new idea of my own."

"Want to share?" Sonya asked her.

"Not yet. But I can make tea for three if you want."

"Tea on a cool, rainy night sounds good." Sonya took Trey's hand. "We'll all go down. I need to put this presentation aside so I don't obsess."

After they brewed tea, Cleo took hers, and Pye, upstairs.

"Is she making herself scarce because of me? I don't want that."

Sonya shook her head as they started to take their tea to the parlor with the idea of starting a fire. "If that was it, she'd have said she was just going up. If she said she has an idea to play with, she has one."

As they approached the music room, music—slow and dreamy— flowed out.

"That doesn't sound like Clover's style." Sonya stopped at the doorway. "It's a record. It's the Victrola playing a record! That's new. And here I am finding that really charming."

"I'd say that's old—as far as the music goes. Ah, 'Body and Soul.' I've heard my grandparents do this one."

As charmed as she, Trey took her hand, drew her inside the room. Then setting his tea and hers aside, took her in his arms.

Swayed into a dance.

And here and now, he thought as they held close, matched steps, while the old music played, and the rain fell, it felt perfect.

Chapter Seventeen

Through the night, while others walked, wept, plotted, or grieved, they slept undisturbed.

The gray haze of dawn held back the light, shrouding the day to come, and all its demands. In the hearth, the fire simmered low, adding warmth, bringing a hint of gilded light as Sonya woke. Content, she curled a little closer to hold on to the quiet, and him.

Bodies fit, curve to angle, angle to curve.

In that gray haze, his lips found hers. Soft, slow, sleepy. And on a sigh, she answered in kind. They embraced the warmth and each other in the old bed while the sea drummed its steady beat, while the last of the stars winked out.

As his hands moved over her, slow and sure, contentment became a yearning.

With tender touches, with gentle tastes, in the stillness of that softening edge between dark and light, yearning spilled into need.

His heartbeat quickened against hers, hers against his. Answering that pulse, she moved over him, rose up. Silhouetted in the firelight, she took him in, took him, on a sigh, deep.

And she joined them together in a rhythm as sweet and dreamy as the dance they'd shared hours before.

For this dance, they glided up together, rose and fell together, rose and fell with her surrounding, him filling. As she moved, his hands slid up her sides, down again, matching her lazy morning pace.

When she sighed again, it sounded to him like music.

In those moments, their needs, like the sea's drumming, found a rhythm more steady than urgent. Pleasure, and the desire to hold on to that pleasure, beat by beat, drew those moments out, and out.

Moments where, in the soft, silky light, their eyes met, their eyes held. When release came at the top of that glide, it swept through them in a long, slow, rising wave.

One they floated on when she lowered to him with her head cupped in the curve of his shoulder.

"I wish it were Sunday," she murmured.

"Why Sunday?"

"Then we could stay just like this for another hour. I love my work. I love having work that needs to be done. But right now, I wish it were Sunday."

"Why don't we make a date for Sunday morning—right back here?"

She crossed her arms over his chest, lifted her head to look down at him. More light trickled in the windows, the terrace doors, as day passed the edge of dawn to start its blooming.

"I'd like that. I like waking up with you when everyone else, ghosts included, are sleeping."

He brushed at her hair. "You think ghosts sleep?"

"I hope they do, or can. I hope they can dream. Well, I hope a certain one has regular nightmares, but the rest? I hope they can dream."

Turning her head, she looked through the glass doors at the bright blooming of day. "Waking up to that every morning? It's nothing I ever imagined for myself. Now it's hard to imagine anything else."

"I wasn't sure you'd stay. Even though I could see you'd fallen for the manor, staying here? Big step, big change. I gave it about fifty-fifty."

"Probably better odds than I gave myself. It's strange, but I think your father knocking on my door that day came at exactly the right time. And then . . . the sketches my father had done of the manor made it impossible for me to not at least try."

With some reluctance, she rolled away and got up. "Then I saw this house." As she pulled out workout gear, she shook her head.

"Sunk. And of course the very sexy, incredibly patient lawyer son of the lawyer, who gave me my first tour of Lost Bride Manor."

She turned to him as she dressed. "I'll add *unflappable*, because you were, and nearly always are. You and your family made this tremendous change in my life easy. I didn't imagine the easy either."

"You took care of a lot of that yourself. And you don't flap easily. Since you're putting on the sexy fitness gear, I'm guessing you're going to work out."

"Coffee first, but it's a hit-the-gym day for me. You're welcome to join."

"I need to head straight into the office from here. Shower and change there. But I'll take the coffee."

Understanding, she nodded. "I know Marlo's situation preys on your mind. I wish I could help with more than flyers for a yard sale."

"You did. You pushed me to air it out. One of my least favorite things, so it takes a push."

"It does? Check out my surprised face!"

He did, and laughed. "Yeah, and you figured out just how to push."

"You're involved with a woman who insists on equal ground. I dump on you, you dump on me. Get used to it."

"May take a little while," he said as they started downstairs with the dogs, then the cat.

"Does the cat just not wake up Cleo?"

"Pye's smart enough to know how things work around here. I'm going to work on those flyers once I'm at my desk. Cleo will give her input when she's up and has had coffee."

"Thanks for that. I mean it."

"*It takes a village* isn't just a saying. Cleo and I are part of the Poole's Bay village. Mookie can eat with Yoda and Pye when they come back in. It'll save you time."

"He appreciates it." Trey let all three out on a sparkling after-the-rain spring morning. "I'm putting the manor on our subscription list."

"For what? *Vogue, GQ*? Porn?"

"You don't have to subscribe to porn as long as there's the internet. Not that I know anything about that."

"Of course not. And this is my I-believe-that face."

He studied it. "You need more work on that one. Anyway. Subscription for pet food and treats. Mookie eats here often enough—Jones, too, for that matter—so he's paying for it."

"Out of his legal consultant paycheck."

"Naturally. It's good stuff, and they'll ship it out." He took the coffee she handed him. "Thanks."

"I'll grab something after the gym, but you should have a bagel, or risk your life with a Toaster Strudel. Have some cereal."

"I'll get something when the dogs come back in."

She walked to the window to look out. "Look, Trey, a deer. I see her now and again."

He glanced out, saw that the dogs hadn't noticed the visitor yet.

"I showed you the stuff you mix up for the sprayer in the shed. The deer repellant. You'll want to start using that."

"Oh, but . . ."

"Unless you want to have a garden for the deer to eat. That doe has friends and family."

"I don't." And yet. "You're sure it doesn't hurt them?"

Finding her worry for wildlife endearing, he tugged on her hair. "Repellant, cutie, not poison."

"All right. Owen says no bird feeders out there because the bears would come calling."

"He's right."

"We've got a lot to learn."

"Lucky you're both quick at that."

He filled the pet bowls while she finished her coffee.

"Go on, get your workout started," he told her. "I'll let them in and grab that bagel. I'd rather avoid possible mutilation over a pastry."

"Cleo might give you a pass. Once." She put her arms around him. "Since Owen's coming to dinner, you'll come, too?"

"I'm planning on it."

"And you'll let me know how things go."

He tipped her head back, kissed her. "I'll let you know how things go."

When she came back just under an hour later, she found Yoda sulking outside the servants' passage.

"Oh now, he'll be back. I guess I could've told Trey to let Mookie stay, but I didn't think of it. You've got me," she reminded him as she walked down to her bedroom. "And Pye, and Cleo. And I bet Jack'll show up to play later."

In the bedroom, she pulled out work-at-home clothes. "I'm going to shower and change, then you can hang with me while I work."

But when she'd showered and changed, he wasn't sitting on his bed waiting for her. As she started down the hall, she heard the sound of the ball bouncing on the main floor.

"Looks like Jack came to play already."

Since the boy remained skittish, she started to announce herself as she approached the stairs.

Then she saw it.

The mirror stood beside her desk. The predators framing it snapped, snarled, slithered. Its glass gleamed and showed her reflection.

A woman frozen in place, her hair loose, the tie to draw it back still around her wrist. Her face seemed pale, her eyes too big.

Then the reflection blurred so she saw only colors, vague shapes.

The pulse at her throat began to hammer.

She heard the ball bounce, the dog give chase. She heard the laughter of a young boy who'd died long before.

"I'm awake." The sound of her own voice made her jolt. "I'm not dreaming, not sleepwalking. I'm awake."

But as the gooseflesh ran over her arms, she started to back away. To call to Cleo.

Even as she stepped back, the glass of the mirror swirled. Those colors, those shapes shimmered behind it. She heard something— voices, music? But distant, like sounds echoing down a tunnel.

And she felt the pull.

Awake, aware, she walked to it. Though her hand trembled, she lifted it to the glass, watched it pass through as if through water.

She drew it back.

The tablet on her desk played Pink's "Just Give Me a Reason."

"I guess I have seven reasons," she said, and walked through the mirror.

Into the library.

Not quite the same, she realized. A fire simmered, and a different sofa faced it. Flowers flowed over the mantel, graced the table. Lamps spread light as the windows showed the dark.

She'd walked from day to night.

Why here? she wondered. And when?

Why here, she thought again, when she heard music from . . .

She closed her eyes. "The third floor," she murmured. "The ballroom?"

But she felt no need to go there, and every need to stay where she was.

"What's here?" The sound of her own voice brought a chill to her arms.

Could the rings be here? she wondered. In the library where she worked every day? But in a different time.

She started to turn, to begin a search.

Then she heard footsteps, the distinctive click of high heels on wood.

A woman stopped in the doorway, elegant in her long midnight-blue evening gown. It flowed down her tall, slim body, with a neckline that accented a teardrop sapphire pendant framed in diamonds.

She'd dressed her sandy brown hair up in a sleek and severe French twist that left a face with knife-edged cheekbones unframed. Not a single curl or wave escaped the sparkling comb that held it in place.

Matching sapphire-and-diamond earrings dripped from her ears.

The face was striking, creamy skin, faintly flushed along those prominent cheekbones with the drama of lips painted a bold red. Her eyes, wide-set, a cool pale blue under thin, sharply angled brows, scanned the room.

But passed over Sonya without a blink.

Sonya knew the face. She'd seen pictures.

She'd seen the photo of this woman in this dress. One taken, Sonya understood, on this same night. Decades before.

Patricia Youngsboro walked into the library with the air of a woman who owned it, and everything else she wanted.

As Patricia glided through the room, fingers trailing over furniture, books, flower petals, Sonya heard the music more clearly.

A woman's throaty voice sang. *Long ago and far away, I dreamed a dream one day.* The diamond on Patricia's left hand flashed light as she turned it to admire.

She gave it a satisfied smile. "And now, within the year," she murmured, "Mrs. Michael Poole of the Poole's Bay Pooles. Of Poole Ships. Mrs. Patricia Youngsboro Poole, mistress of Poole Manor."

She crossed her arms in a delighted self-hug. "And all this, when I take the Poole name, is mine. And well-earned."

She seemed amused as she took a compact out of her evening bag, and in its mirror carefully powdered her nose.

"There, perfect. As Mrs. Patricia Youngsboro Poole of Poole's Bay, of Poole Manor, must and will be, at all times. In all ways."

As Patricia turned, as Sonya watched, as the orchestra in the ballroom segued into "That Old Black Magic," Hester Dobbs stood on the steps leading to the library's second floor.

Still holding the compact, Patricia jolted, then eyed Dobbs with unfiltered distaste.

"I believe I know all the invited guests, but perhaps we haven't yet met. Who are you?"

"I am the mistress of the manor. As you will never be."

Distaste snapped into anger and flooded color into her face. "What nonsense is this! You will leave this house at once, or I will have my fiancé remove you."

"Ignorant woman. I have ruled in this house more than a hundred and thirty years." Dobbs came down another step. Her hair, her long black dress flowed as if caught in the wind. "You will have hours only."

She lifted her hands. Four rings gleamed on her left hand, one on her right.

"Hours to bask in your bride-white gown, to dance and drink champagne. That I'll give you, for the end is sweeter with it. Then like these five brides before you who sought to replace me here, you'll die a painful death in my house."

Eyes dark, gleaming dark, Dobbs came down another step.

"And the ring, so new and shining on your finger, will shine on mine."

"Get out!" Though she'd gone pale, red flags of temper flew on Patricia's cheeks. "How dare you speak to me in such a manner? I'll have you thrown out. Have you arrested."

As she turned to stride out, Dobbs sliced a hand through the stirring air. Crying out in shock, Patricia stumbled to the floor. The compact she still held fell with her, and skidded away across the floor.

The glass in its mirror shattered.

"I give you this warning, as I gave none before you, because like me, you seek power for the sake of power. This I respect."

Dobbs stood over Patricia now as the woman cowered, her face as white as another ghost.

"Come to the manor as a bride, die as a bride. Perhaps I will not revel in your pain as I did the others, but I will not regret giving you death."

Dobbs smiled, tossed back her hair as it blew in the rising wind. "Come to the manor as a bride," she repeated, "live in the manor as a wife, and know your death follows. Your pain, your blood, your tears will only feed my power."

"Stay away from me! Stay away! You're mad."

"So they say." Laughing, Dobbs lifted her arms.

Outside, thunder boomed. In the library, an ice-edged wind whirled so the flowers on the mantel, on the tables withered and died.

Books and blackened blossoms tumbled to the floor.

"So they say," she said again, with a kind of glee. "But I am mistress here, and if you enter my house as a bride, I will make your wedding gown your shroud."

Dobbs looked down at her, almost kindly. "He's weak, Michael Poole, and will never be faithful. He'll choose another, and one I'm sure to enjoy damning to death more than I would you. Go now. Make your choice."

She laughed again as Patricia pushed herself up and ran from the room.

Much as Patricia had, Dobbs wandered the room, touching, indulging.

She stopped less than two feet from where Sonya stood, turned slowly. Stared.

"Something there, something there." She muttered it as her dark eyes narrowed, as confusion clouded them. "A Poole. Yes, a Poole. One of the five, are you? Dead, all dead by my hand, by my power. You think to haunt me? I am mistress here!"

She stepped closer, and it seemed to Sonya looked directly into her eyes.

"Your blood, Poole bitch, on my hands. Your ring on my finger, dead whore. And your tears forever on my tongue. As will be the next and the next, generation by generation. I am mistress here and ever shall be. And damned to you."

When she vanished, Sonya let out the breath she'd held. She could still hear the music. She could see the glittering shards of glass from the broken compact.

Following impulse, she crossed to it. Could she touch it? she wondered. She was as much a ghost here as Dobbs had been. But . . .

She reached down, felt the shock go through her when her hands closed around the lid. Her heart skipped as she picked it up, then the puffs: one, she noted for powder, one for blush—no, rouge, she corrected.

Both had fallen out.

Carefully, she replaced them, closed their twin lids, then the cover on the oblong of gold.

Holding it, she walked to the mirror. And through.

She lowered into her desk chair. The ball bounced along the hall downstairs as she stared at the compact in her hand. Clover greeted her with Katy Perry's "Roar."

She'd brought it back, she thought, dazed. She'd brought this object back through the mirror with her.

Maybe she wasn't up to roaring because everything felt so shaky, but she'd brought it back with her.

As Cleo came down the hall, the ball stopped bouncing.

Cleo lifted a hand in her usual half wave, then stopped.

"Jesus, Sonya, you're dead white. What happened? What—"

She broke off as she rushed in, and Sonya held up the compact.

"It's beautiful. Art Deco. Where did you find it?" As she asked, Cleo opened it. "Oh, the mirror's broken. That's a shame."

"It broke when she dropped it."

Cleo put a hand on Sonya's shoulder. "Who dropped it?"

"Patricia Poole. Well, not Poole yet. I think it was her engagement party. No, I know it was. The dress, like in the photo Deuce had. The same dress and hairstyle."

"Did you dream that? Did you go through the mirror again last night?"

"No. Just now, here. In the library. I need to—"

Shifting in her chair, Sonya lowered her head between her knees.

"Are you going to be sick?" Instinctively, Cleo pulled back Sonya's hair.

"No, no, just . . . a little lightheaded. A little shaky."

"Just breathe, baby." Gently, Cleo rubbed Sonya's back. "I'll get you some water."

"No, I . . . I think I need air more. I'll go outside, get some air."

"You wait. I need shoes and a sweater. You stay right there for a minute."

Sonya didn't argue, but did sit up again as Cleo dashed to her room. She raced back wearing sneakers and dragging on a cardigan.

"We'll go slow."

"It's already better. I just want some air." But she picked up the compact to take with her. "I came up to shower and change after a workout. We were up pretty early. God, you haven't even had coffee yet."

"Don't worry about it." Cleo kept an arm around her as they walked down the stairs.

"Yoda, Jack." As Sonya said his name, the dog raced back down the hall. The cat came with him. "I guess Pye, too. I was going to call out that I was coming down, then I saw it."

When Cleo opened the front door, the cat and dog ran out ahead of them.

"God, that feels good." Sonya took two deep gulps of fresh air. "Better, really better. I saw it, the mirror, in the library."

"Why didn't you call me?"

"I was going to," Sonya said as they walked. "But then . . . I needed to go through. It was as if I had to go through right then. And when I did, I was in the library. But before. Different sofa, different lamps, flowers. Music and voices from upstairs. The ballroom. And it was night. Fire going, the lamps lit.

"And she walked in. Patricia came in."

Sonya told her, from start to finish, pulling out the details. Ones she'd never forget.

"They didn't see me, Cleo, neither of them. Patricia went from arrogant, superior, furious to terrified in a matter of minutes."

"Being knocked down by a ghost who threatens to murder you will do that. Dobbs warned her, warned her off because she actually liked her."

"I don't know if she's capable of liking anyone, but she understood and respected the thirst for power. And figured Michael Poole would pick someone else, more to her taste, I guess it is."

"But Patricia married Michael anyway. Just didn't come back to the manor."

"Terrified," Sonya concluded, "but calculating. And Dobbs had to wait a full generation more."

"For Clover."

"Yeah, God. Dobbs didn't see me, Cleo, but when Patricia ran out, when she wasn't there for Dobbs to focus on, she felt me. It confused her, pissed her off, I could see both all over her. She thought I was one of the five brides she'd killed at that point. And when she vanished, I walked over to this."

Sonya pulled the compact out of her pocket. The gold gleamed as if freshly polished in the sunlight.

"I didn't see how I could actually pick it up, but, like with the mirror, I felt I had to. And I did. Picked it up, picked up the puffs, closed it up."

She stopped, turned to Cleo with the compact in her hands. "I brought it back through. From then to now. She dropped this eighty years ago, but I'm holding it."

"In your father's sketches, he had ones of him and Collin, as boys, exchanging toy cars. But that's not the same. They were in different places, but the same time. You were in the same place, but different times."

"If I could bring this back, doesn't it mean I could bring something else back?"

"Like the rings."

"Yes, yes! Like the rings. Somehow get them from her, or get there before she takes them. I don't know. But I think I felt compelled to try to pick this up off the floor because I needed to see I could. I had to go through at that time so I could see what happened."

"We know why Patricia closed the manor, refused to go back into it."

"The thing is, Dobbs didn't see me. She did before, even spoke to me when Marianne died. Knocked me on my ass when I tried to get to Lisbeth in the ballroom."

"More than that. Yeah, you were awake when you went through with Owen, but you hadn't been. And every other time, you haven't been aware."

Puzzling it out brought a light throb to her temple. Rubbing at it, Sonya puzzled more. "So maybe deliberate—awake, aware the whole time. I don't know. It's a lot to think about. But I have this."

She looked down at the compact, ran her hand over the raised design in the gold. "And we know Dobbs scared off Patricia from moving into the manor. From having her wedding reception here, from being mistress of the manor."

She turned the compact so the sunlight caught the gold and the raised Art Deco design on the top. "It is beautiful. I'm taking it with me when I go to see Gretta Poole. I'm going to call the memory center and make arrangements."

"I'm going with you. I'm not taking no this time," Cleo insisted. "I really don't think you should make the trip alone. Look, I doubt they'll give you much time with her. If it's an hour, I'll be surprised. Yoda and Pye will be fine while we're gone."

"Okay, all right, I just hate taking you away from your work when you're close to finishing."

"I'm going to be done in a day or two, ahead of deadline, so taking a morning or afternoon off is fine. And I hope it's afternoon."

"I'll go up and call now. And you need your coffee."

"All this gave me a wake-up jolt that beats the hell out of coffee. But I still want it. Oh! Look!"

Cleo pointed out to sea where a whale sounded.

"That's never going to be a *So what* for me. And I'm taking it as a sign," Sonya decided. "A good omen."

"Now you sound like me."

After its strange start, the rest of the day ran smooth. So smoothly, Sonya worked past her usual hour, and only surfaced when Yoda raced downstairs barking his greeting.

"I was going to change." But the clock told her she'd missed that opportunity. "Oh well."

She saved her work, shut down.

Cleo played "It's Raining Men," and made her laugh.

"Fun, but it should be only two of them."

As she went down, it occurred to her she hadn't heard anyone come in. Since Yoda didn't sit, wagging, by the front door, she assumed Trey or Owen or both of them went around back for the dogs.

She found Cleo in the kitchen. "You're already cooking. I got caught up."

"Under control. Main's in the oven, and I'm going to mash these potatoes, do some peas—but not the mushy kind. I let Yoda and Pye out because I saw Mookie there. Trey didn't come in?"

"Not yet." Curious, she walked to the door herself. When she opened it, she squealed and ran out.

"What? What is it?" Cleo followed after her.

"Yoda's house!"

She watched Trey and Owen, and the ever-obliging John Dee, muscle it around the corner.

"Side of the shed," Owen ordered.

"Oh, but—"

He ignored Sonya. "Side of the shed. It's got electric and the concrete pad extends under the overhang."

Too charmed to argue, she followed them.

It looked exactly the way she'd drawn and designed, with its mansard roof, the turret, and arched windows. He'd arched the doorway, too, and above it he'd put a sign bearing Yoda's name.

"It's really big," Cleo said.

"So he can have guests over. Oh, it's just stately! I love how it reflects the manor. It's got a little chimney!"

When they set it down, with a trio of grunts, Yoda went straight in.

"He likes it. He already likes it."

"He's got himself some cool digs." John Dee scratched his beard under his grin.

Owen got down on the ground, reached between the back of the house and the shed.

"I have to see." And Sonya crawled in after her dog. "Oh, oh, oh!"

The tray ceiling, the fancy tile floors, a regal little bed with—as she reached over and tested—a trundle for overnight guests. The little electric fireplace and a toy box, already filled.

"Hit the switch on the fireplace," Owen called out. "On the right."

When she did, low, simulated flames came on.

"It works! It's wonderful."

"Floor heat's set on low. Leave it alone."

Yoda snagged an orange bone out of the toy box, and wagged.

"He loves it, Owen. I love it." She backed her way out. Before she could stand, Mookie and Jones went in.

"They all fit! It's perfect. You're a genius."

"You designed it." He nodded at his work. "Fair trade."

"I'm going to agree," Trey said, "since I've seen the oiled and polished-up desk in his workshop. It's a beauty. Thanks, John Dee, for the hand. This thing's a monster."

"No problem. That's a hell of a doghouse."

"Stay for dinner." Cleo bent to look through the arched window. "We've got plenty."

"Ah now, that's real nice, but Kevin's already got that going. I'd better get on."

"Wait just a minute." Sonya ran into the house, then back with a bottle of wine. "For your dinner. You and Kevin."

"Ah now, you don't have to do that. But I'll take it."

When he left, Owen got down, switched off the fireplace.

"It's a nice night. They don't need it. What's for dinner?"

"Crap! I need to finish." Turning on her heel, Cleo headed inside.

"Thank you." Sonya kissed Owen, then turned to Trey. "And thank you to the assistant builder." And kissed him before she laughed.

The cat perched on the roof of Yoda's house.

"Another seal of approval. Let's go in. I've got another tale to tell, and I'm ready for wine."

"Trey filled me in on the last one. What's she cooking?"

"I don't know. Something that goes with mashed potatoes and peas."

As they trooped into the kitchen, Owen sniffed the air. Then he moved around Cleo while she riced boiled potatoes, and opened the oven.

"You made meatloaf."

"I decided to try my hand at it."

Before she could reach for another potato, he swung her around, dipped her low, and kissed her.

Then swung her back up, fluidly. "Meatloaf does that to me."

"I'll keep that in mind."

She went back to her potatoes, but smiled.

"And I say Cleo's meatloaf calls for red wine," Sonya announced.

"I'll get it." Trey went to the butler's pantry for a bottle. "Let's hear the tale."

Sonya got out plates. "You could say the mirror came to me again. Only this morning, when I was wide awake. And in the library."

She put the plates on the table, went back for flatware.

"Your instinct's going to be to get upset." She glanced over as he uncorked the wine. "Try to hold back on that until I finish."

He poured wine, handed her a glass. "You can't finish unless you start. Let's hear it."

Chapter Eighteen

He didn't interrupt, nor did Owen. It was Cleo who interrupted the story.

"We're going to eat this while it's hot. Sonya can finish while we do. Owen, take this bowl of potatoes to the table. Trey, you can take the peas."

At the table, Cleo sliced the meatloaf, served it while Sonya told them about Dobbs and her appearance on the library stairs, and all that happened after.

When she was done, Trey took a slow sip of wine.

"We agreed you'd call me."

"Trey, Cleo was just down the hall. I could've shouted for her, or gone to get her. And I started to. But . . . I can't explain it, not rationally, but it was the same as the night in the ballroom. I had to go through. I needed to. Not a whim, not thinking I'd just handle it myself. A need."

"It wasn't like that for me," Owen said. "I didn't feel that—pull, you called it. I felt something, but not that. But I know you did."

He met Sonya's eyes, then shifted his gaze to Trey's.

"You know that, too. It's hard not to be here when shit happens, but shit's going to happen."

"I was wobbly when I came back," she admitted. "Then Cleo was right there. I know it sounds crazy, but I think it was, somehow, timed that way. Timed for me to go in, come out, for Cleo to get up and come."

"It doesn't sound crazy." Briefly, Trey laid a hand over hers. "It doesn't. And Owen's right, I do know, and it is hard. And getting past that, there's a lot more here. She didn't see you, and she has before. And you brought something back with you."

"The compact. It's in my desk. I'll go get it."

"After dinner." This time he gave her hand a squeeze. "And it's great, Cleo."

"No, my meatloaf's great," Owen disagreed. "This is, and it hurts a little, superior. I'm having some more."

As he took a second helping, of everything, he looked back at Sonya. "A guy wants to protect the ones who matter to him, especially if you're Trey. Tough for you. You're dealing with things most people wouldn't just walk away from. They'd run like hell. That goes for both you and Lafayette here."

"You're not running," Cleo pointed out.

"Jones and me? We like a good fight. Add that bitch killed some of my family. Back when doesn't matter. It's family."

Trey looked over at his friend, raised his glass. "And there you have it."

"Speaking of family," Sonya began, "I've arranged to visit Gretta Poole tomorrow. I kept putting that off, and it feels like, after this morning especially, I should at least make that connection."

"I can shift some things around and go with you."

"You would, you would shift things around, and I appreciate it. But Cleo's going with me. We're both at a point in our work where we can take a few hours away from it."

"Don't expect much," Trey warned her. "I went with my father to see her right after Collin died. She didn't recognize him at all, probably because she thought I was Deuce. Went on about how she knew I'd talked Collin into going into the manor. I got a lecture on that.

"A couple minutes later, when Dad tried to explain to her that Collin wouldn't be able to come see her, she talked about having an uncle named Collin who'd died in the war and left a young widow and baby behind."

"Did she? I don't remember reading that in the Poole family history."

"No. Dad and I figured she mixed together Collin, the family history, and the fictional fiancé her mother made up for her. At the end, she got agitated, claimed her mother would be there any minute, and didn't approve of her talking to strangers."

"I went to see her once."

Cleo lifted her eyebrows at Owen. "Once?"

"With her reaction to me, her doctors didn't recommend a return trip. She thought I was Charlie, her brother. Your bio grandfather."

Sonya studied him, thought of the wedding day dream. "There's a definite family resemblance, but not really all that close."

"Close enough for her. She was happy to see me at first, but that didn't last. She got . . ."

He trailed off, shrugged. "We can use Trey's *agitated*. Everything was my fault. I ruined her life, she'd never get away now, go to New York, and be an artist. Why did I come back? Suddenly this old lady's calling me a cocksucker and screaming at me to go away and never come back."

"Everyone's told me Gretta was weak and subservient and mild," Sonya said quietly. "I'd say there's a lot of pent-up rage inside."

"Well, she sure as hell let it out that time."

"You left out the part," Trey reminded him, "where she went at you, thinking you were Charlie, her brother, and scratched up your face."

Owen shrugged again, ate more meatloaf. "It healed up."

Clover went with Beyoncé's "Crazy in Love."

"I know you were. And none of this," Sonya said firmly, "is Charlie's fault or yours. It's Patricia's, and if Gretta didn't stand the fuck up to her, that's on Gretta, not her brother. I'm going to get the compact."

"Guess I shouldn't've mentioned it." Owen watched her storm out of the room.

"No," Trey disagreed. "She, and you, Cleo, have to know what you're going to be up against. She's pissed because she takes responsibility for her own actions and decisions and doesn't toss the blame for them around."

"I'll repeat." Now Cleo raised her glass. "And there you have it. The three most important qualities a woman, a smart woman, wants in a partner? In no particular order. That they understand and respect the woman for who and what she is. That they're sexually compatible. That they're not an asshole. I can't speak from personal experience about one of those qualities, but you nail the other two."

"Thanks."

Obviously still . . . agitated, Sonya streamed back in.

"You know, I really regret neither of those women could see me this morning, so I could tell them just what I thought of them."

She sat, set the compact down on the table.

"And I'm already reminding myself I can't tell Gretta Poole what I think of her. She lived a lie, was culpable in separating brothers. She had a choice, and she chose the lie. Instead, she wants to blame her own brother for doing what she didn't have the freaking balls to do. Live his own life."

"She's sick, Sonya."

"Yes." She nodded at Trey. "And by the time I see her, I'll have that in the forefront. But not right now. Okay."

She swiped her hands in the air as if clearing it.

"This is a Lucien Lelong compact. He was a French fashion de-signer. He also had a perfume line, designed compacts, lipstick cases, and so on. I looked it up."

"Of course you did." Trey picked up the case. "So you'd carry this in your purse?"

"Yes. Or evening bag in this case. Other than the broken mirror, it's in perfect shape. And inside?" She waited for Trey to open it. "The powder, the rouge barely show use. Same with the puffs. She could've replaced those, but . . ."

"You think this was fairly new," Trey finished, "when she dropped it."

"I can't date it exactly, but it's from the forties, so it may have been a few years old. But I think it's not. It just feels new. Which really doesn't matter."

"But it's curious. It's interesting."

"Can I see it?" Owen held out a hand. He closed it, turned it, frowned over it. "I don't know anything about this stuff, but I think Clarice has something like this." He ran his thumb over the raised design.

"One of the cousins?"

"Yeah." He flicked a glance at Sonya. "Yours and mine. Yeah, she's got a couple of things like this in a display cabinet in her house. Tubes, cylinders? A couple of them and something like this."

He handed it back to Sonya. "Queen P—I remember hearing people call her that behind her back when she was still coming in to the shipyard—liked Clarice. Clarice has a serious head for business and a get-it-done-right work ethic. Plus, she's not stupid otherwise, and knew how to play the old lady. I'm remembering she left Clarice some of her personal stuff."

He gestured at the compact. "Like that."

"So a set," Cleo concluded. "Lipstick case, perfume case, maybe a mirror case, or just a powder compact."

"Probably. Same design, so some sort of set anyway. I didn't know her all that well. She wasn't especially fond of me. Liked my work fine, but on a personal level not so much. After all, I hung out with bad companions."

"Which would be me," Trey put in with a laugh. "And the mystery of why she wasn't fond of the Doyles is solved by learning my grandmother told her to suck it."

"Do tell," Cleo said, so Trey did.

"Your grandmother sure as hell stood up for herself." Sonya rose to let the animals out. "And that's currently my favorite story."

"I do know the old lady was obsessive about things matching," Owen continued. "Her office was like some static showroom, same with her house. I guess it's a style but with no imagination."

"Rigid. It fits." When Cleo started to get up to clear, Trey waved her back down.

"We've got it. Meatloaf."

"That's fair." Owen rose, grabbed plates. "We'll get this done before I have to take off."

"You could stay."

He started to tell Sonya thanks but no thanks, then caught Trey's eye. "Yeah, why not?"

"Look, Cleo, Pye's on top of the doghouse again."

"She likes heights. She's loving her new cat tree. Speaking of cats. I was wondering, Owen. Sonya and I have to go to Boston in a few weeks."

"Yeah, the Ryder deal."

"Trey's going to take Yoda. I was wondering if you and Jones would take Pye."

He glanced over his shoulder. "You waited until I had two servings of meatloaf in me to ask that. Smart. I respect smart. Sure."

"Thanks. Is anyone in the mood for video games? We've got the whole setup, but Sonya refuses me."

"Because I'm crap at video games."

"No, not really."

"You say that because whenever you talk me into it, you beat me into the ground."

Trey glanced over. "Don't tell me you're a sore loser."

"Okay, I won't tell you. But if everyone plays, I'll play."

They headed back to childhood with *Super Mario*, with *Sonic*, then changed it up with sports.

They trounced her. Sonya came close with baseball, but still went down.

Owen set down his controller. "You're really terrible at this."

"I know! Didn't I say? It's not hand-eye coordination. I have good hand-eye coordination. It's not reflexes because mine are just fine. It's—"

"VGCD," Trey suggested. "Video game controller deficiency."

"That's it!" Laughing, she leapt at it. "I have VGCD, and it's nothing to be ashamed of. And due to my VGCD, I'm permanently excused from participating."

"At least I have new gaming partners. Worthy ones." Cleo waggled her controller. "One more round?"

"One more." Owen picked his up again. "I like retiring a winner."

Happily enough, Sonya settled back to watch. She might suck due to VGCD, but the bright spot? They'd put yet another room in the manor to good use. Bright, noisy use.

And by the time they all went up near to midnight, no one and nothing had complained about it.

It started at three. First the trio of chimes, and the drift of music. The heartbreak of weeping, the sounds of doors opening, doors closing, and the ominous creaking.

Sonya reached for Trey's hand and closed her eyes again.

A driving guitar riff blasted from both their phones.

Even as she shot up in bed, Trey was rolling out of it. Both dogs sprang up to growl. As the single word, shouted, repeated, *Thunder!* joined the guitar, it boomed like cannon fire outside.

Wind, screaming like an animal in pain, hurled rain against the windows.

And downstairs, something beat, giant fists, against the grand mahogany doors.

"Stay close," Trey ordered, and was already moving fast out of the room.

Seconds after he started down the hall, Owen came out of his room, then Cleo hers.

"'Thunderstruck,'" Owen said. "And I'm all about AC/DC, but that's a fucking rude awakening."

"She—Clover—wanted to warn us." Cleo reached for Sonya's hand. "Even if it was only seconds."

"It's coming from upstairs, too."

Trey glanced up as Sonya had. "Yeah, it is." Up and down the hall, every door slammed. "And here, too."

"She's been saving this up," Owen said as smoke crawled along the stairs from the third floor.

Something began to wail, and the sound seemed to come from everywhere at once.

Every light went out.

"Shit, shit, I didn't grab my phone. Everybody, stay here, right here," Trey ordered. "I'll go back for it."

"Hold on." Owen switched on a little flashlight. "Always have this in my pocket. Good thing I pulled on my pants."

"There's one in my room," Cleo said. "On my nightstand, right-hand side of the bed."

"I'll get it. Like the man said: Everybody, stay here."

"It's like the time she made me think there was someone outside in a snowstorm. Only worse. When I went down, opened the door, it stopped."

"We'll try that." Guided by the sound of her voice, Trey took Sonya's other hand.

Owen came back with two narrow beams cutting through the ink-black dark. He handed one to Cleo, then aimed his toward the stairs. "She's pulling out the special effects," he said as smoke curled up the walls and blood ran down them.

"We're going down. You've got the light and the lead, Owen," Trey told him. "Watch your step."

They started down as the wailing turned to moaning, then the moaning to shrieking.

The cat abruptly turned, streaked back up. As Cleo turned to call her, she saw Pye run up the steps toward the third floor.

"Damn it!" Calling, she ran after the cat.

"Well, shit!" Owen shoved his flashlight at Trey. "I'll get them. Go."

"We'll get to the door." Sonya fought panic. "We'll get to the door and open it, and it'll all stop. Like before."

"Don't rush. This light doesn't help much."

"She wants our fear. She can't have it."

Since the dogs all barked in front of the door, she followed the sound as much as the narrow beam of light.

"Take it." Trey pushed the light into her hand, grabbed the door handle.

But when he wrenched it open, the storm didn't stop.

The gale blew in.

As the dogs went wild, Trey put his shoulder against the door. "Need to close it," he shouted over the roar of wind.

The light in Sonya's hand bobbled as she pushed with Trey.

"That smoke, it's coming down, it's coming down."

Cleo felt the icy brush from the smoke on her ankles as she ran. She'd brought the cat, a living creature, into the house. She'd be damned if she'd let Dobbs cause her harm.

As she reached the third floor, something grabbed her from behind. Sucking in her breath, she jabbed back with her elbow. Owen grunted, but held on to her.

"It's me, goddamn it. Stop!"

"Pye—"

"I'll get her." He snagged the flashlight from Cleo's hand. "Stay here."

"In the dark? How about no. The door, Owen, the Gold Room door."

"I see it."

He could hardly miss the fiery red glow around it or the way the wood pulsed. Or the smoke that billowed out from it.

The cat stood less than a foot away, back arched.

"Stay behind me."

"Because you have a penis?"

"We can go with that. I also have the light, and I'm keeping it."

He didn't bother to call the cat. In his experience cats came and went as they damn well pleased. And this one was currently very pissed.

Instead, he sang, his voice calm as a lake even as he lifted it over the storm.

"Yesterday, all my troubles seemed so far away."

On a glimmer of understanding, Cleo sang with him.

The cat looked in their direction, and as they walked closer, her back relaxed.

"Yesterday came suddenly." On that, Owen scooped up the cat.

The door swung open. He didn't see Dobbs, saw nothing but dark. But he heard her.

"Poole blood will run like a river. I'll bathe in it."

"Well, that's disgusting." He handed the cat to Cleo, who murmured in his ear:

"Don't you dare go in there."

As she spoke, the door slammed shut. The storm died; the lights flashed on.

"Show's over," Owen decided.

"I couldn't let Pye just—Oh God, Sonya. Trey."

"We're fine, they'll be fine." Or nothing would stop him from going in that room. "Let's go."

When she heard their voices calling, Cleo closed her eyes in relief. Then setting the cat down, threw her arms around Sonya when they met on the second floor.

"I'm sorry, I'm sorry. I broke the first rule. Stay together."

"I'd have done the same. You're all right?"

"Yes, we're all okay. You?"

"Yes. It didn't stop when we opened the door. It got worse. But it stopped when we finally got it closed again. We're okay. Everyone's okay."

She reached back for Trey's hand, dropped it again when he hissed.

"Are you hurt? What—your hand!"

"Ice burn." Red slashed across the palm. "The door handle. It's not bad."

"I remember what to do. I remember."

"Let's have a look." Owen took Trey's hand, gave it a study. "No, not too bad. We'll fix it up. Why don't you let these guys out," he said to Cleo as they started down to the main level. "They can let off some of this middle-of-the-night energy."

"Did anything happen upstairs?" Trey asked.

"The usual." Since it was over, Cleo indulged in a quick shudder. "Smoke billowing, door glowing and pulsing. Shrieking, moaning. Pye was in front of that damned door, hissing. And Owen started singing.

"Why 'Yesterday'?"

"The melody. Soothing."

"Well, it worked. Pye calmed down. Then the door opened. I was afraid for a minute Owen would go in. What was disgusting?" she asked as she opened the door for the stampede.

"Huh?" After making sure Sonya did know what to do for an ice burn, he turned back to Cleo.

"You said, 'Well, that's disgusting.' I didn't see anything inside the room. It was too dark."

"You didn't hear her?"

"I didn't hear anything—well, other than the shrieking and moaning and blowing and thunder."

"I guess it was just for me. She said Poole blood's going to run like a river, and she'll bathe in it."

"That hits disgusting." Trey breathed out as Sonya treated his hand.

"I'm having a beer. Want a beer?"

"Yes," Trey said definitely. "Yes, I do."

"Half a glass of wine," Sonya told him.

"I'll have the other half."

"This is more red than mine was. My burn was more pink. Are you sure—"

"It's not bad." Trey leaned forward to kiss her forehead.

As he set Trey's beer down on the counter, Owen took another look at the burn. "Truth. I'd tell you if he was being Mr. Stoic. It's already calming down. Good work."

"And while she's working, I'm thinking." Trey picked up the beer with his good hand, drank. "Was it closing the door that did it? The singing—that's interesting. Or maybe all of it. You said she wants our fear, and she can't have it. You wouldn't let yourself be afraid. That's not just interesting, it's downright impressive."

"I know that's what she wants. I'm not going to give her anything she wants. But I had a couple of moments," Sonya admitted. "A hell of a couple of moments."

"Clover hit all our phones at once," Cleo pointed out. "Either she knew what was coming, or felt it. It was right before, just an instant really before it all started."

"She's looking out for us." Sonya's stomach jittered with relief when she saw the red on Trey's hand fading to pink. "All of us. And that helps me not be afraid."

She straightened, drank some wine. "It looks better, it really does. One more round," she decided. "And maybe the late-night drink will help us all get some sleep."

Trey considered as he watched Sonya apply another warm compress. "She knew we'd open the door. You had before. Logically, we'd do that again."

"She did that to the door handle, wanting whoever touched it to be hurt." Sonya removed the compress long enough to kiss the burn. "And you, Owen, I think she wanted you to go in that room. To hurt you."

"She'll have to take a bath in something besides my blood. Since everything's cool now, I'm going to let the gang back in, go up. I can grab a couple more hours of sleep."

"We'll all go up. No, this is good," Trey assured Sonya. "We've got a staff meeting at eight, and you and Cleo have that drive to Ogunquit."

"Practicality works." Sonya carried the bowl of hot water and her wineglass to the sink. "Plus, I think going back to sleep is like a thumb in her eye."

"Let's go put four thumbs in her eye." Cleo wrapped an arm around Sonya's waist. "And a number of paws."

On the second floor as Sonya and Trey continued down the hall, Owen hesitated.

"Look, Jones and I can bunk in your sitting room if you're nervous."

Cleo gave him a long look with those tiger eyes, and smiled. "That's a sweet offer, but we're fine." To prove she meant it, she gave him a kiss on the cheek. "Sweet dreams."

In his own room, Owen stripped down, dropped into bed. And lulled by the sound of the sea, fell, in his habitual way, instantly asleep.

And did dream.

Of playing chess with Collin. Chess wasn't his game, and he figured Collin dragged him into these occasional competitions just to kick his ass.

He didn't mind.

Music played, which suited them both. Collin often filled the house with sound—music, an old movie playing in the background. It occurred to him he'd developed his own affection for old black and whites here at the manor.

He didn't make it up here as often as he once had, before work and life crowded his time. But he tried to make a point of stopping in every couple of weeks, bringing up books Collin ordered from A Bookstore, or coming up with Trey.

Video games, conversation over a beer, an old flick in the movie room. Just time spent.

The connection mattered, family mattered. And he simply enjoyed Collin's company.

After pondering his next move, Owen advanced his king's pawn.

Collin sipped some of his evening brandy, and didn't ponder his next move before choosing his bishop.

"How's work?"

"It's good." Brows drawn together, Owen studied the board. "I'm working on one of Mike's designs. Fancy pleasure yacht. Client's more interested in the fancy than performance, but we'll give him both."

He moved to block the bishop, and opened his own to capture by Collin's knight.

"Well, shit."

"You have a gift."

"Not for chess."

"Not for chess," Collin agreed. "For building. For seeing something on paper, even just in your head, and making it real. For animals," Collin added with a glance to where Jones slept by the fire. "Not everyone would've taken on a wounded dog no one wanted."

"Wounded but scrappy. Scrappy counts."

Owen reached for his beer.

It didn't seem odd, in the dream, Collin's hair showed no gray, his face no lines. They sat at ease, the chess board between them, as contemporaries rather than relatives separated by a generation.

"You understand the value of friendship, as I do."

"You and Deuce go back. Like all the way back."

"We do, all the way back. You and Trey have the same sort of brotherhood, and that's a precious thing, Owen. You'll both need that precious thing to face what's coming. She needs to stop it, my brother's daughter, but you and Trey and the woman who stands as her sister have to play your parts."

Owen captured a white pawn with a black. "Like pawns?"

"Not at all. Knights, capable of crafty moves in defense and offense."

"I've already lost one of those."

"But this is only a game. Your bond with Hugh, your own brother, is strong, but you and Trey, like Deuce and I, forged that bond by choice. She saw to it I never knew my brother, my twin."

"Patricia."

"Yes." Collin looked toward the fire. "Her, and the other. And still, despite that, we had a bond. I made the choice to leave her, my brother's daughter, this house and all inside it. I would have done that regardless, but I did it with a lighter heart because of you and Trey."

"Why her? Why Sonya?"

"She's my brother's daughter," Collin said simply. "A Poole as much as you, me, the rest of us. My father and my true mother's granddaughter."

He sat back again, looked toward the fire, and at whatever he saw in the flames.

"I lost my Johanna because I refused to believe. I lost my love and any chance to have children of our own. She's what I have. Sonya's what I have, and what the manor has."

He tapped a finger on his queen. "The white queen faces the black."

Owen looked down, saw his queen had changed. He saw Dobbs, the hair, the flow of the black dress, the face carved in hard lines. Seven rings glinted on the black queen's hands.

The chess board became the manor, where shadows moved behind its windows.

"It's more than a house," Collin told him. "A man who builds knows that. Defend the white queen and cast out the black."

"How?"

"Courage," Collin said.

And Owen woke in bed to the sound of the sea breathing and the dog softly snoring.

"Okay, that was a kick in the ass."

He checked the time, decided what the hell, and rolled out of bed.

The second he did, Jones stopped snoring with a snort and lifted his head. When he saw Owen heading for the bathroom, he settled again.

He showered, dressed, and when he walked into the hall, Jones came with him. By the time he got to the kitchen, he had three dogs and a cat in tow.

Grateful that animals didn't insist on talking before coffee, he let them all out. Since he had time—or he'd decided to take it—and a long day ahead, he opted to scramble up some eggs.

But coffee first, always.

He drank the first mug watching a trio of deer come out of the woods, then retreat as the dogs—and damn if the cat didn't join in—gave chase.

They'd still need the repellant, he figured, but the dogs, and possibly the cat, would help keep the local wildlife from making an all-they-could-eat buffet out of the gardens.

He remembered that Collin had loved the gardens.

He wouldn't mind having a big yard himself, Owen considered. But when the hell would he carve out the time to deal with it? Same for the various designs he'd drawn up for finishing and expanding his house.

No time, no real motivation.

He finished the coffee, filled the food and water bowls before letting the animals back in.

Then he got down to making his own breakfast.

As he whisked eggs in a bowl, Trey came in.

"I thought you'd be gone by now."

"I'm taking another twenty." Without asking, Owen added a couple more eggs to the bowl, and waited until Trey had coffee in his hand. "If you've got twenty, I've got a story this time."

Chapter Nineteen

Before Trey could respond, Sonya came in. Something in the beat of silence had her gaze moving from man to man.

She said, "Uh-oh."

"Nothing like that." Owen held up the bowl. "Want scrambled eggs?"

"No, thanks." She went for coffee.

"I was about to tell Trey about this weird dream I had." As he spoke, Owen poured the eggs into the hot, melted butter in the pan.

Despite the lack of coffee, she whipped straight around. "You went through the mirror."

"No. And yes, I'm sure," he added before Sonya could ask. "I woke up in bed, with Jones still snoring. When my feet hit the floor, he's up. I leave the room, he's with me. It's how we roll."

"This is true," Trey confirmed.

"It's like he needs to be right there in case he has to help me fight off a horde of roaming zombies or invading, eye-sucking aliens."

"I saw that eye-sucking alien movie." Reassured, and boosted by coffee, Sonya dropped bread in the toaster. "It was terrible. I liked it."

Trey just shook his head. "Good to know. So you had a dream."

"That I don't think was just a dream. About playing chess with Collin."

Now Trey smiled. "He'd double-dare you with chess, then beat the crap out of you."

"That's why he double-dared me. It wouldn't have been so weird if that was it, even though it was way lucid. Like I could feel the chess pieces in my hand, smell the fire, taste the beer. But what really hit the weird is he was young. Like our age, Trey. His still had blond hair—not a trace of gray."

"Like my father," Sonya murmured.

"Yeah, I guess so. And his face—it's not how I see him when I think of him. I've seen pictures, sure, but it's not how I remember him."

He finished the eggs, plated them as he told them about the dream. Sonya added toast to their plates, put in more for herself, and topped off their coffee as they listened.

"It sounds like he wanted to explain to you why he left the house to Sonya. Not to you or the other cousins."

"Not necessary, but yeah, I think that was part of it."

"And the more important part? To warn you," Sonya added. "The black queen. It's a good symbol for her. He thought about my father, and I'm what's left of my father. But he clearly loved you, both of you."

"Family," Owen said simply, "and the Doyles were family to him as much as the Pooles. Maybe more. And this house? A lot more than a house for him. He took the history, the legacy, all of it to heart, and whatever he added or changed, he kept that in mind. Anyway, I sure as hell never had a dream like it."

"You're a Poole," Sonya pointed out. "And sleeping in the manor. Now that it's happened, I realize I should be surprised it hadn't happened before."

"And it could be because you've gone through the mirror now," Trey added. "But you're both missing an important point. A key point."

"Says the lawyer." Owen got up to take his plate to the sink.

"That's right, and the evidence supports that if you dreamed about Collin, and in the now, Owen—since you talked about a boat Poole's building now as well as about Sonya—Collin, some part of him, is still in the manor."

Sonya's phone erupted with "You Got That Right."

"Lynyrd Skynyrd," Owen muttered. "Never wrong. I missed that."

"Right there with you," Sonya told him. "And it makes sense. I mean if you follow manor logic, it makes sense. He's here, too. I . . . What aftershave did he wear?"

"Strange question I actually know the answer to because Anna and I got him some for his birthday once when we were kids. Eternity."

"Calvin Klein." Sonya nodded. "I should've known. Same as my father. I've caught a trace of it a few times. Just a trace, but I recognized it. Collin's still here, not just because this is home, but . . ."

"Because Johanna's still here," Trey finished.

"Yes. And he either found a way or decided it was time to connect with Owen."

"It was good to see him, talk to him. Even though, given how he looked, I'd have been a toddler."

Pausing, Owen looked at his cousin.

"He didn't have to tell me to have your back on this, Sonya. Already there."

"I know it."

"I've gotta get going. Got a fancy yacht to build among other things."

"Do you have one?" Sonya wondered. "A fancy yacht?"

"What would I want with that? I've got *The Horizon*. A sloop, a beauty who heels and hardens up like a dream. Let's move it, Jones. Later," he said, and with the dog beside him, went out the back.

"I've done a little sailing with Cleo, and I have no idea what *heels* and *hardens up* mean."

"I'd explain, but I have to get going, too. You're okay."

It wasn't a question but a statement Sonya appreciated. "I am. And if it follows pattern, after that explosive show last night, she'll need some time to gear it all up again."

"Good luck with Gretta." He kissed her, lingered. "I'm afraid you're going to need it."

He took his plate and hers to the sink.

"Do you have one? A boat?"

"I don't need one. I've got *The Horizon*. Come on, Mook."

When he left, Sonya smiled over her coffee. She'd never had a brother, but she recognized brothers when she saw them.

It seemed silly, maybe shallow, to worry about wardrobe for this visit to her great-aunt, but Sonya wanted to appear friendly and respectful.

Whether Gretta noticed or not.

By the time she got upstairs, she discovered the decision had already been made.

The sage-green dress with its high V neck and fabric belt lay on the neatly made bed. As they were paired with her earthy brown pumps, Sonya agreed with Molly's choice.

"Friendly but not frivolous, simple but not stuffy. Nice work. Nervous." She pressed a hand to her stomach. "I don't know why, but I am. She won't know me, probably won't even talk to me. This whole trip is most likely a waste of time. But I'm nervous anyway."

Clover's musical response was Bachman-Turner Overdrive's "Takin' Care of Business."

"Yeah, that's what I have to do. Take care of business, family business."

Dressed, makeup done, she debated—too long—whether to wear her hair up or down, then settled on using a clip that allowed a combination of both.

"Nearly ready!" Cleo called out from her bedroom when Sonya walked by. "Two minutes."

"I'm going to let Pye and Yoda out so they can do everything they have to do until we get back."

She found herself reluctant as she stood alone in the kitchen checking her purse one more time. Reluctant to leave the manor, to take this drive, to meet this woman who, in a very real way, had betrayed her own brother, the woman her brother loved, and two helpless infants.

But Clover had it right. Until she took care of this business, it would hang over her.

"Very nice choice," Cleo said as she came in. "You look approachable but not malleable. I overrode Molly this time, and went with the black. I thought I could fade into the background if necessary."

"This is the right thing to do."

"It is, Son. Whatever it accomplishes or doesn't, it's the right thing to do. And a necessary thing.

"I'm grabbing a couple of Cokes for the road. After last night, there can't be too much caffeine."

"Speaking of last night, Owen had a dream."

Cleo turned quickly, a Coke in either hand. "A mirror dream?"

"No. I'll explain in the car. We need to let Yoda and Pye back in. Maybe we should put out some treats for them, or more toys, or—"

"I think Jack will take care of that." Cleo handed a Coke to Sonya and went to let the animals in. "Be good, be good, my sweets. We'll be back before you know it.

"You're jumpy, I get it." Cleo patted Sonya's arm. "You drive. It'll take your mind off it. And you can tell me about this non-mirror dream I'm assuming I didn't star in."

"Not this time."

They went out to the car, where Sonya programmed the GPS. "I'm not worried about Pye and Yoda. If they need to go out again, somebody in there will let them out, and back in. I don't know why I didn't think of that before."

"Neither did I, but I'm betting you're right. In any case we're not going to be gone all that long."

"No." But the nerves kept jittering. "Couple hours. Just a couple hours. Okay, mind off what's on the other end of this drive, eyes on the road. Owen," she said, and told Cleo about the dream.

"I think that's just lovely. I think it's lovely the way Collin wanted to reach out to him, and how he did it. Take away the damn black queen for now."

"Boy, wouldn't I love to."

"For now," Cleo repeated. "Sitting over the chess board together— just the two of them—beer and brandy, music, the dog, the fire going."

"You know, I didn't think of that. He made it comfortable. Familiar."

"Exactly. Letting Owen know he was proud of him, he loved him. Things people sometimes forget to say until it's too late to say them. And the way he spoke about your dad, Deuce, Trey, the Doyles. It's meaningful."

"From my take on it, Owen understood that. He got that, and it mattered."

"So did and do you, matter. He trusted the manor to you because you're his brother's child, and because the manor matters. And he's still part of it, like Clover and Molly and the rest."

"That's what Trey pointed out, and both Owen and I missed. I should've known you wouldn't. So why did he look young? Owen's age?"

Angling her head, Cleo adjusted her sunglasses. "I've always wondered, if you need to, or choose to, stay after you die, couldn't you be any age you were?"

"You would wonder that."

"Jack, for instance, can't be a grown man because he never was. But Collin was Owen's age once, so why not? And wouldn't it put them on more even footing?"

"I thought the last part, but I never gave any thought to the other until now. Again, in manor logic, it makes sense. Some sense anyway.

"We're going to be there soon. I've thought of a dozen different ways to approach this, and still can't decide which is best."

"You can overprepare," Cleo pointed out. "I think this is a case of playing it by ear."

The memory center, housed in a rosy brick building, spread long and low over expansive grounds. It stood quiet behind gates, with a flow of gardens waiting to bloom flanking each side. Paths wound through them where people walked in twos or threes or sat together on stone benches. Bright red tulips circled a small fountain with the spill of water catching the sun in rainbows.

Trees showed their April haze of green or the first brave blossoms.

It all looked almost bucolic, but Sonya saw a woman with tears on her cheeks crossing to the parking lot.

Such was the cruelty of forgetting.

Inside, they checked in, had their identification verified, then got an overview by one of Gretta's caregivers as they walked past a common area.

People sat together, sat apart. A trio of women worked, intently, on a jigsaw puzzle.

"We offer group and individual activities, designed to stimulate or soothe all five senses. Music therapy, photographs, animal therapy. Art—which is Gretta's interest. She wanted to stay in her room this morning and draw."

The caregiver, Jen, gestured them down a hallway.

"She draws?"

"Art engages her, and comforts her. Her drawings are childlike now, but she takes pride and pleasure in them. I understand you don't know your great-aunt."

"No, I only learned about this part of my family recently."

"She wanted to be an artist when she was younger. Her son often brought her art supplies when he visited.

"We were sorry to hear of his passing."

"Does she ask about him?"

"No. She'll ask about her mother. While she still has good days, her condition has deteriorated over the last year. Though rare, she can have bursts of violence or verbal abuse. Understand, this is the disease."

"I do."

"She's having a good morning, and most often enjoys visitors."

They walked into a pretty private suite with the cheer of natural light. Dozens of drawings and paintings lined the walls. Childlike depictions of flowers, of houses with a big yellow sun overhead, Christmas trees, stick figures.

The room had a cozy sofa and chairs, a colorful floral rug.

And a table by the window where a woman sat drawing with crayons.

Her hair was stone gray and cut short. Over faded blue eyes she wore white-framed glasses that slid down her nose. And over her thin frame, she wore pink pants and a crisp white blouse.

With her tongue caught in her teeth, she hummed tunelessly as she drew.

"Good morning again, Gretta. It's Jen, and I've brought you visitors."

"Did Mother come? She said she would."

"Not today. Oh, what pretty flowers. They're so cheerful."

"Need to finish, hang it up. Pick the ones I want for my show when I go to New York."

"We'll hang it up for you, but these nice women have come to see you."

She looked up, wrinkling her nose as her glasses slid down a bit more. "You're pretty. I like pretty things."

"Thank you." Sonya offered an easy smile. "I like your art."

"I'm very talented. There are several artists on the Poole family tree. Such talents often come through the blood."

"I'm sure they can."

Gretta offered a hand. "I'm . . ." Her eyes clouded a moment. "Miss Poole. Are you an art dealer?"

"No, I'm not. But I appreciate art. I'm Sonya. Is it all right if I sit down while you work?"

"Company is always invited to sit. Manners are essential to a decent society."

"I'll be close by," the caregiver murmured, and stepped out of the room.

"It's very kind of you to pay a call. May I offer you some refreshment?"

Though surprised by the offer, Sonya smiled again. "No, thank you. We're fine. Is there anything we can get for you?"

"Oh, I have everything I need, and Mother will be here soon. We'll have a civilized tea when she arrives. I will have to start packing shortly. There's so much to do before I leave for New York. And I still have to pack and buy my train ticket. Is that where you're from?"

"New York? No, I'm from Boston originally."

"Mother and I travel to Boston twice a year to shop for the season. Mother has an image to maintain at work, and hosts important dinner parties for important people. One must be appropriately dressed at all times. Mother selects my wardrobe, of course. Mother has excellent taste."

Sonya had an image of a young woman led around on a leash. But pushed it away.

"I'm sure she does. I always enjoyed shopping in Boston, but Cleo and I live in Poole's Bay now."

"Who is Cleo?"

"My friend." Sonya gestured to where Cleo sat.

"She's very pretty. She could be an artist's model. I don't use models for my art. I enjoy painting still lifes and landscapes primarily. It's good to have friends, but of course, when you're a member of an important family, they must be carefully chosen."

The leash she'd envisioned now ended in a choke chain.

"Do you have friends in Poole's Bay?"

"I'm very busy with my art. Very busy." Then she frowned. "I know you."

"I'm Sonya."

"No. No. I don't know that name. It sounds foreign, and I don't know that name. But I know those eyes. Poole green. Mine are blue, like Mother's."

Sonya thought of Trey's word—*agitated*—as Gretta picked up another crayon.

"She'll be here soon. Mother is a very busy woman, and is always punctual."

"I have something of hers." Sonya reached in her purse, brought out the compact.

"Where did you get that!" Gretta started to reach for it, then snatched her hand back. "Not supposed to touch Mother's things. So pretty, so shiny! But mustn't touch. No. No. She'll be angry."

"You've seen this before?"

"Not that, like that. You shouldn't have that."

"I found it," Sonya said carefully. "In the manor. Cleo and I live in the manor now."

"No, you don't!" The words whipped out as the eyes behind the white-framed glasses went hard and bright. "Nobody does. Mother says it's an albatross, but Papa won't sell it. I'm not allowed to go there. No one is."

"Charlie went there. Charlie lived there with his wife, Lilian."

"Charlie was bad! He never listened, always in trouble." Her voice went to singsong, like a child's. "He went away. I stayed. I was good, he was bad."

"He was an artist, like you."

"He had responsibilities to the family, to the business. He—he shirked them. The manor is bad. I painted it once, and Mother destroyed it. It's cursed," she said in a whisper. "Locked up tight."

Then smiling, she continued to draw.

"But I'm going to New York. I'll have my own apartment. Are you from New York?"

"Charlie unlocked the manor and lived there with Lilian."

Gretta's mouth twisted, and the point of the crayon broke as she dug it into the paper.

"Gold digger, digging for Poole gold. Deserved what she got. And Charlie, too. Didn't listen." She began to color furiously, dragging Scarlet over the paper like blood.

"Go against Mother, pay the price. Lock it up, lock it all up and throw away the key."

She set the Scarlet aside, picked up Midnight Blue. Scribbling, scribbling, she formed odd figures beneath a bloody sky.

Understanding she might never be able to ask again, might never have the answer, Sonya pressed.

"How did she choose? How did your mother choose which baby to keep, Gretta? How did she decide which of Charlie's sons to keep?"

Gretta laid a finger over her lips. "Family secret. Just between mother and daughter. Not Lawrence. Useless. He likes boys instead of girls. More secrets. Nobody can know. He's dead anyway. Lawrence is dead. It's just Mother and me. Just us two now."

"I'm family, Gretta. I'm a Poole." Sonya glanced down at the crude drawing of two babies, fists raised as if for a fight as the sky above them bled red. Sonya tapped both. "How did you choose?"

"'Pick one, pick one. Doesn't matter which.' Only one to preserve the line. They looked the same. One stays, one goes. And never, never tell."

"You picked."

"I didn't want either. I'm going to New York." Again she put her finger across her lips. "Another secret. Lots of secrets. Mother said I had to pick one. And now I'm Mother, too. Mother said I had a fiancé, oh, very handsome! His name was . . ."

Frowning, she stared up at the ceiling.

"Doesn't matter. Doesn't matter. He's tall and brave and had to go to war and fight. He has blond hair and blue eyes, and we love each other so much. He died, though, very sad, but I had a baby anyway.

"I didn't want a stupid baby! Poole blood, Poole line, Poole business. Poole secrets. Never, never say Charlie's baby. Gretta's baby. Do my duty. Fucking duty."

She grabbed Black, drew angry slashes over one of the babies she'd drawn.

"Charlie's dead, and that's that. He cried and cried and cried, but he's my baby now."

"And his brother?"

"What brother?"

Angling her head left, right, left again, she chose Mountain Meadow to create flower stems.

"Collin's brother. His twin brother."

"Who knows? Who cares? I only had one baby. Mother named him . . ."

"Collin."

"Collin Poole hanged himself. Everybody knows that."

"The baby you raised was Collin, too."

"I wasn't a good mother, because he didn't listen. Like his father. 'You chose poorly, Gretta.' They looked the same, didn't they?"

Gretta clenched her teeth: anger, exasperation.

"How could I know I'd pick the one who wouldn't listen and behave? I followed all her rules, I did my best."

"I'm sure you did."

"Stayed, didn't I?" Her mood darkened again as she grabbed Wild Strawberry for petals. "I stayed in Poole's fucking Bay saddled with a stinky crying baby. I did my duty, not like goddamn fucking Charlie."

Snarling, she drew a stick figure with Black, and put it in a hangman's noose.

"Hanged himself. Pooles do that. Selfish bastard ruined everything for me. He didn't do his duty, did he? Went where the fuck he wanted, did what the fuck he wanted, getting some gold-digging street whore pregnant. The manor killed him, so he got what he deserved."

The fury exploded out of her as she stared at Sonya.

"You've got his eyes. Poole-green eyes. You'll die there, too. Mine are blue, like Mother's. Stay away from the manor. Everyone dies there."

As quickly as it had erupted, the anger died. She sent Sonya a vague smile.

"This has been a lovely visit. I hope to have a showing of my art in a few months at an important gallery in New York. I'll see you receive an invitation."

"Thank you." Sonya rose.

"The maid will see you out. Please ask her to have Mother come in when she gets here, and bring tea. Mother's so busy, I wouldn't want to keep her waiting."

Outside, Cleo put an arm around Sonya's shoulders. "That was sad and horrible."

"It's a sad and horrible disease, and after what seems like a very sad and horrible life. I'm sorry for her."

She stopped at the car, just leaned against it, because she wanted the air for a few minutes.

"My take—and tell me if yours is different. She lived under her mother's rule, and rules, where Charlie didn't. He got away. But I think she was planning to do the same."

"To New York."

"She was a bit older than Charlie, so she'd probably come into some of her trust fund. It sounds like she had plans to use that, move to New York, get an apartment, focus on her art."

Cleo nodded. "And then."

"Yeah, and then. Browbeaten into choosing one of the twins, taking it as her own, a product of some bogus engagement."

"The resentment." Cleo looked back at the building. "It's still festering. All these years."

"Because she was too weak to refuse to live that lie, to refuse to go along, to stop her brother's sons from being separated."

Again, Sonya took the compact from her purse. "A woman nearly eighty still afraid to touch her mother's things."

"And yet, waiting with some anticipation for her mother to come. Why don't I drive back?"

"Would you?" Sonya handed over the key fob. "She remembers," she said as she got into the passenger seat. "Just as they told me. Remembers things from back then better, I think, than she remembers things from yesterday."

"That spurt of rage? And that was rage—like Owen told us about. That's bottled up in there."

"That horrible drawing."

"She drew her rage," Cleo decided. "What would it do to someone, living a lie like that, resenting every minute of it? Doing what she saw as her duty and giving up a dream?"

"And never having a life of her own. Never, that I've heard of, having real friendships, a relationship. Living under her mother's roof and rules, even after for the rules, after her mother's death."

"You know more than you did before we came."

"I can see it, but I'll never understand it. Can you imagine Patricia standing with Gretta over those babies and telling her to pick one? Like they were puppies in a kennel, or worse, shoes on a shelf."

"All in all, Son, your dad was lucky. He had parents who loved him instead of a woman who did what she felt forced to do. Her duty."

"You couldn't be more right." She thought of the compact in her purse, then pulled out her phone. "I'm going to call Poole Shipbuilders, see if Clarice is in and will talk to me."

"Now?"

"While it's all right here in my head. You can drop me off if she'll make time for me. I'll get someone to give me a ride home."

"I'll drop you off, run some errands. You can text me when you're done, and I'll pick you up."

"Great. First, I'd better see if I can have some time with Cousin Clarice."

Sonya got her first up-close look at Poole Shipbuilders. The original brick building Arthur Poole had built as a young, enterprising man had expanded over the centuries, the generations.

It spread and dominated its portion of Poole's Bay, and its shipyard that had spawned a village. Had, she thought, built the manor where she now lived.

"It's bigger than you think," Cleo commented as she wound through the lot, section by section, toward the area designated for visitors. "It's impressive."

"Intimidating and strange. Strange that I own a piece of them. A tiny one, but still a piece. That building there, that's the offices. Clarice is on the fifth floor.

"Okay." She took a deep breath. "Wish me luck."

"You know I do, but why would you need it? Text when you're done."

Sonya got out, crossed to the entrance with its careful landscaping and dignified sign.

POOLE SHIPBUILDERS, ESTABLISHED 1781.

She went through a wide glass door and into a lobby that immediately put her more at ease.

They'd stuck with tradition with models of ships, portraits of generations of Pooles from the founder, Arthur Poole, she noted, right down to Owen.

Floors—wood planked rather than tile or carpet—gleamed. A waiting area with comfortable chairs boasted a brick fireplace with a thick wooden mantel. It held a model of a sailing vessel and a pair of antique lanterns.

When she crossed to the reception counter—wood again, not sleek but smooth—the woman behind it smiled.

"You must be Ms. MacTavish. Ms. Poole said to expect you. If you wouldn't mind signing in. I'm Noelle, by the way, Corrine Doyle's niece."

"Oh, it's nice to meet you."

"You, too. If you take the elevator to five, Ms. Poole's admin will be waiting for you."

"Thanks."

She crossed to the elevator. Before she could push the up button, it opened. Owen got off, carrying a design tube and looking rushed.

He pulled up short when he saw Sonya. "Hey. Are you looking for me?"

"No. I'm here to see Clarice."

"Okay. Gotta go." Then he stopped again. "Do you know where you're going?"

"Fifth floor."

"Yeah, then take a right, all the way down. Corner office. Later."

As he strode away, Noelle called out, "Owen, you've got that four o'clock with Mike. He's coming to you."

"Yeah, yeah, yeah."

When he kept going, Sonya stepped on the elevator, took a last look at Arthur Poole's portrait, then pushed five.

Chapter Twenty

On five, she stepped into a smaller, busier lobby, where a woman with flaming red hair and wearing a spring-green suit waited.

"Ms. MacTavish, I'm Adele Loring, Ms. Poole's assistant. I'll escort you to her office."

"Thank you. It's a lovely building, and an amazing view," she added as the wide, sea-facing window drew her gaze.

"We think so. Can I bring you in some coffee, tea?"

"No, thanks. I appreciate Clarice making time for me, and won't keep her long. I know she's busy."

"Always. Busy and tireless. They seem to be Poole traits."

They passed offices—doors open, doors closed, and the productive sound of keyboards.

Doors stood open at the end of the hallway, and the wall of windows didn't just draw the gaze, it astonished it.

They ran floor to ceiling, offering the sweep of the rugged, rocky coastline. It opened the room to the flow of bay and marina into the sea. And the sweep of boats—pleasure and work—that plied it.

At the large desk that looked as if it might have belonged to Arthur Poole himself sat a woman who carried her forty-six years lightly. She wore her dark blond hair in a short wedge that suited the diamond shape of her face, and a sweep of bangs that accented those Poole-green eyes.

She rose when the admin stepped in with Sonya, and added surprise as she barely topped five-two.

Sonya had expected tall and formidable, but the woman who came around the desk was petite in a pair of red running shoes and an all-business dark suit.

She held out a hand.

"Sonya, it's great to finally meet you."

Petite or not, the handshake hit formidable. "It's great to meet you. Thanks for taking time out of your day for me."

"Don't be silly."

Clarice waved that away, but Sonya knew when she was being measured.

"How about a cappuccino? I'm dying for one."

"I'm not silly enough to turn one down."

"Coming right up," the admin said, and slipped out.

"Let's sit over here. I've been glued to my desk all morning."

She gestured to a seating area with a cream-colored sofa, two chairs the color of the sea, and a table that looked as old as the desk.

"First, Owen tells me you've settled into the manor very well."

"Yes. It's an amazing home, and I love it. I understand Collin felt an obligation, but—"

"No buts." Without hesitation, Clarice pushed that aside. "Of course he did, and rightfully. None of us knew about your father, about you. I understand Collin learned about him, and you, from Deuce not long before your father's death. I'm very sorry you lost him, and sorry Collin felt unable to share he had a twin. It must have been painful for Collin.

"Thanks, Adele," she said when the admin brought in the coffee.

"We're all pleased you're in the manor, and if it troubles you, I can assure you none of us wanted it. It's beautiful, yes, and contains so much family history. But we're all very settled in our own homes."

"I'd hoped to talk to you about some of that history. I've just come from seeing Gretta Poole."

"Oh." Clarice took a sip of cappuccino. "That would've been difficult. We've tried to take turns going to see her since Collin had to put her in the center. It rarely goes well."

Over another sip, Clarice studied Sonya, and seemed to come to some decision.

"I don't remember her as a happy woman, and in the past several years her mental health has deteriorated.

"Even though he knew what she'd been a part of, that she wasn't his biological mother, Collin looked after her as a son would. I'll be frank, as that suits me best. I don't know if I'd have been as generous or forgiving."

"I think she felt, though I don't agree, she had no choice. Her mother . . ."

"If you think I'd take offense at anything you say about Patricia Poole, don't. This was her office. It's mine now. She had her way of running the business, and the family for that matter. I have mine. We have two children, my husband and I. Teenagers, twins. I can't imagine the heartlessness it took to separate the brothers. Except . . ."

She took another sip of coffee. "I knew Queen P very well, as I've worked for this company since I was sixteen—summers then, of course. She respected my business acumen, but made it clear she disapproved of Hank—my husband. She offered me a promotion and a ten-thousand-dollar bonus if I broke our engagement."

"I see."

"Bet you do." Clarice smiled and drank more coffee. "She reluctantly respected my backbone. In any case, we got along because we both invested our time and talents in the family business. Then again, I didn't know until well after her death what she'd done to the family."

"She made Gretta pick."

"I'm sorry?"

"She made Gretta pick which twin to keep, which to put up for adoption."

"How do you know?"

"From what Gretta told me."

Obviously surprised, Clarice sat back. "She told you about it?"

"Some of it. I think I opened the door by showing her this."

She took out the compact.

"I—Patricia left me three pieces with that design. May I?"

Sonya handed Clarice the compact.

"This is such a surprise. I admired the lipstick case. She always carried it. And she told me it was part of a set her husband—Michael Poole—gave her for Christmas right before their engagement announcement. She never mentioned this piece. Where did you get it?"

"I found it in the manor. The mirror's broken."

"Yes, I see."

"Gretta recognized it, too, and I was able to ask her some questions. Her mother told her to choose one baby, as only one was needed to continue to the family line. And they would say Gretta had been engaged, but the fiancé died. The baby was his. It seems people believed that."

"Not everyone," Clarice murmured. "My mother didn't. She knew Gretta, and I heard her—overheard her—talking to my aunt once, saying there was no way Gretta Poole had gotten away from her mother's hawkeye long enough to get pregnant.

"I'm sure there was a lot of gossip and speculation about it back then, but by the time I was born, it had largely died out. Except for the occasional comment like my mother's."

She started to hand the compact back.

"You should have it," Sonya told her. "It's a set, after all."

"Owen said I'd like you," she replied. "I would very much like to have it, thank you. Not because it was Patricia's, but because it's a lovely set."

"If there's anything else in the manor you'd want, I hope you'll tell me."

"Here, at the company, we display history and tradition. My home, on the other hand? I like clean, simple lines. Contemporary.

"Collin saw to it I got what was most important to me, as he did with all of us. You have a small share of the company. If you want to take a more active part—"

"Oh, I absolutely don't."

"And I'm very pleased to hear that." Laughing, Clarice finished off her cappuccino. "I'd have thrown you a bone, but we have a damn good rhythm around here. I will offer you a tour whenever you like."

"Thanks. I have to get back now. I left a cat and a dog inside the manor. But I'm glad I finally came."

"So am I. And thank you for this." She set the compact down. "It not only completes the set, but I find the broken mirror very symbolic. The woman who owned it cared far too much about appearances."

On the way out, Sonya texted Cleo, then stood in the brisk spring breeze and watched a group of people launch a boat into the bay. Curious, she moved around for a better view as they hauled the boat on some sort of wheeled platform down a long, slanted track.

Voices carried on the breeze as they worked. While she couldn't hear the words, she caught the accents—pure Maine—a bark of laughter, what sounded like a sharp command.

By the time Cleo pulled up, white sails billowed, and the couple on the deck of the boat shouted and waved to the crew on the dry dock.

The boat glided on the waters of Poole's Bay.

"I think I just saw someone take their first sail in their new boat." Smoothing her hair back, she smiled at Cleo. "It's a process."

"I want that process with my own. And Clarice?"

"I liked her, Cleo. You'll like her. She was wearing red On Cloud sneakers with—I'm pretty sure—a classic Armani suit. She probably has gorgeous Italian pumps at the ready. I gave her the compact."

"You really did like her."

"I did. She strikes me as the no-bullshit type."

As Cleo drove, Sonya related the gist of the conversation.

"As strange as this has all been for you," Cleo commented, "it's been strange for all of them, too. Learning what Patricia and Gretta did, then having you take up residence, someone they never knew existed. I have a lot of respect for the way Owen's handled that, and now I can spread that respect to Clarice Poole."

"I'll say she was relieved when she asked if I wanted a more active part in the family business and I gave her an unqualified no."

"I bet. So two new Pooles for you today. And I'd say polar opposites. And now we're home," Cleo added as she pulled into the drive.

When they opened the door, Yoda wagged with his ball clamped in his mouth—no doubt courtesy of Jack. Pye leaped down from where she'd perched on the newel post, and from the tablet on charge in the library, Clover greeted them with the Isley Brothers' "Shout."

Yes, Sonya thought. Now we're home.

The rest of the day flowed into a quiet night, and Sonya found her creative juices churning in the morning. Routine settled in, and she welcomed it with enthusiasm.

Neither she nor Cleo mentioned the quiet, as they agreed: Talk about it, jinx it.

On Saturday morning, they did discuss whether or not to go by the yard sale.

"God knows we don't need anything. But."

"But," Cleo continued, "we go to show support, and because we're part of Poole's Bay."

"Same book, same page. How about we plan to leave about two?"

"Okay. That gives me time to give my last illustrations another good look. Then I'm sending them off. Then?" Cleo swiped her hands together. "Done."

"I want to see them. I'll come up before we go. I need to do more testing on the Gigi's job."

"We have a plan." As she filled her water bottle, Cleo looked at Sonya over her shoulder. "And it includes you having a little time, which you haven't, with Trey."

"He and Owen have been busy with their own work, then the whole yard-sale thing."

"It shows character they've taken the time and trouble to repair some of the things that drunk son of a bitch damaged."

"It does, and I've missed him. We can invite them to dinner tonight. I could do that scallop-pasta thing. It's actually quick and sort of easy."

"We can pick up the scallops on the way home, so part two of a plan. I'm going up to get to it."

Before she did the same, Sonya checked the recipe. And reminded herself it sounded harder than it was. Mostly. She'd made it for her mother, so she could make it again.

Satisfied, she headed upstairs. As she and Yoda settled in, Clover used Def Leppard's "When Saturday Comes" to communicate.

"Just a couple hours' work. Then Cleo and I are going out for a while. And this Gigi's job is going to rock just like Def Leppard."

At just after one, thoroughly satisfied, she shut down to do her makeup. Then wandered up to Cleo's studio.

"Perfect timing. I'm going to send these last six, and unless my editor has issues with them, I'll be officially on sabbatical."

Sonya came around the desk to study the work.

"Oh, Cleo, no one's going to have an issue with this group of mermaids."

"Gossip."

"About what?"

"Anything at all works for me. But that's what you call a group of mermaids. A gossip. Sexist, I know, but that's the term."

Cleo studied them herself, and smiled. "I liked the idea of them getting together, like a girls' night out."

"I love it, and this one, a family unit—the way he's holding the little girl, and she's cradling the baby. Oh, and this one! I swear you can see her hair moving in the current. Fire and water."

"They're going. When you know you've done the best you can do, you stop."

"They're amazing, and yes, send them." She wandered to the windows. "I think we're doing our best work here, Cleo. And I'm happier doing it."

"I don't disagree. I was happy in Boston, and fulfilled, too. But I'm happier and more fulfilled here. I'm going to paint my ass off, Son. I've got so many ideas."

"Speaking of paintings, have you checked today?"

"Right before I sat down to look these over."

"I might as well take another look before we go. Oh, and we need to pick up angel hair pasta. I think we have everything else. Maybe—"

She broke off when she opened the door. Her heart kicked up its beat until it pulsed in her throat, in her ears.

"Cleo, it's Agatha."

"And they're off! What? But—"

She jumped up from her chair, rushed over. "Well, Jesus! Two—maybe three—hours ago, that wasn't there."

"It's my dad's work." Now tears wanted to clog her throat. "I'd know that even without the signature. My father painted this, Cleo."

"It's like they're taking turns."

"I don't know how this could be, but there it is. There she is. Agatha Winward Poole. The fourth bride."

"It's beautiful work. She's . . . more stately than beautiful. The gown's amazing. Look at that train, and the detail of the lace. A tiara over the veil. The diamonds actually sparkle."

"She's different from the others we've found. More regal, I'd say. But more than that, Johanna looks serenely happy, Clover almost giddy, and Lisbeth, well, sparkles like those diamonds. But she looks—"

"Smug."

"That's the word. Smug or not, she didn't deserve dying on her wedding day. We'll take her down, and when we get back, hang her portrait with the others."

As they studied the portrait, Cleo draped an arm around Sonya's shoulders.

"I hate it makes you sad."

"I saw her die, and here she is, regal, proud, and yeah, smug. It is sad. And it's strange and awful knowing if she hadn't died, I wouldn't have been born, would I?"

They carried the portrait down and propped it against the wall in the music room.

Being out on a sunny spring Saturday chased the sads away. When they arrived, the yard sale was already in full swing.

Up and down the block cars and trucks lined the quiet little street.

People carried lamps, small tables, a toaster, chairs along the sidewalk.

More, a great deal more, milled around the yard, browsing or bargaining for items rigorously organized by type or use.

Corrine, with a floppy-brimmed hat over her hair, stuck orange dots on price tags—SOLD.

Anna sat at a folding table with a cashbox. Money changed hands briskly.

More women worked the crowd, laughing, counteroffering.

Sonya watched Trey and Owen muscle a sofa and carry it toward the sidewalk.

"Hey, cuties. Didn't expect to see you today."

"We wanted to see how it was going, and wow. Is there anything we can do to help?"

"Stop talking," Owen suggested, "so we can cart this damn . . . damn good-looking sofa," he amended as the woman leading the way turned, raised her eyebrows at him, "down to Ms. Bridge's truck."

"Dolly's truck," she said. "You graduated high school some time ago, Owen."

"Ask Mom," Trey said to Sonya. "I think they've more than got it, but she'd know."

"You ask," Cleo told her. "I'm going to browse."

"Cleo."

"Browse isn't buying. Probably."

Shaking her head, Sonya made her way through the people, the tables, to Corrine.

"What a turnout. Is there anything Cleo and I can do to help?"

"You already did. Word of mouth's one thing, but those flyers you did? We've got people stopping by—and buying—who are staying at the hotel, even just passing through the village. Marlo's going to have a nice nest egg, and your flyers made a difference.

"That fifty's firm on those nightstands, Harry, so don't even try. They're a set and in good condition. Since Owen and Trey fixed them," she muttered to Sonya.

"Look at this cute little purse!" Cleo came over with a cross-body bag. "You know I love a red purse. And it's only twelve dollars."

"Cleo, in all the years I've known you, I've never seen you carry a purse that small, except an evening bag. And even then."

"It could happen. It's red. It's twelve dollars."

"Ten for you," Corrine told her.

"Sold."

Sonya spent the next two hours—twice as long as intended—while Trey and Owen hauled nightstands—fifty dollars, firm—and side tables, an easy chair, and more. While Cleo hunted bargains, she chatted with people she knew, with others she'd just met.

And if she bought a few things as well, she told herself she did so to be supportive.

"You're running out of stock," she said to Trey when he had a minute.

"Yeah, it's good to see. I had to tell her what Wes did, and she's been pretty down. This is going to lift her up again."

"If you and Owen aren't worn out after this, come to dinner. Stay the weekend."

"Dinner sounds great. The weekend even better. I'm sorry I haven't had any time in the last few days."

"For a good cause. I'm going to get Cleo away from here before she buys something else. Come up when you can."

"Hey." He pulled her in, kissed her on the lawn where strangers and neighbors, clients and family browsed what was left.

In the end, Trey and Owen helped load up the borrowed folding tables.

"Thanks, Mom, seriously."

"Neighbors help neighbors, but you're welcome. I'll see the money's deposited, and the firm can cut Marlo a check on Monday morning."

"Great. Got a total there, mistress of the cashbox?"

"I do." Walking over, Anna handed her mother the cashbox. "Three thousand, three hundred fifty-eight dollars and fifty cents."

"That's a damn nice haul," Owen commented.

"It is, but that's not all. And remind me whose idea it was to put out that giant pickle jar that said *For Marlo and the kids*, with their picture on it?"

Trey gave her a brotherly eye roll. "Yours."

"That's right, I nearly forgot. And I'm going to admit it wasn't just hormones that had me tearing up when Bob Bailey stuffed a hundred in there. Fifteen hundred and eighty-three dollars—for a grand total of forty-nine hundred forty-one dollars and fifty cents."

"Make that five thousand and whatever." Owen dug out his wallet. "Hell, I've only got eighty-five on me. I'm keeping the five. Lend me twenty."

With another eye roll, Trey pulled out his wallet, passed Owen twenty.

"And here's another hundred and fifty-eight dollars and . . ." Trey dug in his pocket. "Fifty cents. That makes it an even fifty-two hundred."

Teary, Anna kissed them both.

Seth jogged up. "Deuce and I got the trash bagged up and stowed in the back of the truck. What's this?"

"With these last contributions, fifty-two hundred goes to Marlo."

"Let's make it fifty-five. Solid number." He took out a money clip, peeled off bills.

"Show-off."

Grinning at Owen, he passed the bills to his mother-in-law.

"You're very good boys," Corrine said. "I'm proud of you, and of my very good girl. Proud enough I'll spring for pizza and a bottle of Chianti."

"Baby girl says: Pizza, yum."

When Anna put a hand on her baby mound, Seth laid his over it. "So do Mom and Dad."

"Gotta rain check that, Mom," Trey said. "Owen and I have an earlier invite to dinner at the manor."

"What're they making? Because," Owen said, "pizza."

"Don't know. We need to get the dogs from Mom's. I should probably clean up a little."

"Clean up later. It's past have-a-beer time."

Because he couldn't disagree, Trey didn't argue.

When they arrived at the manor, both women rose from where they sat in the main parlor drinking wine.

"They've got adult beverages. I want an adult beverage."

"We'll get you that." Sonya stopped Owen before he could head straight back to the kitchen. "We want to show you something first."

She led the way to the music room.

"Another one." Studying the portrait, Owen slipped his hands into his pockets.

"Bride number four," Trey said.

"Agatha Winward Poole. Owen Poole's—son of Marianne Poole—first wife. Died of anaphylactic shock via poisoned petits fours on her wedding day."

"When did you find it?"

Sonya glanced over at Trey. "Right before we left for the village. The yard sale didn't seem like the time or place to mention it."

"No." He moved closer. "That's your father's signature. The same as on Clover's."

"Yes, my father's work. Cleo and I hung it there when we got back from the village."

"She's a looker. They all are," Owen observed. "But this one's got an edge to her. So, four down, three to go."

"Maybe just two? We already have the portrait of Astrid."

He shot Sonya a sidelong glance. "You're a graphic designer. You know space better than that. Taking the width of these four, the spacing between. Three more."

"I did notice that, and thought about it."

"They have to paint them. Your dad, Collin. One each so far," Cleo pointed out.

"Cleo had looked in the closet two hours or so before I did. Nothing there when she looked, then this. I'd almost forgotten what

it's like to be jolted like that. It's been—not saying the *Q* word—
workplace productive for a few days."

"Take it when you can get it," Owen advised. "Now I'm getting a
beer. What're we eating?"

"I hope you like scallops."

"I'm a Mainer."

"I assume that's a positive for scallops."

"All-around positive," Trey assured her. "I haven't really been able
to talk to you, not in depth, about your visit to Gretta."

"And dropping by Poole Shipbuilders." Owen handed Trey a beer.

"I can head that up by saying Gretta's difficult and sad, and Clarice and what I saw of Poole is great."

"Can't argue with either. Why is nothing cooking?"

"Here." Cleo pulled a tray out of the refrigerator. "I did a char-
cuterie."

"Fancy word." Despite the fancy, he popped a slice of summer
sausage. "Good."

Between bites and sips, Owen set the table while Sonya began the
process of cooking while having conversations.

She muttered Bree's recipe's warning as she sautéed the scallops.

"Do not overcook, do not overcook."

"So Gretta recognized the makeup case?"

"Mmm." She nodded at Trey. "And I think that's how I was able to
get her to say more about what happened with my father and Collin.
A lot of pent-up rage there, which came out in the nasty drawing and
a lot of f-bombs."

"Who wouldn't have rage, pressured to give up what she wanted,
to pretend she'd given birth, to raise a child she didn't want?"

Owen shrugged at Trey. "She could've said no. And yeah, yeah,
nobody's saying it was easy to say no to Patricia Poole, but she was
an adult, and Jesus, had the advantage of money her mother couldn't
take away from her. If she'd had a spine and half a heart, she'd've
taken both those kids and told the goddamn truth."

"I'm going to agree with Owen." Cleo gave Sonya's back a quick rub. "It seemed to me she was blaming everyone but herself. Charlie, Clover, her mother. But she doesn't take any of the responsibility."

"She has dementia," Trey began.

"True, but did she ever take responsibility?"

"No, not that I've ever heard," Owen added. "But she is, and was, who she is and was. It's too bad. There would've been plenty of Poole relations who'd have taken both kids.

"And fuck, sorry, Sonya. That sounds like I'm tossing your father's parents aside."

"No, it doesn't. I understand what you meant, and it's true. But we've said it before. My father got the happy end of that situation. Gretta played Collin's mother out of duty, and under duty was that pent-up rage and resentment. And as far as I know, she never let that rage or resentment out, never took it out in an abusive way on Collin."

"No." Trey shook his head. "I'd have heard from my father if she had."

"Flat," Owen said. "That's how I remember her. No real ups, no real downs. Just flat."

"Because she gave up." Cleo put a platter by the stove. "When she gave in to her mother, she didn't just give up New York, she gave up everything."

When they sat down to eat, Trey sampled a bite, then grinned at Sonya. "Hiding your talents."

"More of a limited skill. But I've got this one down. It's good."

"It's damn good. A damn good reward for a couple of long days." Owen toasted her with his beer.

Clover chimed in with Bowie's "Heroes."

All in all, Sonya considered it one of the best weeks at the manor.

And though she woke at three, she didn't walk. Instead, she stood with Trey at the glass doors and watched Hester Dobbs take her fall.

PART THREE

The Living and the Dead

I can call spirits from the vasty deep.
—William Shakespeare

Chapter Twenty-one

May arrived and brought tulips, and fat buds on the twisty branches of the weeping tree. And May meant another Saturday in the village, at Bay Arts' May Day event.

She loved seeing Anna's work displayed, and her friend cheerfully talking to customers and other artists.

Maybe it was barely more than another week before Boston and the promised shopping trip, and maybe it was only May. But there was so much right here, so many interesting, unique things.

She started her Christmas shopping.

"Oh, those are beautiful wineglasses." Cleo took one, studied it.

"I know. Handblown, and I love that pale green in the stem. I'm getting them for my aunt Summer, for Christmas. And this dragonfly bowl? My grandmother—Dad's mom—loves dragonflies. And see that adorable birdhouse with the copper roof? My grandfather's big into birds, so—"

"Christmas." Cleo pushed the wineglass back at her. "Why didn't I think of that? I'm going to get busy."

By the time they drove home, with the back seat full of shopping bags and boxes, they'd decided to reimagine one of the third-floor rooms into a gift/wrapping room.

"I think the sitting room that faces the back. Still a terrific view, woods, gardens, but not as distracting as the water."

Cleo hunched her shoulders in a happy sigh. "Great minds. It's just big enough, has a small but decent closet. We should have shelves in there, though. And we need a good table for wrapping."

Sonya tossed her hair, shot Cleo a grin. "Let's go find one."

An hour later, they stood in the sitting room with Trey and Owen.

"The sofa and the little side tables stay, but we'll move them over there." Sonya gestured as she talked. "Those two chairs would go into storage. We'll switch out the art later, put some of our own up, we think. But there's a cabinet—a wardrobe—up in the attic that can go over there, and a table—it's just right—that'll go by the windows."

She sent Trey her most charming smile. "It'll all fit. We measured."

"How did we get to be weekend furniture movers?" Owen wondered.

"For beer and food," Cleo told him. "I'm making shrimp étouffée. You'll like it."

"Well." Trey scratched his head. "From that mountain of shopping bags, I get the concept. But are you sure you want to do all this up here?"

"Cleo already works up here, right across the hall. It's a good purpose for this room, this space. And it's another way to take ownership."

"The last is more the answer to why here."

"Maybe. Yes, maybe. She doesn't get to dictate how we use the manor or anything in it. Except," she had to admit, "the Gold Room. But that's temporary."

"Let's get started. At least we're not hauling stuff all the way downstairs." Owen shook his head at the shopping bags. "I don't even want to think about the insanity of buying Christmas presents in May."

When they stood in the attic in front of the wardrobe they'd uncovered, Owen ran a hand over the wood. "She's a beauty, and weighs about as much as my truck."

"It'll be perfect," Sonya enthused. "The doors on the side have some shelves, and the drawers at the bottom are great. The center mirrored doors, just lovely." She pulled it open. "If we just take out the hanging rail and—"

"No." Owen cut that off like an axe through wood. "This doesn't move an inch if you're going to fuck it up."

"We were just thinking of—"

"No."

"He won't budge on that," Trey said.

"Then we'll need more shelves. In the closet."

"He can do that." Owen jerked a thumb at Trey. "That's grunt work he can handle."

"Thank you very much."

"Truth." As if already feeling the pings and knots, Owen rolled his shoulders.

It might not have been as heavy as a truck, but it took the four of them to move, carry, maneuver it. The table Owen identified as a huntboard proved easier.

When both pieces sat in place, Sonya did a little dance, and Clover fell back on one of her favorites with Queen and "We Are the Champions."

"They're perfect. You're the best!"

She kissed Trey, then Owen in turn.

"You need to clean them up some." Not a suggestion from Owen, but an order. "Oil them."

"We will. We'll do that tomorrow between addressing invitations."

"You're going to hand address a hundred and fifty invitations tomorrow?"

"Please." Sonya laughed at Trey. "I have a program for that."

"And we're going to add some protection to this room, like in my studio. I have some things."

"If you can do that," Owen wondered, "why don't you do the whole damn house?"

"Have you seen the size of this house? And honestly, I don't want to press my luck."

"But right now, we're going to make dinner for a couple of strong, handsome men."

"We?" Cleo said as Clover chimed in with Mary Wells's classic "My Guy."

"I'll do the grunt work."

* * *

It started at three with the chime of the clock, the trill of piano music.

In the nursery, a grieving mother wept. In the servants' quarters, a young girl from Ireland cried out in pain. A boy lay dying of fever in his bed.

A man sat in a leather chair enjoying his post-dinner brandy and cigar while another split wood to add to the stack.

In the ballroom, people danced, ghosts among ghosts as time slipped. Musicians played reels, then waltzes, then fox-trots.

The dead raised glasses to the brides, the grooms.

A midwife delivered twins of a dying mother while another nursed hers for the first and last time.

The voices, the music, the weeping grew like a storm that had Sonya covering her ears.

"Do you hear it? Do you hear it?"

"Yeah." Trey wrapped an arm around her. "I'm going to check it out."

"No, don't—"

The fire came on in a roar; the terrace doors blew open.

The dogs sat up, barking, and Sonya swore she heard dozens, inside and out. Barking, baying, howling.

She rolled out of bed along with Trey, and with him fought to secure the doors again.

And saw Dobbs on the wall, facing the house, arms lifted, her smile hard and brilliant in the moonlight.

"That's not right. It's not right. She sees us."

"None of this is right." Teeth gritted, Trey shoved the doors closed.

The room changed around them. Flowers with pink-tipped petals covered the walls. Wood logs crackled in the fire.

A woman wearing an apron over a gray dress, a cap on her head, stood by the head of the bed. A woman, her dark hair matted with sweat, labored in it while others knelt on the bed between her legs.

"Trey, God, Trey, do you see?"

"Yeah, I see. We need to get the others."

Her heart broke as she gripped Trey's hand. As the midwife said, "The babe's coming!"

Then, even as they rushed out, unseen, the room changed yet again. She saw Clover, pale as the ghost she was, racked with the pains of labor.

"I have to help her." Sonya broke away, and though her hands simply passed through the woman on the bed, she felt a jolt, like an electric shock.

"Someone's here, Charlie." Breathless, Clover tossed her head from side to side. "Someone's here."

"No one here but us, babe. It's just you and me. I'm here. Don't worry."

"Sonya." Trey gripped her hand again, pulled her back. "Sonya, stay with me."

In the hall people scurried along or strolled. A couple shared a kiss outside a bedroom door before the woman giggled and drew the man inside.

A man in a stiff black suit carried a tray with two brandy snifters out of the library and turned toward the stairs.

Owen already stood outside his room with a growling Jones.

"Looks like we've got a lot of company."

"Cleo!" Even as Sonya rushed toward the room, Cleo stumbled out.

"There's someone in my bed. Jesus, there's someone in my bed."

"I'll take a look."

Before Trey could go in, Sonya grabbed his arm. "Together. Stay together."

Not someone, but a couple, naked, lost in the throes.

Sonya couldn't stop the laugh that bubbled up. "No. Just no."

She turned to go out and the doorbell bonged. And kept bonging even as something beat against the front doors.

As they went back into a hall, a maid carrying a stack of linens walked straight through them. She stopped a moment, shuddered as she looked behind her.

Then continued on.

A woman in a green velvet riding outfit with a tall hat cocked on her head came out of another room and strode toward the stairs.

A man in a white suit, red bow tie, and spats jogged up them.

"It's not now," Cleo murmured. "But not really then."

"From the looks and sounds of it, it's whenever. She was out there," Trey said to Owen. "Dobbs, on the wall, and facing the house. She saw us. She waited to see us."

"Let's go see if she still is."

The dogs raced ahead of them to bark at the door. The cat arched her back and hissed.

Screams and racing feet sounded from the ballroom.

"They're dying," Sonya said quietly. "The brides. They're all dying."

As they started down, Astrid Poole limped through them, her hand pressed to her bloody white gown.

Sonya's heart shuddered as she fell. More screams filled the air. And as she looked down, Sonya saw not only Astrid, but Johanna.

And it all stopped, it all vanished.

Trey pulled open the front door to cool, clear air.

"She's not there."

"She finished." Sonya stared out at the seawall as the animals raced outside. "She ended with the first and last bride. She killed them, showed us, and she finished."

"Trey's right about the whenever. Let them run around awhile," Owen added as he closed the door. "The guy in my room was smoking Camels and there was one of those phones—candlestick deals. And when I first came out, there was a girl wearing bell-bottoms. It wasn't Clover. She's blond and this one had dark hair."

"Not just people who died here. Whenever," Sonya repeated. "All the music and voices from the ballroom. Servants and the rest. Not all of them died here."

"Illusions." Trey kissed the top of her head. "Most of it illusions, or memories."

"The manor's memories."

"Yes!" Sonya turned to Cleo. "Yes, that's it."

Cleo rubbed her chilled arms. "Barely a peep out of her for two

weeks so she could do this. Then we pissed her off, Son, taking another room on the third floor."

"Good. Good! Let her waste her energy on bullshit like this. She
can keep right at it because it doesn't change what fucking is. This is
my house!"

"Okay then," Owen began, and she rounded on him.

"A Poole built this house. Pooles made this house! It's our house.
A house for the living."

From the tablet in the library came Simple Minds and "Don't You
(Forget About Me)."

"Not now, not ever. This house is ours," Sonya repeated, fury under every word. "And anyone who lived here and loved it. I don't care
if a thousand ghosts make their home here now, then, or goddamn
whenever. There's only one who's not welcome.

"Reclaiming another room pisses her off? Just wait until we're finished, and she can piss herself back to hell."

Shoving at her hair, Sonya let out a long breath. "Now I'm going
back to bed."

As she strode toward the stairs, Trey grinned after her.

"I get why you're gone over her," Owen commented.

"Way gone. I'd better catch up. Call the dogs and Pye in, will you?"

"Sure. Go on up," he told Cleo. "I'll bring them in."

"I will, but I want a good shot of whiskey first. Want a whiskey?"

"Now that you mention it. Look, the offer to bunk in your sitting
room sofa still stands."

"And is appreciated, very sincerely. But I'm fine—or will be after
about a couple of fingers of Jameson's. I can't say I would be if I'd
seen someone murdered in my bed. But sex? It's healthy."

"Let me know when you want to get healthy."

Cleo got a bottle from the butler's pantry and smiled. "You'll probably be the first."

After a late start all around in the morning, Sonya kissed Trey goodbye, waved both men off. She gathered what she needed and went

to the third floor. After shooting up a middle finger in the direction of the Gold Room, she went into the new gift room to do as Owen instructed and clean and oil the furniture.

And found everything already gleaming.

"You beat me to it, Molly. A very big thank-you."

Hands on hips, she turned a circle.

"It's going to be perfect. I'm going to order supplies—after we get the invitations out, and probably after the trip to Boston. And you know what? After Boston, Cleo and I are going to pick another room, put our stamp on it."

They spent the day dealing with invitations, going over the proposed menu—in detail—Bree sent them.

"I can run into the village and mail these tomorrow. Or"—Cleo wiggled her eyebrows—"we could see if Anna and Bree are up for lunch. Hang out, finalize the menu."

"I like that or."

"I thought you might. Plus, you're starting to count down the days to Boston." She tapped Sonya's head. "And this'll distract you in a fun way."

"It will. I'm telling myself I can be as nervous as I want now, so I'm finished with it before Boston. I'll go text both of them."

It did distract her, and in a fun way. And likely reading her nerves and her countdown, Trey took everyone out for pizza the next night, showed up for dinner the rest of the week.

And one night he arrived with shelves for the closet.

"These are perfect. Thank you."

"You got very specific about spacing when I asked."

"I did. We measured."

"We're about to find out if we're both right on it." Before he picked up the first shelf, he took a look around the room. "You've added some things in here."

"Cleo mostly, seeing as she's on sabbatical. Crystals, candles, the suncatcher in the window—hers. Protection, apparently."

"And you switched out the art. Nice choices. Cleo's work?"

"Most of it."

"Wait a minute." He walked closer to a meadow of wildflowers, hills shadowed in the distance. "S MacT? This is yours."

"Just something I did in college."

"It's great."

She sent him an indulgent smile. "So says the man who sleeps with me."

"So says the man looking at something beautiful. And this one, too. Boston, right? The river. I didn't know you could do this."

"It's not what my mother calls my passion, and she's right. I enjoy it now and then."

"Only now and then?"

She lifted her shoulders. "Artistically, I guess my interests and talents fall into the more practical areas. So graphic art suits me, and satisfies me.

"Cleo dug them out, hung them up. And it is nice having our work here together, like our personal gallery."

"Any objections from down the hall?"

"Not so far. They'll come." She glanced behind her. "Let them come."

Bells rang, windows rattled, the doorbell bonged now and then when no one was there. Sonya brushed those off as she did the occasional slamming door or cold wash of wind.

She had more important things to deal with than the tantrums of a dead witch.

Top of her list as she packed for Boston: what to wear for her presentation.

Trey looked both wary and aggrieved as she held up yet another choice.

"It's nice."

"Nice? God." She immediately hung it back in her closet and reached for another.

"I don't know why you're asking me. It's a trap, it's a classic trap."

"I'm asking you," she began as she studied the navy suit in the mirror, "because you're a professional, a man who takes meetings, goes to court, and . . ." The suit joined two previous choices on the fainting couch at the foot of the bed. "I don't know why I'm asking you either."

"Whatever you wear, you're going to do great."

She could only sigh at him. "This is not the answer."

"Right. I'm going to go let the dogs out."

When he escaped, she texted Cleo.

Wardrobe help. STAT!

By the time Cleo came in, Sonya had three more choices draped over the couch.

"I sense a crisis. Presentation day wear."

"Trey was no help, at all."

Cleo shot her a look between baffled and amused. "Well, of course not."

"Of course not," Sonya agreed. "Which shows how screwed up I am at this moment to have even asked him in the first place. He ran away."

"Because he's nobody's fool. You've got to respect the tactical retreat."

Cleo, dressed in rainy day painting gear of an oversized shirt and leggings, perused the pile on the couch. She picked up three suits, the navy, the black, and a gray.

"No, no, and no. Put them back."

"But—"

"Too expected. Great cuts, excellent fabric—you've always had exceptional taste in clothes—but you don't want the expected."

"I don't? No," Sonya realized. "I don't."

"This sage green's lovely, and it looks great on you, but again, no. Go a little bolder. No prints," she decreed, and walked into Sonya's closet herself.

"No, possible, I wish I could wear this, but no."

"Maybe separates."

"And no. This one."

"Oh, but Cleo, do you really think pink?"

"It's not pink, it's coral. It's warm, feminine without fuss. I remember this hits you right at the knee, so the right length for this, good neckline. You want my necklace, the tiny gold beads."

"I love that necklace."

"It's just right for this, and your twisty hoop earrings I covet. You could pair it with this cream-colored jacket, but I say no jacket. Having your own home gym and using it's given you happening shoulders and arms. Let them see a strong woman. But in these."

She pulled out a pair of cream-colored stilettos.

"Those kill my feet. They killed my feet when I tried them on. I should never have bought them."

"They're gorgeous, you'll suffer, but you'll look fabulous. Strong, capable, feminine, professional, and fabulous. I'm going to do your hair in a fishtail braid. I've got a lipstick that matches this dress. You'll wear that."

"I love you, Cleo."

"How could you not? Crisis averted."

Cleo's phone sang out with "Count on Me."

"And Clover agrees. Pack it," Cleo ordered.

On a cloudy morning, Trey loaded suitcases in the car. If he wondered why they needed so much for a two-day trip, he wisely said nothing. And valuing his life, he didn't suggest, with the load they had, they take the truck Sonya had yet to drive.

Both women had dressed for the road in jeans, T-shirts, and light jackets. Sonya wore a Red Sox fielder's cap.

He thought she looked adorable.

And she stroked and cooed and fussed over Yoda as if she and Cleo were headed to the South Pacific instead of Boston.

"We're going to be fine," Trey assured them as Sonya continued to coo to Yoda and draped an arm around Mookie's neck. Cleo cooed, too, and cuddled the cat, who appeared mildly interested.

"You have the keys and there's plenty of food if you decide to bring them back and stay at night."

"We'll see how it goes."

"I'm going to check my list one more time."

"Sonya, you've checked it three times. Everything's in the car." Swinging her to him, he kissed her. "How can I miss you if you won't go away?"

"Funny," she said, but she did laugh. "Thanks, really, for looking after Yoda. You be a good boy. You're going to have so much fun. Trey, don't forget to—" She broke off, laughed at herself. "You won't forget. You never forget."

"And you'll take Pye to Owen." With some reluctance, Cleo passed the cat to Trey. "He's expecting her."

"I will, and he is."

"Okay, all right." Sonya took a last look around the foyer and couldn't think of anything else to delay the start. "We're ready."

She wrapped her arms around Trey. "Miss me a little."

"I already do. Text me when you get there. You're going to kick ass tomorrow."

"That's the plan. Let's do this, Cleo."

As they walked to the car, got in, and he stood in the doorway with two dogs and a cat, his phone played Fleetwood Mac's "Go Your Own Way."

"Looks like they are."

Since he'd juggled his schedule just enough, he closed the door and went back for another cup of coffee.

And to give the manor and its residents time to get used to having him in the house alone.

After Collin's death and before Sonya's arrival, he certainly had been. But everything changed with that arrival. Activity at the manor had certainly kicked up.

Barring emergency, he had every intention of staying there for the two nights Sonya and Cleo were gone. He expected Owen would join him, but either way.

He wanted to see what Dobbs might have in store when the current object of her wrath wasn't around.

As he sipped his coffee, three doors above slammed in sharp, rapid snaps.

He just smiled. She'd have to do a lot better than that.

He finished off his coffee, rinsed out his mug.

"Okay, gang, we're going for a ride."

Knowing cats, he picked Pye up in case she decided to make herself scarce, because cat.

Outside, the dogs jumped—or in Yoda's case, more clambered—into the back seat of his truck. The cat settled down to curl in the front. He glanced back, saw the shadow move in the library window.

He thought, what the hell, and waved.

He half hoped the window would open, that Clover would once again lean out. But the answering wave struck him as too hesitant and shy for Clover.

As he drove away, the manor fell silent, like a breath caught and held.

Then, from the Gold Room, came a peal of wild, triumphant laughter.

Chapter Twenty-two

As she hit Boston traffic, Sonya adjusted her mindset and her behind-the-wheel strategy.

And added that to her list of reasons she didn't miss the city where she'd been born and raised as much as she'd expected to.

Oh, there were things she missed, she admitted. Her mother hit number one with no competition. But she missed the Charles River, the botanical gardens, the Boston Common. No more impulse attendance at Fenway, or trips to her favorite restaurants, cafés, and shopping haunts.

But not, excepting her mother, as much as she'd expected when she'd made the trip in reverse in the deep freeze of winter.

She'd always loved the house where she'd grown up, and every memory inside it. She'd loved her condo, her neighborhood, but she'd always considered that a temporary stopping point on the way to finding her forever home.

But being back, she realized Boston had been another stopping point. An important one, a foundational one, but she'd moved on from it.

And didn't regret it.

"How does it feel?" she asked Cleo.

"Like we're visitors. Just the way I feel when I go back to Lafayette. I loved it there, I loved it here. But now? A visitor. You?"

"I wondered, and maybe I worried and that's why I haven't come back until now. But I feel just the same way. If all this hadn't happened, I think I'd have been happy here. But it did, and now I wouldn't."

She handled the traffic—it had been a few months, but she'd had years of practice—and finally slipped out of it and into the leafy neighborhood of her childhood.

Dogwoods bloomed, tulips popped, pink blossoms dressed ornamental cherry trees.

"We'll see this at home in another week or two," Cleo predicted.

At home, Sonya thought, in the manor by the sea.

Yes, they were visitors here now.

But there was the sweet, two-story house where she'd grown up, with the red maple leafing out in the little front yard, and her mother's car in the drive.

That would be, always, home, too.

"I told her she didn't have to take the day off."

"And you thought she wouldn't?"

Sonya shook her head as she pulled in behind her mother's car. "I knew she would. I'm so glad she did."

Even as she said it, Winter rushed out of the house.

She wore stone-gray jeans, a light sweater in popping pink.

Sonya shoved out of the car, felt her eyes sting as her mother threw her arms around her.

"Oh, I missed you. Missed you, missed you." Sonya burrowed in. "I didn't know how much until right this second."

"My baby. I'm so glad to see you, really see you." When she drew back, Winter's hazel eyes were damp. "Oh, and you look so good."

"I want some."

"Cleo." Winter turned to embrace her. "I'm so happy you're here. You're both here. Let me get a good look at—Oh! You both look so good! I can't complain when I see how good Maine looks on the pair of you. My girls!"

She pulled them both in for another hug. "Let's get your things inside. I want to hear everything about everything."

"We FaceTimed two days ago, Mom."

"That's different. Oh! The displays for your presentation tomorrow. I want to see them. I want to see everything."

When they hauled a load inside, everything was so wonderfully familiar. The cozy living room where her mother had cleaned out the fireplace for warm weather and placed candles, her father's painting over the mantel—the path through the misty woods. Spring flowers bright and happy in a vase.

And she sniffed the air.

"Something smells amazing, but I told you not to cook."

"You don't get to be the boss of me until I'm old and decrepit, and even then you'll have a fight on your hands. It's lemon chiffon cake."

"My very favorite."

"Right there with you," Cleo said.

"We're going to have a nice spring salad with pretzel rolls first. And mimosas."

"I just moved ahead of you," Cleo claimed, "but if I don't pee pretty damn quick, I'm going to disgrace myself. I'm going to take this up to my room—it's still my overnight room?"

"Always."

"I want to hang up my assistant's dress. Son, you should do the same with your dress unless we want to add ironing to our list."

"And I don't. Unpack, then—No, text Trey, unpack, then mimosas."

"He asked you to text him when you got here? Another mark of my approval," Winter decided. "Final marks when I finally meet him. Now let's get you both settled in."

When they had, Cleo took another few minutes before coming down to give mother and daughter a chance to just be.

"Look at the pretty table. Your best dishes, tulips and baby's breath, your grandmother's lace cloth."

"I liked having an excuse to fuss. Now, I know you said you wanted to take me out to dinner tonight, but—"

"That's firm." Sonya pointed a finger at her mother. "You're not cooking. Neither is Cleo."

"I still can't believe Cleo does cook."

"I'd say it surprised her, too. Not only that she can, but she likes it."

"And look at you." After she got the champagne out of the fridge, Winter flexed her biceps, patted it.

"I know, right?" Sonya flexed her own. "Who knew that was there? And surprise for me, I actually enjoy my solo, in-my-own-home-gym, mostly-every-other-day workouts."

"Well, Maine and those workouts look really good on you. So does being in love."

"Oh, well . . ." Smiling, she rolled her shoulders. "We haven't brought up that major four-letter word yet. It's a really big word."

"I know love when I'm looking at it. And it makes me realize I didn't see it when I looked at you with Brandon."

If she couldn't say it all to her mother, then who?

"I've never felt this way about anyone else, and more? I really *like* Trey, for so many reasons. I don't know what it says about me that I didn't have that, not really, not honestly, with someone I planned to marry."

"It says you nearly made a mistake. But you didn't, and that's what matters. You told me you thought he'd head up By Design's presentation tomorrow."

"It'd be surprised if he didn't. He's good, Mom, Brandon's very good."

"You're better."

With that, Winter popped the cork.

"I heard that!" Cleo came in. "Before you pour, I have something for you."

She handed Winter a package wrapped in embossed white paper with a pink ribbon.

"A thanks for hauling my stuff up to Maine before I moved, for sending me recipes, and for being, since college, my Boston mama."

"The first was no trouble at all, the second's my surprised pleasure, and the third? My absolute delight."

When she unwrapped the framed painting, Winter teared up again. "Oh, Cleo."

"When did you do that?" Sonya came around the counter. "You didn't tell me you did that."

"You don't have to know everything."

The dreamy watercolor showed Sonya, in profile, sitting sideways on the seawall, hair caught in the breeze. Yoda has his front paws on her knee, and she her hand on his head.

"It's beautiful, Cleo, just so beautiful. Baby, look how *content* you are."

"I looked out one day, and there you were, just like that. And I knew then and there it was a gift Winter had to have."

"I'll treasure it, and every day when I look at it, I'll know my baby's where she's happy."

Over lunch and mimosas, cake and cappuccinos, they talked about everything.

At Winter's insistence, they set up the displays and ran through the presentation.

She sat quietly, face impassive, legs crossed, hands folded on her knee.

At the end, Winter applauded politely, then let out a cheer, jumped up.

"Brilliant!" She hugged Sonya tight. "My daughter's brilliant! And so's her best friend. Ryder Sports would be idiots not to go with your campaign. It's the best."

"You haven't seen By Design's."

"I don't need to." She flicked that away. "Yours has punch and it has heart. And the displays?"

Clasping her hands together, she studied the slick posters that had once been only ideas on a mood board.

"Brilliant again. Cleo, you look fabulous."

"I just can't help myself."

With a laugh, Winter gave her a one-armed hug. "And Trey? Very handsome. And this is Owen, also very handsome. But all of you, all the rest? People, not models, not actors—and that's part of the brilliance."

"I'm going into the presentation with my ego pumped."

"Good. You should. I want you to do something for me."

"You know I will."

"I'd like you to order me this display. I want to have it."

"Sure, but—"

"It's your work, it's your art. I want to hang it in my office. And now," she said, "let's go shopping."

That night in the manor, Trey split a pizza with Owen.

"Dobbs wasn't happy when I came back."

"Yeah?" Owen shrugged. "Screw her."

"Clover was. My phone played for half an hour. How'd the cat handle it?"

"She was fine. Jones was a little miffed, but it's all fine." He glanced around when the doorbell bonged. "Expecting someone?"

"It's nobody. The dogs are out, and they'd've barked. That's one of her new deals. It's gone off—that makes the fourth time—since before you got here."

"I could turn it off."

Trey tilted his head. "You figure that'll stop it?"

"You got a point. How about when we're done here, we go down, find a flick where lots of shit blows up. That'll piss her off."

"Sounds good."

While shit blew up on-screen, the cat curled on the chair between them, and the dogs sprawled on the floor, the servants' bell rang incessantly. The doors to the theater opened and shut twice.

Trey ate some popcorn. "Pretty weak sauce from her."

"Flick's got better action."

And at three, Trey stepped out on the balcony. Owen opened his window, leaned out.

Together they watched Dobbs jump.

Trey looked over at Owen. "See you in the morning."

"Yeah."

Trey went inside; Owen shut the window.

And the manor settled into quiet.

* * *

The next day, Sonya put on the coral dress, Cleo's gold beads, her twisty hoops. She spent twice as long on her makeup to be absolutely sure it wasn't overdone or underdone.

She'd skipped breakfast—her stomach wouldn't take it.

Cleo walked in with a tray holding half a bagel, a small bowl of berries, and two Cokes.

"I know," she said before Sonya could refuse. "Didn't I room with somebody who couldn't eat if she was worried about the exam she was about to take? But your presentation's not until two, and you need something in your stomach before that."

"You're right. I know you're right. I swore I'd get done with the nerves before today. I've failed."

"Still time. Now sit. I'm doing your hair."

"Which also takes me back to college. You know why Mom went to work this morning?"

"So she wouldn't hover and make you nervous, and make herself nervous because she made you nervous." Cleo sighed. "I love Winter."

"So do I."

Since they were there, she ate a couple of berries, then decided she could, at least, nibble on the bagel.

"I texted Trey this morning. He and Owen stayed at the manor last night. They did pizza and a movie."

"I texted Owen to see how Pye did. He texted back: 'Fine. She slept on my ass.' You know, she doesn't sleep on mine, but his? It's a little annoying."

Sonya watched the magic in the mirror as Cleo's long artist fingers worked.

"I feel, as his cousin, I can say this without sexualizing. He's got a great ass."

"I have noticed that truth."

"Plan to do more than notice? I'm talking about this to distract myself, so indulge me."

"That was still under consideration until Dobbs had one of her wild tantrums. He came after me and Pye, and he didn't bitch about it. He said he'd have done the same thing. So I plan to try him on when the time seems right, and see if we fit in this elemental area."

"I suspected as much."

"No rushing in. I think, I really think, what needs to happen at the manor needs all four of us. Since I firmly believe that, I'm not going to mess it up for sex."

"I think you're right about the four of us, and I don't think you'll mess things up." After another bite of bagel, Sonya reached for her Coke. "He doesn't strike me as the type, any more than you are, to let sex interfere with friendship and family. The four of us are both."

In the mirror, Cleo smiled at Sonya. "We are, aren't we? And that's what's going to beat her. And this hair? If I do say so myself, is perfect, and is going to add another reason they'll want to hire you."

"The hair's great, and you were right about eating something. Also—you're on a streak—right about the outfit, even though I now have to put these murder-my-feet shoes on."

Cleo patted her shoulder. "Suck it up."

Sucking it up, Sonya put on the shoes and rose to study them both side-by-side in the mirror. Cleo had gone with a mustardy yellow that brought out not only the varied tones of her hair but her eyes.

And worked—like magic again—with Sonya's coral.

"I see the genius in your plan. Female, but not soft. We look like spring done in strong colors."

"Nothing stuffy or expected. Smart women who know how to take the time to put themselves together well."

"And now I'm not as nervous."

"Look confident, be confident," Cleo declared. "Let's get this party started."

What nerves remained, Sonya knew she'd handle. The drive to the Ryder building gave her time to settle into herself. She knew what to do and how to do it, so she would.

The rest? Out of her control.

She parked in the underground garage of the many-storied brick-and-glass building, shouldered her laptop case as Cleo shouldered hers. Between them, they carted the displays, the box of folders for the attendees to the elevator.

"What song do you think Clover would play now?" Sonya wondered.

"Ah . . . Let's go with Kesha and 'Woman.'"

"That's it. That's the perfect one. We're motherfucking women."

"Baby, that's right."

Buoyed, they rode up to the lobby.

Sonya remembered it from her previous work for Ryder as steeped in tradition. The Ryder logo flew behind a small reception counter; the tile floors in a soft, smoky gray worked well with pale blue walls. Two navy chairs flanked a table, and over it hung a portrait of the founder.

Sonya signed in, then, as directed, they took the elevator to the seventh floor.

As they rode up to seven, Cleo hummed "Woman" and made Sonya laugh.

"It's the day you've been working for, my friend."

"It is, and I want it, Cleo, but I realize it's not the alpha and omega for me. Visual Art is doing just fine. I'm doing just fine. More than fine. And realizing that takes some of the edge off."

"Whatever works."

As they stepped off the elevator, a Ryder staff member greeted them. "Ms. MacTavish. I'm Lauren Cooper. I'll escort you to the conference room, assist you in setting up."

"Thanks. Ms. Fabares will be working with me today."

"Good to meet you both. If you'll come with me."

As they started along the hall, bright with windows, with framed displays of various Ryder equipment between, Brandon Wise strode down.

He wore a sharp navy pin-striped suit (thank God she hadn't gone with the navy), crisp white dress shirt—they'd have French cuffs, she knew, with monograms—and a navy-and-burgundy-striped tie done in a double Windsor. His oxfords exactly matched the dark brown leather of his briefcase.

His blond hair, perfectly styled to suit his smooth "no, I'm not a movie star, but I look like one" face, caught glints from the sun streaming through the windows.

His smile, all charm, spread like the sunlight.

"Mr. Wise, I didn't realize you were still here."

"On my way out now, Lauren. Miranda and I started chatting after the rest of the team left, and time got away from me. Hello, Sonya. You look . . . well."

"Thank you. I am."

He gave Cleo the slightest nod. "Cleo."

She gave him one right back. "Asshole."

His smile wavered, but didn't quite fall.

"So how are things in the backwoods of Maine?"

"It's on the coast, and it's lovely. Now, if you'll excuse us."

"If I could have just one minute. Lauren can show your . . . assistant where to take your supplies."

"One's all I have to spare. I'll be right behind you, Cleo. It's fine," she added.

"Let me take those for you." Sending Sonya a look of apology, Lauren took what Sonya carried. "The conference room is at the end of the hall."

"Yes, I remember." As they walked away, Sonya glanced at the watch she rarely wore. "Minute starts now."

"The hardcase act doesn't suit you," he said lightly. "Looks like you've put on a little weight. Trying to run your own little company, and away from the action? Can't blame you for stress eating."

"I haven't, and I'm enjoying freelancing. If you want to take your minute to comment on my appearance—"

"Touchy, but you always were. I thought it only fair to let you know, I've got this account sewn up. Miranda just confirmed it. I understand Burt has a . . . let's be delicate here and say a fondness for you, and pushed to give you this exposure. But I've got the account, and that shouldn't be a surprise."

She stiffened when he put a hand on her shoulder.

"You're going to want to move that hand."

He moved it, and sighed. "I wanted to spare you some embarrassment, for old times' sake. Stick with your minor league websites, Sonya. Ryder's big league, and you're just not. Never will be."

"I'll give your advice all the consideration it's due. Now, if you'll excuse me, you've gone over your minute, and that's all you're going to get."

"All that time together, and I really missed how much of a bitch you had in you. Breaking our engagement was the smartest thing I've ever done."

"Jesus, Brandon, you really are pathetic."

"You've already lost, Sonya," he called out as she walked away. "You never had a chance."

"We'll see about that," she muttered. "We'll fucking see about that."

When she reached the conference room, the displays were up, the packets laid out on the long table. Yet another staff member filled water glasses.

"Ms. MacTavish—"

"Sonya."

"Sonya," Lauren corrected. "I want to apologize. By Design's presentation completed nearly forty minutes ago. I had no idea Mr. Wise remained behind."

"It's fine. He wanted to give me some advice."

"Asshole," Cleo muttered. "Ambush."

"It doesn't matter," Sonya repeated.

"In any case, I apologize. Miranda Ryder and the rest you'll present to are in the executive dining room. Obviously, Mr. Wise wasn't. They're due back in about ten minutes. Is there anything I can get you?"

"Just water's fine. Cleo?"

"That'll do."

They set up the slide show for the big wall screen, ran a quick test.

When Lauren went out, Cleo turned to give Sonya a hug. "I'd ask if you're okay, but you look more than okay."

"It's not my alpha and omega, but I want it. He made me want it more."

"You've still got a couple minutes. Want a quick trip to the ladies' to kick something in those fabulous shoes?"

"Don't need it. His—*ambush* fits—energized me, and I'll use it."

Burt Springer came in first, a tall, robust man with threads of gray through dark hair and deep-set brown eyes. He strode straight to Sonya and took her hand in both of his.

"Sonya. I wanted a second just to say I'm glad you're here, and I'm looking forward to seeing your ideas."

"I can't tell you how much I appreciate you giving me the opportunity."

"You earned it." He turned to Cleo. "Burt Springer."

"Cleo Fabares. It's lovely to meet you. Sonya's told me how much she enjoyed working with you."

"It's mutual." Then he frowned. "Why is that name so familiar? Now, I know we haven't met before—how could I forget? Wait! Could you be the Cleo Fabares who illustrated my granddaughter's favorite book? *Jessie's Best Day*?"

"I am."

On a look of delight, he snapped his fingers. "I knew that name. Small wonder. Eva's four, and she loves that book. I bought a second copy for Grandma and Pop's house. I can't count how many times we've read it to her. Though at this point, she reads it to us. She loves the pictures, especially the one of Jessie jumping in the ball pit. If I had a copy with me, I'd have you sign it for her."

"I'll see you get one, signed by me and the author."

"That would rank me as best Pop ever." He took out a card. "Wait until I tell my wife. Are you and Sonya working together at Visual Art?"

"Sonya and I have been friends since college."

"And currently we're housemates," Sonya added. "Cleo's helping me out today."

"I don't have to tell you I wish you the best of luck, but I'll tell you anyway. And here come the rest. Knock our socks off."

She knew some of the fifteen who took their seats at the table from her previous work for Ryder, and others by reputation and research for her presentation.

Windon Ryder served as CFO, Lowell Ryder as VP of marketing. And Miranda Ryder, head of the table, as, Sonya knew, head of everything.

She had three generations of Ryders in the room to impress, and twelve others who'd weigh in.

She was ready.

"Good afternoon. I'm Sonya MacTavish of Visual Art, and this is Cleo Fabares, who'll assist me today. I want to thank you for this opportunity to—"

"I understood you were a one-woman operation," Miranda interrupted. "Have you expanded your company?"

"I haven't, no." Sonya met the steel-gray eyes directly. "Ms. Fabares is a friend and today a volunteer."

"Before you begin, you understand By Design, a company you once worked for, has already presented."

"I do, yes. And no doubt, as By Design is an exceptional and creative organization, their presentation met those standards. I believe mine will as well."

"Why did you leave their employ? Laine Cohen and Matt Berry have, as you said yourself, built an exceptional and creative organization."

"And I owe Laine and Matt a great deal. They were wonderful to work for. The decision to leave By Design and build my own business was neither easy nor impulsive, but was the right decision for me. Only more so as I relocated to Maine."

"As a one-woman operation?"

"Yes, which I could never have done without the foundation I was given at By Design. In your packets, as requested, I have samples of work I've done since starting Visual Art. I've found freelancing both challenging and fulfilling, and I appreciate the opportunity to present my vision for Ryder Sports, a business rooted, as I am, in family and community."

She glanced at Cleo, who cued up the slide show, and began.

She stayed in the moment, though afterward, all the moments blurred. She fielded questions—those tech questions did come up—and when it was done, forgot her answers.

What she remembered, and always would, was Burt coming out into the hallway to take her hand again, and whispering in her ear:

"Socks knocked off."

Sonya didn't speak until the elevator doors shut.

"Was she as tough as I think? Miranda Ryder?"

"Tougher." Cleo blew out a breath, rolled her eyes. "Scary tough. I liked her. I sort of want to be her in thirty or forty years. Now let me say this, not as your friend, not as your temporary assistant. Ready?"

"Yeah."

"You. Were. Awesome!"

"I can't remember it." Because they felt cold, she rubbed her hands together. "It's like a big blur now. Maybe later I'll remember."

"I was watching, looking at faces when I could. They liked it, Son. They really did."

"I'm putting it away. I have to put it away."

"Uh-uh. You're going to tell me what that asshole said to you."

"In detail. But I'm going to change out of these shoes so I can feel my feet again, take several long breaths. And I'm going to take you and Mom out to dinner."

"I'm going to tell you now, your mom has other ideas. She's home now, and she's making her famous garlic and sage roast chicken. She wanted you home tonight, Son. Wanted you to relax. For us all to relax."

"You know what? I want that, too. We did a good job, and I'm letting it go. Doing a good job's enough."

Chapter Twenty-three

She enjoyed every minute in the home of her childhood with her two favorite women.

Some of the presentation blur faded, and what didn't, Cleo filled in.

After dinner, now cozy in pajamas, they sat in the living room with wine and lemon chiffon cake.

"I can't believe that son of a bitch came after you right before your presentation."

"Winter MacTavish!" Cleo snorted. "Do you kiss your daughter with that mouth?"

"I do." Winter leaned over, kissed Sonya to prove it. "And he actually claimed *he'd* broken the engagement."

"It's easy to rewrite history and make yourself the hero of the piece." Sonya shrugged. "Seeing him like that? So slick and smug and patronizing? It just made me more determined to show off my stuff. And it made me appreciate Trey even more.

"They're there again tonight," she added. "Trey and Owen at the manor. I called him when I went up to change. He—they—didn't have to do that. I think he feels, and Owen, too, they're not just taking care of Yoda and Pye, but the manor, and what's in it."

She sipped some wine. "They both watched Dobbs jump again last night."

Winter shuddered. "I can't imagine that. And don't really want to. I like better imagining the girl—because she was just a girl—who gave birth to your dad playing music for you, looking out for you. I like knowing you have four pieces of your father's art in the manor. The one you took with you, and the three you found there. It matters to me. It puts him there with you, too."

"And here with you," Sonya murmured.

"Always. I wonder if knowing he is—with me—made it easier to accept what goes on in your manor. I worry about you, both of you," she admitted. "But I worry less knowing you're there for each other, and Clover and Molly, and the rest you've told me about."

"And next month, for a couple of days, you'll be there, too."

"Can't wait. Summer called me today. She got your invitation. I didn't ask if you'd included her because I didn't want to pressure you."

"Mom, I don't blame her for what Tracie did. It was her choice to get naked with Brandon, several times. It's not her mother's fault."

"She's coming. Her and Martin. She's booking a room at the hotel."

"We have room for them. They're welcome to stay at the manor."

"Martin? Ghosts? Never." Winter laughed at the idea. "If Summer and I ever take a sisters' trip up there, she'd stay. But Martin, that's a hard no."

"I forgot. He won't watch scary movies either." Remembering now made Sonya grin. "He wouldn't make it through a single night at the manor."

"Your grandparents, both sets, will want to come. If they can, the hotel's a better fit there, too. You let me worry about that end of things."

In the morning, they loaded the car again.

"Drive safe and—"

"Text when we get there." Sonya hugged Winter hard. "I'll see you soon. I love you."

"I love you right back, both of you. Oh, and let me know when you hear from Ryder."

"I will, either way."

"I'm proud of you either way, but now I really don't want that jerk to get it."

"Right there with her," Cleo said when they got in the car. "If it's as pretty at home as it is here today? I'm unpacking, then taking my easel outside. Paint with me."

"Cleo."

"Come on. I know Trey texted and said not to worry about getting Yoda and Pye. They'll bring them and dinner tonight, and yay to that. But it'll be noon easy before we get home. Then we have to unpack, take a breath. Who starts their workday at like one in the afternoon? We worked hard. Let's play."

The day stayed pretty, making up for a couple of rounds of ugly traffic. The sight of the manor, rising up when she rounded the last turn, made Sonya's heart clutch in a way she hoped never got old.

"Cleo, the tree."

"I see. Oh, when all those flowers open, it'll be spectacular."

A few had, giving a hint of beauty to come. Delicate pink dripping from those curved and twisted branches whispered *Spring, spring, spring.*

"The garden center's going up a couple places on our do-it list."

"I'm buying a hat." Cleo got out of the car, stretched. "Next trip to town I'm getting a cute gardening hat."

"You have your adorable painting outside hat."

"And your point?"

"I have none," Sonya admitted.

"God, what a gorgeous afternoon. We're painting. I won't take no."

The minute Sonya opened the front door, her phone broke out with "Can't Stop the Feeling!"

"We're happy we're back, too."

They hauled in suitcases, shopping bags, laptop cases, and ignored the counterpoint of doors slamming on the third floor.

Sonya took a breath.

"It's big, it's beautiful, it's haunted. And it's ours."

"Unpack, gather supplies, then we'll paint this gorgeous day."

"Quick stop to check my email, texts, and so on. Text Mom we're home, and do the same with Trey."

"That's allowed."

"It's too soon to hear from Ryder, but I have to check or I'll obsess."

"Of course you do, and of course you would. When do you think?" Cleo asked as they started upstairs.

"By the end of the week, maybe. Better if it's into next week. I'm thinking the longer it takes, the better my chances. A quick decision probably leans toward By Design. So I'm going to check, then put it out of my mind."

When she found no communication from Burt Springer, she considered it a good sign. Maybe she couldn't put it completely out of her mind, she thought as she unpacked, but she could push it into the back.

She dug out the shirt of her father's she used as a smock on the rare occasions she painted. It made her think of him, feel close to him.

She had a set of his brushes she'd packed away, and one of his easels, a palette.

When she walked out with Cleo to set up, she looked around.

"Are you doing the tree?"

"No, I'm waiting for it, full dress." Cleo gestured. "I'm looking at the view of the bay, the lighthouse from here.

"I'm doing the tree," Sonya decided. "A between-seasons thing."

As they set up, Clover went with Elvis and "Spring Fever."

On a laugh, Sonya set her canvas. "I guess we've caught it."

They chatted off and on as they painted, and Sonya found herself enjoying it all. The air, the scents, the call of birds. And experimenting with color and shape that had nothing to do with work.

Though the tree with its few brave blooms and fat, waiting buds stood as the focus, she had the turret rising behind it, the rounded shape, the golden stones, the tall windows.

And the shadow that came and went behind the glass in the library.

An hour in, Cleo stepped back from her own to wander over to Sonya's.

"Sonya, you know that's good."

"It's not bad."

"Good. You've caught the light, and the delicacy of the blossoms. The scatter of them gives impact to the witchy shape of the tree. The way you've used the turret, it's good perspective, and impactful again with the contrast. Then there's the hint of shape in the window. Just a touch of spooky."

"It was there. I feel like it's Clover this time."

When her phone played "Say My Name," Sonya looked up again. "Looks like I'm right about that. I like her there, and in the painting."

"We're hanging it."

"Let's see how it finishes up." She glanced around, then walked to Cleo's canvas. "You know this is wonderful. Dreamy, almost fanciful, but real. Rocky coastline, the perfect blue of the bay sliding out to sea, and the boats—at dock or gliding. The bits of the village, there's a sturdiness to that, the weathered brick of the Poole building.

"And the lighthouse guarding it all. Sabbatical, my ass. Where will you put it?"

"If it turns out the way I hope, I think I'll talk to Kevin at Bay Arts. We'll see. Right now, I'm painting for me, so that's the sabbatical."

They went back to it, painting through the afternoon to Clover's musical interludes.

"We're going to do this more often." Cleo wiped most of the cerulean blue off her hand. "But that's it for me today. I need to step away from it. Bring it out again tomorrow."

"I'm done. I got what I wanted. If I keep playing with it, I'll end up with something else."

"It's really good, Son. You painted something you love, and it shows."

As they started to pack up, they heard the truck coming. So did Clover, as she hit it with Thin Lizzy's "The Boys Are Back in Town."

As it had when she'd seen the manor again, her heart clutched when Trey's truck rounded the bend.

This is love, she thought, and it feels amazing. Terrifying, over-whelming, and amazing.

She ran to the truck the minute Trey parked. Yoda and Mookie leaped out first to greet her like a long-lost lover.

"I missed you, too. Missed you! I know you were good boys. You're such good boys. And you." She threw her arms around Trey. "Hello."

Because she couldn't help it, she put that clutching heart into the kiss. And it opened like the buds on the tree when he answered in kind.

"Come on, boys, what about me? Give those two a minute and come see Cleo."

"Welcome home," Trey murmured, and drawing back, laid a hand on her cheek. "I missed your face."

"I missed yours, and everything else." With a sigh, she laid her head on his shoulder. "Thanks for looking out for everything while I was gone."

"I want to hear all about it. What's this?" He gestured toward the easels. "Art class?"

"Cleo's idea of an afternoon playdate. And it was actually fun. A good way to shake off the traffic and travel."

"Let's have a look."

He kept her hand in his as they crossed the lawn. He came to Cleo's canvas first.

"You did this in an afternoon?"

"It's not finished, but I had the concept in mind for a while. *Light Over Poole's Bay.*"

"It's terrific, seriously. You did this?" he said to Sonya.

"And it is finished. Cleo's going to do the full bloom, so I decided to do *Between Seasons.*"

"You should play more. If I could do this, I'd play all the damn time."

"That's when play becomes work," Sonya reminded him. "Let's get all this inside."

"Owen's bringing Pye?"

Trey nodded as he helped them break down. "He had a few more things to do, so he'll pick up dinner."

"Great. We can take all this up to my studio. I'll clean the brushes, Son."

As they started up, so did the banging.

"There she goes. Did she do much of this while we were gone?" Sonya asked.

"She lets you know she's pissed. Nothing major the last couple days. More when you come up to the third floor. We checked the studio closet every night," he added, "just in case, but nothing."

"I looked before we went outside, but take another look now, Sonya."

"Nothing yet." Sonya closed the closet door.

"I've got the brushes," Cleo said again. "Go pour me a glass of wine."

"How's your mom?" Trey asked as they started down.

"Wonderful. It was so good to see her, to have that time with her."

"And Boston?"

"I asked Cleo how she felt when we got there, and she said exactly what I felt. She said she felt like a visitor. And when we got to the house, I realized that would always be home. How lucky I was to have all the memories of growing up in that house, to know it's a place I'll always be welcome. And what a difference a few months can make, because other than Mom, I missed Boston so much less than I thought I would.

"I missed this guy more." She bent to rub Yoda. "And you," she added, giving Mookie the same treatment." Then straightened. "And you."

She paused at the music room, looked at the portrait. "I missed this house with everything in it. Except . . ."

"Goes without saying."

When they went into the kitchen, she saw the pet treats, a ball of string, and Yoda's ball on the island.

"Somebody missed the pets," Trey told her. "The first night you were gone, when we came in, those were there, plus all the cabinet doors were open, the counter stools, the chairs turned over on the floor."

"Poor Jack. What did you do?"

"Had what most people would consider a monologue. Talked about how Owen and I had to look after the pets since you had to be away for a short work trip. How we'd come back with them after work every night."

When he pulled out two dog biscuits, two dog butts hit the floor.

"Last night, the stuff was on the counter again, but everything else stayed in place. So I guess he got it."

She watched him pass out the biscuits. "You're a sweet man, Trey."

"And that's usually the kiss of death."

"No. Just the opposite for me. You took my dog to work with you."

"He won Sadie over. That's not a snap."

"And you brought him back after work—you and Owen brought Yoda and Pye back, stayed here because you didn't want to leave the house empty after all that's happened. You talked to the ghost of a little boy who missed having the pets around to play with."

She ran a hand down the sleeve of her shirt. "My father was a sweet man. Not a pushover, not—what's the word for it? Treacly."

"That's a good word."

"It is. So I know and value a sweet man when I see one."

The dogs leaped up, raced toward the front of the house seconds before the doorbell bonged.

"That's Owen. Pour that wine—I'll go for that, too." Trey kissed the top of her head. "I'll get the door."

While he did, Clover played the Pretenders' "I'll Stand by You."

"It's true. I would. Will. And knowing he will? It changes every-thing."

She poured the wine.

Then smiled at Owen, reached for another biscuit and the cat treats when Pye and Jones came in on either side of him. "There's beer," she told him.

"I don't mind that." He nodded at the wine, so she got out another glass.

"So, welcome back. What's this about the asshole ambushing you before the deal?"

"What? What ambush?" Trey demanded.

Sonya poured the fourth glass. "How did you know about that? Telepathy?"

"That'd be cool, but no. Cleo texted me right after you got home, I guess to make sure I hadn't lost one of her cat's nine lives. She mentioned it."

"There she is." Cleo all but purred herself as she came in and scooped up the cat for a snuggle. "Thank you." She gave Owen a chaste kiss on the cheek that had him eyeing Trey.

"I bet you got better than that."

"I can't lie. What ambush?"

"Brandon decided to needle me before the presentation."

"He should've been gone," Cleo added as she set the cat back down. "He was lying in wait, and that's an ambush. Asshole."

"Which Cleo called him, to his face. My favorite part. He gives her one of these." Sonya put on a superior look, added a slight nod. "'Cleo.' And she gives him the same nod, with an 'Asshole.'"

Both women broke into laughter as Owen grinned at Cleo.

"Well played. Major points."

"You didn't tell me about any of this."

"I wasn't going to text you about his bullshit," Sonya began, then stopped. "You're mad. It barely shows, but you're mad. I wasn't holding something back, I swear. I just didn't want to get into that stupidity in a text."

"Then let's hear it now."

"All right, yes, he should've been gone, so he did lie in wait. Our escort was surprised and embarrassed when he came strutting down the hall."

"He looked like a mannequin." Cleo peeked into a take-out box. "Lobster rolls, perfect."

"Fries, too. Better put them in the oven on warm," Owen warned, "if this is going to take a while."

"It won't. It didn't."

"Going in anyway, and my mannequin comparison wasn't a compliment. Fake man covered in designer smug."

"That's true. He lied about why he was still there. The escort told us later. He was just trying to get under my skin, claimed he'd been chatting with Miranda Ryder—she's top dog—and had the account sewn up. He claimed she'd confirmed it. That I only got the offer to present because of Burt—Burt Springer—and he made that sound salacious."

"Another good word," Trey said.

"I'm full of them today." Because that insinuation still stuck, she gulped wine to swallow it down again. "Burt's another sweet man—a man old enough to be my father. A family man. It turns out Cleo illustrated his granddaughter's favorite book. He reads to his four-year-old granddaughter. That's the kind of man Burt is."

"That's something you didn't mention to Burt Springer," Trey assumed.

"No. Would you have?"

"No."

"He called her a bitch."

"Well, shit." Owen looked at Trey.

"Cleo."

"Well, Son, he did."

"He said, after I told him to fuck off—in classier words—that he didn't realize I'd had so much bitch in me, and he was glad he'd dumped me. Which he didn't, and which, at this point, doesn't matter. I handled it, okay?"

"And then some" was Cleo's opinion.

"He wanted to make me nervous, undermine my confidence, and he did just the opposite. He revved me up."

"And she crushed it. Outside of college presentations and run-throughs like we did here, I've never actually seen my girl in action. Crushed. It."

To emphasize, Cleo clinked her glass to Sonya's.

"I want to hear about it. But if he contacts you or gets in your way again, I want to know about it. And not," Trey added, "two days later."

"There really wasn't anything you could have done," Sonya began.

"You'd have known you had someone pissed off for you."

Owen just held up two fingers, so Cleo held up three.

"No, make that four," she said. "Winter. But in Sonya's defense, she did her Taylor Swift and—Clover, bring it."

"Shake It Off" rocked out.

"And I did." Sonya rocked her hips and shoulders to prove it.

"I've got a question, but I want food, and so do the animals. I've got this part covered." Owen went to feed the pets.

"What's the question?" Sonya asked as she got plates.

"How you hook up with an asshole?"

"Jesus, Owen."

"No, Trey, it's a fair question—and I've asked myself the same. The answer's really twofold. First, he hid the asshole really well for quite a while."

"I have to agree there." Cleo pulled out the fries. "I nearly liked him. I mostly liked him because of Sonya, but I nearly liked him, and I've got an excellent asshole meter."

"He was great with my mother, and that's important to me. He was supportive at work, interested—or seemed to be interested in what I had to say. Attentive without being smothering, easy with my friends, and all of it."

When they sat at the table, she hunched her shoulders. "It wasn't until after the engagement that I started to see little things, then bigger ones. For the most part, I thought it was just my own nerves or the stress of planning this big, elaborate wedding. Doing a house search, all of it at once."

"Which you didn't want," Cleo pointed out.

"Which I didn't want. On that fateful day—before I knew it would be that fateful day—I realized there were things we had to address, talk out, come to better compromises on. Then, well, no need for that."

She sampled a fry, smiled. "The second part, and it's really the first? I wanted, I really wanted, to start to build what my parents had. The problem with that, other than him being a lying, cheating asshole?

We didn't want the same things at all. I'd just started to understand that when—fateful day.

"I'm grateful for that fateful day because—and I've done a lot of soul-searching on it—I wouldn't have gone through with it. The wedding. I'd probably have sent the invitations out, gotten that close, which would've been horrible. But the closer we got, the more he showed me, and the more unhappy and just unsettled I felt.

"So there you have it."

"Legit," Owen decided, and pointed at Trey. "Howie Queller."

"Yeah." Trey shook his head. "Friend of ours. High school and beyond. A few years ago, the three of us are having a beer, what, about a week before his wedding?"

"About that. And he all of a sudden pops up how he doesn't want to do it. Doesn't want to get married, how he's stuck now. Trey's soothing him some. Got the jitters, you love her, right? And Howie's saying how he thought he did, but he doesn't. He's not ready, and she wants this and that, and he doesn't. Trey's, man, you gotta talk to her, figure this out. How you don't want to make promises you can't keep."

"And you?" Cleo asked.

"Owen said: 'You don't put a ring on someone's finger unless you want it to stay there. If you don't, don't.'"

"Now Howie's all but crying in his beer about how excited his mom is, how her dad's spent all this money, how Alma—that's the bride—can't talk about anything but the wedding. So he gets married."

"We handled the divorce under a year later," Trey finished. "And it wasn't pretty."

Sonya ate some lobster roll. "I could've been Howie."

"Nah." Owen grabbed more fries. "Howie's a moron."

When they'd eaten, talked, when the kitchen was put to rights again, Cleo moved toward the mudroom for a jacket.

"I'm going to walk out with Pye and the boys, and call it early."

"Early's good. Thanks for bringing dinner, Owen."

"No problem. I'll walk out with her, and go from there. I still have things to get to."

When they went out, Sonya turned to Trey. "I'm trying to be sorry you were angry on my behalf. A little at me, but mostly for me."

"Mostly for, yeah. I know his type; I see them in court. I don't like that you had to deal with him."

"That's why I can't really be sorry. Come upstairs with me. I missed you. I missed being with you."

But first she held him. "I'm really, really glad I wasn't Howie."

"Since I'm thinking about getting you naked, I'm thrilled you're not Howie."

Outside, Owen started to call Jones.

"I've got a question first. What was your immediate thought when I said the asshole called Sonya a bitch?"

"That Trey and I should take a ride to Boston, then flip for who got to punch him first."

"That's what I thought."

"Trey wouldn't do it, not for words. But if that fucker goes after her again, even with words, he'll find a way to make him pay for it. That's what Trey does."

She nodded as they walked, as the sea beat its drum and the moon sailed overhead.

"I took a pair of his boxer shorts when we packed up his crap. I buried them with a curse. I really hope it worked at least some."

"What kind of curse?"

"Jock itch."

Owen winced, shifted. "Remind me to stay on your good side. I've got to get going."

"Mmm. Do you snore?"

"Nobody's complained. Why?"

"I like my sleep, so I need to know if I'll let you stay after we have sex or boot you out."

She turned, wrapped around him, and kissed him in the moonlight like a woman who'd already made up her mind.

"Is this because I talked about punching that guy?"

"That put a cap on it, but there are several more reasons in the bottle. Do you want to hear them now?"

"Not really. Do you snore?"

She smiled, took his hand, and drew him toward the house.

"Why don't you come in and find out?"

Dobbs didn't wait until three.

Just after one, the doorbell began its bong. And smoke alarms through the manor began to scream. The dogs leaped up barking.

Trey was out of bed in a flash and dragging on pants.

"It's Dobbs." Sonya scrambled up. "It's got to be."

"It's Dobbs, but we need to check. The alarm company's going to call, give them the code, tell them to hold off the fire department."

"I don't remember the code. Damn it!" The echoing boom from the third floor nearly drowned out her voice.

"LBM-1794."

Trey was out of the bedroom a step ahead of her and hit the hallway as Owen and Cleo rushed out of Cleo's room.

He said, because he couldn't think of anything else, "Okay. Ah, Sonya's going to hold off the fire department. You head down, we'll head up. If you see any smoke, any fire, send me a nine-one-one."

Shoving at his hair, Owen nodded. "It's Dobbs, but we look."

"It's Dobbs." But Trey began opening doors as he worked his way down the hall. "And we make damn sure."

"I told them it was some sort of a malfunction and we're working on it." As Trey did, Sonya checked rooms on the way to the stairs. "God, Trey, she wouldn't actually start a fire. She wants the manor."

"She's a lunatic. We check."

"There's no smoke. Not even her kind." But Sonya's heart hammered as they hurried to the third floor.

Her phone played Tom Petty's "Makin' Some Noise."

"That's right, that's right, Clover. She's just making some noise."

Enough that Sonya wanted to cover her ears.

But she worked her way down the hall with Trey, opening doors, checking rooms.

"The door to the Gold Room's already open."

"Yeah, I see it."

She grabbed his hand. "Don't even think about it."

"Too late not to think about it."

"Stay!" She snapped at the dogs. "And that means you, too."

"I got it." Maybe it grated, but he got it. "We decline the invitation." But he shined his flashlight into the thick, deep dark of the room.

He expected to see her, floating above the floor, arms outstretched, hair blowing, eyes lit. But except for furniture, the room stood empty.

"She's not in there." Sonya tightened her grip on Trey's hand. "She's somewhere else in the manor. Cleo, Owen."

"They're fine. So are we. We finish this floor, then the ballroom, the rest."

But when they started toward the ballroom, the cold washed over the hallway in an ice floe of air.

The lights they'd turned on snapped off.

Sonya felt it, actually felt it move by her. Like breath on the back of her neck. The dogs let out a growl that turned to a whine as it passed.

In the dark, a shadow darker still flowed down the hall.

A whisper came. "Death lives here." And a scream followed it.

The Gold Room door slammed; the lights flashed back on.

Silence fell so fast, so complete, Sonya's ears rang with it.

"Back in her cave," Trey muttered.

"I felt her. I felt her right behind me."

"Did she touch you?" Trey shoved the flashlight back in his pocket to run his hands over Sonya.

"No. At least—no. But I felt . . . Like someone breathing down the back of my neck."

He spun her around, pushed up her hair. "Nothing. Does anything hurt?"

"No. No. It was just a sensation. And I saw her, or the shadow of her. Did you see that?"

"Yeah, I saw it. I want to check the rest. We want to be sure, but I think it's over for tonight." He took her hand again. "Okay?"

She went with him, room by room.

"I'm texting Cleo to let them know we're nearly done. You must've noticed Owen didn't go home after all, and came out of Cleo's bedroom."

"I was a little distracted at the time, but it was hard to miss."

"Thoughts?"

"I'll go with Joe Pesci and 'There's a fucking surprise.'"

After an hour of stress, she laughed. And with considerable relief as they started back down, she leaned her head toward his shoulder. "You're okay with it?"

"Why wouldn't I be? They're both all grown up. You?"

"Cleo's my person, Owen's my favorite cousin, so I'm absolutely fine with it. And I'll ditto your *My Cousin Vinny* quote."

They reached the bedroom level as Cleo, Owen, Jones, and the cat came out of the servants' passage.

"All clear," Owen said.

"Same. A lot of noise and disruption, which was her point. She left the Gold Room," Trey added. "Wandered around some."

Sonya suppressed a shudder. "We saw her go back in. That's when the noise stopped."

"She did what she set out to," Cleo pointed out. "Got us all up and searching the house like the Scooby Gang."

"I'd say she's not happy you and I came back from Boston, Cleo."

"Oh, there's that," Cleo agreed as they started down the hall as a group. "And I think she got bitchy because there were four people sleeping in the house."

"That's happened plenty before."

"It has." She smiled at Owen. "But this time four people were sleeping after, let's say, they'd enjoyed the pleasures of the flesh."

"Jesus." As Sonya snickered, Owen scrubbed his hands over his face. "That's a way to put it."

"She's not flesh, and she can't enjoy its pleasures." Cleo shot a look at the ceiling. "I'm saying the old witch is jealous. I'm going back to bed."

Cleo turned to her room, gave Owen a look over her shoulder. "Well?"

"Well. Yeah." He glanced at Trey. "It's been a night," he said, then followed Cleo.

Chapter Twenty-four

In the morning, with the men gone and Cleo sleeping, Sonya settled in to work.

She expected her first order of non-business business would come in a conversation with Cleo about the change in sleeping arrangements.

The idea made her smile.

Since she'd already dealt with her emails and texts, she opened her first file.

Dobbs might have disrupted her night, but she damn well wouldn't screw with her workday.

And a bunch of pissy noises wouldn't drive her out of her own home.

Banging on the wrong door, she thought, and started another test of the Gigi's job.

At exactly nine-oh-one, she heard the ping of an incoming email. She nearly ignored it, but paused her work. If her client wanted another change, best to know now.

But the message came from Ryder, and Miranda Ryder's assistant, informing her Ms. Ryder wished to arrange a Zoom call at Sonya's earliest convenience.

"Shit, shit." Sonya pushed up to pace.

Too soon for good news, she calculated. But maybe, maybe, they just wanted a follow-up. Like a callback? Or they had a few questions.

Possible, she decided. Not probable, but possible.

"Just get it over with, Sonya."

Clover offered classic optimism in "Don't Stop Believin'."

"Right. It's fine. Absolutely fine. It's been a valuable experience."

She sat, emailed back that she was available now or would make herself available at a time that suited Ms. Ryder.

Then she gulped down water, wishing she'd grabbed a Coke instead. Especially when the response came immediately with the link.

"I guess that means right freaking now. God, I didn't think how I look!" Panicked, she grabbed the emergency video call makeup out of her desk drawer.

After a quick application, she took a breath, squared her shoulders. And clicked on the link.

"No music now, Clover," she murmured, and entered the room.

"Good morning, Ms. MacTavish. Thank you for your quick response."

"Good morning. It's nice to speak with you again."

Behind Miranda, the bookshelves held books, awards, photos. On a counter, and to the left of her shoulder, stood a vase holding an arrangement of white flowers.

"Again, on behalf of Ryder Sports, I'd like to thank you for the creativity and energy of your presentation."

At the words, so cool and polite, Sonya felt her stomach sink, and braced for the kiss-off.

"It was a valuable opportunity for me."

"As a woman in the first year of running her own . . ." Miranda trailed off. "Are you in a library?"

"In my home, yes. I work at home, and use the library as my office."

"It is a turret?"

"Yes, it is. My uncle . . ." Too complicated, she decided instantly. And it only postponed the inevitable. "I inherited the family home in Maine last winter."

"It's very impressive. In any case, we've given your presentation and direction serious consideration, as we have By Design's. I will say, those directions are divergent. You did an excellent job with yours, Ms. MacTavish."

"Thank you. I can say, sincerely, I appreciate the opportunity, and enjoyed stretching into a creative challenge of this scope. I understand a company with Ryder's longevity and reputation requires a more established team."

"Do you?" Miranda offered the barest hint of a smile. "There are some who agree with that. I'm not one of them, and I'm not alone in my opinion. Or in the decision to go with Visual Art and in your direction.

"Congratulations."

For two slow beats, Sonya's mind went and stayed blank.

"You're . . . giving me the account?"

"That's correct. Burt Springer wanted to make this call, but I overruled him. He will, however, be in touch later this morning to discuss the terms. He feels confident you'll come to an agreement."

"Yes. I'm sure we'll come to an agreement."

Her brain felt numb. Her body felt numb. But she knew her mouth moved, as she heard her own voice.

"Thank you for your confidence. I won't let you down."

"I trust you won't. Would you like to know why we decided to go with a freelance one-woman company in her first year of business?"

"I would, for a variety of reasons."

"You respected the history of this company, and the family behind it, while looking forward. Without the history and the family, there would be no Ryder Sports, and no looking forward. In addition, Ryder Sports isn't just for professional athletes, but for everyone. Your vision embraced exactly that."

"My father taught me how to ride a two-wheeler. It was a Ryder."

Now Miranda smiled fully. "Was it?"

"Yes. And I still remember that wild thrill when he let go. I think I'm about to feel it again."

"It's going to be a pleasure working with you. Burt will be in touch. Oh, one more thing? There are offices very near where Mr. Wise spoke with you before your presentation, and some with doors open."

"Oh."

"You won this account through your own merits and because we believe your vision aligns with ours. If we had opted to go with By Design, it would have been contingent on Mr. Wise being removed from the campaign. We don't tolerate dishonesty and bullying at Ryder. We'll speak again," she concluded, and signed out.

Instantly Tina Turner banged out with "The Best."

Still numb, Sonya just sat, staring at nothing, counting her own breaths.

When the numbness broke, she curled up in her chair and wept.

Cleo started her morning shuffle down the hall, and when she saw Sonya, it turned into a run.

"What happened? What's wrong?"

"Ryder," Sonya managed as Cleo wrapped around her.

"Oh, baby, I'm so sorry. I don't know—" She broke off when she drew Sonya's face up to swipe at her tears. "Wait, wait! I know that face. I know those kinds of tears. Oh my God, you got it! You got the account."

"I got the account."

Weeping with her now, Cleo dragged her up to embrace.

"I'm so happy for you. I'm so proud of you. Tell me what they said. Everything. I don't even need coffee!"

"They liked my direction—the history, the family, the everything."

"You were right about that direction, from the get-go. That was your instinct, your insight, and you ran with it. You made it work."

"I went numb, I mean like a full mind/body shot-of-Novocaine numb. Burt's going to contact me about terms. Terms. Oh my God, Cleo!"

"I'm going to dance now."

When Cleo did, Clover went with ABBA's "Dancing Queen."

"I've got to text Mom, and Trey, and oh, Corrine. Her photographs. Cleo."

"Dancing!"

"Cleo, somebody heard what Brandon said to me. Somebody overheard our conversation, and it got back to Miranda. That's who called to tell me."

"Good." Cleo stopped dancing long enough to shoot out a vicious smile. "I say that's good. And don't think for a second you got this account because of that."

"I probably would have thought that, but she told me I didn't. She said if they'd gone with By Design, they'd have stipulated he be removed from the team."

"I like her. Give me thirty years to grow up into her. Text your mom, text everybody! We're going to celebrate tonight. I'll figure out how after coffee."

"Would you bring me a Coke when you come back?"

"Can do."

When she did, Sonya paced her office. "I can't seem to sit yet. Mom's over the moon, maybe three times over it. Trey said they're picking us up at seven. Dinner at the hotel's fancy restaurant."

"I'm all in on that."

"This isn't how I thought I'd spend my morning. I was running tests, then I intended to stop them when you came out so I could grill you about Owen."

Cleo's lips curved in a slow, satisfied smile.

"I know that face, so things went well there, despite the disruption."

"Oh, Dobbs can stick it. I'm pleased to say things went exceptionally well there, twice, before the disruption."

"I thought he was going home last night."

"So did he." With a laugh, Cleo smoothed a hand over her hair. "I changed his plans. You're okay with this, aren't you, Son?"

"I love you both. I've loved you a lot longer, but I love you both. Still, if he hurts you, I'll . . ." Eyes narrowed, Sonya punched her right fist into her left open palm.

"You know, Son, you and Owen have a lot of similar traits. Now, since it's another gorgeous day, I'm going to put myself together and paint outside."

Sonya picked up her phone when it rang. "It's Burt."

Cleo blew her a kiss and walked away.

*   *   *

Once she finished the call with Burt, she cried again. Then she washed her face, drank her Coke, and got back to work.

She couldn't and wouldn't neglect her other clients because she'd just netted the big fish.

Toward the end of the day, Bree sent her the finalized menu, with vendors for each dish, for the open house in an email attachment.

Bree's message was:

> **Discuss again if you have to, but this is what you want.**
> **Gotta go out if you want a blowout!**

Damn right they wanted a blowout, especially now.

She printed two copies, carried one into Cleo's room to lay it on the bed beside what she assumed was Molly's choice of a short, sexy, lipstick-red number.

On her own bed she found the flirty periwinkle with its low back that Cleo and her mother had talked her into buying in Boston.

"If not now, when?" she decided, and further decided the dress, and the night, called for her curling iron.

When she went back to Cleo's room, her friend sat and slipped on her shoes. "Winter and I had it right with that dress."

"You did. And Molly picked a winner for you. Did you have a chance to look at the menu?"

"I did, and it gets a big wow. We could probably have done it, in at least twice the time and with considerable headaches and anxiety."

"Agree. So that's the discussion. I'll let her know it's a full-out go. How's the painting going?"

"I think it's finished. Letting it sit now, and I started another. I'll be down in two minutes."

Sonya heard the front door open, then Trey and Owen walked in.

Both men wore suits. She couldn't say why she found that so endearing.

Trey took one look at her. "Wow. If we didn't have a reason to celebrate, I do now. You look amazing."

"I feel the same."

Owen's gaze lifted as Cleo came down the stairs. Tilting her head, she crossed to him. "Don't I look amazing?"

"You always do."

"Clever man," she murmured. "Man in a suit."

"Only under duress."

"Duress looks good on you."

She ran a finger down his tie, and laughed when Clover played "Sharp Dressed Man."

As celebrations went, Sonya decided this one topped her current list. A couple of sharp-dressed men, a restaurant with a stunning view of the water, crystal sparkling in candlelight, and the delight of a bottle of champagne.

"This is beautiful. Really beautiful."

She tore her gaze from the view long enough to glance around. The white linen, the quietly flickering tea lights, servers in formal black, the whisper of music all combined in elegance.

"Trey figured pizza and beer didn't hit the mark."

"Not this time." Trey lifted his glass. "To a job well done, a victory well earned."

"Thank you. And here's to all of you for playing a part in it."

"Tell them about the bonus round," Cleo insisted. "Son's not petty enough to consider it a bonus, but I am. The asshole overplayed his hand."

"I actually am petty enough. Someone overheard his hallway bull-shit, and it made the rounds, I guess."

After she'd told them, Owen added another toast. "Almost as good as a punch in the face."

"I want to know if he tries to come back at you," Trey reminded her.

"I will, but . . . I see him in a hot-air balloon, and the wind is taking it farther and farther away. I can barely see it now." She narrowed her eyes. "You know, I think it's sprung a leak, and look at those clouds! Oops, now it's gone."

She sipped champagne.

"He will not be missed."

They drank champagne, ate perfectly prepared food.

"I can see why Bree wants these crab cakes at the Event." Sonya offered Trey a bite. "I've never had better. They do a mini version, so that's what we're having. And their mini beef tourtières."

"What the hell is that?" Owen asked.

"I admit I had to look it up. It's like a little pastry."

"Fancy stuff," Trey commented.

"We're also having pizza bites, jalapeño hush puppies—"

"Now you're talking." Owen gave her another toast.

"RSVPs started coming in." Cleo smiled, pure satisfaction. "We're going to have a packed house."

"Word's going around." Trey offered Sonya some of his salmon. "You've got the hot ticket of the summer."

"And we're going to do it up right. Cleo and I are hitting the garden center, and we're going to meet with the florist. We ordered the party lights, but we need a couple of handsome handy men to help with that."

"It's always something," Owen muttered. "You want that boat, don't you, Lafayette?"

"I do." Cleo gave him a lash flutter. "How long does it take two handsome handy men to hang some fairy lights?"

"How many did you get?"

Now she just smiled, said, "Mmmm."

"That's what I figured."

"You can be bribed with meatloaf and sex."

"Probably."

"Definitely," Trey corrected. "Are you worried about what Dobbs might pull with so many people in and around the house?"

"I'm trying not to think about it, but yeah, I do think about it. Still, when my mother came before for a couple days, things were benign, and relatively quiet."

"I'm counting on the good energy outweighing her dark energy. Lights, music, people?" Cleo lifted her hands. "It's what the manor was built for."

"She won't win." Sonya spoke decisively. "Maybe it's naive, but I feel like getting the Ryder account, and it was against the odds, means that just standing up, pushing forward counts. And maybe if—when—I go through the mirror again, I'll learn something more. Some way to get the rings. I wouldn't be here, Cleo wouldn't, the four of us wouldn't be here together if things hadn't happened the way they happened. So . . ."

With a shrug, Sonya picked up her water glass. "Keep standing up and pushing forward. What?" she said when Trey just smiled at her.

"She doesn't have a chance."

"I can give you some time on Saturday for the damn lights."

Cleo raised her eyebrows at Owen. "Without a bribe?"

"Oh hell, I'll still take the bribe—no sane man turns down meat-loaf and sex. But family doesn't need bribes."

"As much as I liked Clarice, you're secure in the favorite-cousin slot. I'm probably going to regret this, but let's order dessert."

They lingered over dessert and coffee, over easy conversation. Then Trey rose to extend his hand to the man who walked to their table. Owen did the same.

"Good to see you. Sonya MacTavish, Cleo Fabares, this is Anson Miller, Seth's dad."

The first word that came to Sonya's mind was *distinguished*. Flecks of silver dashed through a head of gold hair brushed back from a narrow, sharp-boned face. He had hazel eyes with a hint of green and a ready smile.

"It's nice to meet you. You have a beautiful hotel."

"Thank you for that. I had a dinner in the private dining room with some VIPs, and saw you when I came out. I just wanted to say hello, and don't want to interrupt."

"You're not," Sonya assured him. "Can you join us for coffee?"

"Thanks, but coffee at this time of night's only for the young and adventurous."

But when the server offered a chair, Anson took it.

"Just for a moment. I couldn't pass up the opportunity to meet the new mistresses of the manor. From Louisiana, aren't you, Ms. Fabares?"

"Cleo, and yes, originally."

"Anson knows what's what in Poole's Bay," Owen put in.

"Got a little Poole in me, from way back."

"Of course! On the family tree in Collin's book," Sonya remembered. "Ah, down from Connor and Arabelle's daughter. Um, Gwendolyn, and, oh wait—Sebastian Haverton?"

Anson's eyebrows lifted. "Well, someone else knows what's what. Collin was a good man. I'm sorry we never had the chance to know your father."

"He was a good man, too."

"No doubt. I hope you're both happy in the manor, and we—my wife and I—look forward to seeing it and you next month. Hospitality's been my business since I was younger than any of you, and I appreciate when someone offers it. My best to your family, Trey, Owen," he said as he rose. "Enjoy the rest of your evening."

"Another cousin," Sonya said when Anson left, and smiled at Owen. "You're still my favorite."

On the drive home she looked back and thought, yes, a perfect way to celebrate what was, for her, no small victory.

An elegant evening out, a respite from the routine she fell into—and admittedly embraced—a chance to dress up and share that celebration with people she loved.

It didn't get much better.

And tomorrow, she thought, she'd dive right back into routine. Happily.

But when she looked up, caught a glimpse of the manor, she laid a hand over Trey's. "All the lights are on. I swear every light's on."

"I see it."

"She wouldn't turn on the lights." In the back, Cleo leaned forward. "If anything, she'd shut them all off."

"I gotta go with Lafayette on that one. Dobbs goes for the dark."

"That may be true, but they're still on." Sonya craned her neck as they came around the last turn. "Except the Gold Room. God, we left all the animals inside. If she's—"

"Owen and I'll check it out." Trey pulled up. "You and Cleo wait here."

"My house," Sonya said, pushing her door open even as Cleo did the same.

"Pig's eye" was Cleo's answer.

They heard it before they reached the door. Barking, music, laughter.

"What the actual fuck?" Owen said as Trey opened the door.

They caught a glimpse—quick, but clear—of a boy as he tossed the red ball, of people dancing as music—Lady Gaga's "Bad Romance"—blasted.

They vanished, smoke in the wind. For an instant longer, one remained, the pretty young blonde with her fall of shining hair, her bright blue eyes. She flashed a happy smile before she, too, was gone.

The three dogs panted, and Yoda let out a sad little whine. The cat stretched on the newel post as if a hand stroked her, then leaped down.

"Bon Dieu de merde," Cleo said, and laughed.

"Say what?"

She flicked a glance at Owen. "Holy shit. When I'm that surprised, the French comes out. They had a party!"

"They had a party," Sonya murmured. "There were so many, but it was all so fast I couldn't . . ."

"The kid throwing the ball." Trey bent to pick it up, studied it a moment as if he held an alien object. Then he tossed it for the dogs to chase. "And Clover."

"Yeah, caught her." When Mookie won the race, returned with the ball, Owen gave it a toss. "And you had that right. Hot babe."

"It—it was happy." As the music continued, Sonya wandered the foyer. "And loud. I guess, maybe, they didn't hear us? That sounds crazy, but given the circumstances. And now I wonder if they do this when we're not here."

"I think they were celebrating for you."

Touched, stunned, Sonya turned back to Trey as the music switched to Whitney Houston and "I Wanna Dance with Somebody (Who Loves Me)."

"And there you go," he said.

"So do I." Cleo grabbed Owen's hand. "I wanna dance with somebody."

"Me, too!"

As she kicked off her shoes, Sonya decided this made it the perfect celebration.

So they danced in the light as the spirits of the manor had danced.

Chapter Twenty-five

Maine bloomed in May. To add their part, Sonya and Cleo decided to hit the garden center.

"Son, we need to take the truck for this."

"But do we really?"

"We do, really. Even if we just do the dozen pots we picked out, washed out, we're not going to have room in your car or mine. We have to buy potting soil, and the peat moss. I really want to try herbs and tomatoes. Maybe peppers, too. Add all that to flats of flowers, and there's just no way."

"But it's so big."

"That's the point." Along with a bolstering smile, Cleo tried an encouraging shoulder pat. "You can do this."

"I've got an idea!" Sonya shot a finger in the air. "Why don't you drive the big, scary truck?"

Cleo shook her head. "You first."

"There's only one solution. Rock, paper, scissors."

A moment later, Sonya looked down as Cleo's rock crushed her scissors.

"Damn it. I know you're right about taking it. I hate you're right about taking it. I should've done a test run. Like just driven up and down Manor Road a couple times."

"We're going for it." So saying, Cleo pulled out the remote she'd stuck in her pocket and opened the garage door.

It sat in there. Big, black, terrifying.

"It's a monster." Sonya approached it with dread. But she opened the driver's door.

She wanted to fill those damn pots with flowers, didn't she?

"Okay. I'm getting in." When she did, she sat staring straight ahead. "I can't reach the pedals, so—"

"That's why you adjust the seat."

She did, fussed with the mirrors, put on her seat belt.

"Maybe it won't start."

Of course it did. Either Trey or Owen had run it every couple of weeks since she'd moved in, so it started right up. With a roar.

"Oh God. One step at a time," she muttered. "One step at a time. I'm taking off the brake. I'm putting it in drive. Just FYI, I will not attempt to back it in again if we survive this trip."

Holding her breath, she eased on the gas. "We're moving."

"If we move at this speed, we might get there in time for the end-of-summer sale."

"All right." Face grim, Sonya vised her hands on the wheel. "Remember, you asked for it."

She made it down the drive, turned onto Manor Road.

"I'm driving a freaking truck."

"I'm driving it back!"

Somewhere along the twenty-minute drive, Sonya's legs stopped shaking. She almost enjoyed it.

What she enjoyed, thoroughly, was wandering the big garden center outside Poole's Bay, debating with Cleo on what to buy, asking for advice from staff, other customers.

She figured what they didn't know about gardening they made up for by knowing color, shape, texture. And they'd both studied up on the basics.

Maybe the bare basics, but the basics.

They wanted scent, too, and herbs. And because she got completely caught up, what she felt were adorable tomato plants, some peppers, bags of soil, cute gardening gloves, fertilizer, a shiny new watering can, wind chimes.

Then they saw her, the fairy with the dreaming face and spread wings. She held a crystal ball in her hand, powered by solar, as she bent over as if to sniff the blooms.

"Son, we must have her."

"Cleo, we must."

In the end, they bought so much—even with the fairy and what they deemed a goddess holding a solar lantern riding in the back seat—it all barely fit into the bed of the truck.

"We lost our minds," Sonya decided.

"I can't argue, but God, this is fun." Cleo rubbed her hands together. "I'm taking the wheel."

After they got home, it took a full hour to haul everything to the back, to place the statues where they felt they belonged while Yoda and Pye sniffed at everything.

They put up and filled the hummingbird feeder, assured bear wouldn't come calling there.

Then armed with spades, gloves, soil, and a bevy of plants, they started on the pots they'd already placed.

A kind of art, Sonya thought as she mixed colors, shapes, varied heights.

"I need one of those spilly-over things." As she reached for one, she studied Cleo's pot. "That's beautiful, and you know, so's mine. We can't kill them, we just can't."

"We won't. We're going to take good care of them, and if we mess something up, we've got Jerome. Plus, if Eleanor takes care of the solarium plants, maybe she'll keep an eye on these, too."

Pausing, she looked over at Sonya.

"You had to see where he—it had to be Jerome—prepped that area where I can put the herbs. I can walk out of the kitchen and cut what I need. The tomatoes and peppers can go over there, too. It's good light."

By the time they finished the pots and realized they had enough left for half a dozen more, Anna dropped by.

"I heard you two loaded up the truck. And now I see my information was accurate. Just wow."

"We went overboard." Sonya pulled off her gloves.

"Not possible. You can use what's left to fill in the beds, and still go back for more."

"Really?"

"Oh, absolutely." As she gave Sonya a nod, Anna gestured. "You could mass that half flat of impatiens over there, and pop some of that heliotrope there."

"Wait." Sonya held up a hand. "You know what you're doing. If we haul, will you point?"

"Got ginger ale?"

"All you can drink."

They hauled, Anna pointed, they placed. Digging in could wait until after a break. But it didn't take long to realize Anna was right.

They could actually buy more.

"I love your new statues. I love what you're doing here. These chairs." She sat in one Cleo had painted on her sabbatical. "So fresh and cheerful. The flowers, all of it. Now I'm going to tell you, after much debate, discussion, consideration, Seth and I decided on the mural. Do you really have time to do it?"

"Try to stop me," Cleo told her. "Which one?"

"You made it tough, giving us two fabulous choices. But we want number one. And I can see that's what you were hoping we'd want."

"My personal favorite."

"And mine," Sonya added. "Both are adorable, but that one just had a little more touch of whimsy."

"Tell me when you're ready for me to start on it."

"Can we say anytime after your open house?"

"We can."

Yoda let out a bark and dashed.

"I think our handsome handymen have arrived. We talked Trey and Owen into hanging some lights," Sonya explained.

Mookie and Yoda raced around the side of the house, body-bumping each other in insane joy. Jones swaggered behind them, giving them his one-eyed look of disdain.

When the men came around, Trey took a study of pots and beds. "Been busy, and you drove the truck."

He came up on the porch, bent down to kiss his sister's cheek. "How's my niece?"

"Active. Very. We're considering starting up an infant soccer league. She'll be captain."

"We'll cheer her on," he promised as he pulled Sonya up, kissed her. "You drove the truck," he repeated.

"Like Owen wears a suit: under duress. But we needed it for this."

"Obviously," Owen replied. "I like the new girls. Anything left at the plant place?"

"We left a few things," Cleo told him. "And since Anna's given us some pointers, we may go back for more."

"And I've got my own selections still in the car." Anna levered herself up. "So fill-in-the-blank Kate Miller and I are going home to plant."

"Should you be doing that?"

"I'm pregnant, Trey, not disabled. And we're going to go enjoy this gorgeous day. Talk soon."

Trey watched her go, then turned to Sonya. "Should she be doing that?"

"I have no idea, but she's a smart woman, so I'd say she does. And our break's over. We'll show you the lights and where we want them—thanking you in advance—before we start digging again."

Shortly, the men, hands in pockets, stood studying the weeping tree with its thick, curved branches and delicate pink blossoms.

And exchanged a look.

"I'll get the ladder."

When Owen trudged off to the garage, Sonya and Cleo went back to planting.

She'd helped her mother—a little—planting things in the spring, Sonya remembered. And she'd done a little more at her condo. But nothing, she thought as she dug, to this extent.

She liked it more than she'd anticipated.

Not just the pots, which had been blank canvases, but now digging in the ground, filling in canvases already begun by another hand.

She worked on Anna's suggestions while Cleo focused on the herbs and vegetables.

More taking ownership.

The dogs wandered front to back, as if supervising light stringing and planting, while the cat curled up on the deck to take a nap in the sun.

When the men came around to add lights to the deck, she simply filled with happiness. She sat back on her heels, swiped a gloved hand over her forehead, and left a smear of soil behind.

Owen stopped by Cleo. Sonya couldn't hear the words, but a moment later, Owen shook his head. He walked to the garden shed, then came out with a bag of something he took to her.

She'd reached the end of the bed, noted Cleo worked in another spot, when Owen and Trey walked to her.

"Done," Owen said.

"It's going to look great. Any lights left over?"

"You bought enough to light up half the forest," Trey pointed out.

"I was just thinking, if there's enough, there's that kind of pergola with the big, twisty vines?"

"Wisteria."

She looked up at Owen, smeared more dirt on her face. "Is it? I know wisteria—the blooms anyway. They're gorgeous! Maybe, since we have them, we could put lights there."

Trey didn't bother to sigh. "I'll get the ladder."

"What was in the bag you took to Cleo?"

"Epsom salts."

Frowning, she rose, stretched her back. "Like what you put in the bath for aches—which I may do later?"

"That, and what you add to the soil when you plant tomatoes, peppers, other stuff. Magnesium," he added. "They want it."

"Oh."

"Did you mix up deer spray?"

"Not yet."

"If you don't want to look out here tomorrow and see stumps, mix it, spray it."

"All right, but some of what we got is deer resistant."

Owen said, "Uh-huh," and walked over to study the pergola.

Sonya walked over to Cleo.

"Owen says to mix up the deer spray and use it."

"He gets bossy, but he's probably right. The last thing we want is those pretty deer coming in and nibbling on all this. Go look at my herb bed! And the rest. And it smells so good already."

"I will. And if you've got the rest of this, I'll go make sandwiches."

"I've got it, and I'm hungry." Cleo glanced up. "You've got dirt all over your face, Son."

"I do?" She swiped at it. "They could've told me."

Annoyed, she went around to see the herb bed. So pretty, she thought, and hadn't they been smart to get those sweet little plaques to stick in the ground that identified the herbs?

Since she'd gone that far, she continued around the front to admire the tiny lights running along the branches and the blossoms dripping from them.

She drew in the warm spring air, the scent of it carried on the steady sea breeze.

A good day's work, she thought. Lights, flowers to dress her home.

When she went inside, Clover greeted her with Ella Fitzgerald and "A Flower Is a Lovesome Thing."

"Sounds like an old one, but a new one for me. You're expanding my musical vocabulary."

After she washed up, she just had to look out the windows. Flowers on the deck, flowers in the beds, Cleo in her adorable garden hat, men hanging lights among the wisteria she imagined dripping color and scent before much longer.

Still brimming with happiness, she got out the sandwich rolls, the deli meats, cheeses. Ice-cold Cokes—unless the men wanted a Saturday afternoon beer—good sandwiches, plenty of chips.

A kind of inaugural garden picnic.

As she worked, she heard the dumbwaiter hum its way up to the butler's pantry. It made her smile and wonder what Molly sent up. Maybe another pretty platter for the sandwiches, or picnic plates.

She stopped to go into the butler's pantry and open the dumb-waiter.

The rat, big and black, stared back at her with feral red eyes. Its long, skinny tail swished. It bared its teeth.

She couldn't stop the scream, or the second that ripped out of her as she slammed the door shut again and stumbled back.

She heard it scrabbling inside, even as she heard the laugh, the long, terrible laugh, echo from above.

Cleo burst in, rushed to her.

"What is it? Shut the fuck up!" she shouted when the laugh came again.

"Don't open it. Don't open it."

Trey ran in, and Owen, and the dogs, even the cat as Cleo wrapped around Sonya.

"She's shaking," Cleo said, and wrapped tighter. "I don't know what happened."

"In there." As she pointed, smoke leaked out of the dumbwaiter. "God, oh God. A rat. There's a rat."

Immediately, Cleo hauled Sonya several feet away.

"I don't think so," Trey murmured, and even as Sonya shouted, "Don't!" he opened it.

A trail of smoke billowed out, then nothing.

"It wasn't real." For whatever reason, the realization made Sonya shake harder. "It wasn't real."

"You sit down now. Come on, you sit." Cleo pulled her to a counter stool. "I heard her laughing. This was one of her nasty tricks."

"It looked so real. I slammed the door, and I heard it inside. It looked so real."

"Nothing there now." Trey took over for Cleo, drew Sonya against him, stroked her hair. "You don't have any rats or rodents in the house. No sign of them anywhere. We've been all through it, remember?"

"I know, I know, but . . . God. God." Then she pushed away, color flooding back into her face. "Goddamn it! I screamed. She made me scream, and she laughed. I fell for it."

"If I open a door and see a rat, I'll probably make some noise."

Owen's comment got a look of approval from Cleo.

"You shut the door," Trey pointed out. "You didn't run."

"More from being frozen in place than anything else. It was big, really big, and solid black. Red eyes, pointy little teeth. When I slammed the door on it, I could hear it, like it was trying to claw its way out."

"I'll get you some water."

"No, Cleo, I'm okay now. I really am. I'm just pissed she made me scream."

"Then I'll give that dumbwaiter a good scrubbing out."

"I got it. No, I've got it," Owen insisted. "Maybe somebody could finish making those sandwiches. We'll take one to go if everything's settled back down. If Cleo wants her boat before next season, I've got work—and Trey's working with me."

Sensing Trey about to object, Sonya squeezed his hand. "That's fine. I'm fine. Nothing's going to screw up this very good day."

"If you come back about seven, I'm going to grill some chicken."

As he filled a bucket with hot, soapy water, Owen glanced back. "You know how to grill?"

"I can figure it out. Sit, Son. I'll finish these sandwiches."

"We'll be back by seven," Trey promised. "Sooner if you need."

"We're fine," Sonya said again. "Cleo and are going to take our sandwiches out to the deck and admire our work, and yours. She hates that, so she sent me a rat. She hates we've added color and light and scent. Hates we're putting our mark on the manor. We're going to keep doing just that, and she can send a swarm of her fake rats."

"Let's not go there," Cleo said, and finished making sandwiches.

They ate on the deck with the cat and all three dogs. Then, vowing to be wise gardeners, mixed up the deer spray. When the animals deserted them, they agreed the smell would keep anything with a nose from munching on the garden.

Cleo spent the rest of the afternoon painting while Sonya worked on the cards for the open house dishes.

When the men came back, Cleo proved she could grill. They ate on the deck, and lingered to watch the sun go red behind the trees.

And to Sonya's delight, watched the solar lights twinkle on.

"You were right." Trey stretched out his long legs. "Worth it."

"I want to see the tree. Let's go see the tree!"

When they did, Sonya felt that happiness brim over again. "It's perfect. It's exactly how I imagined."

"I hate to say it." Owen scanned the tree, then gestured. "You've got enough left to do that giant rhodo on the other side of the house. Nice counterpoint."

Trey shot him a look. "I'm not getting that damn ladder. It's dark. Tomorrow," he said to Sonya. "We'll take a look at it tomorrow."

The week passed quick and, thankfully, quiet. Even through another meeting with Bree where they went over logistics, took another tour of the house, the grounds.

RSVPs poured in, with barely a regret. They ordered flowers for delivery the day before, rented stanchions to block off the third floor.

Flowers bloomed in the sun. Lights twinkled in the dark.

Cleo painted, sometimes at home, sometimes in the village. Sonya filled her days with work—with breaks for walks with Yoda in the garden or by the seawall.

If she kept an eye on the Gold Room windows, it wasn't a fearful one, but one of defiance.

In the evenings when Cleo cooked, she sat at the counter going over the checklist for the open house.

"We're really set. I'm obsessing," Sonya admitted. "But we're really set. With a big cheer for Bree."

"Cheer! We'd better be set at this point. Family's going to start pouring in, so we'd better be. And I'm thinking we have a kind of buffet for the ones who come in on Friday. I think I can do a ham."

Slowly, Sonya repeated, "You think you can do a ham?"

"I talked to Corrine about it, and I think I can do it. A ham, those roasted potatoes I've got down now, a veg, maybe some crudités, a cheese platter."

"I call the crudités and cheese platter. And I can do some beer bread, since I've got that down. You're right. We have to feed them. It's going on the list. You know, at this very moment, all this seems like such a good idea."

"And we're hoping it still feels that way after."

"Yeah, we are."

"Positive thoughts bring positive vibes," Cleo declared. "How's work going?"

"Really well. Gigi's is officially up and running, along with the Ogunquit law firm, and Ryder's really happy with me. And the painting?"

"I was going to wait until I had some wine to talk about that."

"I'm getting it now. Spill."

"I took three framed canvases down to Kevin. He took all three."

"All! Yay—but . . . not the watercolor of the tree."

"That stays here. He also asked if I'd do a showing in the fall."

"Cleo!"

"I think I will. Sabbatical will be over, but I'll have enough. Even with doing the mural for Anna."

She handed Cleo a glass of wine. "I love our life."

Cleo clinked glasses, then smiled when Yoda scrambled up to run to the door. "Looks like a part of that life's coming around for dinner."

Sonya did love their life and the sharp turn it had taken months before. She loved her work, the result of another sharp turn into freelancing. Though it came with stunning challenges, ones she was determined to meet, she loved her home.

She loved Trey. Maybe they hadn't said those words to each other yet, but she knew love. Hard to say it, she could admit, as a year before she'd designed her wedding invitations to another man.

And she loved their life, so why rush it?

After ending a virtual meeting with Burt and some of Ryder's marketing team, she sat back, satisfied.

Her work, she thought, her art, her vision would soon come to life on a big-ass billboard in Portland.

"It's a hell of a thing, Yoda." She rubbed his back idly with her foot. "Consider this a quick victory lap before I start the mood board for a new client."

As she worked, Clover's music played, and the breeze wafted in the open windows.

A pretty perfect way, she decided, to end one month and start another. She hoped Cleo enjoyed the same, painting down in the village at the marina.

If part of her stayed braced, always braced, for whatever Dobbs would try next, she wouldn't let it interfere with what she loved.

When her phone rang, she stepped back from the beginnings of her new board.

Sonya picked up the phone, and her heart dropped a little when she saw the display.

By Design.

No, she wouldn't let the fact it might be Brandon stop her from answering her own phone.

"This is Sonya."

"Sonya, Laine Cohen. Can I put you on speaker? Matt's here, too."

"Yes, of course. Hi, Matt!"

She pictured them both, in Laine's office, the view of the Boston Common behind her. Laine with her sharp wedge of hair the color of Sonya's formal dining room table. She'd have a pair of readers—some bold color—on a chain around her neck.

And her partner, Matt, sitting on the L of Laine's desk, his glossy blond hair catching the light through the big window.

They'd been good for her, good to her from her start as an intern right through her resignation.

"How are you doing?" Matt asked. "How's Maine?"

"I'm doing really well, and I love Maine. Wait just a second."

Because they'd been good to her, good for her, she walked to the open window.

"Hear that? That's the Atlantic. I'm looking at it, and the boats on it, from my office window."

"You sound happy," Laine commented.

"I am, very. How are both of you?"

"Busy, which makes us both happy. Sonya, Matt and I wanted to call you and congratulate you on the Ryder account."

"Thank you. That's so . . . that's so you."

"We've spoken with Miranda Ryder, and with Burt," Matt put in. "Both speak highly of you, and your work. I hope you know Laine and I feel the same."

"I do. I wouldn't be where I am, professionally, without the foundation you gave me."

"That's not to say we're not disappointed to lose that account, but," Laine added, "you earned it. Now, after considerable . . . discussion, Matt and I agreed we needed to speak with you on another matter. We were informed about Brandon's behavior and actions at Ryder."

Sonya walked away from the window, began to pace. "That door's closed for me."

"I hope it is. Matt and I met with Brandon before his presentation, one that was scheduled so as to avoid any overlap with yours. At that time, we directed him, clearly, firmly, that if for any reason the two of you crossed paths, he would remain professional, polite, refrain from discussing your past history. He was there to represent By Design, and we expected him to meet those standards."

"He failed. Laine and I want you to know we're sorry for it."

"It's not your fault. Not what happened at Ryder, not the past history."

"Regardless. He represented us. Matt and I were very clear. Brandon chose to ignore our directive."

"Childish," Matt muttered. "Petty."

"We met with Brandon regarding this incident. He claims you deliberately waylaid him, insulted him, Matt, me."

That fired her up. "I did no such thing! I promise you, I—"

"We're aware of that," Laine interrupted. "Even if this business hadn't been overheard, we know better, Sonya."

"We know you," Matt said. "Miranda thought Laine and I should know, he also did his best to undermine you and your work during his presentation. She found it very . . . what was her word for it?"

"Unbecoming," Laine supplied. "As a result of our meeting with Brandon, and by mutual agreement, he is no longer with By Design."

"Oh."

Sonya's mind went temporarily blank.

"Under normal circumstances, we'd keep this as internal company business. Matt was very persuasive otherwise, and, frankly, I really couldn't disagree with him. However fond we are of you, Sonya—"

"And we are!"

Laine gave a light laugh. "And we are, we didn't come to this decision for you, but for the company we've built, for its standards. We're telling you these details in case Brandon attempts, in any way, to malign your personal or professional reputation."

"Forewarned is forearmed," Matt tossed in.

"Yes, thank you. I don't take blame for any of it, but I'm sorry."

"As we all are. We wish you nothing but the best, Sonya. While we're disappointed about the account, Matt and I take some pride in your accomplishments. I'll add Miranda also mentioned that when asked, and in contrast to Brandon, you spoke with respect and affection for By Design. We appreciate it."

"You earned the respect and affection."

"If you ever decide to come back to Boston, our door's open," Matt told her.

"Thanks. This is home now."

When she hung up, Clover tried Billy Joel's "A Matter of Trust."

"I guess it was. He broke it with me, now he broke it with them. And I can't figure out how I feel about it. Taking a break. Come on, Yoda. Let's go for a walk."

Chapter Twenty-six

She opted for the gardens. While the sea always enthralled, she decided she needed the peace of the gardens, the simple joy of knowing she'd played a part in adding to them.

She tested the soil on the deck pots, found it—as always—moist. What she and Cleo had planted had already begun to fill and spill.

While Yoda wandered and sniffed, she noted that irises had begun to bloom, some purple, some butter yellow, some tender peach.

And the wisteria dripped from the pergola. A dwarf tree spread an umbrella of snowy white blossoms.

She'd yet to spot a single weed, and found none now as she, like Yoda, wandered and sniffed.

When she couldn't identify a plant—which was often, even if she'd planted it herself—she used her app. One of these days, she promised herself, she'd know them all.

But now it calmed her, settled her to just walk as the wind chimes they'd hung tinkled or gave their low, muted bong.

She decided to circle around, check Cleo's herb bed, see if any blossoms—a daily hope—had opened on the tomatoes or peppers.

But when she called to Yoda, who'd wandered closer to the woods than she'd realized, he just kept going.

"Yoda, come back here!" She started jogging in his direction as his stubby legs picked up speed. "Yoda! Damn it, don't go in there today. I don't have the bear spray!"

But he ran straight in, and muttering curses, she had no choice but to follow.

Trees had leafed out, so the sun shimmered its way through them. Though she felt the charm of it all—almost like her father's painting over the fireplace back in Boston—she wasn't prepared for a walk in the woods.

She heard him barking now as she continued to call. Probably after a squirrel, a chipmunk, a rabbit, whatever.

"Come on, Yoda, this isn't like you. You're such a good boy. Come on, and we'll get you a treat!"

Wildflowers reached up where they could catch the sun, and the deeper shadows showed hints of green.

If she heard rustling, she imagined squirrel, chipmunk, rabbit. And refused to let her mind drift to bear.

She prayed her adventurous dog stuck to the path and didn't end up getting them both lost.

A rustling—bigger than squirrel, chipmunk, rabbit—made her heart skip. Then a deer leaped across the path and vanished in those green-hued shadows.

Birds sang out; the pines whispered.

And she felt it, that pull. Just a tug at first, but irresistible.

"Oh God. Here? Now? Why?"

Though she slowed her pace, it pulled her forward, a thread she simply couldn't break. So she went deeper into the shadows and light, deeper yet until all she heard was her own heart pounding.

It stood on the path, dappled in that light and shadow. And here, in the deep woods, the predators framing the glass seemed at home.

Yoda sat at its feet, his head ticking back and forth.

Did he see himself? she wondered.

She didn't. She saw a blur of light and shadow, the green of trees, the brown of the path. But not a reflection. A continuance.

"How is this even possible? How could it be out here?"

When Yoda wagged at her, she crouched down. "You have to stay because I have to go. I have to."

She straightened, stared at the mirror as she heard—distantly—the sound of hooves.

"If anything hurts my dog, I swear, I'll make them pay for it."

She went through the mirror.

And into the woods, on the path. The same path, she knew it, but different. The air so much cooler, and if she hadn't felt fall in that air, she saw it in the trees flaming with it.

1805

Arthur Poole slowed his horse from gallop to a light trot. No hurry, after all. He had nothing but time today. And his mood stayed lifted high after the gallop.

He was a contented man, a successful man, and one who considered himself in his prime. As hardly more than a boy, he'd sailed from London and near poverty to the rough and rugged coast of Maine.

With a dream. With ambition. With a strong back and determination.

And with those, he'd built ships, and a thriving business. He'd built a home worthy of a successful man, and soon—after he'd ridden out of woods that belonged to him—he'd sit by the fire in that home—Poole Manor—put his feet up, and have a glass of whiskey.

But now he enjoyed the ride, the solitude, and the time for reflection.

He'd built a family as well, and had such pride in them. More, and it surprised him, even more pride than he had in his business, his great house, the village below that carried his name.

The scrappy boy from London.

And he felt joy that his eldest son—four minutes ahead of his twin—had asked for the hand of Astrid Grandville. Not simply because she came from a good family, a wealthy family, but because she had a spine and mixed it with a sweetness.

And above all, she loved his son, and he loved her. He could see it, feel it, and felt that joy in knowing it.

Collin would marry for love. He hadn't, Arthur thought. He'd married for need, for ambition, for the wealth that came with the wife.

But he had grown to love, and deeply.

Perhaps it had been the birth of their first children, Collin and Connor, that had opened that part of him. And as years passed, as the family grew, so did his love for the woman who made that family with him.

Now, older and wiser, he was content to—slowly—turn the reins of the business over to his sons. Good, bright, steady young men, both of them. And he could and did trust his eldest to tend to his siblings when the time came for it. To make a home, as he had, in Poole Manor.

But today wasn't about a far-flung future. He had more ships to build, plans to expand the manor again.

After all, he'd have grandchildren coming before too much longer.

The thought made him laugh at himself.

"Wedding first." He gave his mount a pat on her long neck. "And we'll see to it the manor shines like a jewel for it. The most important wedding Poole's Bay has ever seen."

The woman stepped onto the path so he had to pull up his horse. The woman dressed in black, her black hair a tumble rather than modestly restrained. And her dark eyes full of uncanny light.

He knew her, Hester Dobbs. He knew her for a witch.

A chill ran through him as she smiled.

"Woman, you have no place here."

"I will have. I will have my place here, in these woods, in the grand grounds before them, in the manor that rises over the sea. I will have all."

"Go back to your cottage, woman, and stir your witch's brew."

"Oh, I have, Arthur Poole. I have. And your son drank that brew thinking it was no more than a cup of water after a long ride. And when he did, I bedded him in my cottage in the deep woods."

Rage rose up. "I can have you hanged for it."

"But you won't." She stepped closer to him, laid a light hand on the horse's neck. "I tell you now, Collin Poole, your firstborn, your heir, is mine. As these woods will be mine. And I will be mistress of the manor for all time."

"And I tell you, you will have nothing. You will not touch my son again, and I will make certain of it. I will see you dragged from your cottage, banished from Poole's Bay. You will have nothing of mine, and never will you step foot in my home as long as I live."

"This is true. This I know. I have seen it, and so."

She lifted her hands.

"In this place, I call the wind. And as it blows, your life I end."

The horse shied as the wind swirled, as it moaned like a wounded man and sent leaves spinning.

With a curse, Arthur controlled it.

"Be damned to you, witch!" Arthur shouted it, but Dobbs continued.

"Father to son, the manor will pass, and under my spell, he will do all I ask. With my power your life I take. Now turn and turn and bend and break!"

His head turned at an odd angle on his neck. For an instant, his eyes, Poole green, bulged, and his mouth opened as if to gasp for air.

Then something cracked, a hideous sound. And he fell, limp and lifeless, to the ground.

With a laugh, she gave the horse a swat to send the mare running down the path. Stepping over, Dobbs looked down at Arthur.

"You thought you could stand against me? Keep me from what I desire? Your death only brings me closer to what is mine, what will always be mine."

She lifted her arms again, turned in the swirling wind. "I am and will be mistress of the manor. All who stand against me will meet death."

She started to slip back in the woods, then turned her head sharply.

Her eyes looked mad, wild and mad, as they stared down the path. The path where Sonya stood by the mirror.

"No one there. No one. And yet . . ."

As if in pain, Dobbs lifted a hand to her temple, pressed.

"Seven? Seven? A number of power. Seven. What does it matter?"

She looked back at Arthur's body, and smiled.

"They'll find him here, and mourn and grieve. And I will feast on their tears."

As she gathered the skirts of her dress around her, Dobbs slipped into the trees.

Shivering in the brisk air, Sonya stood as she was. And shed the first tear for Arthur Poole.

"I come from you. You were standing up for your son, your family, your home. So will I."

She stepped back through the mirror, into the warm where her faithful dog waited.

She crouched down, gathered him to her for comfort, and to wait until the dizziness passed.

It would, she thought. It would pass. Just as the mirror no longer stood on the path.

Still holding Yoda, she rose, walked back to where Arthur Poole's body had fallen.

"They found you here. Worried, had to be worried, when your horse came back without you. So they looked for you, and found you here. And thought it was an accident. They never knew what she'd done. But I know now. It matters I know now."

She walked back out of the woods while her head cleared and the leading edge of the horror dulled.

She went inside, splashed cold water on her face. Clover tried Bad Company's "All Right Now."

"Yeah, mostly all right now. Need a few more minutes."

She gave Yoda a treat, and because Pye came out as if to say *where the hell have you been*, she gave the cat a couple.

Then she sat, texted Trey.

I know you and Owen planned to work on Cleo's boat tonight, but can you both come? I'm fine. I'm okay, but I went
through the mirror again, and saw something. I need to tell
you in person. I'm fine, I promise, but I need to tell you.
We'll be there. Is Cleo with you?

Not right now, but she will be. I'm going back to work. I
wouldn't if I wasn't okay. And I promise, I wouldn't tell you I
was if I wasn't. I just need to tell you.

**We'll be there. Tell Cleo not to cook. We'll bring some-
thing. Work if it helps, otherwise, take a break.**

I took one. That's how it started. Don't worry. Bring pizza.

She added that in hopes it would help ease the worry she knew he
felt.

Done. By six, earlier if you need.

Six.

She added a pizza emoji, then a heart.

Back at her desk, Sonya wrote it all out while the details stayed fresh.
It seemed to her they'd stay fresh forever, but she documented.

Maybe, someday, she'd put everything she'd documented since
moving into the manor into a book. Like Deuce Doyle had done for
Collin on the family genealogy.

A kind of legacy, she thought, for those who came after her.

For now, she filed what she'd written, then pushed her mind into
work. Work could stand as sanctuary as well as purpose.

Later, when Yoda scrambled out from under her desk to run downstairs, she shut down. She started down the steps as Cleo came in
carting her guerrilla box she used for supplies and carrying wet canvases.

"What a day! I nearly finished one painting, then had to stop to
sketch this kid—three, maybe four—sailing in a little sloop with, it
had to be his mom. I swear he looked like he'd woken up on a day
that melded Christmas, his birthday, and Halloween together.

"I haven't forgotten about dinner," she continued. "I'll throw us
something together. I lost track of time, which is when you know it's
really going well."

"Trey and Owen are bringing pizza. About six."

"Oh." Cleo pulled the band out of her hair, shook out her curls. "I thought it was just you and me tonight, but pizza sounds . . . Shit. Something happened."

"It did. Not Dobbs—or not one of her tantrums. The mirror. I went through again."

"Damn it, Sonya, why didn't you call me, or text? I'd've come right back."

"Exactly, and I promise, no need for that. Go on, put your things away. I'm going to go pour us both some wine."

"This can wait."

"I need time to get my head out of work mode and into this anyway. It's nearly six, so by the time you finish they should be here."

"And you'll only have to go through it once," Cleo concluded. "Okay. I won't be long."

Case in hand, Cleo jogged up the steps, and Sonya turned to the portrait of Astrid Poole.

"You didn't know. You, your Collin, his twin, his sisters, Arthur's widow. You didn't know he'd been murdered, just an obstacle for Dobbs to remove. If you had, somehow, you might have lived."

She started back, pausing at the music room to study the portraits. It would all have been different, she thought. But the first domino fell with Arthur Poole.

In the kitchen, she opened a bottle of wine and stood looking back at the woods.

So peaceful just now, and so welcoming in the green of spring. She'd walk there again; she promised herself that. She wouldn't let Hester Dobbs block her from any part of what was hers.

When she heard dogs barking, she turned back to pour the wine.

Trey came straight back, and after setting pizza boxes on the island, took her face in his hands. He gave her a long, careful study, then nodded.

"Okay."

"Yes. Okay. There's beer in the butler's pantry," she told Owen.

He took two out of a six-pack, then took the rest to the pantry fridge. "Now there's more. I can go through the mirror," he pointed out. "I could be here inside fifteen minutes."

"I couldn't wait. I mean that literally. Let's get started on this pizza. Now that you're here, I realize I'm starved. And here's Cleo."

When she came in, Owen tapped a finger to her hand. "Missed a spot."

Cleo glanced down at a smear of red paint. "I'll get it later. Now, Son, you can tell us what happened without interruption."

By the time they sat, she had the narrative clear in her head, and a lot of appreciation for three people who understood her.

"I'm going to start at the beginning, which has nothing to do with the mirror. Laine and Matt—they own By Design, where I used to work—called. They wanted to congratulate me on the Ryder account. And to let me know word had gotten back to them on the crap Brandon pulled before my presentation, and that he no longer works for By Design."

"Well, I'll absolutely drink to that." And Cleo did.

"He maligned me and my work in his presentation—something Miranda Ryder didn't care for. Then he lied to Laine and Matt about that, and about what happened between him and me. So, he's out."

"If he takes a step toward you, or continues to bad-mouth you, personally or professionally, I need to know about it."

"And you will," she assured Trey. "I promise. That door's been closed and bolted on my side for nearly a year. If he can't do the same on his side?" She shrugged. "He's going to end up taking more lumps.

"After, I just wanted to clear my head, and Yoda needed a walk, so I took him out back. Everything looks so good. All the work we did, just so beautiful. So satisfying. I wanted to check out the herbs before I went back to work, and I saw Yoda walking into the woods. I called him back, but he kept going. He always comes when I call him."

She paused, drank. "He went right in while I'm running back there, calling him. I could hear him barking, and I thought he must be chasing a rabbit or squirrel. Then I felt it."

She took a breath, closed her eyes a moment. "That tug, then the pull. The path turned, and there was Yoda. He sat in front of the mirror on the path."

"Something happened in the woods," Trey concluded. "And you needed to see it."

"Yeah. The glass was blurred, and I could hear hoofbeats. Distant, but I could hear them. I had to go in. I was worried about leaving Yoda, but it's irresistible. I told him to stay, and he lay down like: Sure, I'll wait.

"And I went through."

"Eat something." Trey nudged her plate, and the slice she hadn't touched, closer.

With a nod, she took a bite and felt it ease the stress in her head, the hunger in her belly.

"I was still there, on the path, but it wasn't spring. Fall, chilly, brisk, leaves gone red and gold and orange. But more than that, I could— like in one of the dreams—hear what he was thinking. Almost like he was telling me."

"Who?" Cleo demanded.

"Arthur Poole."

She told them, detail by detail.

"He was thinking of his family," she continued, "of expanding the manor, as he hoped to have grandchildren before much longer. Then she stepped on the path. Dobbs. They didn't see me. They were ten or twelve feet away, but didn't see me. He called her a witch, told her to get off his land. She told him she'd tricked his son, Collin, into drinking a potion. That's how she got him into bed."

"She bespelled him," Cleo murmured. "Then she tried to use that as a claim to the manor."

"He was the eldest, so he'd inherit. But he's engaged or maybe about to be, right? That complicates things, so she tries sex." Owen reached for another slice. "But it didn't do the trick."

"It wasn't an accident," Trey concluded. "Arthur Poole didn't die in an accident."

"He was furious. He looked so formidable. Then she brought the wind. He controlled his horse, but she said these words."

As Sonya repeated them, Cleo pulled out her phone to note them down.

"And she twisted her hands, like you would when you're wringing something out. I heard it. God, I heard his neck break, then he fell."

To give herself a moment to steady again, she lifted her wineglass.

"She slapped the horse, and the mare ran down the path toward the manor. She ran right by me like I wasn't there. Dobbs looked crazy, she had all along, but now she looked jubilant and crazy. He'd been in her way, now he was dead, and she'd be mistress of the manor forever.

"She started to go back into the woods, but she stopped, looked over where I was standing. She didn't see me. She said, like a question: 'Seven?' She said it again and again, said it was a number of power, but I could see she didn't understand. And it was like she had a sudden headache."

Sonya pressed her hand to her temple. "She looked confused, and just stark raving mad. She went back in the woods, and looked at him, at Arthur Poole. I realized his family would never know she'd murdered him. Later I realized Collin probably never knew she'd used witchcraft to get him into bed."

"So guilt on top of grief played a part in his suicide," Trey concluded.

"I really think so. I came back through. It was spring, Yoda was waiting, the mirror was gone."

She picked up the slice, set it down again. "I know it's important to understand what really happened. But it feels so damn useless when there's nothing we can do to change it, stop it."

"It's always better to know than not," Trey told her. "I can wish you weren't the conduit, but that's the reality of it."

"You accumulate knowledge." Owen got up to get himself and Trey another beer. "And knowledge is power."

"So, accumulated knowledge from this latest adventure."

Cleo ticked off fingers. "Collin Poole didn't roll around with Dobbs of his own free will. Dobbs murdered Arthur Poole. For Dobbs, it was always about the manor, not the people. They were just obstacles or stepping stones."

"Like the day in the library, I was awake, aware. It felt dreamlike on the other side, but I was awake and aware."

"After Poole was dead," Trey continued, "and she wasn't focused on him, she sensed something. Sensed you without knowing what or who."

"I hadn't been born yet—but I was there in that time and place, and awake, aware."

"Exactly. Despite what she'd done, Collin Poole married Astrid Grandville. But that day, on the path, she didn't know she'd kill Astrid, take her ring, create the curse."

"I can only think she believed she could force or seduce Collin into marrying her, so she could have the manor. It was and is what she wants. To be mistress of the manor."

"Forever. You told us she said forever," Trey added.

"Yes, but . . ."

"She always intended to have it, to hold it. If it took her death, her blood to do that—forever—clearly she'd do whatever she needed to do. I imagine she didn't see it happening so soon, but nobody lives forever."

"She's batshit." Owen took another pull of his beer.

"No one can argue that one. But"—Cleo held up a hand—"could she have foreseen that Astrid, and all the ones who came after her, would stay? I don't think so. This house? It has a power of its own. And it doesn't want her."

"It doesn't," Sonya murmured. "It doesn't want her."

"It must burn for her to know that." Cleo continued, "To know people, the spirits of them, go on day and night, tending to it, while she's trapped in a hell of her own making."

"She can't break the spell," Sonya said slowly, "or she's gone. She tied herself with her own words, her own blood magic. Every generation, and a bride. She sealed that with Astrid's blood, then her own. She's as caught in that cycle as the brides she killed."

"She hopes to scare you out, push you out," Trey said. "You're a threat. It may be a hell of her own making, a cycle she's trapped in, but it's what she has."

"Seven—she repeated it. Maybe she got it from me. Maybe I thought of the rings, the women, the brides, and how it started with the murder of Arthur Poole. She sensed me, or something, maybe she sensed that, too. It confused her, and I swear it hurt her."

"Looks like we have to find a way to hurt her again, and harder."

Cleo smiled at Owen. "I like the way you think."

Clover weighed in with Aerosmith and "Don't Get Mad, Get Even."

"Words to live by." Sonya picked up the pizza she'd barely touched, and ate.

Chapter Twenty-seven

The day before The Event, they had a foyer full of flowers. Cleo had a ham in the oven, and her fingers crossed. They'd put together a simple buffet menu for family in what they hoped would serve as a prelude to the feast the next day.

Every inch of the manor shined.

They arranged and rearranged tables and chairs outside, and lit countless candles that the forecast for the next day—sunny, low seventies—held.

Sonya hauled flowers upstairs to place arrangements—hours of debate on those—where they'd selected.

When the doorbell bonged, she nearly ignored it. Dobbs's rumblings had been few the last couple of days, but that remained one of her favorites.

Then she remembered Yoda had gone down to the apartment with Cleo so she couldn't count on his bark to tell her.

She opened it, found Winter.

"Mom!"

"I came a little early to help, whether you need it or not." Scanning the foyer, Winter laughed. "Are you sure you got enough flowers?"

"Mom," Sonya said again, and threw her arms around her mother. "You're by yourself? I thought—"

"I convoyed with your grandparents, and they headed straight to the hotel. They wanted to unpack, settle in a bit."

She wheeled her weekender aside. "Summer and Martin are driving with your other set. They're all coming. Now put me to work."

"I absolutely will, but let's get your bag upstairs first. Cleo took flowers to the apartment; her parents and grandmother are staying there tonight and tomorrow night before they head back on their road trip."

She started to pick up Winter's suitcase, was brushed aside, so grabbed more flowers.

"I can't believe they're driving all the way from Louisiana and back."

"Melly, Cleo's mom, told me. They wanted to see some sights."

"And according to the texts and photos they've sent to Cleo, they're having a hell of a good time."

"That's the word," Winter agreed. "Everything looks fabulous, Sonya. The tree in full bloom out front, that enormous rhododendron, they're just spectacular."

As they passed the library, Sonya's tablet played Three Dog Night's "Joy to the World."

Winter sent a look back over her shoulder. "I guess you've gotten used to that."

"Not just used to. I love it. You have to see the view from your room with the gardens blooming."

When they went in, Winter walked to the window. "Talk about spectacular. You and Cleo did this?"

"A lot—most, really—was already done. The perennials. But we did the pots, planters, the annuals. I loved that, too. Who knew?"

"You've made a home, baby. I knew it when I was here before, but if I had any lingering doubts, they're gone. And the squatter on the third floor?"

"That's a good one. *Squatter.* We're not going to worry about her. Why don't I help you unpack, then we'll go down and fix you a snack?"

"I'm here to help, not be waited on. I'll unpack, and when I'm done, I'll help you with that ocean of flowers."

"All right. I'm nearly done up here. When you're unpacked, we can start on the main level."

When Winter came down, Sonya handed her a vase. "Casual dining table. I'm putting these three low ones on the formal dining table. Cleo should be back in by now, so we'll start there."

"Give me one of those. Now we've each got two. Something smells amazing."

"Flowers, and we hope the ham Cleo's doing."

"Wonders really do never cease. Oh."

Winter stopped at the music room. "Your father's work again."

"Yes. Johanna, Clover, Lisbeth, and Agatha."

"It's stunning and it's all so strange. And yet, I can see him, I can see Drew standing there in front of the canvas with his palette, his brushes."

"Still the One" played on Sonya's phone.

"Yes," Winter murmured. "He is."

As they walked into the kitchen, Cleo was opening the oven to check on her ham.

"What! Nobody tells me! Put those flowers down and give me my hug. We've got a gallon of iced tea if you want," Cleo said as she got and gave the hug. "Or we can get you some wine."

"I'll start with that iced tea. You're making a ham."

"A whole, big-ass ham." Cleo said it with glee. "Bree said if I don't screw it up, and there's any left over, she can make it work for tomorrow."

"The size of that ham?" Sonya poured iced tea. "There'll be leftovers. I already made a card for it. *Cleo's Honey-Glazed Ham from The Manor.*"

"Then I really better not screw it up."

They placed flowers, then helped Cleo quarter potatoes for roasting. Cleo pulled the enormous glazed ham out of the oven, set it aside to rest.

They arranged a bar in the butler's pantry, and worked on a colorful platter of crudités.

"I have to say it's nice seeing you girls work together in the kitchen. I won't worry about you going hungry."

Yoda raced to the front door before Sonya heard it open. Then raced back with Mookie.

"Oh! Look at this dog! Aren't you something! Look how Yoda's introducing me to his friend."

Mookie sat and looked up at Winter with eyes full of desperate love.

When Trey came in, Winter stopped crooning to the dogs and gave him a long, assessing look.

"Mom, this is Trey Doyle."

"I've seen his picture on the law office's website, along with this handsome boy. Winter MacTavish."

"It's nice to meet you." He took the extended hand. And he smiled. "I see you in her. I saw her father because I knew Collin. Now I see you, too."

"I can't look out for her anymore. Do you?"

"Mom, seriously?"

"When she'll let me."

"That's a very good answer."

The dogs raced; the doorbell bonged.

"I'll get that."

When she opened the door, it was Cleo's turn to throw her arms around her mother. Then her father, then her grandmother.

In the kitchen, Sonya heard the excited mix of French and English.

"That's Cleo's mom, dad, grandmother. Trey, why don't you get my mother a glass of wine? She likes the pinot grigio."

"Sure." When he went into the butler's pantry, Sonya shot a finger at her mother.

Winter just smiled.

Melly came in first. She didn't have Cleo's stature, and her hair was true black and pin straight. But she'd passed on her eyes, tawny and tipped at the corners.

She hugged Winter first, said: "Mmm-mmm-mmm." Then embraced Sonya the same way as Trey came back with a glass of wine.

"My goodness, aren't you handsome? I'll give you a hug, too, if you give me a glass of that."

"Melly Fabares, Trey Doyle."

"Well now, Sonya, I see your taste in men has improved considerably. Winter, look at our girls living in this big old beautiful house. I think it must take half a day to walk from one end of it to the other."

When Trey brought in more wine, Melly kept her word, hugged him. "Mmm. Got yourself a good, solid build there, too. Jackson, you come on back here and bring Mama."

"She's taking her time with Cleo." Jackson, a tall beanpole of a man, came in, offered his slow, shy smile. He kissed Winter's cheek, then Sonya's before shaking hands with Trey.

"Um, Jackson Fabares, Cleo's daddy."

"Trey Doyle. It's nice meeting you. Can I get you a drink?"

"Wouldn't say no to a beer if you got one handy. Something sure smells good in here."

"Cleo baked a ham," Winter told him.

"She did what now?" he asked while Melly let out a bark of laughter.

"She makes a damn good meatloaf," Trey added, and handed Jackson a beer.

"I might just have to sit down. This sure is some place you got here, Sonya. Some place."

Imogene Bea LaRue Tamura, long-legged and lanky on the cusp of seventy, stood inside the music room with her granddaughter. She had a mane of wild butterscotch curls that time had liberally streaked with white. She credited her remarkably smooth, dusky skin to the melting pot of her genetics, and a life well lived. Her eyes, caught somewhere between brown and gold, studied the room.

She wore her traveling jeans and a red T-shirt with low-top Converse sneakers of the same bold color. Half a dozen chains bearing crystals, an ankh, symbols of sun and moon hung around her neck.

On her right hand, she wore a wide silver band carved with the astrological sign for Libra, and a moonstone cabochon on her middle finger.

A widow for twelve years, she wore her wedding ring, a hammered gold band, on her left.

Her left biceps bore a tattoo of the fivefold symbol.

"They look out for you, these and more. And look to you, you and Sonya, these and more. This house is full, *chère*, sorrow and joy, blood and sweat, tears and laughter, as a house so long in years must be."

Her voice, fluid and rich, carried the easy flow of her native New Orleans.

"This is a good house, a good, strong house, *ma fille*."

"I know it, and feel it. But it makes it better and stronger to hear you say it."

"Still, it holds a powerful, dark force." Imogene glanced up as she spoke. "Greedy, and mad with that greed. It wants your fear."

"Doing my best not to accommodate."

Imogene smiled. "You got a head on your shoulders, my boo, and always did. I got some things for you. Your daddy—and I credit my girl for picking such a man as Jackson—didn't complain, not one time along this way, about the weight of what I had him haul down."

"He loves you, Magie."

Imogene smiled at Cleo's childhood endearment. "I love him back with cake and ice cream. Now, you take this."

Imogene lifted one of the chains from around her neck.

"Oh, but that's your special tourmaline, the one Paw gave you."

"Now we're giving it to you. It's protection, *chérie*, and powerful strong, as it comes with love." She hung the chain with its three thick black stones around Cleo's neck.

"Love's a circle, when true, never ends. A circle protects against what wants to bring harm. Hold your circle, Cleo."

Imogene glanced back as Owen paused in the doorway. And her smile lit like the sun.

"Why, there you are! I wondered when you'd come along. You're a looker, aren't you, boy?"

"You sure are," he said, and made her laugh. "You must be Cleo's mom."

On a laugh, Imogene fanned herself, fluttered her lashes. "I do believe I'm in love."

As Owen grinned back, Cleo shook her head. "This is my grand-mère. Imogene Tamura, Owen Poole."

"Get out" was Owen's sincere response.

"Now I know it's love. So this is Owen Poole who builds boats and ships. Building one for my *bébé*, I hear."

"Yes, ma'am."

"Oh, there's no ma'aming between us. It's Imogene, or my grand-babies turned that to Magie. You pick one of those, and come over here and give me a kiss."

Once he did, she slipped an arm through his. "Now, I believe I'm ready for a cocktail. Do you know how to mix up a whiskey sour?"

"I can learn."

"Then I'll show you how it's done."

Sonya had imagined it, and hoped for it. Seeing and feeling the manor filling up with family. Her mother chatted away with Melly, and now that her aunt and uncle had arrived with her maternal grand-parents, Summer joined that chat fest. Jackson and her uncle had wandered outside with the dogs. With a glass of wine, her grandfather—an avid gardener—did the same.

At her grandmother's request, Sonya gave her a tour of the house, or some of it, before dinner.

Louisa Bane Riley, a formidable woman, had let her hair go silver and kept it short, sharp as a blade. She wore glasses with frames of searing blue, discreet diamond studs, a straight-lined navy dress with white piping, and low-heeled Pradas.

As they toured the first floor, she made noncommittal noises, gave a few approving nods.

If Sonya knew anything, she knew her grandmother was a hard nut to crack.

But when they reached the library, Louisa stopped, held up a hand as she studied the room.

"Well." The single word held her straitlaced Boston roots. "Well," she repeated, and turned to Sonya. "You found your place, haven't you?"

And the tension in Sonya's shoulders dissolved. "Yes, I have."

"I had my doubts, as I'm sure you know."

"You're nothing if not honest in your opinions, Grammy."

"I am, and I had my doubts about the choices you've made in the last few months. You're a talented young woman, Sonya, with an exceptional work ethic. I worried you'd made these choices due to your . . . unfortunate experience."

"Was it unfortunate?"

Louisa's lips curved, very slightly. "I have to forgive Tracie. She's my grandchild. I don't excuse her abhorrent behavior, but I have to forgive her. One day you may as well. Without excusing her, she did you a monumental favor. I dislike, more than I can say, that I was duped by that *person* whom I refuse to call a man. But seeing this, seeing you here, takes a bit of the sting away."

Clover added her opinion by playing Beyoncé's "Ring the Alarm" on the tablet.

"That's . . . unusual."

"Not around here."

"So I've heard. I've never believed in that business."

She brushed a hand over the desk. "Still. Your home is full of character and history, and beautiful things well cared for. By all appearances, you're happy in both the work you've chosen and the direction you've taken with it. You're my grandchild, and I love you, so what more could I want for you?"

"That means a lot to me, Grammy."

"You can show me the rest later, as it's clear that will take some time. I've barely said two words to the rest of your guests."

The doorbell sounded as they started down.

"That must be Nan and Grandpa. Everyone else is here."

Sonya answered, and went straight into hugs.

Her grandfather, big and broad-shouldered, her grandmother, delicate and petite. She felt her grandmother tremble, just a little, and understood this visit was bittersweet.

"I'm so glad you're here. I'm so happy to see you."

John smiled, stroked her hair. "Got yourself a mansion here, little girl. It's a whopper."

"It really is."

"I hope we're not late."

Sonya looked at her grandmother, the sweet heart-shaped face, the quiet blue eyes struggling to hold back tears.

"You're not. It's family."

"Martha, John, it's lovely to see you." Louisa offered cheek kisses, then took John's arm. "John, I'm more than ready for a glass of wine if you'll take me back. The house is a maze, but I know the way. And how was your winter in Savannah?" she continued as she led him away.

Her grammy might be brutally honest, Sonya thought, but she also understood another woman's pain.

"It's a beautiful house, Sonya, like something out of a painting or a movie. You always wanted a rambling old house."

"I did." Sonya hugged her again, and held on for a moment. "I want to show you something."

With an arm around Martha's waist, she led her down the long hall.

"Oh, it's so much house, isn't it? And so beautiful. No wonder you're happy here. We're happy for you, Sonya, so happy you . . . Oh."

At the music room, with the sound of voices rolling down from the kitchen, they stopped.

"Oh, I see. I see Drew in her smile. So young, so pretty, and she looks kind." The tears came now, slowly, softly. "She would have loved him, loved them both. We would . . ."

"I know, Nan. Believe me, she knows you gave Dad what she couldn't."

The phone in Sonya's pocket went with "Loves Me Like a Rock."

"We loved him so much. Drew was such a loved and loving son, a loved and loving husband and father. I hope she knows what a good, good man he grew up to be."

"She does, Nan. I'm sure of it."

"So young," Martha said again. "Sonya, could you give me a minute or two? I'd like to sit here for just a minute or two."

"Of course. Just follow the voices when you're ready. Take all the time you need."

Alone, Martha sat, dried her eyes, then looked into the eyes of the portrait. "I wish we'd known about you and Charlie. If we'd known, we would have told him about you. If we'd known, we would have loved his brother just as much."

As she struggled for composure again, the phone in her purse played "Martha My Dear."

She jolted, then pressed her lips together. "I see him in you. Thank you for the greatest gift, the most precious gift."

Pausing, Martha folded her hands.

"Drew was always a bright boy. Not always a good boy, but who wants that? Ah, he took his first steps at ten months, then there was no stopping him. He liked grape popsicles and Matchbox cars. And drawing. He always loved to draw and color."

She cleared her throat.

"Once, he was only three, he got the crayons. Those big, thick ones? I'd put them up where I didn't think he could reach, but I should've known better. He could climb like a monkey."

She had to stop another moment, fight back more tears.

"He drew pictures all over the wall in his bedroom. I thought he was napping. Again, I should've known better. Drew was so proud I couldn't get mad at him.

"John and I didn't paint over it for years, and when we did, John cut out a section, and patched the drywall. And we framed the piece we saved. I still have it."

She sighed, and when she drew in a breath, drew in the scent of wildflowers, like a meadow basking in sunlight.

"There's so much more I could tell you. I wrote some out, some memories." Opening her bag, Martha took out a manila envelope, thick with pages. "But most of all, I want you to know, he was loved from the first second they put him in our arms. He was loved. He was a beautiful boy who became a beautiful man.

"And he was loved."

She rose, set the envelope on the piano.

She jolted again when the phone in her purse played Alanis Morissette's "Thank U."

Then she smiled.

Cleo's ham proved a success, with enough left over to feed everyone again. Twice.

Sonya got exactly what she'd hoped for—an easy evening with family that blended well. She watched Cleo's grandmother flirt outrageously with Owen, and Trey simply slide in with the various personalities as if he'd known them all his life.

"A much better choice," Louisa muttered to her at some point. "But I'll save my full approval until after I meet his family tomorrow. Something that never happened with that *person*."

She patted Sonya's hand. "He has honest eyes."

They took a walk around the gardens, people and pets, with the lights twinkling just as she'd imagined.

When she kissed her grandparents goodnight, she saw no tears in Martha's eyes.

"We needed this." Martha gave her an extra squeeze. "To see, to really understand. I left a long letter for Drew's birth mother in the music room, on the piano. Silly of me. I think you'd like to have it."

When the rest left, and Cleo went down to help her family settle into the apartment, Sonya's mother sat with Trey and Owen in the parlor.

Sonya walked back to the music room, but saw nothing on the piano.

Her phone told her why with Carole King's "Child of Mine."

"All right," she murmured. "You have it, and I hope it brings you some joy."

As she walked back into the parlor, Winter rose.

"I just promised these two a big pancake breakfast in the morning to get them started on what's going to be a long day. This was the perfect prelude, my baby, especially for Drew's mom and dad. They needed this bridge."

"Nan spent some time with Clover. She left a letter on the piano in the music room, but it's not there. So I guess Clover spent some time with her."

"I may not ever get used to that, but I'm going to say good. Now I'm going to follow along with these dogs sprawled on the floor, and the cat curled up on that chair, and get some sleep."

She bent down, kissed Owen's cheek, then Trey's before she walked over to hug Sonya.

"I'll see you all in the morning."

As Winter went out, started upstairs, Trey glanced at the doorway. "Well, she's amazing."

Sonya plopped into a chair. "She is. And this next stage of The Event is successfully done. So, Owen, you aren't planning to run off with Cleo's grand-mère, are you?"

"Tempting. She's all that and an ice-cold beer. She's got some stories, man, and knows how to tell them. Nice group. Your grandmother— the tall one—she's a little scary."

"Tell me about it."

"She liked me." Trey's smile reeked of satisfaction. "She googled me, and decided I might do."

"Oh God. Sorry."

"I kind of liked her little-bit-scary style. An interesting evening to be a part of. One thing's for certain: They all enjoyed it, and each other."

Cleo came in, dropped down, said: "Whew!"

"Are they settled in?" Sonya asked.

"They are. My grand-mère brought us a box of about two dozen bottles. Witch bottles to hang. Good mojo. And some more white sage cones she made herself, candles ditto. A gorgeous hunk of fluorite, another of rose quartz, a pretty brass gong for when we meditate."

"I didn't narc on you and tell her you never manage over ten seconds."

"I made it to thirty once."

"You'd been drinking," Cleo reminded her. "Doesn't count. She put crystals and candles around the apartment before she unpacked her clothes, and my father gave me a list of more plants he tells me we need. My mama just oohed and aahed over everything. She said to tell your mama she'd help with breakfast in the morning."

"She's gone up to bed."

"That's a damn good idea. I'm going to do the same."

She pushed up, tossed her hair, then gave Owen her arched-eyebrow look. "Interested?"

"Am I alive?"

He got up, and so did Jones, then the cat.

"Job well done," Cleo said to Sonya. "See y'all in the morning before a reasonable hour."

"I'm still a little wired," Sonya realized. "You might be able to help with that."

"Bet I could."

She pulled the tie from her hair, slipped it on one wrist as she ran her other hand through.

"You know what I noticed tonight?"

"There was a lot going on."

"There really was," she agreed. "But I noticed just how easily you slid right into all of it. Didn't take you two minutes. You're just good with people."

"It helps to be when you deal with them on a daily basis."

"Not just deal with. You like people."

"By and large. Don't you?"

"*By and large* fits, I guess. I'm not shy, and I like the interaction. But I'm not sure how I'd deal if I couldn't balance that with the quiet time. Which I like more than I realized I would when I worked in an office.

"Tomorrow? Really looking forward to it. All those people, all that interaction. But then, I'll be glad to sock myself back into the quiet and the work."

"Another reason this house fits you like a glove."

"You're right. It does. Everything, one exception, suits me to the ground. I loved showing it off to my family. Which gained me Grammy's very hard-won approval. Louisa."

"I got it. Grammy, Louisa. Nan, Martha. Granddad, Bill. Grandpa, John."

"You would get it. And I expect, after meeting your family tomorrow, you'll also get Grammy's very hard-won approval, if that matters."

"It always matters." He trailed his fingers through her loosened hair. "She loves you. They all do. And everyone here loves Cleo. It doesn't always work that way, believe me. But I know when it does. My family loves Owen, his loves me. It adds the special when it works."

"You're right about that, too. Now, about helping me smooth things out."

"I've got some ideas." Rising, he pulled her to her feet.

"I'm counting on it."

She woke at three, wired again. But she didn't feel the pull, felt no need to get up, to walk.

"Okay?" Trey reached for her hand.

"Yes."

Still she nestled close to him as the chime of the clock echoed away, as the weeping drifted like the piano music.

She heard nothing from the third floor, and closed her eyes again, grateful.

It wouldn't last, she knew. But maybe with so much positive energy, they'd get another day, another night.

Because tomorrow, no matter what came, they'd open the house, and fill it again.

Chapter Twenty-eight

In the morning, Winter, Melly, and Imogene took over the kitchen. They allowed any who wandered in to get coffee, then summarily booted them out.

Booted, Sonya listened to the mix of voices, a lot of laughter, and the occasional musical interlude from Clover.

While it wasn't anything she imagined, she realized she wanted this, too. Wanted to listen to a group of women laughing in her kitchen.

With their own agenda, she and Cleo began dressing tables with the hot pink cloths they'd chosen. In lieu of centerpieces or formal arrangements, they placed pale blue mini mason jars to hold single fat, colorful blooms. Peonies, dahlias, hydrangeas.

They drafted whatever male came within shouting distance to haul out more tables, more chairs.

"Hey, all y'all!" Melly shouted out the window. "This big old platter just came up on the dumbwaiter thing. All by itself! This is one wild house. Breakfast in ten!"

They feasted in the dining room, with platters and bowls spread over the big table. Pancakes, bacon, eggs, biscuits, berries, hash browns, and grits, as Imogene decreed no breakfast complete without them.

Sonya crossed another want off her list. A big family breakfast in the dining room.

Then they got back to work.

With their delivery, they placed the portable bars according to Bree's chart.

Sonya found the flurry of activity, the busy hands, the mix of ideas exhilarating.

When she saw Imogene and her gangly son-in-law hanging witch bottles from tree branches, or her mother and Melly designing a tablescape for the dining room, she wondered how she and Cleo had ever imagined they could do all of it alone.

A last-minute decision to add some conversation areas to the front had Trey and Owen searching through storage.

Then Bree arrived with two servers and the rented dishes and glassware.

"I got my outfit and all in my car. You got a place I can change after we're set up?"

"Absolutely. I—"

She cut Sonya off with a wave. "Later for that. I need the bars stocked. Misty and Wayne, get cracking. Follow the chart. You've got enough hands around here to cart out and set up the plates, the flatware. You've got that chart."

"We have all your charts," Cleo told her.

"Good. I want to see what you've got out there. So, Tall Guy."

"Ah, Jackson," he said, and offered a hand.

She shook it. "Bree. How about hauling some of these plates out there? I'll show you where once I see."

She grabbed a carton of dessert plates and led the way.

"Okay, this is good. Looks good. Jackson, that table there. Under it for now. We're going to do four stacks of twenty-five dinner plates, same with dessert plates. When they get low, servers will bring up more. Kitchen crew will take care of washing and sending more out as needed. Flatware—"

"We found these cute lined baskets."

Bree frowned at Sonya. "Let me see them."

While Sonya scrambled back for them, Bree worked her way along. "Hot dishes here, replenished as needed. Salads and whatnot, breads, rolls, your condiments. Desserts over there.

"This is good. You did good. This'll work."

Obviously satisfied with the arrangements, she paused.

"So who is everybody?"

"The tall guy bringing out more dishes is my father. The woman right behind him with I guess it's dessert plates is my mother, Melly."

"She's got to be a foot shorter than him."

"Fourteen inches as I recall. And there, the woman coming out with Sonya's her mother, Winter."

"Got it. Who's the smoking chick coming out of the apartment?"

"My grand-mère."

"Like grandmother? Hot grandma. You got some lucky DNA in there."

She took one of the baskets from Sonya, studied it, nodded. "Okay, all right. These are nice. They'll work fine. Hi, Sonya's mom. Bree."

"Winter. I've heard you're an amazing chef and organizer."

"I am all that. She got your hair. More lucky DNA. Okay—Wait, where are Trey and Owen?"

"They're getting some chairs or benches or whatever works to set out front. A couple conversation areas," Sonya explained.

"I'll take a look when they've got it set up. So, here's the schedule."

Since she had it down to the minute, Sonya wasn't sure whether to be relieved or terrified.

Bree approved the conversation areas, and Owen decreed all of it went back inside when the day ended.

They hauled, set up, hauled some more. And as intimidated as impressed with Bree's efficiency, Sonya showed her coordinator a guest room, then dashed to her own to change for the party.

"She's terrifying," Sonya said when Trey came in. "I love her."

"Given that, you must mean Bree. Nice dress, cutie. Really nice."

"Is it? Not too much?"

She studied the look of the pale green dress in the mirror. Sleeveless, it had a square neckline she thought suited her, and an easy, fluid skirt that would dance around her knees.

"It's just right."

"You'd say that even if it wasn't, which is just as well because by Bree's clock I've only got ten minutes left. You've only got ten minutes to change."

"Okay."

"I hate that." With genuine feeling she pushed at her hair. "Just hate that you can get ready in ten minutes. I was thinking about wearing my hair down, but—"

"I like it down."

"Fine, settled, but now I need different earrings. What are you wearing?"

"Clothes."

"Oh, shut up." Laughing, she changed her earrings.

He went with dark gray jeans, a pale blue shirt, and managed to get ready three full minutes before her.

"I really hate that."

"But you look amazing."

He laid his hands on her shoulders from behind, kissed the top of her head. She turned, started to lift her mouth to his, then nudged him back.

"No time! I don't know what she'll do if we get off schedule, and I don't want to find out."

Grabbing his hand, she pulled him into the hall just as Owen stepped out of Cleo's room.

"She's still in there, fooling around."

"No! She can't! Schedule."

When Sonya dashed into the room, Owen just shrugged. "She asked me which dress—she had two—and went with the one I didn't pick."

Trey only nodded. "Don't be insulted, trust me. I've got a sister. Let's head down where we can probably be useful."

Bree, the general to the army she'd amassed, had everything under control. The vision Sonya and Cleo had imagined for the first opening of the manor came to vivid life with flowers, music, the glint of silver and copper and glass under clear blue skies.

Family came early, as requested, because family, as Sonya saw it, was the heartbeat of the manor. Guests arrived in a trickle, then a flood. And as she'd wanted, wished for, the manor filled.

She enjoyed seeing her mother laughing with the Doyles, and her aunt in deep conversation with Anna.

She split tour-guide duty with Cleo and Trey, and while the third floor stayed quiet, the servants' bell for the Gold Room rang insistently.

She met more Poole cousins, and felt gratified they'd come. Though she'd been assured, more than once, they held no resentment over her inheritance, it relieved her to see and feel the lack of it herself.

Connor Poole Oglebee, head of sales, a big man on the cusp of fifty with a big laugh and deep brown eyes, drew her aside into the music room.

"An impressive gallery. Sad and beautiful at the same time." He stepped closer to Agatha's portrait.

"My branch of the family tree comes through Jane Poole, Owen's twin, and the child she had shortly after Agatha's death. Seeing this, the lost brides together this way? It makes me wonder what might have happened if Jane had been married in the manor. I'm here because she wasn't."

He turned to Sonya. "We're both here due to choices made along the way. I'm sorry Patricia Poole made the choices she made, and glad—very glad—Collin did what he could to rectify those choices."

"My father had a good life. Too short, but a good life, a happy one."

"Yes, I believe that. I met his parents, and your mother. And you." He took her hand. "Collin would like what you've done here, what you're doing. He never took his eye off the business, even though in the last few years he rarely came in. But he guarded that legacy."

He looked back at the portraits, scanning from Johanna to Agatha.

"I'd come here every four weeks or so, on the excuse of giving him a report. One he didn't need, as he kept his eye. He guarded that legacy," Connor repeated, "as he guarded the manor, another legacy. But this was more than that to him. It was home. Despite all its . . . quirks, he loved the manor."

"So do I."

"So I've been told. And so I see. You look after this part of things, and you can trust me, Clarice, and all the rest to look after the business that helped build it."

* * *

She'd never thrown a party anywhere near this size and scope, and discovered just how much skill it required to engage with so many guests, individually or as a group.

There, Cleo's talents outpaced hers by a mile, but she did her best, chatting with the mayor, the historical society, merchants, restaurateurs, teachers, servers, the police chief, the fire chief.

And took time to sit a few minutes with Lucy Cabot, who'd fostered Yoda, and Pyewacket.

"You have a very happy dog," Lucy commented.

"He makes me a very happy human."

"I see Owen built him a dog palace."

Sonya glanced over to where Pye sat on its roof, the queen of all she surveyed. Out nearer the tree line, a young boy—around Jack's forever age—threw the ball for Yoda and Mookie to chase. Jones, too dignified for such public displays, sat and watched with mild disdain.

"He likes it, but I think he likes it better when he has company. He's a sociable dog."

"He sure has plenty of company today. It's a terrific party, Sonya. You and Cleo made an impact here."

"We couldn't have done it—and boy, do I realize that now—without Bree."

"She's a wonder. I'm still coming to grips with how perfect she and Manny seem together. Who knew?"

Rock Hard's drummer with his flop of hair and Buddy Holly glasses kept the beat. And the chef with her flaming cap of hair and tattoos danced.

Danced, Sonya noted, with Sonya's uncle, Martin.

"Well yeah, she's a wonder."

She rounded more tables, stopped by more groups. She sampled some dishes, sipped the manor's signature drink. She danced with Ace—the man had the moves.

She told him exactly that.

He responded with a wink and a grin as he twirled her. "Men who can dance get the girls. That's how I won my own darling, the prettiest girl in Poole's Bay."

When he spun her again, lowered her into a dip, Sonya believed it.

She remembered her mother telling her about one of her father's dreams of the manor, of people strolling the grounds, standing on the terraces.

Like this, she thought, but this was the now.

She danced with Trey, held close, just swaying.

She thought he had the moves, too.

"Got yourself a hit here, cutie."

Smiling, she looked up at him. "It feels good, and right and real. It may take me days to recover, but so worth it."

Resting her head on his shoulder, she looked over at the manor.

And saw. Shadows, shadows at the windows. They were part of it, too—the good, the right, the real. Those who walked the halls, who built the fires and polished the wood. Who'd lived and died inside those great walls.

They weren't alone in the house facing the sea.

And neither was she.

People came and went, some came and lingered long after the lights twinkled on in the trees, along the pergola, the deck.

She said goodbye to her grandparents, her aunt, her uncle.

When the last straggler drove away, Bree plopped down, kicked off her shoes. "Somebody get me a drink."

"I've got you," Owen said.

"And don't be stingy on the pour! Manny lost the toss, so he's DD and driving me home. Band's breaking down, kitchen crew's finishing cleanup."

"I saw that myself," Sonya put in. "And wow. They're on top of it. Everyone's been on top of it."

"Biggest bash around here in God knows. They're hoping you'll do it again, and sign them up."

"Done." Cleo sat back with her own drink. "If you head the team."

"I can do that. Thanks." She took the glass from Owen, drank deep.

"I worried we'd have some . . ." Bree sent a sidelong look toward the manor. "Incidents. But other than some of the crew's phones playing when the band took a break, or somebody going to clear finding it already cleared—that kind of thing—nothing much. And nothing too spooky, I guess."

Imogene sipped her drink. "It won't hold for long, but for now."

With interest, Bree studied her. "You're pretty spooky, but in a cool way."

"Best party I've ever been to," Melly declared, "and I've been to plenty. I lost count of the number of jaws I saw drop when people got a load of this place, the spread, the sparkle. You girls did yourselves proud."

"There was one thing." Winter lifted her hands. "A man wearing a tux, sitting in a big leather chair, smoking a cigar. I passed by, and stopped. He said he'd missed parties at the manor, and was glad my daughter and her friend knew how to throw one. I said I'd bet it wouldn't be the last time they did.

"Somebody passed by, asked me if I knew where to find the powder room. I told them, then turned back. And the man wasn't there. I swear I could still smell the cigar smoke, just a hint of it, but he wasn't there."

"Okay, that's seriously spooky." Bree downed the rest of her drink. "And I'm heading out. No, sit, stay. I've got Manny. We'll talk."

Imogene leaned over to pat Winter's hand. "He wanted you to know he appreciated the party. There were more who felt the same. Some watched from the windows. You saw them, Cleo. Sonya?"

"Yes."

"A young girl in a maid's uniform, so busy," Imogene said, "helping where she could. Happy to. A little boy, such big eyes, watching the other children. The pretty thing from the portrait, Clover, with all that shining blond hair. So full of joy. And more. So many."

Imogene sighed. "She watched, too. The dark one. So much rage. But the protection held, and held strengthened by all the joy, the energy, the life.

"But be ready. It won't hold long. Now I'm going to put my old bones to bed. The energy won't fade tonight, so sleep easy." She rose. "You'll need to."

Sonya slept like a stone, gratefully. The morning brought more good-byes, as Cleo's family loaded up right after breakfast. Imogene drew her aside, gripped both of Sonya's hands.

"I left you something on your big fancy desk. It's an amethyst obelisk."

"Thank you. I—"

"Now, I know you don't set much store in such things."

"More than I used to. Maybe."

"Don't matter a bit. The stone, the shape, it'll help push out that dark energy and bring some calm into the place you work and create. You've got a big job to do, *bébé*, but you won't be alone.

"It's a good house, else I'd never leave my precious girl or you in it. But you're going to fight for it." She gave Sonya's hands a last squeeze. "You fight for it."

She stepped away, shook her head. "Let that girl go, Melly. I need my hug, too."

"Just one more." Melly squeezed Cleo tight. "Be as good as you can."

"Sometimes I'll be better. Y'all text when you stop for the night so I know where you are." She embraced her grandmother in turn. "And travel safe."

"I got that covered. We're having an adventure."

"Every day with the pair of you's an adventure. Come on now," Jackson urged, "or you'll be goodbying till nightfall."

Before she got into the car, Imogene looked back at Owen. "We're going to have us a fais-dodo when you come down to see me."

"I don't know what that is, but I'm already looking forward to it."

On a laugh, she slid into the car.

"What's a fais-dodo?" Owen asked as they drove away.

"It's a party. Are you planning a trip to Louisiana?"

He shrugged at Cleo. "I guess I must be, but right now, we're hauling those chairs and the tables back inside. We're due for some rain
tonight."

"I'll help you put what goes where, then I need to head home."

"Maybe you could stay another night."

Winter slipped an arm around Sonya's shoulders. "Not this time.
My work's waiting. Yours, too."

So Winter bided her time until she wrangled Trey into helping her
carry chafing dishes down to storage.

"I really like your family," she began.

"Me, too. I really like yours."

"Me, too. We're lucky there. It was hard, so hard, on Sonya to lose
her father that way, so young. She adored him."

"I know. It's easy to see when she talks about him."

"I won't say that loss defined her life, but it did influence her direction. Her choice of career. Her talent and interest led the way there,
but the early influence played a part. This house? Her father was born
in this house, and that matters. She always wanted an old rambling
house, and I wonder if, somehow, like Drew, she just . . . knew."

Winter jolted when the servants' bell rang furiously.

"You don't even flinch when that happens," she murmured. "I can't
tell you how much that reassures me. You're a steady sort, Trey, and
she needs that steadiness. This past year turned her life upside down,
so she needs the steady."

"She's got plenty of that herself."

"She does. She really does. Looking back, I can see so clearly what I
didn't. Her relationship with Brandon, her gradually letting him run
more and more of the show. She wanted family, to make her own, so
she ceded little pieces of herself. Then he betrayed her, and she was
done."

"I won't. If you're worried about her and me, where we're going—"

"No. That's between the two of you. What I'm asking is for you to
keep looking out for her—when she lets you. You have a way of doing
that, and it doesn't ask or demand she give up little pieces of herself.

"This beautiful old house." She wandered as she spoke. "So much hers—I can feel it. And part of me wants to drag her out, and Cleo with her—lock the doors behind them."

She turned back. "I can't, and I hope I wouldn't if I could. I worry less because Cleo's with her, and together, they're—"

"Downright awesome."

She smiled. "Downright awesome. I worry less now that I've met you, met Owen, your families. You don't need my approval, but you have it."

"I might not need it, but I can value it. I do."

The bell rang and rang. The lid on one of the chafing dishes began to rattle and shake. Trey simply put a hand on the lid to still it.

"Didn't even flinch. I can head back to Boston with some peace of mind."

After Winter left, and all the pets sprawled out in a post-party coma, Sonya dropped into a chair in the parlor.

"It's so quiet. I almost forgot what quiet's like."

"It's going to get quieter. I'm taking Trey and working on the Sunfish."

Cleo straightened in her own chair. "When can I see it?"

"A week. Ten days tops. Or next month if I don't put some time into it."

"Go away."

Trey pulled Sonya from the chair. "Dinner tomorrow? Anywhere you want."

"Right here. My social battery needs some serious recharging. Thank you. Both of you. It was a hell of a good party."

"Maybe the next thing to a fais-dodo."

Because that amused her, Cleo rose, walked to Owen, gave him a long, smoldering kiss. "My grand-mère throws the best fais-dodos in Louisiana. Now go build my boat."

"Let's go, Jones."

"If you need me," Trey began.

"I'll call."

When they left, Sonya dropped into the chair again. "It was a hell of a party. They did a lot to help make that happen."

"They did. Job well done all around. Now I've got an urge to work. Studio work. What about you?"

"I've got some work I could get done. How about we do that, then cocktail time on the widow's walk?"

"I'm there." Cleo rose again. "We've got enough party food left over to have a nice smorgasbord. Dinner and a movie?"

"And I'm there. Cleo? I know it can't last, but the house feels settled. Like everybody's taking a nice long breath."

"I feel that, too. So if we've got some of that quiet time, we'll use it. See you around five."

Sonya went up to her office. She sat, and smiled as she ran her fingers down the smooth sides of the obelisk. Maybe she didn't put a lot of stock in such things, but it couldn't hurt.

Plus, really pretty.

With Yoda curling under her desk, she booted up.

Work she'd put aside sprang right back. Maybe most wouldn't look forward to a working Sunday afternoon, she decided. But it suited her.

She laughed when her tablet geared up with the Young Rascals and "Groovin'."

"Yeah, that's right. This is my idea of grooving on a Sunday afternoon."

She laid a hand on the tablet.

"I'm glad you got to meet Dad's parents, and you could see how much they loved him."

She caught the scent—wildflowers blanketing a sun-washed meadow. Closing her eyes a moment, she breathed it in.

"It made you happy. I can feel that. You carried him, you gave him life. They gave him a life, a really good life. Then he built a really good life with Mom. And me. So I'm glad you got to meet them."

Opening her eyes, she smiled. "And it was a seriously kick-ass party."

Clover went with "Party in the U.S.A."

"Good choice. Suits my mood."

An hour into the work, Yoda scrambled out from under the desk. She started to pause her work to let him out, then heard the bounce of the ball down the hall below.

And that, she thought, suited her, too.

Chapter Twenty-nine

The quiet didn't hold long, but it held for most of a week while the gardens grew lush and the air warmed like a kiss.

A door might slam, a window might rattle. The clock chimed at three, and spirits walked. But life and work in the manor went on.

Twice that week, Sonya took an hour or two away from her own to help Cleo work on the mural for Anna's nursery.

In an old tee and jeans, her hair bundled under a well-worn Red Sox cap, Sonya worked on the petals of a fanciful rainbow flower while, on a step ladder, Cleo finished detailing a dragon sleeping on a cloud.

Pleased with her petals, Sonya stepped back to take stock. More dragons—and a baby dragon just peeking out of its egg—a pair of winged horses, unicorns, a purple griffin inhabited the forest with Cleo's colorfully striped moncoons.

A trio of butterhounds fluttered.

Trees dripped with jewel-colored fruit where bright birds nested. In the mist of a waterfall, fairies danced, and in the impossibly blue pool, mermaids swam.

"It's a dream, Cleo. There's not a kid in the world who won't love waking up to this."

"It's coming along. I want two or three more elves, and I think a Titania-like fairy in a bower."

"I'm coming in!"

Forewarned, Sonya looked over as Anna stepped into the nursery.

And watched as the mother-to-be pressed her hand to her lips, watched her eyes fill.

"Oh. Oh! It's amazing. I can't believe . . . Every time I come in there's more wonderful. Cleo, Sonya, honestly, it's just magical."

"That's the goal," Cleo said, and stepped down to study her sleeping dragon.

"You added a castle."

"Sonya's idea."

"What's a magic forest without a castle on a high hill in the distance?"

"I love it. I love it so much. And she will." Anna pressed her hand to her belly. "She'll love it. Iona or Eliza or possibly Fiona will love it."

"Last time," Cleo recalled, "you were leaning toward Laurel."

"I was—we were. And maybe. Anyway, I was just taking a break from the studio, and I wanted another peek."

Now Anna laid a hand on her heart. "I'm enchanted. It's enchanting. Let me fix you some lunch."

"I have to pass," Sonya told her. "I need to get home. I've got a video conference coming up."

"I'll take you up on lunch," Cleo said. "Give me another twenty."

"Whatever you want. Wait until Seth sees what you've done today."

"I'm thinking an elf here, peeking from behind this tree, and another—maybe two, one over here, another sort of blending into these flowers. Like they're playing hide-and-seek."

"So cute!"

"I'll leave you to it. See you later, Cleo."

"Oh, I'll walk you out."

"I know the way. Bask awhile."

She left them talking about elves.

She'd had a good week, Sonya thought. Productive at work, pretty quiet in the manor, and with the added element of mural fun.

Trey and Owen would come later, bringing dinner with them. They'd eat outside, she decided, take advantage of a gorgeous June day.

On the way home, she stopped for fresh flowers, then again at the bakery. Who didn't want brownies for dessert?

She thought how lovely it would be if her life just flowed along as it had this past week. Good work, a good man who cared about her, good friends, a good home, and a growing community around it.

And in a little over an hour, she had a meeting about the biggest job in her career. A job she'd earned.

But first, she'd let Yoda and Pye out, tuck the brownies away, arrange the flowers.

When she drove up, the windows stood open. And why not? she thought. The sun shined, the sea breeze came soft and warm and sweet as summer whispered in spring's ear.

As she carried the bakery box and flowers to the door, she heard Yoda's welcoming bark. He greeted her with wags and happy whines while the cat leaped down from the newel post and sauntered to the door and out.

"You go ahead with Pye. Tell you what. I'll leave the door open while I take care of these flowers. Then if Jack hasn't already stuffed you, you'll both get a treat."

She went back, stored the bakery box in the butler's pantry, then started to prep the flowers.

The tall blue vase, she thought. Anna's work would set the new flowers off.

Then she felt it, that pull and the slight lightheaded sensation that often came with it.

"Oh, not now, not now. I have a meeting in just over an hour."

But she couldn't deny it, couldn't resist it. Even as she thought to text Trey, that thought slipped away from her. And she followed the pull.

Back through the house. The sound of the sea rising against the rocks through the open door, open windows seemed distant. Seemed a mile away, more a dream than real as she climbed the stairs.

Her heart began to trip as she continued on, as the pull drew her past the library, past the old nursery, and up the stairs to the third floor.

Not the Gold Room. She wouldn't go in, she promised herself. She'd find a way to break this need.

She saw as she walked down the long hallway, the door pulsing, the heartbeat of it. Heard it pound in her ears. Even with fear squeezing its clammy hands on her throat, she walked on.

And into Cleo's studio, where the mirror stood. Waiting.

Cleo had a large canvas on her easel. Her studio work, Sonya knew. Some figures, some color, it all barely registered as the mirror drew her.

You've got a big job to do, Imogene had said.

"All right. All right," Sonya repeated, and stepped through the glass.

The studio smelled of paint and brush cleaner, and a hint, just a hint, of Calvin Klein's Eternity.

Not Cleo's studio now, she realized, not with the pair of old chairs shoved against the far wall and canvases stacked against the back wall.

The light streaming in was almost silver. A storm rolled outside the windows, lashed at the sea so its waves whipped up, white-tipped.

The storm echoed on the canvas, just as fierce and full of wild movement.

The man at the easel painted the storm at sea, a brush in one hand, a palette knife in the other.

He wore jeans, a faded denim shirt rolled up at the elbows, both splattered with paint. His hair, the sun against the storm, fell messily over his collar.

How many times, she wondered as her heart wept, had she watched her father just like this? Legs spread, hair tumbled, his whole being focused on what he created?

She watched Collin Poole paint, and thought it a kind of magic how much his technique matched his brother's. Even how his hand held the brush, how his body angled.

And the music. AC/DC's "Heatseeker."

Yes, her father would have gone with hard-pounding rock when painting a storm at sea.

But couldn't Collin hear the heartbeat from the Gold Room? Couldn't he feel the rage inside it? She wondered it didn't swallow everything else up.

Then she heard something else—footsteps—just before Johanna came in.

She paused there a moment, just looking at Collin, and everything she felt for him shined in her eyes.

She had her auburn hair back in a tail and, like Collin, wore jeans and a shirt rolled to the elbow. Her feet were bare, and she carried a mug.

Sonya could smell the coffee, dark and rich.

"I'll set this on your worktable." Her voice, strong but quiet, held something else. Sonya heard the frisson of excitement in it. "I don't want to interrupt."

"You're not." He turned to her, turned down the music.

And what he felt for Johanna shined in his eyes.

Sonya saw her father's face, heard her father's voice. A tear slid down her cheek as he smiled.

"I got what I wanted, and I'll always want you more." He gestured toward the painting. "What do you think?"

Walking to him, Johanna tipped her head to his shoulder. "I think it's glorious. Passionate, full of wild movement and drama. The way you have the lightning striking the sea, you can all but hear the snap of power."

"You're so good for me." He gathered her in. "My whole world opened when you came into my life. I put color on canvas, but I didn't know what color was until you. I didn't really believe in love, until you."

Tipping her face up, he kissed her. Then they stood together, looking out at the storm.

"Just a few more days, and we'll be married." He brought her hand to his lips. "We'll be the Pooles of Poole Manor. Let's hope this storm passes, and doesn't decide to circle back on our wedding day."

"If it does, we'll weather it. Damned if some rain will stop me from being your wife."

Like Collin, Johanna didn't seem to hear the pounding that came, not from the storm, not from the music, but from Dobbs's lair.

Instead, Johanna smiled and laid a hand on Collin's cheek.

"I thought about waiting until I was—your wife—until we were the Pooles of Poole Manor, but I just can't. And I know we'd planned to wait until after we were married to get started, but . . ."

She took his hand, pressed it against her stomach. "Close enough?"

It took him a moment, just a moment for puzzlement to turn into shock and shock to explode into joy.

"You're—Are you sure? Of course you're sure. You wouldn't say unless. My God, Johanna."

She laughed as he lifted her off her feet, spun her.

"Johanna, Johanna. Shit!" He set her down, ran his hands down her sides. "I shouldn't do that. Are you all right? How do you feel? Did I hurt you? Him? Her?"

"Of course not, and I feel amazing. I feel strong and sure and so happy. I'm fine. We're fine."

"Maybe you should sit down. Maybe we both should sit down. I swear my knees are weak."

"Then maybe we should lie down." She circled her arms around his neck. "Together."

"Maybe we should." He scooped her off her feet.

"Let's not tell anyone until after the wedding, Collin. Let's keep this ours, just ours, until after."

"Not a word about it," he promised as he carried her out. "Until you say so, I won't tell a soul. And then I'm telling everyone. Johanna made me a husband. Johanna made me a father. Johanna, my Johanna, gave me the world."

They were gone, with the coffee she'd brought him cooling on the workbench, the storm falling away.

Another tear spilled as Sonya walked to the mirror, and through.

The sun shined through the windows and sparkled through Cleo's hanging crystals.

And the closet door stood open.

Already shaky, already grieving for people she'd never met, she stepped over.

The bride wore her dark hair in a cascade of curls that fell down the nape of her neck. The wide skirt of her gown formed with a mass of ruffles that rose from the sweeping hem to a tiny waist. More ruffles fell from the bodice, and down the shoulders to her elbows.

She carried a single pink rose. Her face was radiant with joy.

On a sigh, Sonya said, "Marianne."

She carried the painting downstairs where the cat sat on the newel post and Yoda ran to meet her.

The front door, closed, told her someone had seen to their pets while she'd gone into the past.

With Yoda trailing her, she took the portrait to the music room, set it against the wall. She thought of the woman she'd seen dying in childbirth, the grief of her husband.

And looking at Johanna's portrait, thought of the woman she'd just seen, the one with a ponytail and bare feet. And like the third bride, radiant with joy.

A woman who, she now understood, died with the potential of life inside her.

"Marianne. We'll put you with the others tonight. Right now, I have to pull myself together. I have a meeting. But I'm not forgetting you. I'm not forgetting any of you. I have a big job to do."

Her phone played Roy Orbison's "Crying."

"Later," she murmured. "I can cry after the meeting."

She'd promised treats, so walked to the kitchen only to find them sitting on the counter. With a note, in the careful cursive she'd seen before.

I closed the door and gave them the cookies.

"Jack. Thanks for that."

Centered on the island stood the flowers, artfully arranged in Anna's blue vase.

"And Molly, thanks. I just . . . forgot about them."

She got out a Coke, drank some of it standing by the window, and waited for the boost. But her heart stayed heavy, her head light.

She got through it, and though Clover stayed silent, the scent of wildflowers drifted throughout the meeting.

Not alone, Sonya reminded herself.

After the meeting, she worked another hour, incorporating her careful notes before checking her email. She found two local inquiries for website designs. She couldn't find the joy in them, not yet, but responded before putting them aside.

Tomorrow, she decided. She'd find the joy in them tomorrow.

Instead, she worked on changes requested for a book cover. After her checks on and posts to various social media, she admitted she needed to shut down for the day.

No amount of work, no amount of focus could block that portrait, that luminous face, out of her head.

She'd hang the portrait.

Like a faithful guard, Yoda stuck with her when she went downstairs again. She found the cat sitting on the piano in the music room—another watchful guard.

"You're just the right cat for Cleo, and the manor." She gave Pye a long stroke, then crouched down to snuggle Yoda. "And you're perfect in every way."

When she hung the portrait, she stepped back to take in the five lost brides. Clover reached out to comfort with "Let It Be."

"But I can't, can I? I can't let it be. I'm here to stop it, and I don't know how. And God, *God*, I look at this beautiful bride in her lovely ruffled dress, and I see her dying in blood and pain. I hear the babies she fought to bring into the world crying. I see Hugh Poole grieving.

"And I see that bitch slinking in to take her ring."

The doorbell began to bong, and Sonya swore she heard laughter, wild and crazed, along with it.

"Oh, go to hell." Disgusted, she shoved at her hair. "I need air."

With her four-legged guards flanking her, she strode to the front door, threw it open. She walked to the seawall, where the waves crashed, where the water stretched—shimmering blue—in an endless roll.

The perfect June day, as spring eased its way to summer, brought out the pleasure boats. She watched them glide, over the ocean, down in the bay. Sails full, motors racing.

Then a school of dolphins, bulleting along, leaping up, diving down.

It calmed her. And still, she couldn't find the joy.

Windows banged shut in the house behind her. She ignored them.

Today I give you nothing, she thought, even as the grief rose up from her heart to clog her throat.

She didn't hear the truck coming up the road, but Yoda did. He let out his happy bark, and when she turned, she saw Trey's truck pulling in.

It flooded her now, all the grief and sorrow she'd walled off to get through the work, to stand against the viciousness, the violence that shadowed her home.

Mookie leaped out, long tail whipping as he and Yoda held a sniffing, wagging contest. Then Trey, hair windblown, in a gray suit, the blue tie loosened around his neck, the battered briefcase over his shoulder.

And it all broke through as he walked across the lawn toward her.

"Last client of the day just down the road, so—"

His easy smile of greeting snapped away. And with a look of worry, he quickened his pace.

"What happened?"

As the tears burst through, she simply fell into his arms.

"Sonya—"

"Just hold on to me a minute," she managed. "Just hold on to me."

"I've got you. But tell me if you're hurt." Stroking her back, he pressed his lips to her hair. "Just tell me if you're hurt."

"Not that way."

She wept against him, and as the dogs tried to push their way in, as the cat circled, Trey shook his head.

"Go on now. Go on."

He held on, half afraid the sobs would shatter her like glass. He gave her his silence, and the time she needed to purge herself of what struck him as a terrible grief.

A grief that stabbed at his heart as she wept it out in his arms.

When her sobs subsided, she gave one long shudder.

"I hate I gave her that. I hate I gave her tears."

"I hope she drowns in them. Come on, let's go inside."

She shook her head, then laid it on his shoulder with a sigh.

"I need the air. I thought I needed the sea, but I think I need the garden. The color of it. The life. Can we walk?"

Easing back, he took her face in his hands. Ravaged eyes, still brimming, and tears clinging to her lashes.

"Sonya." Undone, he kissed her. Gently, gently, even as some part deep inside him wanted to pound to dust whatever had caused that storm of grief.

He took her hand, and with his other reached in his pocket for a handkerchief.

"You have a handkerchief," she said as he dried the tears on her face. "You're wearing a suit, and you have an actual handkerchief."

"I had court this morning, and an emotional client."

"Oh, right. You told me—about court, not the client. You're too discreet to talk about your clients. Did you win?"

"As a matter of fact."

"That's good. You're early, aren't you? I'm so glad you're here. I'm so glad you came early. Then I cried all over your nice suit."

"Going to tell me why?"

She nodded, began to walk. "I had a meeting, virtual, so . . . Let me go back. I took a couple hours late this morning—late for me, not Cleo—to go with her and work on the nursery mural. It's pretty damn fabulous."

"I've heard. Cleo's still at Anna's?"

In her time, he thought, at her pace.

"I guess, or on her way home by now. I had to get back for the meeting. I stopped for flowers and brownies. You were bringing dinner."

"Owen's getting it."

As they circled around the house, he glanced up at the Gold Room, then banked his murderous thoughts.

"I let Yoda and Pye out, left the door open until I put the brownies away, dealt with the flowers. But before I could . . ."

She trailed off again as it struck her. "She didn't greet me. Clover always greets me with music when I come home, but she didn't. I just realized that. I guess she knew. Does it matter? Maybe, maybe not.

"You're letting me ramble," she said. "Just ramble away. No *What the hell happened, Sonya?* No *What the fuck's going on?* Not from you."

"Things come out in a ramble, if you pay attention."

"And you do, pay attention. And because of that, I feel more myself than I have since—the mirror."

"You went through?"

"I was going to prep the flowers, and I felt it. That pull. I didn't want it. I had the meeting, and I wanted to prep for that, too. I wanted to text you, but I couldn't. I just had to go."

She drew in the gardens, into her mind, into her lungs. The scents, the colors, the life.

"The third floor," she continued. "I was afraid it would be the Gold Room. I told myself I wouldn't go in, no matter what. But that was a lie. If it had pulled me there, I wouldn't have a choice. But it didn't. It was in Cleo's studio. And I went through, into Collin's studio.

"Maybe we could sit, sit on the deck."

He walked with her there.

"Do you want some water? Some wine?"

"Later. I'm going to get through this. There was a storm, and he painted it. Collin. He was young, and God, he looked so much like my father. Younger than my clearest pictures of Dad, but I've seen photos. And he stood like him, he held the brush like him. Sleeves of his shirt rolled up just like—"

She broke off, pressed a hand to her face.

Trey rose from his chair, plucked her up from hers, and cradled her in his lap.

"Yes, that's better. Johanna came in, brought him coffee. She looked so happy, content, and more, I could tell, I could see excitement. And when he spoke to her, Trey, I heard my father's voice. And the tone of it? Just the way Dad would talk to Mom sometimes. That love. I could see in them what I'd seen in my parents. That unity. That rightness.

"They talked about the wedding, just a few days away. Then she told him. She was pregnant, Trey."

"Johanna was pregnant? I've never heard that. My parents were really tight with Collin and Johanna, but—"

"That's the thing," Sonya interrupted. "They were so thrilled, both of them, just over-the-top happy. And she asked him not to say anything until after the wedding. To keep it just theirs until after the wedding. He said he wouldn't say a word until she told him it was okay. But she never got the chance to, Trey. She never did, so he never told anyone. At least I think that."

"I never knew him to break his word. So he carried that alone."

"It makes you sad," she murmured, and laid a hand on his cheek. "You loved him."

"Yeah, I did. He carried that loss, the woman he loved, the child they'd started together and wanted. And he carried it alone. It's goddamn tragic. But . . . they had that, Sonya. For a few days, they had that absolute happiness. Not everyone gets that, even for a few days."

"Trey, if she'd lived, if they'd had the baby, we'd be the same age. My parents would have been expecting me at the same time."

"And that hits hard."

She closed her eyes, rested her forehead to his. "They met in the mirror. I know that. From the time they were boys. And I think, I really believe, somehow, my father came through. He painted the manor, he had dreams about it. What he thought were dreams. It makes me wonder what would have happened if. And it broke my heart to know there's no if at all."

She laid her head on his shoulder. "Then I came back to Cleo's studio. And found Marianne Poole. Her portrait."

"Cutie, you've had a hell of a day."

He surprised a laugh out of her. "Oh God, yes. I brought it down.

Yoda and Pye were back in, the door closed, and I had a note from Jack."

"You're not messing with me now?"

"I am not. He left me a note saying he'd let them back in, closed the door, gave them treats, and Molly—had to be—had put the flowers in a vase. Kind, just so kind, and it helped a little.

"But I had to take the meeting, then I did what work I could get my head around. I came down, hung the portrait. I thought it would make me feel better. It just didn't. It was all right here."

She put a hand to her throat.

"And she started on the doorbell, and worse, I heard her. I heard her laughing. So I went outside, for the air, for the water. It didn't help either.

"Then you came, and I fell apart. Because I knew I could. I could fall apart because you were here. And that, finally, helped. I wish I hadn't given her those tears, that grief, but it helped."

"You gave her nothing. You mourned her victims, and gave her nothing."

Clover went with Christina Aguilera's "Fighter."

"And she's right," Trey said. "You are."

"There you are!" Cleo stepped outside. "I was wondering—"

Breaking off, she whipped off her sunglasses. "What's wrong? Son—"

"I'm fine. I'm fine now." She got up to prove it. "And honest to God, I can't go through the whole thing again without a glass of wine."

"I'll get it." He shot Cleo a look as he rose. "And I'll go through it again. You can fill in anything I miss."

"I don't think you miss much."

"I try not to." As he walked down from the deck, he signaled to Cleo. "Give her a minute, okay?"

"She's been crying."

"She needed to. She may need to again, but she's all right. Just give her a minute."

When he went inside, Cleo went up on the deck. She shoved her sunglasses on again, sat. "It goes against my nature, but I'm going to listen to him. I'm giving you a minute."

"I appreciate it." Sonya sat again, closed her eyes.

And basked in the silence.

Trey came out with a bottle of wine, three glasses. After he'd poured, he sat.

He went through it all, and Sonya marveled at his recollection of details, some she barely remembered recounting herself.

Part of being a good lawyer, she decided.

As he spoke, Cleo reached over, took Sonya's hand.

Solidarity.

"I'm so sorry I wasn't here, Son."

"Don't be. I wasn't alone, and I knew that all through it. And now that I did get through it, and I cried all over Trey, I'm glad I saw them together. Collin and Johanna. I'm glad I could see how much they loved each other, and would've loved the child they'd begun. I saw my dad in him, and in a way, I saw my parents at that stage of their lives. So full of love and excitement and plans.

"Sitting here now?" With people she loved, with the gardens blooming and the evening just starting to go soft. "I know, I absolutely believe, the purpose of seeing them, of finding Marianne's portrait right after, was a reminder of what's at stake."

She lifted her glass to Trey. "You said I didn't give her anything. I mourned for her victims and gave her nothing. I needed to hear that. And I can believe it."

"Her victims deserved to be mourned."

"Yes, they do. My father and Collin painted those portraits, and there's purpose in that, too. They deserve to be displayed together, remembered. That's what we're doing. They deserve to have their rings back. And I don't know how, but we're going to make that happen."

"I'm with you, all the way," Cleo told her. "Now, I want to go see her. See Marianne. You're right, there's purpose in that art. We see who we're fighting for."

"Let's all go see her."

They went inside, into the music room.

"She's beautiful," Cleo murmured. "Lit."

"Radiant," Sonya agreed. "That's the word that sprang for me. Young. She, Clover, Lisbeth, all close to the same age."

"Collin's work again." Cleo nodded as she moved in for a closer study. "They've taken turns."

"Honoring them," Trey put in. "Not just the woman Collin loved, or the woman who gave birth to both of them. But all the ones who came before. And the way it looks, this is where they're meant to be."

"In a room made for music." Sonya smiled at him.

Both dogs let out a yip and raced for the door.

"That'll be Owen, and dinner." Cleo stepped back to the doorway, waited. "We're in here," she called out when he came in with a bag from the Lobster Cage and Jones. "With a new addition."

He walked back, passed the bag to Cleo, then studied the portrait.

"Marianne Poole. Very Scarlett O'Hara." His gaze shifted to Sonya, held. "What's up? Dobbs give you trouble?"

"Not very much."

"I've had women cry over me, and on me, so I know what one looks like. What's up?"

"So gallant of you to let her know she looks like hell."

"I didn't say she looks like hell," he corrected Cleo. "Exactly," he added, and made Sonya laugh.

"And somehow still my favorite cousin."

"So, again, what's up?"

"We'll tell you over dinner—outside. It's too nice for in. I have crying jag face because I had a crying jag. And they make me hungry."

"Works for me."

While they ate, and the dogs roamed, and the cat watched, Owen listened.

And said little until the end of it.

"You okay now?" he asked Sonya.

"Yes."

"It had to be a jolt, seeing him like that. Like your father."

"They were so alike. I've seen pictures of both of them now, but this was . . . more."

"He said something to me, after Hugh moved to New York. How I was lucky I had a brother I was close to. Even though we wouldn't be in the same place, we'd always have that bond, growing up together, sharing memories and all that. Hugh and I always got along, mostly anyway. He said how odds were we'd make each other uncles one day. How being an uncle was close to being a father."

Owen winced as Sonya's eyes filled. "Oh man, don't start up again."

"Just a little. It's a good thing to know. They couldn't be close, but they knew each other. Through the mirror. I think that mattered to both of them.

"It's a good thing to know."

Chapter Thirty

On a bright, breezy Saturday morning, Cleo launched *The Siren*. She took the cat, and, at her insistence, Sonya took the dog.

As Cleo drove to the village, Sonya cast another dubious glance in the back, where Pye curled on the seat and Yoda planted his stubby front paws against the partially open window to catch the air.

"I'm really not sure, especially this first time, it's the best idea to take them on the boat."

"We all go. It's going to be a moment."

"Yeah, but what kind of moment? Joy and delight, or chaos and capsizing?"

"The first. I feel it in my bones. You had a tough week, Son. It's time for some silly fun."

She couldn't deny the tough week, but she'd handled it. And she'd handled the uneasy nights, waking at three to the sound of the clock, the music, the weeping, and waiting for the pull of the mirror to take her . . . somewhere.

Worse, waiting for Dobbs to strike out yet again.

"Friend of mine, you're stressed. Maxed-out stressed. Today, we break that. I'm excited." Cleo gave her a light punch on the shoulder. "Be excited! I haven't seen a peep of my boat except on paper. And today? We're going to sail the bay! All four of us."

She'd sailed with Cleo before, Sonya reminded herself. And considered herself a more than adequate first mate. But she'd never sailed with a cat or a dog, much less both at once.

Rather than breaking her stress, the idea just piled more on.

"Trust me," Cleo insisted as she pulled in beside Owen's workshop and parked next to the pair of trucks already there.

"Famous words."

But Sonya got out and, though Yoda sent her a sad look when he saw it, hooked the leash to his collar. Cleo gathered up the cat and an enormous bag.

"You know, the man's workshop's bigger than his house. I wonder what that says about him."

"That he loves his work?" Sonya suggested.

"Could be that. Could be he isn't as invested in his home, yet, as he is in his work."

"Your workspace in your apartment in Boston took up more room than your living space."

Cleo smiled, tossed her hair. "It did, didn't it?" She gave Sonya a one-armed hug. "I predict you're going to thank me after we sail."

"I may. I sure as hell plan to thank the gods of sailors, dogs, cats, and loyal best friends upon our safe return."

"You can do both, but Owen built it for two adults, and we're sticking to the bay. We all have PFDs, but we won't need them."

Hope not, Sonya thought as they walked around the workshop to the dock where Trey stood with Owen and two more dogs.

The Siren sat trim and glossy in the water, the mermaid at its bow with her head lifted, her hair flowing. Her companions swam port and starboard.

The boat gleamed in the sun, its red sail rolled and ready to hoist. Cleo let out a squeal and shoved Pye into Sonya's hands, dropped the bag.

She ran forward, and nearly toppled Owen off the dock when she leaped up, hooked her legs around his waist, and locked her mouth to his.

"I helped," Trey said. Then he sent Pye and Yoda as dubious a look as Sonya's thoughts. "Really?"

"Apparently. Wow. It really is beautiful. Owen, the carving."

"Busy here." He went in for another kiss, but Cleo jumped down, pushed him back. And moved closer to the boat.

"Oh, she's just gorgeous. She's . . . she's so me!" Kneeling, she reached down to run her fingers over the carved figures.

"It's beautiful work, Owen. Seriously beautiful work."

"She turned out pretty good. And she's stable, built for up to three hundred and fifty pounds, so she'll hold both of you, no problem. Plus, she's got the hiking strap you wanted."

Now he looked at Pye and Yoda. "Looks like you were serious about them. That cat's wearing a hot pink PFD."

"Naturally. It matches mine. I got Yoda the more masculine but still stylish purple."

She went back for the bag she'd dropped, then handed Sonya her PFD—also purple—before putting on her own. She took out two water bottles, handed them to Owen.

"Toss those to us, will you?"

"Maybe we should go over a few things," Trey began.

"I've grilled her already," Owen said. "She knows what she's doing."

To prove it, Cleo put the cat under her arm, stepped off the dock onto *The Siren*'s deck.

She got her balance, set the cat down.

Pye walked toward the bow, sat. Like a masthead.

"Oh God, here we go." Sonya unleased Yoda.

"Pray for us."

She kissed Trey for luck.

Obliging, Yoda jumped onto the boat. Hoping for the best, Sonya followed.

Trey watched them paddle away from the dock. "That looks promising. But hey, maybe we empty our pockets, ditch shoes. In case."

"They're fine."

And they watched Cleo move to the windward side, stepping over the cockpit where Yoda planted himself. She took the tiller with one hand.

And hoisted sail.

Her shout of triumph echoed back as *The Siren* glided over the waters of Poole's Bay. Sonya's laugh flowed back with it.

"She's sailing with a cat." Owen pushed up his sunglasses. "And a dog. The cat's wearing a pink PFD, and the woman's handling that boat like she was born at the tiller. I'm done. That's it. She's it. Jesus, she's just it."

Trey clapped a hand on Owen's shoulder. "You're just figuring that out?"

"I should've known she was trouble. Fuck it, I did know she was trouble. Now I'm sunk."

Trey looked out where Sonya lifted her arms to the sky.

"That makes two of us."

In the boat, Cleo tacked, and *The Siren* flew.

"You were right. So right! I forgot what it was like to just *go*! Yoda's loving it. Look at him."

Pointy little ears pinned back by the wind, he had his head lifted to it. And wild delight gleaming in his eyes.

"And Pye!"

Sure-footed, the cat had walked back to sit beside Cleo. And looked like a queen pleased with the performance of her barge.

"We needed this. We deserve this. Man oh man, Son, this boat handles like a dream. That man's amazing."

"He sure gets you. Everything about this boat say Cleopatra Fabares. Oh, what a day. But you were wrong about one thing. It's not silly fun. It's just fun."

"And how's that stress?"

"What stress?" With another laugh, Sonya waved to a boat as one of its passengers took pictures of them.

She supposed they made one. Two women, a cat, and a dog in a mermaid of a boat.

They sailed for an hour before Cleo guided *The Siren* back to the dock. As Sonya secured the lines and removed Yoda's PFD, Trey wandered out of the open double garage doors of the shop. Yoda leaped out, shook the spray from his brindled fur, then pranced into the shop.

Trey took the cat, then offered Cleo a hand. "How'd she handle?"

"She's perfect. I've never sailed anything like her. Small but mighty."
She took the cat, nuzzled it. "We love her. Owen in there?"

"Yeah. Cold drinks, too."

"Right now I want both."

When she walked away, Trey ran a hand over Sonya's windblown
hair. "It looks good on you."

"What does?"

"Everything, but right now? Happy and relaxed."

"I'm both. And I don't know half of what Cleo does about boats
and sailing, but from my perspective, she's right. That one's perfect."

She took his hand as they walked toward the shop.

"We had other boats come abreast, some taking pictures of us."

"That's no surprise."

"And a couple called out asking where we got the boat. If Owen
ever wants to take on more solo custom work, I could build him a
hell of a website."

They stepped inside the cavernous space, and Sonya goggled.

"It's even bigger than it looks from outside."

She'd never seen so many tools. Hand tools hanging on a wall, bigger ones sitting on shelves, others that looked powerful, and more than
a little scary to her eye, standing on their own. Massive standing chests
with drawers she supposed held more. Workbenches, stacks and more
stacks of lumber, another shelf holding what she thought were antique
tools—including the sander he'd taken from the manor.

More holding cans of resin, paint, sealer.

And tucked back, a battered old couch and what looked like someone's grandfather's recliner from the sixties, a dog bed, an ancient
refrigerator.

And the desk.

"Is that—that's the rolltop you found in storage."

Marveling, she walked to it, ran a finger over its now-silky surface. "How did you manage to let it look old, wonderfully, and shiny
new?"

"Elbow grease mostly. I got Cokes, I got beer."

"A Coke, thanks."

Cleo, already sipping one, lifted it to the wall above the desk. "You're putting her there, aren't you? *The Mermaid*?"

"That's the plan."

Nodding slowly, she sipped again. "It's a good plan. It's the right place for her. But right now, I need you to sit at the desk. I need it open, and Jones sitting beside you."

"Because?"

She reached in her enormous bag, pulled out a sketch pad.

"You have a sketch pad?"

"I always have a sketch pad. Go sit. It's an interesting setup. Then I'll trade you for a sail, you and Jones, in *The Siren*."

"I don't see why—"

"You will. You see it, don't you, Sonya?"

"I have to say yes. And if Trey will give me a ride home, I'll take Yoda—since I see Pye sitting on top of the desk."

Cleo smiled. "See why we've been best friends forever? Then I want one with you using one of these tools. Maybe just a sander or a chisel. Maybe that band saw."

"You know what a band saw is?"

Cleo gave him a roll of her eyes. "Of course I know what a band saw is."

Owen looked, a little helplessly, at Trey. "Damn it."

"We'll get out of your way. Come on, Mooks."

"I've got a couple ideas for you," Cleo told Trey.

"Definitely getting out of your way." He grabbed Sonya's hand, pulled her out of the shop.

"When she's ready for you, you won't escape."

"I can run pretty fast."

"How about a stroll on High Street instead? I'll buy you an ice cream cone."

"I'll take that deal."

An easy day, Sonya thought, one with no work and all fun. She'd needed it, and considered her balance fully restored as they walked the dogs along High Street.

They stopped often to have a word with friends and neighbors. And that reminded her what she'd made herself a part of.

It pleased her to see some of Anna's pottery in the window display at Bay Arts. As they paused there, Kevin stepped out.

He had a mile-wide grin, gold wire-framed glasses, and sported a bow tie.

"Caught a glimpse of you. First, again, Sonya, amazing party. John Dee and I had an absolute blast."

"We did, too."

"Always good to see you, Trey. I just saw your grandmother yesterday."

"She gets around. How's your mom?"

"Doing good. Just a sprain. Pickleball injury," he said to Sonya before he bent down to scrub at both dogs. "Hello, puppies. Hello there. I wanted to tell you I just this morning sold the last painting Cleo brought in. A couple from Cambridge taking a long weekend. Staying at the hotel."

"She'll be delighted."

"Please tell her, if I don't talk to her first, I'd be delighted if she has anything else ready. And I want to tell you, I'm ready to go with your proposal for the website, the signage, the works."

"Now I'm delighted. I'll start building the website next week."

"Great. We'll talk. I have to get back to it. Enjoy this spectacular day."

She did, from the sail, to the walk, the feeling of belonging, to margaritas on the deck with the men handling steaks on the grill.

Clover kept things upbeat with the music, Molly had the windows open, and three dogs plus cat played in the yard.

"Every day should be today," Sonya decided.

"If only." Then Cleo smiled. "We'd get bored."

"I hate knowing that's true." Sonya paged through Cleo's sketchbook. "These are terrific. You already know that. You want oils for the one at the desk."

"Mmm. And I want to play with shadows and light. *Man Working*

Late, that sort of thing. Right now, I'm feeling lazy. Like a movie after dinner."

"Read my mind."

While they ate in the sunlight, Sonya smiled over at Owen. "I've been looking at chairs for out front, maybe a nice bench, the kind that'll handle being out in the weather. The thing is, I haven't found anything that's not boring and standard. Nothing with the character the manor deserves."

Eyeing her, he ate a bite of steak. "You want me to build you chairs and maybe a bench?"

"You do have that incredible workshop, and all those tools. I drew up some ideas."

"Uh-huh." He glanced at Trey, who shrugged.

"She did it this afternoon. I gotta say, they look good. Interesting."

"Interesting. And say I find them interesting, what do I get?"

"I thought since Cleo would use them, too, she could offer you sexual favors."

"I'm already getting those."

"Yeah? They can be withheld."

He just turned to Cleo. "But can they? Can they really?"

She laughed and lifted her margarita.

"I also noticed you have a nice collection of old tools. There are more of those downstairs. You could take whatever you wanted."

"Maybe I'll take a look at the design."

When he did, saw the generous seats, the wide arms, the carving on the back that represented the weeper in bloom, he hissed out a breath.

"Okay, interesting. But you're going to want to angle the seats and backs some."

"Whatever you think."

"I've got some teak, and that'd work. But black locust, more interesting."

"Isn't that an insect?"

"No. Back when, they used it a lot for outdoor work. And you want character, the been-here-forever feel. It can be a bitch to work with."

"Not for you." Cleo batted her eyes at him.

"I'm taking those sexual favors, Lafayette. And some tools." He pointed at Trey. "You helped get me into this, so you help with the build."

"I'm in. I like them. I'd've talked her out of them otherwise."

"Is that so?" Sonya said.

"It's what he does. Talks people into things or out of them. Mostly," Owen added, "they come out of it thinking it was their idea."

"Let the record show this was Sonya's idea—issuing the challenge— and yours to accept it. So." Trey smiled. "How about that movie?"

At three, the clock sounded. On the drift of piano music, Sonya rose. Trey got up quickly.

"I'm awake," she told him. "I'm awake, but I have to . . . I need to go."

"I'm right here with you. But I'm going to get Owen. You don't have to go through alone."

"I have to go."

When she walked into the hall, Trey started to go down ahead, get Owen. But both Owen and Cleo stepped out of the bedroom.

"Somebody woke me up," Owen told him. "It wasn't Cleo."

"I heard it, too. Like before. Someone saying 'Sonya,' a hand on my shoulder."

"I'm awake, but . . . Do you feel it, too?"

"Not really. Something maybe." Owen shook his head. "But not really."

"I have to go. I have to."

She continued to the end of the hall with that pull growing stronger and stronger. Then she stopped at the top of the stairs, pointed down.

"It's there. Do you see it? It's down there."

"I see it." His eyes on the mirror, Trey took her hand. "You can say no, Sonya. I'll help you say no if that's what you want."

"No, I want . . . I need to."

"I'm with her. You need to stay with Cleo. It's not reflecting. Movement in it, and I can hear music."

Trey kept Sonya's hand. He saw them reflected in the glass as they walked toward the mirror. He heard nothing.

At the base of the stairs, he put Sonya's hand in Owen's, and all his trust with it. "Look out for her."

"I got it."

Cleo grabbed Owen's face, kissed him. "Look out for you, too."

"That's the plan. Ready?"

"It doesn't matter. I have to."

Together, they stepped through.

And stood in the grand foyer with the portrait of Astrid Grandville Poole. The music, the voices, came from outside the open windows.

"'Louie Louie.'" Owen identified the song, the heavy bass coming through. "So sixties or beyond."

"I don't understand—"

Even as Sonya spoke, the front door flew open. The woman rushed in, long auburn hair in tumbling waves to her shoulders. She wore a crown of rosebuds over it, with ribbons trailing behind.

She hiked up the frothy skirts of her white dress as she hurried toward the stairs. In high, sparkling heels, Johanna Poole started up.

"Her feet are killing her," Sonya murmured. "I can hear her thoughts, like with Arthur Poole."

Gripping Owen's hand, she followed the seventh bride.

1995

I'm married. I'm a married woman, a woman married to the best man I've ever known. The only man I've ever truly loved.

From today, we're Collin and Johanna Poole.

And why, in God's name, did I wear these ridiculous shoes on the most important day of my life?

I laugh, pause on the stairs, pull them off. And let out a long, relieved sigh.

"Because they're gorgeous, and I needed to be gorgeous today."

I felt gorgeous when I saw the light and love in Collin's eyes as I walked toward him.

A perfect day. Our perfect day.

I flex my aching toes, lay a hand on my belly.

All three of us.

I can't wait to tell Corry, to share the news with my closest friend. I'm going to be a mom!

But today, I'm a bride, and that's enough.

More than enough once I change my shoes!

At the top of the stairs, I turn a circle and think of all the plans Collin and I have for the manor. He's updated some of it, a lot of it really, but we'll do more.

And we'll need a nursery. Absolutely not the one used by his ancestors. Too far away from our bedroom, and we want our baby close.

Plus, that room makes me sad, just so sad.

We'll fill the house with happiness, and children, and art and music. Love, most of all love.

Collin's been denied love for far too long.

To think his grandmother, his own and only grandparent, refused to come to the wedding. And his mother, so distant, so empty somehow, didn't come.

Too damn weak to stand up to Patricia.

Thank God he's had Deuce and Corry and Ace and Paula—and little Trey and Anna. All the Doyles, his *real* family. And now I'll make a home, make a family for Collin, with Collin. And I'll fill all the empty spaces he grew up with.

In the bedroom, I put my sparkling wedding shoes away, consider other choices.

"Well, the hell with shoes. Barefoot Bride suits me better anyway."

Almost giddy, I roll down my stockings, discard them, then rush out to join the party.

A woman in black waits at the top of the stairs.

A strange dress for a wedding—almost like a bride herself, but one in mourning.

I feel the hair at the back of my neck stand up as she stares at me.

But I'm the hostess here now, so smile at her.

"Oh, hi. Are you looking for a powder room?"

"I look for you. The seventh bride."

"Pretty sure I'm Collin's first. Johanna Poole." I extend my hand.

She doesn't take it, but grips my left, and so hard! She yanks my ring from my finger.

"What the hell's wrong with you?" Fury rises as I try to take back what's mine. "Who are you?"

When she held up her hands, I saw seven rings gleaming on her fingers, and for a moment, a moment only, I thought of the curse. A strange story of witches and death and darkness I'd never believed.

But in that moment, I did believe.

My only thought now, in fear, is to get away, to find Collin.

She speaks.

"Who am I? I am, and always will be, mistress of the manor. I am your death."

I turn to run, run down the stairs. Away.

Something grips my head, my neck. I feel a sharp shock of pain, then nothing. Nothing, as my body tumbles down and down the beautiful stairs.

Hester Dobbs looks down from the top of them, holds her hands up once more so the rings seem to fire on her fingers.

"Seven brides with seven rings, with blood and death their power sings. The rings on my hand make them mine, and I am mistress here for all time."

She flicked a hand, and the entrance doors opened.

"Find her, grieve her. And I feast on your tears."

Turning, she looked into Sonya's eyes.

"I feel you, bitch whelp with Poole blood. You are far too late."

As people rushed in, as the house filled with shouts, screams, she laughed.

"Ah, taste it. Like wine. Delicious."

Like a shadow struck by sunlight, she vanished.

"Too late to save Johanna and the other six, but it can't be too late to send Dobbs to hell. It can't be."

Because she trembled, Owen put an arm around her. "We can't do anything here. We should go back."

As they went back down, people moved through and around the

mirror as if it didn't exist. Before she stepped through again, she saw Collin holding Johanna's body, weeping for her, saying her name as she'd seen the first Collin Poole hold and weep for Astrid.

It broke her heart.

When she stepped back into the now, Trey wrapped his arms around her.

"You're cold."

"A little. It was Johanna. The wedding. She came in to change her shoes. Her feet hurt. She was so happy."

"Come, sit down." He guided her into the parlor.

"I'll make you tea."

Sonya shook her head at Cleo. "Just water. Just some water. I always feel so *off* after. Owen?"

"Water's fine. I couldn't do anything. Not a fucking thing. I thought I'd get to Dobbs first, but I couldn't. It's like watching a play, but you're trapped in your seat."

He sat, scrubbed his hands over his face. Then was up like a shot when Cleo screamed. Screamed again with the sound of glass shattering on the floor.

She stood, frozen, her hands over her mouth as if to hold back another scream. And stared up at the man hanging from a rope near the base of the stairs in the grand foyer.

"Watch the glass." Owen avoided most of it as he picked her up.

"Tell me you see that. You see that."

"It's Collin Poole." Sonya fought to breathe as she looked up. "Astrid's Collin."

As the rope creaked, Astrid lay below him, her wedding dress soaked with blood.

And seconds later, Johanna lay bloody and broken beside her.

They all came, all the dead of the manor, in their moment of pain and fear and despair.

While the house filled with their cries, their sobs, their pleas, as despair clogged the air, laughter—wild, free, mad—rolled over them like thunder.

About the Author

Bruce Wilder

NORA ROBERTS is the #1 *New York Times* bestselling author of more than 240 novels, including *The Mirror, Mind Games, Inheritance, Identity*, and many more. She is also the author of the bestselling In Death series, written under the pen name J. D. Robb. There are more than 500 million copies of her books in print.